Hannah & Emil

BELINDA CASTLES

This edition published in 2013
First published in 2012

This project has been assisted by the Australian Government through the Australia Council, its arts funding and advisory board.

Allen & Unwin
Sydney, Melbourne, Auckland, London

83 Alexander Street
Crows Nest NSW 2065
Australia
Phone: (61 2) 8425 0100
Email: info@allenandunwin.com
Web: www.allenandunwin.com

Cataloguing-in-Publication details are available from the National Library of Australia
www.trove.nla.gov.au

ISBN 978 1 74331 578 1

Printed and bound in Australia by Griffin Press

10 9 8 7 6 5

MIX
Paper from responsible sources
FSC® C009448

The paper in this book is FSC certified. FSC promotes environmentally responsible, socially beneficial and economically viable management of the world's forests.

Author's note

While this novel is based on the events of my grandparents' lives, it should be considered fiction. The main episodes of this novel happened, but almost all of the detail is imagined, and some elements of the narrative have been deliberately altered for the author's purposes. None of the characters in the book, beyond the protagonists, are intended to bear resemblance to specific individuals.

For my father and all the descendants
of Heinz and Fay,
in memory

Prologue

Flora

SYDNEY, 2005

It was the humid heart of summer and Flora had been wading through thick, wet air for days, dreaming of a cool change. She was newly, invisibly pregnant and sometimes found herself kneeling on the floor of the Customs House library, head on the cool metal stacks, waiting for this light-headed exhaustion to pass. Even the air conditioning did not seem to lessen the weight of the air.

When her day ended she walked downstairs to the huge entrance hall, where the model of the city lay beneath the glass floor. She had begun to take a later train home so that she had time to study the model, which took up the floor space of a large living room. She walked above the fanning train tracks of Central Station and along the length of the city centre to Circular Quay, and the Customs House. I am in there, she thought. There's a little Flora, standing on the ground floor of that building, looking down past her feet at an even tinier Customs House, imagining an even tinier Flora. But it was like the concept of infinity, too mind-bending to sustain.

Perhaps she should have been an architect. She would love to make these miniature buildings, to hold a form of her imagined structure in her hands, to shape every detail: to angle the roof carefully between forefinger and thumb, to mould the trees that would be placed around it. Then put it out into the world of other people, let it grow into something thousands of times the size. But she felt her own part in such a process every time she placed exactly the right book in the hands of a visitor. She sent its recipient off with it out into the city and they took it home into their lives, sat down in a quiet place, opened it up and stepped through into a room, a house, a world they had never known.

She trailed her memory along the streets beneath her feet and through the little buildings. She had arrived at Central Station from the airport with her backpack, her excitement spreading and rising, filling the noisy high-ceilinged hall. I am in Australia, she thought. What sort of life will this be?

There was the block at the edge of Kings Cross where she had found her bedsit. From the window she could see the tallest of the gleaming curved points of the Opera House from behind, poking out above the trees.

The Flora she imagined, her miniature, walked down the cool, damp-smelling steps from the Cross down into Woolloomooloo, the city soaring up out of the Domain ahead of her. At first she had walked to a café in the dark windswept tunnel of Kent Street, where she made coffee and counted change, and in quiet moments had spread open the paper on the back counter to look at the jobs section. She was a librarian by training. Surely every city needed librarians? After several months she had seen the ad lift off the page of the *Sydney Morning*

Herald like a banner, cracking in the breeze. They were moving the city library to the Customs House and needed new staff.

And so began her new routine, her new life. Joining the morning flow down into the trains, burrowing beneath the city, emerging above the Quay and disappearing into her own allotted building, like everyone else. Emerging later into the fading day, tired and light, part of the great movement of the city.

The most wonderful thing about this model beneath her feet was that it was always changing. A building had gone up at Darling Harbour and no sooner had it been completed than the workmen came in early and inserted into the model city the building's replica. The city changed while Flora slept.

Two years now of this place. She had come from England, just for a look, because of her family history. She was, after all, half Australian. And she had loved the endless sky, the salty harbour breezes and the hard reflective surfaces of the city's buildings. The lightness of not really knowing anyone, of not being at home. She felt so free it made her dizzy. But now there was David, and this new being inside her. She looked beyond the edges of the model buildings to where the tracks ran out from Central and imagined herself on one of the little trains, carrying the dot inside her home to their house in Newtown.

The light in the hall dimmed and she looked behind her, out to the street. People were hurrying by, bent over. It must be raining. She walked out over the northern tip of the model city, across the void where the harbour would be, if the model didn't end, and through the door towards the real harbour. She stepped into an instant drenching as she crossed the road between buses towards the Quay, the ferries a yellow and green blur in the grey air beyond the station.

~

Flora let herself into the cottage, knowing at once that David was not home yet. She was glad. She liked to be in an empty house before anyone came home, just long enough for a cup of tea, a space between the sound of voices, then company and warmth.

She dropped her bag on the horrible vinyl sofa that creaked when you sat down and made for the kettle. There was a note on the bench. *Picked up a parcel for you. It's huge! In the spare room. Don't try and move it on your own. Stupid dinner tonight. Late.*

It would be the last of her books and photo albums from England. Her mother was moving out of her lovely, messy old house in the country, into a flat. If all my stuff is here, Flora thought, then I suppose it's home. She imagined her mother's new flat as a depressing place on a bland estate and felt briefly bereft. She took her hot mug down the dark hallway to the room where they stuffed their folders of bills, David's toolbox and boogie board, those of her books that wouldn't fit on the shelves in the living room. On the single bed was a parcel the size of a suitcase, wrapped in brown paper and string like something from another age. She found some scissors in the desk drawer and cut her way in to expose a patch of worn brown leather. It *was* a suitcase.

She sat down on the bed next to the ruptured parcel and touched the leather, left her hand there for a moment, and she was small suddenly, eight perhaps, lying between clean-smelling, striped flannel sheets looking at the old brown suitcase next to her pillow. There was a lamp on it, and her book—the Brothers Grimm or Hans Christian Andersen or some old English thing about fairies. Her grandmother Hannah was reading it to her, had just laid it down, the page marked for the following night. It was the moment before sleep, in Hannah's flat in London. This was Hannah's case.

Home, her memories, all that made her, burst into this light new life. Hannah had died a few years before Flora left England. They had all been relieved, in the end. Dementia had eaten away her body and her mind. She asked strange things you could not think how to answer. Now, with this square of leather beneath her fingers, Flora recalled the earlier times: her visits to Hannah in Hampstead, going together to the British Museum, riding backwards on the little fold-down seat in a hackney cab. Playing with the babushka dolls or reading fairy tales while Hannah sat at her desk by the bay window amid her dictionaries. 'Do you know, Flora,' she might say, 'translation is a sort of writing. You are making something quite new.' Hannah still travelled then, but it was a newer, smarter suitcase that stood in the hall, always ready; this old thing with a loose clasp had been relegated to the spare room to serve as a bedside table.

She pulled back the string, tore off the paper. The suitcase filled the little room with a musty leather smell, and she opened the window, let in the hot, wet night, ozone and tarmac drifting up from the alley. The catch was tied shut with yet more string. She cut through it and opened the lid carefully, a breath escaping, a puff of aged paper, ink and unsmoked tobacco. This new sensitivity to smell was overwhelming.

Inside the case was a mess of loose, crumpled papers, photographs, a sliding stack of little black notebooks, a plastic bag with a man's old tweed jacket inside, patches at the elbows. On top of the heap was an envelope with her name on it. Inside was a note from her father. *Hannah left you this case, it's only just arrived from her solicitor. Been sitting in customs for months, apparently. Not sure what to make of it but some of it might be interesting.*

Under the plastic bag was a carved wooden box. Flora opened the lid to find a green enamel plate with flowers painted on it in a child's hand; on top of it, rolling around, a lovely little globe. Beneath these, a couple of medals, an old key, a compass and a tape, and at the bottom of the box a German children's book: Grimm. She picked up the globe for a moment, turned it in her hands. It was the size of an orange but barely the weight of a sheet of cardboard. At its base were marked the initials SL—not the initials of any of Flora's relatives.

Gazing at the jumble of odds and ends in the case, Flora had a vision of her grandmother in her Hampstead flat, rifling through the case in the dead of night, curly hair mad and white, looking for objects, photographs, casting aside papers, gripped by the need to find something lost in her memory, to lay her hands on something, some icon that would return it to her.

Flora pulled loose a photograph. Two dark-haired boys with naughty grins hugged Hannah's legs on the deck of a ship: Dad and Uncle Ben, going to England for the first time. They had been born in Australia during the war and they both lived here now. Two more photos. Hannah in one of them, so young: dark, curly-haired, standing beside Flora's German grandfather Emil. They were in one of those lanes of Flora's English childhood, a tunnel of trees, a lit path. If the picture were in colour it would be a corridor of glowing green. On Emil's shoulders sat a thin blond boy, shirtless, a piece of cloth tied about his neck like a cape. One of Emil's hands held the boy's, and also a cigarette. In the other photo, Hannah had been replaced by a tall, very fair woman who looked like the boy. No one but the boy was smiling.

Flora began to gather the papers together, smoothing out the crumpled sheets on the bed beside her. She lifted one and saw that it looked strange. If she held the page just far enough away not to be able to make out the words, there was something odd about the pattern of print on the page. Not on every page, perhaps on one in three or four, there was a space that did not belong. When she looked closer, she saw that these were spaces in the sentences, the size of a word. And when she read the sentences, she saw that Hannah had recorded her memories. Flora heard her voice the instant she began to read, and yet every few pages there were these gaps in otherwise perfectly structured sentences. As she looked through more and more of these sheets, and found that they could be clustered, ordered, she realised with a start that the spaces were gaps in Hannah's memory of language, marking the beginning of her words failing her. Did she see these for herself? Did she write faster against the spreading of the gaps?

But as Flora started to read the pages she stopped noticing them, inserting suitable words as she read, without effort. She found fragments of Hannah's childhood in the West End with her brothers, of her travels in Paris and Berlin, the boat to Australia. The moments of a life, retrieved from the dark. Flora put a cushion between her back and the cold wall and began to make piles. After a while she went to the kitchen for a bowl of cereal and brought it back to the spare room, her mind still working over the ordering of the pages. When the type began to blur she picked up a notebook from the pile and examined it. These too could be ordered. They were diaries, she realised—the source material for many of the typed pages.

Late into the night, the rain lashing the window as though someone stood in the side alley emptying endless buckets against it, Flora tidied the pages into two piles. One she had sorted into order: the early part of Hannah's manuscript. The other was still a puzzle to be worked through. She laid both piles in the lid of the open case next to her, unable to take in any more tonight. She lay back on the narrow bed and closed her eyes. Her mind, sliding down towards sleep, was reaching towards something. The things in the wooden box, she thought. The medals, the compass . . . But the thought she was grasping towards evaporated and a memory came in its place. When Hannah was very old, she sat with Flora at the round table in the corner of the sitting room. They were surrounded by the piles of papers that Hannah continued to generate somehow but never now cleared away. Hannah was reading to her from a Russian dictionary. *I knew all this once*, she told Flora. *Where has it gone?* It had seemed as Hannah spoke that she was lost in the layers of time, that all her dead were in the room with them, and that it was to them that she was speaking.

For a moment as Flora lay, close to sleep, she was with Hannah again at the table. She saw her face: teeth missing, lips gathering elastically over her gums. She had stopped dying her curly hair red and it was wild and white, like Einstein's. She leaned over her dictionary. Her finger, arthritically curled, nail bitten, pointed at the Cyrillic script as she read out the words. As soon as her lips formed around them, all those soft, low sounds, made for her old, soft mouth, Hannah was transformed into an ancient Russian woman.

She looked at Flora. 'You have his forehead,' she announced. 'Whose?' Flora asked, frowning, sure that Hannah would say her father's, as everyone always did. 'Oh yes. There, dear, when you scowl. Emil's. Do you know my friend Emil? You're very like him.'

Flora was twenty then. She knew that Hannah's mind was failing, and yet she felt a sudden shift inside her, looking into Hannah's face. She does not know me. How can she not know me? She fought the urge to shout, 'It's me, Flora—your granddaughter. It's *me*, Hannah.'

~

When Flora woke there was a cup of tea steaming on the bedside table. She could hear the shower, David singing badly. That boy in the photograph, the fair boy on Emil's shoulders. He didn't look only like the woman. She reached into the case, which David had lifted onto the floor while she slept, and found the photograph, still at the top of its pile. Yes. He had Emil's long nose, and something around the eyes.

She eased herself onto the floor into a patch of morning light next to the suitcase. She took out the wooden box and placed its contents on the carpet next to her, along with the jacket. She felt in the pockets of the jacket and found the source of the tobacco smell, lifted the packet to her face, opened the flap briefly so as not to let it all out at once, breathed it in. A half-packet of tobacco. The one Emil had never finished, had not had time to finish. She tucked the tobacco back inside the pocket and laid the jacket across her lap, put the green plate on top of it and on that the tape, the key, the medals, the compass. She rolled the little globe lightly on her palm. She was not the only one, then, to love small things. It was the most perfect, exquisite little object, its tininess reminding her of what a globe was: a gorgeously intricate miniature of the whole world of people and places and life. And it brought a new knowledge of herself, of her habits and loves having old precedents, that made her skin prickle.

The thought she had lost the night before returned, complete. The tobacco, half-finished, these few silent objects. Somehow, every moment of their lives might be here, in her hands, in her lap. Not just in Hannah's pages, but in these medals that rattled on the enamel plate, this globe with its fading colours.

She returned the globe to the plate and picked up the key, wondered that this object could find her, could follow her across the world. The traffic was growing heavier at the window, the light was changing, a man called out on the street, the day was coming to life. She replaced the key on the tin plate with a little click. She gathered the medals and the compass and the globe into her open hands and the light, rising at the window, fell on them. For a moment they seemed to give off a light of their own, and a heat.

Then the light passed on and the objects in her hand were old, worn things again, relics. Any life in them was a life she imagined.

Part I

Emil

DUISBURG, 1902

In the summer, it did not matter that Emil was shoeless. The soles of his feet were as tough and dirty as leather. His friend Thomas left his own shoes at home in a paper bag stuffed behind the toilet in the outhouse, and so there was no difference between them.

Down along the Rhine, at the edge of the fields, dozens of men were building a huge factory. Ships docked at the pier and swearing workers unloaded bundles of timber planks and steel beams and crates of bolts, tools and machinery, while a crane swung pallets of bricks from the ship onto the bank. The boys were close to the world of how things worked, of metal and machines, and Emil watched carefully. He and Thomas ran around the crane operator as he peered up at the rope on the winch and then at the teetering bricks, wiping his forehead with the back of his hand and then shifting the crank gently, wheeling in the load. They jumped and ran in circles, shouting encouragement, but all the time Emil followed the progress of the bricks, pieces of wire, moulds, pipes, planks of wood to see what would happen to them, to see what their purpose in the world might be.

One day they watched unbelieving as an entire load of bricks was upended into the river. It happened slowly enough to observe properly, to remember afterwards: the pallet dipped a little to the left and the crane operator overcorrected it. The bricks went in, sliding unstoppably, hundreds pouring into the water in a second. The boys hooted and slapped each other, pointed at the operator, a man named Dieter. The foreman came striding down the track from the office-cabin above the steep bank and stood in front of him. He cuffed Dieter around the ear and shouted. Dieter's body crunched forward and he held his head in his hands. Blood was filling one of them, leaking from between his fingers. The boys ran home.

The next day there was a different man working the crane, one with a head like a bulldog's. The boys stood on the towpath at a distance, taking in the impressive size of Dieter's replacement. Emil approached the man, who was loading machinery parts onto a cart to pull up to the factory. 'Come back!' Thomas called from behind. But Emil's curiosity forced him on.

'Excuse me, sir.' The man did not stop loading. Sweat darkened his vest. 'When is Dieter coming back? Is he working inside the factory now?' The man stopped at last, snarled, a wordless grunt from his throat. Emil froze, and then felt Thomas pulling at his shirt. He woke to himself and they ran back along the path, gasping and laughing.

As the building grew, the ragged rows of bricks blocking out more and more sky, they found that there was always some corner of the building site left unattended. They lugged armfuls of sharp-edged bricks stacked up to their chins to a hidden spot behind a hummock and built a den with walls high enough for them to stand inside the structure unseen. They peered over the bricks, watching the builders beyond the little rise of land, small from here, balancing like circus performers as they hurried across steel beams and up and down great ladders, the hods of bricks at their shoulders like no weight at all.

Every day was warm; the grass a little drier, coarser underfoot. Emil woke each morning expecting summer to be finished, for the rain to spoil his days, but it was just blue, over and over again. The men's skin shone red as they worked, like his father's when he came home from a day going door to door at the factories, looking for work. Emil's memories of winter seemed distant: sliding along the iced-over river on Thomas's toboggan, Papa pulling them both along, falling over, laughing, falling again for their entertainment.

Sitting on the grass in the deep shade of the den, he leaned against the wall carefully; they had no cement to make it strong. He said the thing he'd been carrying around all morning. 'Mama says I cannot go to school this year after all.'

Thomas turned from his spy hole and reached down to punch him on the arm. 'Of course you can. You've got to go to school.'

Emil shrugged, picked at the grass. 'She can't get me shoes. The ones Papa got for me last winter are too tight now.'

'You don't need shoes; you only need pencils and a satchel. Mama took me to buy mine last week.'

'You wait till next year too and we'll start together. Ask your mama.'

'She'd whip me. Listen, Emil, have my shoes. I'll get more.'

Emil was silent for a moment. Papa told him all the time that if you had a good education you would never have to look for work. But Mama would not change her mind about the shoes. His parents shouted when he was trying to sleep.

'What would you tell your mama?'

'I'll tell her I lost them. I lose *everything*.'

Emil stepped out of the den and lay on the hummock. The men were on their lunch break. They sat on the pier hunched over their little boxes. His own stomach growled. If Thomas had not taken anything from his pantry, he would have to go home and find some bread and risk his mother roping him into some errand or other. Or they could go along the river, beyond the factories, to the copse where there were berries, but they turned his stomach watery.

Thomas followed him out onto the grass and lay next to him, chin on his hand. 'Tell your mama you found them.'

'She'll say I've stolen them. I'll tell her you grew out of them and gave them to me.'

Thomas nodded. It was decided.

They lay half asleep, the sun on their necks. Because it was summer, Emil's hair was shaved for lice. Thomas's curls rested on his shirt collar, black against the pale cotton of his shirt. Emil began to sweat against the hot grass. 'Come on, let's go for a swim,' he said.

'Are the men still there?'

'No, they've gone back to work. Let's go.'

They jumped down to the towpath and ran along to the pier, warning each other to be quiet, but the sounds of hammers against steel and men calling out to one another were much louder than they were in any case. They reached the pier and flung their clothes behind them onto the bank, naked and laughing. Throwing themselves down on the warm boards to keep out of sight, they slithered out over the water, rolling down the steps and into the river, gasping at the cold. They gripped the poles of the pier as the current pulled their legs downstream.

'Look, I'm swimming!' Thomas shouted, holding one arm in the air, swallowing water.

Emil had watched people swim at the lake on Sundays, had dipped his head under close enough to see their actions through the dark water. They pushed the water away from themselves and kicked out their legs like frogs. He practised the frog kick for a few strokes. Easy, smooth, legs growing warm in the cold water. He let go of the pole with one arm, scooped water out and away, did it again.

'What are you doing?' Thomas asked.

Emil smiled at his friend and let go of the pole. The tugging water pulled him back and thrust him down immediately. He thrashed his way to the surface, saw that he was already several metres away from Thomas and the pier. Flailed, splashed, forgetting the movements he had practised.

'Emil!' Thomas called. 'EMIL!'

Push the water away, he told himself, and he began to do it. It was no good, his head kept going under. He stroked harder but he hadn't got his legs right. Made himself wait for half a second, the river pulling him along, while he coordinated his limbs. There was shouting on the bank, Thomas, the men now. His head stayed clear, he did it again, pushed harder on one side so that he was running forward with the current. Stopped for a split second to take a bigger breath, began to sink, made the movements again quickly, and again. He could keep his head up but he was surging with the water. Thomas's voice was small behind him, like something he was beginning to forget.

The bank was a few metres away. He saw the individual blades of grass, the path. When he needed to he would be close enough to reach them. Movement at the corner of his eye distracted him. It was Thomas, racing along the path, three men behind him, calling out, red-faced. He turned away from them, concentrated on his strokes. They were running hard; he must be going very fast.

One of the men was sliding into the water just ahead of him. Another held the man's arm from the bank while he reached out and grabbed hold of Emil's hand. Emil was ducked under for a moment, water filling his nose and mouth, tasting of petroleum. He was furious, tried to slip from the man's grasp, but he was too strong; he had thick, hard arms. He gathered Emil against his hot chest, his breath loud in his ear. 'Stupid boy!' he said, clasping him too tightly. 'Stupid, idiot boy! Your father will skin you alive.'

Then a couple of men were grabbing at him and heaving him up the bank. They lay him on the path on his back. Thomas's face was above him. 'What did you do? What did you do? You were floating away! We only just caught you.' Thomas's head, his thin chest, were dark against the bright sky.

Emil coughed up some water and grinned. 'Did you see me swim, Thomas? I swam. I swam so fast. You were running, I saw you, but you could not run as fast as I could swim.'

~

One morning at last the sky was grey. Emil's father was standing over the couch which served as the children's bed, shaking his shoulder gently. Papa was smiling, and he had shaved. He smelled of soap and there were little circles of colour on his cheeks. 'Big day for us, boy! School!' In his hand was a book. He laid it gently on Emil's chest. 'It is the Brothers Grimm. Wonderful stories, *liebling*. You will read them all before long.'

Emil picked it up; its paper cover was smooth. He looked at the letters on the cover, the lovely round symbols that meant nothing. Inside the book were pictures: a little girl in a cloak carrying a basket, two children in the dark forest.

He loved this object instantly, its smell and corrugated pages, the smooth inked illustrations.

His father reached into his jacket pocket, drew out a cone of sweets and laid it on top of the book.

'How did you get the money, Papa?' Emil whispered.

'I'm a working man, don't you remember?'

'But you haven't started yet.'

'I start this very morning! Big day for both of us. I'll walk you to school and then I begin. And when you come home for dinner your mother shall have ham on the table.'

'Can I come one day and watch you pour the metal into the mould?'

'Of course, when I have been there for a little while.' Papa embraced him, his face smooth and soft where his beard had been before. He looked so naked and pink and young.

From the kitchen came the smells of coffee and oats. The season changing seemed not such a bad thing with them all here close together, these good smells, Papa happy. Emil stretched out a foot, kicked his sister under the covers. She snorted but did not wake. His father laughed.

'Princess Greta,' he whispered in Emil's ear. '*That's* your sister!'

After breakfast they said goodbye to Mother, who was bent over Emil's new book at the table, and Greta, playing under the table with his tin soldiers. He kissed his mother near her ear. For a moment he wished he could stay, play with Greta. Mother held him briefly, tightly, pushed him gently towards the door, turned back to the book. His feet felt big and heavy as he clomped down the stairs in the shoes. They shone like black water—Papa had polished them the night before—and they had no holes. The boots he had worn the previous winter let the melting snow in and soaked his socks, giving him chilblains, so that his mother would no longer let him leave the apartment on a snowy day. And so he would sit inside while below on the street boys threw missiles at each other and shouted and laughed until it grew dark.

He and his father joined the stream of men walking to work, women off to the market with baskets under their arms, children with comb lines in their wet hair, socks pulled high. Without warning he was flying into the air, raised over Father's head, onto his shoulders. 'You begin school a king, young man. No walking for you!' From here he could see into the windows of apartments: women cleaning, an old man smoking in a rocking chair, a couple kissing in their underclothes at the sink. Papa drummed out a tune on his ankle and Emil beamed at the passers-by, the tallest boy in Duisburg. His father nodded to the people he knew. 'Can't stop, my boy's off to school today.' And then, when his acquaintances had gone on their way, he would tell Emil stories about these people who lived in the streets around their apartment. 'Frau Bern is looking better since her operation. Manning may cough up for beer occasionally now, if she keeps him sweet.' 'Oh, there's poor Gunther. He injured his hand in the smelter and now he can't get work. Won't join the union—too proud.'

Emil heard the children shouting as they approached the school gate. Father swung him down and laid a hand on his shoulder. 'I'm proud of you, Emil. This is the start of great things.' He winked and was gone, running down the street. He was probably late. He often was. Always one to chat and gossip and let the time slip by. Mother laughed at him for it.

Thomas was already in the schoolyard, showing some other boys his new catapult. A tall, thin man in dark clothes approached the group, put his hand out. Emil saw Thomas give up his catapult, his head hanging forward, his hair a mop covering his face. Emil ran to him, brushing past the teacher who was looking around the yard serenely, as though it was his lovely garden. The other boys had their hands on Thomas's shoulders. 'He will give it back at the end of the day,' Emil said. 'He *has* to.'

The bell sounded, just like the beginning of a factory shift down at the river, and the boys looked about them, wondering what to do. The older children were funnelling into the school doors, so they joined the crowd at the entrance and squeezed into the building with the others. A teacher was pointing at the younger ones, beckoning them into a classroom behind him. He grabbed hold of Emil's sleeve and pulled him into a bright room with tall windows and a smell of floor wax. Ahead of him stretched rows of desks, which the other boys were quickly claiming.

'Take a seat, boys,' the teacher called. 'Herr Walter will be along in just a moment.'

Emil and Thomas were the last in and there were only a few desks left, at the front. They took them and waited while all around them boys whispered and laughed. The noise in the hall died down and the teacher entered. 'Oh no,' Thomas murmured. It was that man, who had taken Thomas's catapult: as long and thin and upright as a new pencil.

Herr Walter glanced at Thomas, his face mild, smooth, quite handsome, his mouth set in an attitude of patience. But then something about Emil, sitting next to his friend, caught his attention. The teacher studied him for a few moments, bemused. 'You,' he said eventually, while chairs scraped and someone scratched through their shorts loudly with a ruler. '*I* know you. Your father is the socialist, Klaus Becker. Quite the agitator. Come, stand before the class. I will introduce you.'

Emil stood from his chair, uncertain, and approached the teacher, heart hammering. He felt Thomas's eyes upon his back. He did not know whether it was good or bad to be introduced to the class but he was beginning to wish the teacher did not know him. He wondered about that word, *agitator*, wished Father was here to ask about it.

'Here, by the blackboard.' The teacher took a pointer from a shelf under the board and pointed at Emil, tapping him on the neck lightly, the wood cool on his skin. 'Tell the class your name, child.'

'Emil Becker,' he said quietly, looking at the rows of boys who stared at him without smiling. He knew some of them but there was nothing in their faces. Even Thomas looked blank, as though these were not his shoes Emil was wearing, one pressing now at a blister on his heel.

'This boy, Emil Becker, is a socialist boy from a socialist family.' Herr Walter's voice was gentle. 'They are not like us, children. Aside from anything else, this boy does not believe in the Lord, our dear Father. Now, we must be polite to this boy, because we are Christians. He must learn to read and write like the rest of you. But he will never amount to anything. His life on this earth will be wretched and misguided. It is not his fault, the family he has been born into. But look at this boy, children. If you ever doubt that God sees you, and sees your sins, look at this poor lice-ridden boy with holes in his clothes and sin in his heart, and he will remind you never to stray. Sit down, Becker. We will do what we can for you.'

Emil did not know what had happened. He found his seat in a dream, his face burning, everything loud and bright. He looked down at his clothes. Herr Walter was right. The hem of his shorts was frayed and there was a hole in his pullover. He approached it with his finger, slowly, secretly. It fit perfectly inside.

The teacher was speaking. He was explaining something in the same reasonable tone in which he had spoken about Emil. The lesson had begun, he was pointing out letters of the alphabet on the board with the pointer that had touched Emil's neck. Emil stole a look at Thomas. His friend's face was hidden beneath his hair, a curtain that concealed him. All through the lesson, in which the teacher wrote on the board with taps and scrapes of his chalk and talked in his steady tone, Thomas remained behind the curtain and Emil felt an intermittent disturbance in his bowels.

After an hour in which he could make no sense of anything, the bell jolted them all in their seats and the teacher opened the door, smiling. 'Playtime, children. Don't get yourselves dirty in the yard, now. We will distinguish ourselves from animals.'

The boys packed themselves through the narrow doorway, chattering, chancing little blows and pinches. Thomas was ahead of him in the throng of boys. There was a little space around Emil as they moved along the hall towards the door. No one touched him though all around him there was jostling and pushing. When he reached the yard he continued walking towards the gate. No one spoke to him or stopped him. He could not see Thomas anymore. Outside the gate the streets were almost empty. The sun was burning through the clouds and his shirt stuck to his back beneath his pullover. He fixed his eyes on the street, walking quickly. When he reached his apartment building he glanced up and went on down the street, towards the bridge and across the river. Turning away from town, he continued past the half-built factory to the den.

It felt different somehow to yesterday, when Thomas was here, though he could not have said what had changed. The factory was tall, the frame for the roof was on and the towering eyeless face of the wall was forbidding. He curled up in a corner on the ground. A hare startled him, scurrying past the entrance. He settled down again and fell asleep instantly. Then woke to the sound of a bell, coming from the factory, pulled himself up, moist grass peeling from his face, and looked through his spy hole. The huge shadow of the factory spread across the field behind it. Men poured from the structure, beginning the walk along the towpath, past the other factories, back into town.

He and Thomas always took that as a sign to go home for supper, though they could not resist first sneaking into the factory after the foreman had locked up his cabin at the front and left for the day. There were still no doors on the main building. Emil wandered over now, out of habit: along the path to the pier, up the bank past the foreman's office, into an empty doorway and inside the immense, chaotic space of the half-built factory.

It was dizzying to be in a space so large and yet be indoors. But then you looked up past the steel girders high above and there was the sky. There were piles of bricks, wood and steel beams and crates of machinery stacked everywhere, their innards spilling out onto the floor. He looked at the machines as though they were creatures. He knew from Papa about electricity, and about the work of the blood, and they seemed the same, a force that moved through things, bringing them to life.

In spite of the mass of equipment piled about the place there was space to run about until you fell over. He and Thomas would race up and down the hall, dodging the scaffolding that was going up at one side, where a platform for offices was beginning to take form, way up the wall, a sort of stage from which one could view what was happening on the floor. Today he walked up and down the length of the building, breathing in the smells of brick dust and steel. He saw after a while that in the dust on the stone floor were small, bare footprints among the large booted ones. He wondered what children had been here, that he had not seen.

His feet took him outside again. The factory was a little frightening now that he did not have a friend with him to fill it with noise and movement. He saw how large it was in comparison to himself. It would take fifty boys standing on each other's shoulders to reach the top.

Mother was outside the apartment building when he got home. 'Thomas brought your bag,' she said, pulling him into her chest. 'Where have you been? What will Papa say? On your first day of school.'

He pulled sharply from her grasp and climbed the stairs to the apartment. His sister Greta slept on the sofa. She looked fat and warm beneath the blanket. Her cheeks were soft and pink. He crawled in next to her, breathed in her skin, closed his eyes. His mother moved about the kitchen. He smelled the cooking smells. It was true, she had bought ham. The smell was unbelievable. Juices ran in his mouth, he had not eaten all day. He heard the door open, and voices, quiet, in the corridor; his father's voice: 'No!' in surprise. Eventually they came back in, the door closed. He could not open his eyes, would not look at Papa's face.

'Emil,' his father said quietly, next to his ear. 'Tell me what the teacher said to you.'

Emil shook his head. Greta had gone. His pillow was wet where his eyes had been. Papa stroked his short hair, his hand running over Emil's soft bristles, the skin of his fingers lumpy and calloused.

'Why do I have to go to school?' Emil whimpered. He wished his voice were stronger, deeper.

'Because your education is the most important thing in the world. It is worth more than gold. That teacher, he's an idiot, but he has something you need. He has learning. You need to get it from him. You show him. You are poor, but you are strong and clever. Any boy might be the one to change the world. I would give anything to go back, to be your age again, to have this chance. You will be a good, clever boy. I know you will.' Emil remained still, eyes closed. 'Can you smell that ham?' He nodded. Father kissed him. 'Mama will have it on the table in a minute. We'll have a feast. And luckily, I know this Walter fellow. His apartment is not far. We shall go round after dinner and throw horse manure at his window. What do you say?'

Emil nodded into his father's chest. Something eased and shifted. He imagined bringing back his arm, flinging the clod against the window, the teacher in his nightgown opening it to investigate, peering out onto the street. Emil was a clever boy, Papa had told him. When he heard the window drawn up in its frame, he would have another handful ready.

Hannah

LONDON, 1915

My earliest clear memory, and it is so very clear. Childhood is around me, before my eyes, happening now. I live in that room again. My brothers are with me, and Mother and Father. We shall all live forever.

It was a year into the war. I was eight. In my father's desk drawer, in the box room where he kept his bolts of fabric, my brother Geoffrey found a revolver. I took it from him, felt its cold weight in my hand. Geoffrey grabbed it back and pointed it at me. 'Die, marauding Hun,' he whispered coolly.

'*You* are the Hun,' I replied. 'Give it to me.' And he did. I was the elder and could be frightening, if I wished. I pointed it at his head and moved it around a little, as though he were a German I had spied over the lip of a trench, and I must find my mark. It was a thrilling, heavy thing to hold, as though potential and power had heft. 'Bang.'

He threw himself against the propped-up bolts of cloth, clutching his chest. Lolled his head and stuck his tongue out on one side.

I heard the creak of the floorboards in the hall and then the little one was calling for me: 'Hannah, Hannah! Where are you hiding?' I laid the gun back in the empty drawer and put a finger to my lips. Geoffrey opened the door and Benjamin looked from one to the other of us, small and glowering, excluded.

The gun was not the only reminder of the war across the water. A parade marched past Father's shop door on Tottenham Court Road, dressed in khaki. There were redcoats before the war: smart though less impressive. I could imagine the mud of the trenches on the khaki jackets passing endlessly outside, as though they had marched all the way from France into London, their vast number somehow overcoming the obstacle of the Channel.

When a soldier broke off from the mass in the street and came alone into the shade of the shop where I sat on the high stool behind the counter, I lifted my gaze from the pennies I was piling up on the wooden bench and looked him over slowly from his boots to his strange hat, pinned up on one side. I was prone to staring as a child. It is possible I never quite lost the habit. People are so very interesting. Besides, I wanted to be a writer. You had to be sure what people's faces looked like if you were to go away and describe them in your notebook afterwards. That took staring. The soldier did not smile. It seemed he was a starer too. Outside, the band was passing right by the shop with its brass and drums, and the crowds were cheering. But it was muffled in here, as I studied the man's hands for signs that they might have strangled a Hun. If the silence lasted much longer, I determined I would ask.

'Well, love,' he said eventually, his accent strange, almost English but foreign too. His skin was dark, but he was not an Indian. They were darker, and spoke up and down, as though they were half singing. An Indian officer had stood right here where this man did a few months before and Father had struck up a conversation. It had been mesmerising. This man here said, 'Got a couple of ounces for us, then, have you?'

I jumped down from my stool, the shock travelling through my feet, and turned my back to him, reaching up to the high shelf for the tobacco jar. Having placed it on the counter I climbed back onto the stool, unstoppered the jar and measured the cool moist tobacco onto a square of paper, careful not to spill any, breathing in the smell. It was like Father's clothes, but more concentrated, unsullied by shaving soap and coffee.

He leaned forward as he tipped the tobacco into his tin, his face so close that I caught cologne, brilliantine, saw where the tiny bristles of blond hair ruptured the weathered skin. 'Smells like heaven,' he said, eyes closed. It was as though he had considerately placed his soldier's face there for me to take a good long look. There were beads of sweat at his temple, white bushy eyebrows with the little hairs bursting straight out in every direction, purple threads in an old man's swollen nose, deep lines at the corner of his eyes, furrows at his brow. Yet his head was a grown-up boy's, somehow.

The stairs behind me creaked and the soldier stood up straight. Father came through the doorway, his round stomach brushing my back as he passed. 'Sir! We have whatever you need. Just ask the question. Whatever you are looking for. Whatever at all. Is my Hannah helpful?'

'She's a good girl you've got there, sir. No doubt about it.' I listened to the vowels. They were stretched, flat, long, the consonants soft. I watched his lips and tongue as he formed the sounds.

'Ah!' said Father, studying the soldier. 'You are Australian! Welcome! Welcome to London! Very cold for you, I expect.'

'No colder than a muddy ditch.' He eyed me for a moment, and then Father. More, I thought, say more! It was one of those moments in which a window into adulthood gusts open and is quickly slammed shut. 'Sorry,' he murmured. 'Forget where I am.'

'Oh, that's quite all right. You must relax. Enjoy your stay in London. We are happy to have you here with us.'

Later, in the bathroom, Geoffrey banging on the door, I practised the sounds in the mirror, shaping my mouth in ways I had not shaped them before, stretching my lips around the words, making my whispering voice undulate with the phrases. 'Smells like *hea*ven. No colder than a muddy *ditch*.'

'HANNAH!' Geoffrey was almost screaming. 'I'm about to go on the floor!'

I opened the door, mimicked his agonised face, and after a moment let him by.

~

I slept with Mother in those days. When the zeppelin-raid siren sounded, which I could sleep through if left alone, I was always the first to be pushed out of bed. Mother did not sleep at all, it seemed to me. Mothers did not need sleep like other people. They lay awake, listening to you dream, so that they might shove you out from under the warm covers the instant the siren came. In the quieter moments when the siren faded, before it built up again, Father's snoring throbbed through the wall and the floor. My brothers would try to wake him. 'Papa. *Papa!*'

I bundled up the quilt and pillows into a shape that I could carry and after Mother had intervened in the bedroom we were all stumbling down the narrow twisting staircase to the shop, trying not to knock jars of sweets from the shelves with our loads on our way through, scurrying down Tottenham Court Road with all the other dark figures and their fat bundles of bedding, past the shopfronts to Goodge Street tube on the corner. The streetlights were out and the padded creatures bumped and jostled their way to the entrance by instinct, muttering *Excuse me, After you, Mind my foot* in a number of languages. It was cold outside at night, even with a coat pulled over my nightclothes, but the air between the shuffling people was thick and warm and one could tell from its odour that it had been cycled through living bodies. What I loved best were the searchlights tracing paths in the sky. I walked looking up, hoping for a glimpse of a zeppelin, while Mother hurried me into the station entrance, pressing my head into the scratchy woollen coat covering her soft hip.

In the dim light in the endless stairwell I saw Boris from my class with his parents and his sisters just below us. I recognised him by the silhouette of his glasses and his unruly hair. He was Russian but that was not the language we spoke together. Father had taught me only a little of his language—much of what I knew I had gleaned from inside the curtain around my bed during his late-night conversations with Mother, when he spoke of relatives at home and how they fared: shortages, strikes, the cost of food. And English was unspeakably dull, the language of school, not for down here in the tunnels at night. We might have spoken Yiddish, but never in front of Father. He called it the dead language of the old world. He hated anything old-fashioned, anything he connected with superstition. Mother would not have minded so much. She often made up affectionate names in Yiddish, though not when Father was about. She had an endless store, so many that I often had to ask her what I had just been called. Little bird. Flower of spring. Sweet morsel.

We spoke when we were playing in a language we felt we had invented. Or if we knew we hadn't quite invented it, that we were close to its beginnings. Someone at our school, St John's, used it on us, called us little Jews. It was clear what the boys were saying. They called everyone little Jews. We listened to these and other snippets of tattle and invective in the playground and saw quickly enough that it was a simple trick. One worked out how the word would be spelled backwards, with the odd variation where needed for pronunciation. Yobs for boys and so on. Mother hated it, said we sounded like barrow boys and fishmongers.

'Olleh Sirob.' I fell into step beside him, clutching my bundle as we descended into the crowded gloom, whispers echoing up from deep, deep below us. I loved raid nights.

He had not known it was me behind the pile of bedding. I was just a small girl, even for eight. Boris was not required to carry bedding. His mother did everything. We spoke as quickly as possible, partly to show off, partly to obscure further what we were saying. I was not one to waste a chance to irritate my brothers, who were one step behind, and stuck behind our bulkily laden forms until we reached the platform. We exchanged nonsense until our brains tired and we were forced to whisper in English.

'Do you think there is really a bomb?' Boris said. 'Mama says this is a waste of time.'

'*I've* never seen one. But imagine if we went back up and the streets were missing, and we had to live in the tube forever, like rats . . .'

On the platform my parents manoeuvred themselves into a space where they could wedge their pillows against the curved tiled walls of the tunnel. 'Hannah, come,' Father instructed. 'Boys, come. You want the hoi polloi to crush your skulls?' As we burrowed into position, the ground trembled and the whispering ceased for a moment. Everyone looked at the ceiling. Was that a bomb at last? Or merely a rumbling in some ancient water pipe?

I was forced to share bedding with Mother, but made sure that I could lie next to Boris as well. Mother had brought an extra quilt to lay beneath us, but it was thin, the stone beneath it cold and hard. I had to shift constantly to ease the soreness in my bones. I whispered nonsense to Boris and he murmured back in Yiddish, sleepy, forgetting to use our secret language. The bodies on the ground were quiet. A few latecomers straggled onto our platform, excusing themselves as they stepped on hands and feet, drawing forth some juicy swearwords and then a harsh *shhh*, from someone's mother probably. Children all along the platform giggled. Boris trembled against my own shaking body.

Where is Boris? Sometimes I fancy I see him in the face of some Homburg-hatted relic tottering out onto the heath and I peer into the face beneath the brim, heart racing, but it is never him. One doesn't expect people to survive all the things we did. For all I know the Spanish flu got him before he finished school. Imagine, though, if he were still alive and living in London. Imagine what we would say to one another. Heavens, but you are *old*.

Anyway, the tube, in that war at the other end of the century. The lights were always on, so I had to pull the covers over my head to sleep. Mother lay quietly beside me on her back, with her eyes open, no doubt. Father snored, like the other fathers. The boys slapped each other on the other side of him, saying nothing, as though that were enough for them to remain blameless.

'Boris,' I whispered, my corner of the quilt tented above our heads. He smelled of lavender soap; its aroma filled the little shelter. His father owned a chemist's. 'What if they bombed the water pipes,'

I said, speaking English now that I had something close to my true thoughts that I wanted to convey, 'and we were flooded to death?'

'I'd save you.' But he wouldn't. He was almost asleep, crossing the border, leaving me behind.

'What if there was so much water that it filled to the ceiling, and all our bodies spouted up the stairs and onto the road. What then, Boris?'

Silence.

~

At weekends I was free to do as I pleased. Father had proclaimed the Sabbath archaic before my birth and the shop had been open every Saturday since we moved from Wales. No one passed comment because in London Saturday was the day to do business. When the well-to-do were up west in their traps and motor cars for a new set of shirts, or furniture for their townhouses, or sent the maids out for linen, you would be a fool to lock your door, Father said. They liked to take treats home with them too, and he was happy to take their money any day of the week. I remembered distantly the endlessness of Saturdays in the village we had come from, in the Rhondda Valley, where Mother's family had gathered. I would look at my picture books in a corner of the kitchen while Mother cooked all day. The endless meals, sitting up straight, listening to elderly ladies who were hard of hearing speaking too loudly. Sometimes I would be asked to show my books to Grandmother, Mother's mother, a crow in widow's weeds who smelled of medicine. She was dead now and had disappeared from our lives before that. Something to do with Father, of whom Mother's family had never approved. London was the last straw.

The boys usually disappeared together on a Saturday morning before anyone could protest, tearing down the lane and climbing over the railings at St John's to play football with the other boys. The West End held different delights for me. For a curious child who wanted to know everything of the world, it was all there the moment I stepped off the dented stair from the shop to the pavement of Tottenham Court Road.

This Saturday Mother, generally quiet and slightly elusive, was in a vile mood because Benjamin, the little one, clumsy and in thrall to Geoffrey's wicked suggestions, had covered his weekend clothes in mud by jumping in puddles in the ditch. The clothes reeked because there was horse manure in the mud and Mother was at the wash tub in the courtyard muttering in Welsh. Benjamin sat at the kitchen table in his long johns, a look of black thunder on his face. His tin soldiers were scattered across table and floor, a small chubby hand having laid great swathes of the troops to waste. Geoffrey had long since given up on the game and gone out with a friend who'd thrown stones at the window from down on the pavement to catch his attention. This was how boys communicated, I knew; by primitive means.

I put on my hat and stepped out from behind the curtain enclosing my bed, ready to go and find adventure on the windy streets. 'You *will* do everything he says, won't you, Benjamin?' Benjamin, four then, glowered back at me from beneath his dark curls. His clothes would not be dry until tea, by which time it would be too late for anything, and a whole Saturday would be wasted.

'I hate you,' he said quietly. 'And I hate Mother.' We were always saying such things. What casual horrors children can be.

'Save it for Geoffrey,' I replied, adjusting my boater over my long dark plaits. 'He's the one who gets you into trouble.'

He looked at me thoughtfully. 'Can't I come out with you, please?'

'But you don't have anything to wear.'

'My school clothes.'

'Mother will want to wash those too.'

'She hasn't taken them down yet.'

'We should have to get past Father.'

'He won't care.'

'Oh, come on then. But don't annoy me. No being a baby.'

'Thank you, Hannah. Thank you, thank you.' He sprang down from his chair and began to dress. 'I'll show you where Geoffrey keeps his sweeties.'

I laughed, eight and merciless. 'You think I don't know where he keeps his sweets? And I know where you keep yours too—so watch out!'

~

We walked along Tottenham Court Road towards Great Russell Street for the British Museum, the street noisy with horses and motorcars and fruiterers and paperboys shouting. London smelled of animals and coal smoke and roasting chestnuts, not the food of migrants as it does now. Benjamin insisted on holding my hand. I hoped not to see Boris, or anyone else from school. I had planned to look around Shoolbred's and Pritchard's but Benjamin would just whine and all the glamour of the mannequins with their slender waists and meshed hats would evaporate. And the museum was always worth the walk.

Benjamin *had* to look at the mummies before he could be persuaded to visit any other rooms. There was no point in arguing with him. The dimple in his chin deepened when I hesitated: a warning. He was not too old for public tantrums, and it was best not to draw attention, lest some well-meaning adult sent us home to Mother. It was not that I minded, really. You never grew out of the mummies, though I was not quite so enthralled as Benjamin, his face against the glass before a mummy of a cat, mouth slack. I waited as long as I could. 'Come on, Benjamin,' I said eventually. 'My turn.'

I walked quickly across the wooden floors, listening to the heels of my new shoes clop beautifully with each smart step. The trick at the British Museum was not to look at the same things every time, much as you loved them. I was filled with an idea of adventure, of newness, that kept my feet moving. I could not stop for the gems or the crockery. Deliberately I passed through doors I had not noticed before. Past a hundred glass cases of statues and swords, I was drawn on, another door, another empty corridor beyond the Saturday crowds, through the great halls. I glimpsed rooms of wrapped treasures, cardboard boxes. They were packing things up to store, with the air raids, and so I was engaged in a sort of race to see things before they were gone. I entered a dark room and knew that this was where I had been headed. I turned to hurry Benjamin along. Behind me was an empty corridor. *Benjamin*, I thought. Why must you . . . But no matter, I would retrace my steps in a moment. He would not be far behind.

The cases were lit and under the glass were scrolls of parchment and huge books with leather or wooden covers open at some carefully selected page. A few solitary men, mostly very old, stood entranced in the light at certain cabinets, like figures on a stage at the beginning of a scene, emerging from the dark. I found the way actors did that eerie; I could never quite get over the fact that they had been there in the blackness without my knowing.

I placed a finger on the glass in front of me and stood on tiptoe. There was a huge book before me, handwritten with ink in Latin. I imagined the hand writing on these stiff yellow pages. The inkwell. The candle for illumination. I was enclosed in the pool of light around the box and its miraculous contents as though I had left London and this modern age. The glass was cold against my nose and eyelids. I followed the words, mouthing them quietly, thrilled to be speaking Latin, even if I did not understand it. I had the feeling that I could reach through the glass and touch the page, know it by touching. And if I could touch the paper, just once, it might give me something, transmit some magic.

I saw myself doing it, my finger running over the writing. My mind ran ahead and I could feel it, the ink on the page. I saw in an instant that all the people who created these objects were joined together by a gossamer strand. They were part of a special group, like monks or soldiers. Standing here in this light I believed myself one of them, touched by the glitter of whatever had touched them as they sat at their desks with their ink and their parchment and their dim light. Knowledge seemed suddenly like a cloud of golden dust and something had brought me to this room and drawn me inside it.

A hand fell heavily on my shoulder and I let out a little cry.

'It's all right, my dear. We've got something for you.' I turned to see a guard in his smart uniform, a little round man only as tall as Father. My heart surged for a moment. I believed I might be given some special souvenir, that my connection to these objects was so clear and radiant that I was to be awarded some prize of my own. But then Benjamin stepped from behind the guard, the fat, grubby icon of my responsibilities. 'Thank you,' I sighed. 'I was just coming back to fetch him. Come on, Benjamin.' I took his plump little hand. 'If we go now we can catch the Variety at the Oxford.'

'All right. But will Mother be angry, do you think? And will it be me she's angry with, or you?'

'You. I shall go out again if she carries on. But she'll be angry whether we go home now or at suppertime. Come on, there's a new show playing. Boris tells me it's terrific. There's a funny song they teach the audience. And minstrels!'

On Tottenham Court Road we crossed the street well before Father's shop and I made sure we remained concealed amid the

Saturday shopping crowd, away from the kerb. The long coats and shopping bags formed a shifting but solid wall around us. I felt luxurious in a Saturday crowd, as though I was on a picnic rug on grass with cushions looking up at the trees. On the busy street, surrounded by adults with their purpose and their mysteries, I was warm and safe and tingling with promise. The company of children did not put me at ease as a rule, except for Boris and my brothers. Children were and probably still are brutish and fickle, bored by intellectual conversation. Among the grown-ups I hid if it suited me, to listen and learn the secrets of being older, or if I was among Father's friends when they drank beer in the shop after closing I would recite poetry or Shakespeare and bask, careful not to smile, in their appreciation. 'She has the ear!' Father would exclaim, clapping his hands. 'She shall be authoress! If I had these children's education. You think I would sell tobacco to make my crust? My Hannah, you will make your papa proud.' And the men stood close and raised their glasses in foreign toasts, exhaled thick pungent clouds of cigar smoke. I wanted to be instantly grown, completed, to prove Papa correct. Oh, I was in a tearing hurry to be the marvellous, accomplished person of my imaginings.

We drew level with Father's shop. I saw in a momentary gap in the crowd Mr Poppy, the barber whose shop backed onto ours, emerging from the side door, his huge belly covered by a white apron, chatting to a newly shorn customer who was rubbing the back of his neck. Benjamin was slowing, tugging at my hand. 'Can we go home and get some food? I'm hungry.'

'No! We'll never get out again and we'll catch it from Mother without having even seen the show. If you go back in I'm not waiting for you.'

'But, *Hannah . . .*'

We could not afford a scene here, so close to home. 'Listen, I've got a shilling. We can buy a bag of cakes from Mintz's and sneak in the back of the Oxford without paying.'

'Lor, Hannah. I do like cake.'

'It's common to say *lor*.'

'Father says not to say things are common. It's snobbish.'

'Don't say *lor* and I shan't have to.'

I tugged Benjamin along into the dense tide, past the swirling of bodies around the entrance to the tube, like water down the plughole of the basin, and on towards Oxford Street. He put his foot out off the kerb into the path of a motorcar—I felt the straightening of his arm as he stepped out, and I pulled him back sharply. The car roared past a yard in front of us. Inside the adults sat sombrely, obscured by the reflections of the building and my own face in the glass. I saw that I was frowning, as they were, mirroring the mild scowl of adulthood.

Emil

GALLIPOLI PENINSULA, MAY 1915

It was hard to imagine his body back to the beginning now, from here in the dugout, though he had been that person, new and ready, a month before. In front of him, Thomas lay on his low bunk across the trench, shaking and pale, his attention inward. They lay close, side by side. If Emil put his hand out, he could reach him. He did not know whether he was sick or just frightened but, nevertheless, they had orders to go over tonight. He closed his eyes and tried to remember. He did not know why he did this, except perhaps that it was a version of himself he wanted to return to. It was still perhaps close enough.

Between the flat metal of the Aegean and the dawn sky there had been no line. The ships were suspended for a few moments in a grey globe and then it was light enough to see that they sat on a flat surface, that smaller destroyers were in front of them, coming forward towards the cove. All night he and Thomas had lain on the ridge in the dark until a rocket lit the sky and the guns had started. The noise was greater than factories and mills. They had not slept, waiting, and the long fat launches dropping from the destroyers across the grey water were not quite real. But he watched the water and the men, shells cracking out over the boats, stirring up the water in little cyclones. Between shells he heard the knock-knock of the Turks' rifles in the gullies below like bullets in a cigar box. The boats were close enough to see the matchstick oars and the little men jumping out of them into the water.

He looked for individual men, began to fire his Mauser, and the things in the water began to fall, whether from his gun or others he could not be certain. There were so many that he fancied he saw the survivors wading through pink blooms of corpses, gathering and bumping in the waves. Something opened out in him, emptied him of the usual feelings: tiredness, pity. Over the next hour, his body loading and firing the gun as though it were part of the untiring mechanism, of the rifle itself, enough came through to fill the beach and he watched them disappear into the gullies, wondered when they would reach the top, if they had killed enough to prevent them from taking the ridge.

As he loaded he took a moment to look at Thomas. It was hard to believe that they were here. Emil was awake in every cell, his lungs full of gunpowder, the sun growing warm on his neck. There had been fear but now he found he could do it. He was a soldier. He could go on and on, if asked. He would shoot them even as they drew closer and he could see their faces. Whatever he was ordered to do he would do. His body was ready, sprung.

By nightfall it was hard to know just where the British were, but he was ordered to rest for a few hours and he ate his bread and lamb fat in the dugout he shared with Thomas. It was lined with sandbags and they had built a roof of pine logs and dug long shallow dishes in the soil, filled them in with pine needles for sleeping. They lay in their trenches facing each other, the earth rumbling with mortar fire, the lantern on the shelf flickering. The sound was more incredible when you were not physically involved with the firing, when your body was separate and the guns existed outside you.

'Tell me what Uta let you do. I don't want to die without knowing.' Thomas was shouting but it was through lip reading and long familiarity that Emil understood him. He had known from his smile, before he opened his mouth, what he was about to say.

'I promised not to tell anyone.'

'Come on. It's me.'

'No, Thomas, rest.' He snuffed out the lantern and they turned away from each other. He could not imagine sleeping ever again. It was only decorum that made him turn away, to allow privacy for his friend in the night. He smoothed a patch of soil in front of him with his hand and thought again of Uta, who lived in the apartment building across the road from his parents. The day he told her he had been conscripted, he had waited on the street as she trudged slowly across the road, tired from her work hunched over a sewing machine in the glove factory. She was too far away for him to see her face but her step quickened when she saw his shape in the shadow of the building. There was no one in the apartment. Her parents were visiting relatives. When he told her, sitting on her narrow bed in her room surrounded by dolls, she let him briefly put his hand up her skirt and touch the thin strip of flesh between her stocking and her corset. The skin was cold from her walk home, his fingers warm from his pockets. He had tried before but this time her hand did not stop his until it was there, at her thigh.

He did not want to lie here like this; his body was drawn to go back out and take the gun. He held his watch in front of his face and waited for shell fire above to illuminate its face. An hour until they took over.

They had lost that position, soon enough. This dugout, in which he watched Thomas shiver silently, was further back. He no longer lay impatiently, waiting to take up his gun. He reached out a hand and laid it on Thomas's shoulder. He could not stop him shaking.

~

In the quiet times, leaning against the pine-log wall, eyes closed, face in the sun, when any of them might go mad with the memory of what they had seen and their fingers had touched, Emil took to writing letters to his father in his head. Two months since the British and their friends had landed and he had not written a single real letter, though all around him, even now, the Turks were hunched over scraps of paper, smoking and frowning. He could not manage the performance. It was a gesture he could not make, a falsehood: to have them read a letter, to see his handwriting, to believe these were the words of the boy they knew. Still, he had the same urge to tell as anyone.

Dear Father, he wrote in his mind, Thomas did not want to go out that night. He had formed an idea that God would take a dim view of his skill with a rifle. The odds were evil, he said, with his strike rate. You would be happier going out there with your knife? I asked him, many times. God would be happier, he said. Perhaps you're surprised, Father, that he spoke like this. All I can say is that those who believed in God when they arrived aren't so sure now, and those that were wavering see him in everything. Well, I said to Thomas, for tonight, you have a Mauser, and unless we're to be shot for desertion we had better take our posts. I went along the trench to mine and over we went. I survived another action. When I returned to Thomas at the end of it he was lying across the lip of the trench. He looked as though there was nothing wrong with him, as though he was sleeping off a hard night. The dawn did not wake him. I sat next to him and took his hand. It was still warm and I saw then that his face was not whole, but I'd seen worse by then. I was thinking, when his hand goes cold, it will never be warm again, so I had better stay.

You have taught me that a man must act where he sees injustice, that this is what a man is, that in every moment might be the making of history. Father, if thoughts were treason they would have shot me many times over. But I can tell you here, where there's no one but us, that the only way to act in this place is to die or to run, and a dead man does nothing for anybody.

~

The Germans were drinking in their trench during a ceasefire for retrieval of the dead and wounded. Emil filled his tin mug and passed on the bottle of brandy. One of the German officers, Stemmer, was making a joke about the Australians. He called them armadillos: shell on top, tender meat beneath. He said that he liked to see their faces, feel how soft they were inside in spite of their muscles. Emil played cards in the officers' trench between actions, to hear German, but if this was what he had to listen to he'd rather be among the Turks and understand almost nothing.

Out across the gullies the night was falling, the shadows in the creases of the land spreading across the hills. From the dark cracks came the men, the ones who came at night, more and more of them. Turks, British, Australians and New Zealanders. A German, always the same one, with a face he knew from his past but could not place.

They emerged from the cracks in the land exposing their wounds obscenely. He blinked and banished them, knowing they would be back. They always came at this hour as the shadows spread from the gullies.

A peal of wild laughter from down on the beach. Sometimes, on a hot night, when no one was moaning and the guns were quiet, they did not sound like soldiers. You could smell the fires. They were roasting meat by the sea, eating and talking. For days he had been lying in his dugout with a fever from a mosquito bite, waiting for quinine. He would give anything to swim in the ocean—the water would be warm—and then sit on the beach, clothes clinging to salty skin, eating and talking to other men about something that was not killing or cigarettes or when the post might finally arrive.

Perhaps when the dead had been removed and buried they would stop walking out at him at dusk. He could hear those Turks not on duty in their trench close to the Germans, their murmured prayers. He wondered whether the retrieval parties would find Thomas's body, whether they would pray over it.

He remembered a hot night by the Rhine. He and Thomas played cards by the light of a little fire. They had stolen liquor being unloaded outside their fathers' social club and lay on the damp grass moaning, the stars swirling. Thomas's head lay still on the ground, in the summer field. He was becoming something of a heartbreaker around the town. His sister asked about him in her letters to the front. He had not yet answered her.

He let himself imagine for an instant, his head light, that he had never left Germany, that he had been allowed to simply go from his studies into work as an electrical engineer, to marry Uta. There was no pit burial, no faces to be sprinkled with lime. He felt movement near him in the deepening dusk. It was Captain Hass, gentle behind the lines, softly spoken, yet Emil had seen him shoot an able-bodied Turk for coming back with wounded in the midst of an attack. The captain looked him up and down. 'You've been declared fit, haven't you, Becker? You can go out tonight.'

'Yes, sir.'

'Half an hour.'

There was a rumour that Germans were a prize to the Australians on the beach. They did not really know for certain that they were there, it seemed, or how many, but if they found one they had no interest in taking him back down to the pen. It was said the Australians had been promised extra leave for whoever brought back a German head on a stick.

In half an hour, if he chose to, he could end every sensation in his body: the lice running up and down his neck into his hair and shirt, the dried mud caked around his feet, the rod of electric fear in his back, the hunger that made him dream in his scarce moments of sleep of the cinnamon rolls in the Konditorei on Unterstrasse, the noise of the guns that rattled his brain and made every thought an effort. The memory of Thomas lying in the mud, over the lip of the trench. Afterwards, while Emil's body remained here among the Turks, or was dismembered as a trophy for the Australians, some other part of him would travel to the fields on the edge of the Rhine, away from the factories and the town, where all you could hear were birds and the wind in the leaves. Hares running in the fields, more than you could fit in your rucksack.

But that was not the plan he had formed as he emerged from delirium in the medical tent. He stirred his legs, gave them a little shake, went along the tunnel to wait with the Turks. The insects swarmed and dived. He could hear them in the quiet of the ceasefire, and men's voices, just talking. One he knew, Faisal, gave him a cigarette and they chatted a little in the Turkish he had picked up from the men between actions. A group was returning to the trench from the burial, quiet. He took his position. Can I do it? he asked himself.

The machine gun in the trench started up along the line and he climbed to the lip, ready to go over. He wondered how bad the pain was going to be. And now the Turks were running forward, he with them, firing, some falling. Their voices in the night, the strange words and rhythms, helped him not to believe that anything in this world was real. He let his rifle slip towards the ground. He waited for a mortar flash and looked down, took aim—that is my knee, there are my toes, not those, wait for dark, *now, do it*—and fired.

~

He came to in the dark. His leg lay against another's that did not move and was hard. God was talking to him. He was asking him how you fix a Howitzer that has ceased to fire. *Quickly, while they come forward with rifles, how do you fix it?* No, not God. Father. He always wanted to learn what he could from Emil's education, wanted to add to his own understanding of machinery, and Emil loved to explain to him the smallest details of how a machine worked, how you might fix it when it failed. His voice came, as clearly in the dark as though they were sitting opposite one another at the kitchen table. 'Ah yes, I never would have thought it was something so simple.' But Emil could not answer him. His throat was very dry. The blackness was like velvet across his eyes, and the hard leg did not move.

~

There was no time for gentleness for the Turk who dragged Emil over the pocked mud to the medical tent. The firing had ceased but it was never safe in the open. The Turk let Emil's leg slam and bounce along the ground. Every impact sent a shock the length of his body. The astonishing *pain.* So this, precisely, was how much it would hurt. It obliterated thought. The light was coming. He could smell the burial pit somewhere close, bodies decomposing in spite of the lime. The world was the Turk's stretched face against the fading purple sky, the sharp breaths, the rhythmic jarring of pain. In a shallow ditch the Turk laid him down. Through a thicket of dry grass he saw the man running low, zigzagging like a hare from hollow to hollow, back to the line. It was almost light. Stay down, he thought. He lost him and then his helmet emerged again. He heard German voices. In his head he said, I am breathing. Please, don't put the lime on my face.

They tipped him onto a stretcher and carried him around to the back of the hospital tent where a line of men groaned or lay still and silent in the dark. The medical officer shone a torch into his eye, looking at something at the back of his head, shot something in his arm. The others on the stretchers rose up and gathered around him. They all peered, the Turks; they too wanted to look at something beyond his eyes. They shook their heads, ignoring their own wounds: arms stopping at the elbow, burnt faces with pink eyes and mouths. Then he felt himself pulled backwards towards the green centre of Europe away from the wild cliffs of the coast, to a place where the earth stood still and there were women.

~

The Turks on their beds in a long row were grey in face and limb, some gangrenous and foul. They moaned, day and night, though they received visitors, wives with hips that held the eye. They had only been taken back as far as Constantinople. He wondered whether his injury would take him back to Europe at all.

Be quiet or die, he told them silently. From his own body rose the constant tang of old blood, confusing him. He did not bleed anymore and his dressing was changed regularly.

Early in the morning shafts of light slanting from the high windows onto the beds along the wall opposite made them seem blessed in their disfigurement, as though they were about to be taken away to something better. City sounds—hawkers, children—cooking smells from street vendors, coffee, drifted in. He longed to venture outside to see. The intricate hot mystery of the palaces, lanes and bazaars, the call to prayer.

The sister was a dark woman with a lined face like a peasant, and very strong. She lifted men on and off beds, often without assistance, though it was true that many of them were thin, looked weightless. He could feel the ripple of his own ribs when she dragged the sponge across them. She smiled when he used fragments of Turkish to ask for cigarettes and water.

On the night shift there was an Austrian nurse who he had discovered was nineteen, a year older than him. He slept when he could in the day so that he could talk to her. He didn't know if she was pretty. The hair at her temple was an ordinary brown colour, disappearing under her cap, and her features seemed even enough. He couldn't tell anymore, but she had hips and a bosom and looked soft. Her skin was clear. She seemed clean. She was a quiet girl among the Turkish soldiers, eyes cast down like a Turkish woman, but if she had a few moments she would sit on a wooden chair beside his bed and answer his questions. He tried not to scratch at the memory of lice.

What sort of school did you go to? Do you have brothers and sisters? What writers do you read? Why did you decide to be a nurse? Tell me how the houses look in your street. Who are your friends? Once he found the recklessness to say, 'Describe your room at home,' thinking now she would turn her face away, never answer him again. She paused for a few moments as she did with every question and then she told him, stepping out gently into her description as always. She shared a room with her sister in her parents' apartment in a village in the Alps. They had a bed each along opposite walls. Between them was a window that opened out onto the town square. Over the roofs one saw the mountains. When the war began a year ago the square was filled with people singing and she and her sister leaned out their window and listened to them until late at night. She almost fell, she was leaning so far. Her sister pulled her back as she slipped by grabbing hold of her plait. He closed his eyes. He could see it. The people in the square, the girl wide-eyed, careless, her sister more sensible, alert, grasping the long thick plait. He too had sung when they set off. And Thomas.

But she also told him when he asked of the meals at home: 'There is almost nothing to eat. Old bread. Pea soup that has been stretched out for days. No coffee. Hardly any milk. A neighbour's baby died.' She frowned when she spoke, a little furrow appearing over her nose.

The Turkish sister mostly left them alone unless there was an emergency, a fresh delivery of wounded, the bathing of a burnt man. When he heard the cries of one of these and knew that the nurse, called away from him, was holding him, his heart ached for her and he wished that the answering of his questions was enough to keep her here beside his bed.

They moved him away from her after a while, to a large house on the edge of the city that had been converted into dormitories for recuperation. He was not given a chance to say goodbye and he was surprised at the wrench he felt as he bumped along in the back of an uncovered lorry, his leg jarring, crutches either side of him. Here were the streets of Constantinople that had been calling to him. He glimpsed a shady courtyard filled with flowering vines on the tiled walls, a family meal taking place at a long table. A young woman was serving, bending forward. She looked up and saw him as the truck passed down the narrow street. He saw her eyes, and they were much more beautiful than the nurse's, but it was the Austrian girl's ordinariness that had touched him. He might have seen a hundred girls like her any day of the week in Duisburg.

At the house, there was an overgrown garden to hobble around, games of cards, sudden booze bounties, bawdy talk, even whispers of revolution—or desertion, if you gave it its proper name. *We could just . . . not go back.* Longing glances at the hills that led down to the sea. He avoided these conversations. Such thoughts were a contagion. There were men being shipped home or back to the fighting, newcomers with astonishing afflictions, a former schoolteacher who was coaching the men in French, obscure phrases guaranteed to bewitch any woman into weakness and acquiescence. They bet cigarettes from home on cockroach races. Emil picked them well. He never ran out of cigarettes and was often able to buy liquor and chocolate. But he knew this was a brief interlude of unreality. And soon a letter came, congratulating him on his immediate promotion and providing instructions for transport to Palestine.

Hannah

LONDON, 1917

Miss Taylor had blonde curls and milk-white teeth and stood very straight in front of the class as though she had been trained as a ballerina. I always sat a little more upright, walked more carefully in her presence. She had just asked the class for the capital of Switzerland. There were no hands in the air. It was hot and the boys tipped back on their chairs, the girls with the fashionable hairstyles and nicer shoes showed each other notes, believing themselves clever, unobserved. Imbecilic, I thought, not that they would know what that meant.

'Go on, Hannah,' Boris whispered from the next desk. 'You know it.'

I would not look at him. Berne! a part of my brain shouted, *Berne!* But another part prevailed: Do not speak, it commanded. It is beneath you. Miss Taylor cast her gaze around the class, round blue eyes falling upon everyone before me, until eventually she raised a beautifully shaped eyebrow kindly. 'Hannah, dear?'

'I do know, but somebody else can answer. It's all right.'

Faith, one of the stylish girls, groaned quietly somewhere behind me. I knew her groan of old.

'But I'm asking you, Hannah.'

Just then the raid alarm sounded, starting quietly and quickly building to a deafening blare. We were not used to daytime raids. Miss Taylor blinked sternly and said, 'Quick, children, under the desks, just as we've practised.'

I felt the withdrawal of Miss Taylor's attention like being cast into a cool shadow but I dutifully stood, picked up the Philip's atlas I was sharing with Boris and pulled out my chair from under my desk. We dragged our desks together amid the screeching of the other children doing the same and crouched beneath our shelter, holding the atlas above our heads as though we were running home across Fitzroy Square in the rain with a newspaper for cover. Boris trembled. If our school had been hit, and they unearthed us later, they would have found us preserved in rubble, twenty ten-year-olds and one adult crouching, heads bent, as though what we did not see could not hurt us. Or perhaps they would decide that we were praying for mercy.

The others whispered in their neighbour's ear, hands cupped to their heads, made faces. When I saw that Miss Taylor was under her own desk, staring at the floor, whispering, I shuffled away from Boris, poked my head out from under the desk so that I could see through the window—but there was nothing there. I inched back to Boris, whose eyes were squeezed shut. I closed mine too for a moment and imagined I saw it: the long fountain-pen shape of the German zeppelin, its slow dark mass gliding out from the roofs. I didn't know that they had decided to set the Gotha planes on us by then, that the mesmerising zeppelins were already fading into the past.

I opened my eyes to peek at Miss Taylor. I do it now with air hostesses when there is turbulence: *How bad is it? Should I be scared?*

It seemed I should. She was indeed praying, trying to pretend that she wasn't. Her hands were clasped in her lap and her lips were moving. I hoped that if there were such a being as God, against the insistence of Father, he would be kind enough to listen to Miss Taylor. I felt confident that Miss Taylor would pray for us, or at least for me, and so I considered myself to be insured. I was my father's girl enough to draw the line at praying for myself.

~

When we arrived home from school the shop was empty. As we entered its cool shade and tobacco and cinnamon smell, the bell ringing behind us, there was a space behind the counter where we would usually expect to see Father smiling in his black waistcoat, consulting his chained gold watch and saying, 'Ah, children, I believed the *buka* got you. Why so long to walk one hundred yards?'

On the narrow stairs we heard Mother shouting in Yiddish in the apartment.

'What is she saying?' Geoffrey whispered.

'That she cannot bear it a moment longer.'

'Bear what?'

'I don't know.'

'Hysteria will solve nothing,' Father was saying in English as we entered the flat. And then, '*Tishe, deti.*' Hush, the children.

Throughout dinner Mother clenched a handkerchief and ate nothing. She looked pale and her hair had come loose from its bun. I saw suddenly that she was beautiful. I could not stop staring. Had her eyelashes always been so long, her skin so pale? She seemed to be from some other world, this woman I so often ignored as she moved about the kitchen and leaned over the tub in the yard. Now her white blouse, her long cheekbones, seemed touched by light.

A ghost at our table while the rest were noisy, smelly, ruddy, alive. Father wrapped a dark square hand around hers and she pulled it away. The boys made big eyes at each other over their dishes and Benjamin could not help but giggle. I wished, not for the first time, that my two infantile brothers could be exchanged for an older one, away at war, who came home and spent his pay on taking me to tea at the Lyons Corner House or Selfridges.

As we cleared the table there came a sharp rap at the door. It had to be Mrs Reznik from upstairs; she was the only one with the key to the side passage in the alley that adjoined our staircase behind the shop.

'Come!' bellowed Father. She thrust her head around the door like a mouse, her long face twitching at the smell of food. 'Mrs Reznik.' Father stood from the head of the table. 'Will you eat? There is plenty left.'

'No, no. I have just had supper.'

'But Mrs Reznik! You insult my wife's cooking.'

'Oh no. Well, just a little.' She was already at the table next to me, pulling back the chair I had just vacated, easing her mantis frame into it and waiting for a clean dish. She had money, I had seen inside the biscuit tin of bright silver shillings and crowns that she kept at the top of a ladder in the loft. She wouldn't spend it on food for herself, though, and was as thin a person as I ever knew, though quite vigorous and nimble in spite of being considerably older than Mother and Father. If I had as much money as that I would have spent most of it on chocolate and cake on the black market and rations be damned.

I dragged over the extra chair from beside the bed, behind the curtain, and we sat, waiting for her to finish eating. She hunched over her bowl, a thin person who could never be warm or full, long mechanical arms scooping relentlessly. The borscht disappeared quickly and as she wiped the dish with her bread we were able to stare openly at her deep red moustache, so absorbed was she in the act of eating.

'Do you need Hannah tonight?' Father asked eventually. They spoke in English. Father always spoke in English to Mrs Reznik. It seemed to me like acting, for the benefit of others, for two Russians to speak in English. I could not see why one would bother, but then my interest in manners has always been a little underdeveloped.

'Well . . .' she belched a little behind her hand. Benjamin exploded with the giggles and I kicked him. Mother and Father wore their polite faces, smiles fixed, eyes a little wide, though Mother kept glancing at the window which trembled loosely in its frame with every passing cart and motorbus. 'If it is not a trouble. A short letter only. I have tinned beef and peaches and my cousin's family are very hungry.'

'It is no better?' Father asked. 'We have no letters for a little while. Your parcels are arriving?'

'Some I think, yes. But, you know, there is not even so much milk for the baby.'

'But we have some milk powder,' Mother said quietly, the first thing she had said since we came home from school. Father gave me a look that was technically irreproachable but whose timing made it secret, risqué. I loved him fiercely for a moment.

'Yes, yes,' he agreed, leaving me to stifle a grin. 'Send our milk, while you are making a parcel. The children have milk at school.'

'Never. I cannot take children's milk, Mr Jacob.'

'Of course, take. They are fat. Look at my sturdy little Hannah! The baby must have milk.'

Mother was already in the cupboard, fishing for the box. She knocked a bag of porridge to the floor where it scattered wide. 'Oh my!' I watched her, wondering whether she would cry.

'Oh, Mrs Jacob, look what I make you.'

'It is nothing,' Father said. 'Hannah, you take the milk up for Mrs Reznik. We clean up here. Boys, come. Help Mother.'

He stood and took the box from Mother, who kept her back to the room as she bent down to fetch the dustpan and brush from under the basin. His hand was on her shoulder. What was wrong with her? It was only porridge. None of us liked it anyway. There was never enough sugar to make it palatable. Father let us have sherbet from the shop but that just made it claggy and rather sickly.

I went to Father and took the box. 'That's it, little Hannah. Go and help Mrs Reznik now. Home in time for prayers.' He winked. I did not wink back though it was hard not to smile. It would scandalise Mrs Reznik if we were too brazen. Father was making it rather obvious that there were no prayers in this house.

I followed Mrs Reznik up the stairs. Unlike Mother, who in spite of her current fragility was soft in the bottom and the arms, she had no behind. Father called Mother '*zaftig*' when he whispered to her at the kitchen sideboard. Literally: juicy. Mrs Reznik would be whatever the opposite was of that. I wondered: *unzaftig*? She climbed slowly, talking constantly, so I could stare as much as I chose.

'Now, Hannah, the letter is difficult tonight. I tell to Gregor I don't know what I can send more. My health is bad, I don't have the strength to schlep around the West End looking for the little extras. I should be caught paying black marketeers? My God, prison. Can you imagine, Hannah?'

Eventually we reached her landing and Mrs Reznik unlocked the door while I waited impatiently. After an age she led me inside.

That moment, when she opened her door, never lost its glamour. The flat was the same as ours, but not the same at all. It had the same layout but it was only Mrs Reznik living here since her husband, a draper too, went back to Russia to be a Bolshevik. Mrs Reznik had a separate bedroom and a spare room with a desk where Mr Reznik once did his accounts, so rather than a bed and wardrobe being crammed into the sitting room behind a curtain as in our flat, one stepped from the front door into a proper sitting room. Then it was several large strides between the fireplace and the sofa, or from the door to the window looking out over Tottenham Court Road. In our flat, if you mapped our movements, we were like rats, following little channels between the corridors of tables, chairs, beds, laundry, Father's bolts of fabric for his second business, hatstands, boxes of tobacco and sweets. This room contained simply a sofa, a standard lamp, a small dining table with two chairs, a beautiful rug and a bookshelf against one wall filled with books. Mrs Reznik could not read them, which tortured me—to think that all this, this quiet, spacious place to read and this case of books, was wasted on an illiterate. Mrs Reznik had told me that her husband sometimes took books as payment and now she was *stuck with them* when the money would have been of far more use. She lent them to me, and I would read them, whatever they might be: penny dreadfuls, political pamphlets, a French dictionary—devouring them like food in the dim light before Mother stirred in the morning.

The books were part of my payment for helping her with her letters, and she was so mean she would actually hold on to them for a moment while passing them to me so I had to give a little tug to release the object from her grasp. But so far as I was concerned, the main part of my reward was being permitted to spend time here, in this flat, with space, order and comfort, where there was a gold-rimmed bone china tea set on a tray on a sideboard next to a gramophone encrusted with dust. Every time I entered this place, separated from my own home only by a thin floor, it was a reminder, an affirmation. Yes, this was how my own life would be, how it would look to others. I would have my own flat with books and a sofa and a gramophone and no husband and no vile little boys making a mess and a noise. I would drink tea from bone china while writing poetry at a desk in the window. Playwrights and artists and actors would visit me and we would all go off to the theatre together wearing smart gloves with buttons and exquisite hats and I would visit my brothers in their squalid tenements with their enormous, ill-educated broods only when they were *starving*, and I would take their wives bread, and sweets for the awful children, and only because my heart was too tender for my own good. Everyone would say so.

'Come, Hannah. Up at the table. Here is the paper and the pencil. Careful not to break it, I have not another.'

I knew that in the sideboard there was a thick brick of blank paper and a cup of lovely sharp lead pencils, because I looked once when Mrs Reznik was up in the loft fetching her money tin. And so I unleashed upon myself another source of torture: the vivid and durable image of the beautiful cream paper, the perfectly pointed pencils. Who could say how much more bounty lay secreted in cupboards and in boxes under beds? I asked Mother after that how Mrs Reznik laid her hands on such treasures and Mother told me mysteriously that she was a person with connections. When I asked her what she meant, Father said, 'It is she knows people who do her favours because she has already done favours for them.' I liked the sound of that almost as much as I liked her large and empty flat. Imagine, to live in a world where there was a secret currency beyond coupons and money, which were things that anyone could come by. 'Husband did too many favours,' Father said. 'Safer in Russia, with the Bolsheviks.'

The reason I was here, why I was granted occasional access to this quiet, miraculous place, was in order to read Mrs Reznik's letters from Russia and reply for her. Her relatives wrote to her in Yiddish, thankfully, because I did not have the Cyrillic script, though I assumed without deep thought that it would arrive in my store of knowledge at some point. I had not known until this arrangement began that it was possible once you were past the age of, say, seven not to be able to read and write. Some of the stupider boys in my class still struggled, but I had assumed that even for them the instinct to understand and produce language in its written form would prevail. It was like talking. It just happened for humans at some stage in their development. How could you hold a perfectly sensible conversation and not be able to *read*? And so my pencil hovered above the clean paper, finely grooved, lovely, ready to turn this woman's mix of English and Russian with an occasional Yiddish exclamation into something her cousin might understand.

She took my wrist as always in her cold bony fingers, stared at me with her saucer eyes. 'Please write, "Dear Gregor . . ." and I extricated my hand and wrote the story of Mrs Reznik's failing health, which was how we began every letter, before going on to detail the price of the beef and fruit, and extolling at length the virtues of my parents who had provided the milk. I kept this passage brief. I knew it was meant for me, included simply so that I would relay it back to them. I waited with the pencil ready for her to move on. She complained about the daytime raids and claimed that she would not shelter in the tube station anymore because she had heard from a friend of her husband in Shoreditch that there was looting in the East End recently. And all the time I must correct the grammar of her fragmented language at the same time as finding the Yiddish, and Mrs Reznik going on and on, barely giving me a moment to think, except for the occasional pause for a cough, after which she would peer at my handwriting, her nose creasing.

The nerve, I thought, if this woman were to comment upon my script. But I did have appalling handwriting, bad enough for even an illiterate to turn up her nose. I have my notebook before me now and I see described in a scrawl, the pen pressed down so hard the paper threatens to tear, what a fascinating, awful old witch Mrs Reznik seemed to me. I still see her kind about. Hungry, thin, elderly foreign women, alive in the face of all odds, refusing to make themselves less frightening, their faces lined with long memories, bodies bent with burdens never cast off. Who but a wilful, impatient child could hold it against them?

Mrs Reznik was quiet for a second or two, during which I rubbed the side of my aching fist, before going on: 'Gregor, if you send the girl to me, I help you and Nina. I have a little bit money—' she glanced sideways at me '—and I would take care of her like she is mine. She eats well and goes to good school, and when she is big there are good young men here that would not make disgrace for you. I pray the war ends soon and you send her to me in London. Then she is clever and successful and she brings you here. You can do anything in London if you work hard.'

I shook my hand, blinked my eyes. Mrs Reznik had been speaking more quickly than usual, and it took all my concentration to structure the sentences in my brain as quickly in Yiddish as the woman spoke, to push the pencil across the page without losing the flow. I paused, waiting to see if there was more. After a moment I looked up. Mrs Reznik was staring at the wall. Just *wait* until I told Mother why she tucked all her money away and sent tins of beef to Russia while she herself starved, and hoarded paper and pencils in secret cupboards.

She leaned back on her chair and closed her eyes briefly. I watched a little pulse flicker in the crepey skin under her left eye.

'Come now, Hannah,' she said, gathering herself. 'Is it books you have not read?'

'Oh yes.'

'Come and choose. I find your sixpence.'

I decided I would chance my arm, as the barrow boys would say. 'Mother says not to take the sixpence, Mrs Reznik.'

'She thinks I do not have it?'

'She says only that food is scarce and it is better for you to use it for your cousin's family than to give me pocket money, which I shall only fritter on shows and riding the motorbus.'

Mrs Reznik laughed, a harsh, brief sound that I only recognised as a laugh because I sensed that I might have just said something a certain sort of person could construe as amusing. 'You will take shilling. You tell your mother I pay every bill.'

~

It was a hot afternoon. The weekend seemed far. I trudged along the pavement, brothers at my heel, flushed and ready to pounce on any annoyance. Benjamin was dancing about in my path. 'Hannah, I read from the blackboard. I read my name aloud.'

'Tell Papa,' Geoffrey said. 'You'll get a sweet.'

'Really?' Benjamin asked, still looking at me.

'Yes, really,' I replied.

'Will we all get one?'

'No, just you,' Geoffrey said. 'He gives you one when you start to read.'

We were not short of sweets, what with the shop and an indulgent father, but Benjamin was about to experience something special.

I remembered the day I had run home from school, the boys still small and glued to Mother's feet beneath the table, and I had told Father, as Benjamin had told us, that I had read my name on the blackboard. Father had clapped his hands, made me stand at the head of the table where he had been examining his ledgers, and gone to look in the pantry.

'Close your eyes,' he ordered.

I heard Mother whisper, 'It is the wrong kind of sweet.'

'Shhh,' he replied. 'It is the sweetness who matters.' And then, louder, to me: 'What word did you read?'

'Hannah,' I said proudly.

'You see it now, behind the eyes, how it looked on teacher's board?'

I nodded.

'Open the mouth now, very wide.'

I put out my tongue and felt the chocolate, closed my lips over it, let the sweetness dissolve.

'Still, still you see your name?'

I nodded, my mouth crammed with dissolving cocoa, cream, sugar.

I felt his breath in my hair. 'Knowledge is sweet,' he whispered.

Benjamin was still tugging at my hand as we walked along the street. I looked at his delighted face and felt a stab of envy. Then a siren filled the shadowy space between the buildings and I thought: Oh Lord, what now? We looked at each other. The street was empty of people, traffic. The noise grew. We put our hands over our ears and tried to speak.

'We have to get to the tube,' Geoffrey was shouting.

'It's miles away,' I replied.

Suddenly there was a draft of warm air from a doorway, a hand was slapping down on my shoulder and we were all being pulled off the street and into a baker's that I had never before noticed. It was not the one we used. Mother was particular, though Father told her it did not matter where you bought your bread. 'Bread is *bread*, Maria. It is all the same. Go where it smells good.' A woman with meaty hands and a lot of jewellery said, while the dozen or so people crowded into the shop stared at us, 'You are the children of the tobacconist.' She spoke slowly, as though we were hard of hearing, or simple. 'Wait in here until the all-clear and I will come with you and explain to your father.'

The baker gave us an iced bun each and we sat on the floor in a corner while the customers grumbled about the audacity of the Germans now with these daylight raids. I tore off and devoured large pieces of sweet bread while the boys did the same, Benjamin cramming his into his mouth so fast I was sure he would make himself ill. There was a movement in the earth somewhere close by, as close as I had ever felt it, and the people in the shop were quiet as a fire engine's siren grew louder and louder and soon tore right by the boarded-up window, a flash of red just visible where the ply did not quite meet the frame at the top.

'My stars,' murmured the woman who dragged us in here.

'Bit close for comfort,' replied the baker, and they started up again, more quietly than before, speculating where it might have hit.

'Hope it wasn't the tube,' a man said. 'We'll have to walk to Warren Street. Pain in the you-know-what.'

I grew drowsy among the feet, at least one pair of which were ripe I noticed now I had finished eating, and I leaned my head against the wall and tried not to breathe through my nose. Then Geoffrey was shaking my shoulder, the all-clear was sounding, and the woman insisted on walking with us to the shop, though it was only around the corner and we did it by ourselves every day.

Once more the shop was empty when Father should be waiting for us, and we burst into the flat to find them silently contemplating a long, curved, jagged-edged piece of metal on the table. Mother jumped up and pressed us to her roughly. 'Where have you been, you terrible children?' The buttons of her blouse pressed into my cheek until I wriggled from her grasp so that I could take another look at what was on the table. There was nothing else on it. The usual teacups and ledgers and little heaps of change to be sorted had been cleared as though the piece of metal were some kind of exhibit.

Geoffrey gasped. 'Is that an anti-aircraft shell?' He drew closer. 'Perhaps it's part of a German bomb.'

'Can I touch it?' Benjamin said.

'My God, no,' said Mother.

'Where did you find it?' I asked Father, staring at its deadly edge, allowing myself to imagine briefly it jutting out from Geoffrey's head.

'On the front step,' he told us. 'Your mother has packed your bags. You are going to the country.'

~

We saw when we reached the tube platform that all the adults in the area had conspired to banish their children. Around us parents bellowed instructions, as though their children were already on a train moving off from them. 'Don't eat your sandwich until you've changed trains. Mind your cousin.'

Mother was silent and pale. Her strange light had grown more intense lately while the outline of her seemed to fade within it, reduced to a core of worry. She held Benjamin's hand tightly, he complaining and grimacing, without seeming to notice. When she handed me my new brown case, acquired for me especially for this trip by Father, I saw that the veins in her bony hand were raised.

Father leaned down to embrace me. The wool of his jacket scraped my cheek. 'Hannah, you are strong and clever little woman. These boys rely on your brain now, yes?' He straightened, held my eye.

Mother's hand was cold when I took it. She was little and round. She need only lean forward slightly to kiss me on the brow, though I was always small myself. My heart faltered for a moment, as though I were some other child, not the girl I knew myself to be: stout-hearted, indefatigable.

Father crushed a pound note into my hand, smooth with handling. I had only touched paper money in the shop as I placed it carefully in the register and counted out change. 'Emergency fund,' he whispered. I rubbed my thumb over it in my pocket.

A blast of hot air gusted along the platform and the train's snub engine nosed into the station. All over the platform mothers clutched at their children. I had thrown some wicked tantrums at the idea of being sent to the country, but now that we were packed and standing on the platform I longed to be off. The doors creaked heavily as children climbed aboard. I wished to be with those who were moving, not these old, slow ones remaining behind. It was the first time I had been away from my parents and I felt somehow that my life to now had been lived in preparation for this moment.

The boys clung to Mother while I stepped onto the train with the case, turning to offer Father a brave salute, seeking out free seats that faced each other. I sat down, saw my family through the window, potbellied, waistcoated Father shooing them off the platform and up into the carriage. His eye found me and he nodded as the train began to move and the boys settled themselves down. In the last moment that I saw my parents they were small and old and standing very close to one another. As the train picked up speed I saw the picture repeated along the platform: countless huddles of old people in dark clothes, watching the train filled with their children accelerating away from them. Our carriage hit the tunnel with a smack of air and I had begun my first journey without my parents.

We changed at Baker Street. The next train was more crowded and there were many more adults, some of whom were fat and loose somehow and squashed onto seats all together, men and women. We squeezed our way among them. One group began to sing 'It's a Long Way to Tipperary' the instant the train pulled off, as though the movement were a signal, and they were passing around a hipflask, man to woman to man, no one so much as wiping the rim in between. It was like stepping with Father into the working men's club off the lane behind Charlotte Street: all heat and cigarette smoke and off-kilter laughter.

We were still searching for seats as the train started out of the station, knocking us off balance. Only singles remained. I eyed a narrow space next to a woman's wide behind and sat, reluctantly. The woman's soft flesh at the hip sank against me immediately. The boys sat opposite each other a few rows along, next to a couple of airmen who smoked continually. I watched them for a long time but they never appeared to fish for cigarettes in their pockets or even to light them. Geoffrey and Benjamin stared at them openly, and then at each other. They could not believe their luck, damn them. My neighbour ate an egg sandwich. The airmen ruffled the boys' hair and conjured coins from behind their ears. A conductor went along the carriage closing the blackout curtains, turning off the overhead lights. We were approaching the end of the tunnel, leaving London, or at least its dense, homely core.

I closed my eyes. Mustn't sleep, I told myself. Must count the stations. The singers had started up on 'Keep the Home Fires Burning'. Benjamin was laughing, a snort and a high-pitched squeal. I tried to picture the countryside beyond the blackouts and remembered dimly the Rhondda Valley, my beginnings in Wales. The older children in the village heaping me and my brothers into an old pram and letting it run down a hill until we all fell out in a pile at the bottom laughing, and the walk with Mother to the school in the next village across a field peppered with sheep droppings. The world silent and white one morning, the window frame piled high with snow, the roofs and trees iced thickly by some huge fat-armed cook.

I bobbed for some time at the rim of sleep, not wanting to fall against the soft-hipped woman. Surfacing, I forced my eyes open. The carriage was dark and felt cooler, more spacious. It had thinned out and the boys were sitting opposite me, holding the curtains aside, their curly heads jammed up against the glass. I edged back the curtain on my own side and great cracking showers of light flashed up trees, farmhouses, lines of hedgerow, a bus in a field, its row of windows reflecting the fireworks. The boys' faces too flashed yellow and then slipped back into the dark.

'Is it Guy Fawkes?' Benjamin asked Geoffrey sleepily.

'They're shells, dropped by the Hun,' he replied.

'I thought they only shelled London,' I said quietly. The maze of lanes we had left behind us, the thick buildings, seemed far safer than these open fields.

'Are the shells filled with fireworks?' Benjamin wanted to know. 'I love them!'

I remembered the sigh of the crowd on Guy Fawkes' Night from before the war, which Benjamin had only heard about, never seen with his own eyes, at Regent's Park, the whizzing catherine-wheel, the crackling of the fire around the Guy. The memory was old, there were only little pieces of it left. Older now. Still there though, still bright little fragments.

We had no Guy Fawkes now. Everyone was supposed to stay at home when it was dark with their blackouts closed no matter what night of the year it was, but they didn't in town, I heard them beneath our window, singing and fighting. Weird sounds sometimes that you couldn't place as entirely human. We were only allowed out if there was a raid, to go to the tube. That was the only time you could breathe night air. It tasted different: cooler, sharper, laced with something adult. They spoke to each other differently, at night, as though we could not hear them.

The train slowed. The last of the passengers, dim bulky figures pulling cases off racks, were standing and shuffling towards the doors. I knew that we needed the last stop, that this was the end of the line.

I jumped down onto the platform with my case, put it on the ground and turned to lift Benjamin down. Geoffrey sprang down after us, a dark agile figure, his own man already at eight. We looked around for our people. Black clusters of shapes hovered above the platform making voids against the sky, milky with stars.

We walked in a huddle towards the station house. It was cold, even in summer, away from buildings. The groups of shadows murmured names as we passed: 'Watson?' 'Miles?' 'Webster?' When we were almost at the end of the platform Geoffrey said, 'What if they're not here?' and I said, 'Shhh.' I thought I could hear it, our name in the dark: 'Jacob?' A woman's voice. 'Are you the Jacob children?' A face loomed. My eyes had adjusted. She bent towards us, older than Mother, with a strong jaw and kind smile.

I passed up my case, let my arms hang by my side, the inside of my elbow aching. The boys gathered around the woman, seeking out their new mother. She put an arm around Benjamin's shoulder, he always was irresistible—juicy, sweet—if you did not know him, and led us through the dark waiting room, the same smell in its bricks as when you walked past a urinal at the park. Out onto the cool, black road.

We trudged silently after the woman, Mrs Walton-Jones, towards nothing. It might have been ten or past midnight. There was not a gap in a curtain or a set of car headlights to break blackout. Around us people murmured as they walked along the road, their voices emerging close by from the dark. We drew near enough to the group in front to make out a pair of children being led by a man, perhaps a vicar, a pale collar showing above his pullover. All the thrill of movement had drained from my body. It would be better to be buried under a block of flats in London, surely, than in this wasteland. I concentrated on the long dark cylinder of Mrs Walton-Jones's back, stayed as close as I could to it without stepping on her heels, so that I should not fall into a ditch and be lost in the night among rustling things till morning.

~

The dawn found me kneeling on the dresser, leaning on the cold window, nose to the glass. It smelled like earth. Everything smelled of it. For the first time in my ten years I had slept in a room alone. The silence when I opened my eyes, the absence of breath and bodies shifting. I woke when it was still dark and had been up here ever since watching the sky grow lighter over the fields. Where were the boys? How did the house work? There were two staircases, one from the downstairs hallway which stopped at my door halfway up and then continued to a *real* attic, and the other off the kitchen, that must lead to everyone else's rooms. A man of the house whom I had not yet met existed somewhere.

Against the pale sky were lines of trees and shrubs with their tops cut off, all at the same height, so I could see beyond the garden with its tangle of roses and rocky herb patch to the fields beyond and the roof of a chapel down the lane. I stared at the lopped-off greenery, waiting for it to make sense, and then there was a loud drone and over the fields, perilously low, flew three of those fabulously clunky contraptions: biplane bombers. My heart stopped as I caught a glimpse of the bombers' helmets from within the planes' skeletons. They came by so low, the planes' bellies just about skimming the hedges. Then they disappeared into a field, but I could hear the engine choking as it cut off out of sight. It was one of those things one witnesses alone and has trouble verifying, even to oneself. But that was why the hedges had been shorn. There was proof.

It was still early and so I sat on the stool at the dressing table and wrote in my diary. Usually I was forced to write it under the covers, or sitting on a bench in Bedford Square, where the boys would never think to look for me. There were chickens somewhere, in the garden below perhaps, and eventually banging and clattering from the kitchen, but between these walls, my walls, there was nothing, just the scratch of my pen and the creak of leather when I moved on the stool.

Eventually there came the thundering of boys on the stairs, an abrupt thump on the door, Benjamin's wicked laughter, and I quickly placed my notebook and pen in a drawer meant for powder or hairpins.

'Come on,' Geoffrey said. His face on the gloomy landing was bright and hopeful, not his usual expression of slightly dour calculation. 'She's cooking for an army down there.'

Benjamin was tugging at my hand and we tumbled down the twisting staircase to the hallway and into the vast sunlit kitchen with its broad stove and long oak dining table. At one end was the mythical figure known as Mr Walton-Jones, egg-like head appearing briefly above his newspaper with a little grin, blushing faintly. I sat down opposite the stove the better to observe Mrs Walton-Jones across the clear, waxed table, now that she was illuminated by daylight. There was that square jaw, but when she turned to offer me eggs she had such pretty, soft eyes that her face was not too mannish in spite of her shortish hair, broad shoulders and brisk, heavy way of moving about the place, hefting a log into the range from the basket alongside, stirring eggs. Everything she did was quick and purposeful, unlike the unfolding dream of Mother's movements around the kitchen.

'The village school is quite adequate,' she was saying as she lined up plates along the counter. 'Our boys attended until grammar school so I'm sure it will do for now.'

She placed dinner plates in front of us, thick wedges of toast piled high with glistening, creamy eggs. Astonishing. Didn't they have rations in the country? But I had heard chickens. The real treasure was on Mr Walton-Jones's plate: a pile of bacon, at least four thick, streaky rashers. We stared at them. He began to eat and then looked up, saw our eyes on him.

'Lord! I'm eating bacon right in front of you. You probably view me as some kind of heathen.' His knife and fork hovered above his plate. He looked at his wife who was busy filling the sink with water.

'No,' I said. 'We're actually allowed bacon. When there's enough to go round.'

'Gracious,' Mrs Walton-Jones said, turning off the tap, 'how modern. Are you sure?' We nodded, the boys a little too vigorously. I gave them a stare. 'Well, there's plenty here. The farmer is very generous. He butchered a pig last month and we've all been eating ham like it's going out of style.' She looked at me, a pan of enormous uncooked rashers in her hand. 'Are you absolutely certain it's all right, dear? I wouldn't want to get in trouble with your mother and father.'

'It's really quite all right.' I tried to look at her face rather than the meat in the pan. Cook it! an inner voice commanded. Cook it now! We had not had bacon for as long as I could remember, and strictly speaking while Father allowed it, secretly, in a roll with egg at Harry Hendy's Big Corner Café, Mother would have been horrified. We knew what the bacon in the pan would taste like though. Exactly the same as the salty, smoky aroma filling the kitchen.

Mr Walton-Jones looked up from tucking bacon away into his mouth, knife and fork poised over the next rasher. 'You speak rather well, children.'

'Sir?'

'Well, it's just that . . .' He looked at his wife. 'Weren't we given to understand they were only recently from abroad? Refugees?'

'Yes, well,' his wife replied. 'That doesn't appear to be the case. *Are* you Russian Jews, children? That was what we were told.'

I stared at her. I had never in my life heard the word 'Jews' used by a gentile in a way not intended as an insult. 'Father was born in Russia, and so was Mother's mother. And they are both—Jewish. We were born in the Rhondda Valley, in Wales. We are British.'

Mr Walton-Jones continued with his breakfast. His wife turned and let the pan fall heavily on the stove where it began instantly to hiss. 'Yes, anyway, school. Hannah, if things go on for a while, we may need to talk to your parents about a proper girls' school. You could catch the train to Uxbridge in the morning with Peter.' If I am still here when it's time for grammar school, I thought, looking out the window at the sorry lopped-off foliage, I fully intend to run away. There was only so much that quiet bedroom could make up for. '*Are* you Russian Jews, children?' Honestly.

~

The schoolhouse was just at the end of the lane leading out to the fields from the Walton-Joneses' house, in the building I had earlier mistaken for a chapel. The boys dawdled over bees and ladybirds in what was left of the hedgerow. Benjamin wanted a piggyback but a group of children were coming along behind us, so I refused. As the children reached us I saw that there were more behind them. They stared openly as they passed, as though they were cows and we their only entertainment for the day. I wondered if they were a little slow. Uniform appeared to be optional, some wearing grey shorts or pleated tunics and some boys wearing miniature versions of what their fathers would wear in the fields, dull brown trousers and shirts, the girls in homemade floral sundresses. I felt a little stiff suddenly in my boater and pressed pinafore from St John's.

We followed the other children into the school grounds and waited at the door until the teacher, Mr Bailey, appeared in front of us. My first impression was that this was an old man; I registered the halting gait of a tall adult pass us by as we waited. Then I saw with surprise that he was very young, almost like one of us, an older brother perhaps with smooth skin and an unlined brow. I saw in his profile a large sad eye in a face still slightly soft along the jaw and cheekbones, and that he walked with a cane. In London, young men who moved like the old meant only one thing. He caught my eye, saw my brothers behind me, a little silent group amid the others who shouted and pulled at each other, not noticing that he had arrived. 'You must be the town children,' he said, just loud enough for us to hear, while the others went on with their jostling. 'Hannah? Geoffrey? Benjamin?'

He gave us his mournful smile, leaning towards us, and a little jolt passed through my heart. One of his eyes did not move along with the other. *It is glass!* I said to myself, involuntarily squeezing the elbow of Geoffrey's jacket, a little pit of horror opening up in my stomach. I caught myself. 'Sir,' I said in what I believed to be my discreet voice, 'were you injured in France?'

Well, I must have been speaking more loudly than I imagined, because the class fell quiet at my back. The teacher gave a little cough. 'Egypt. Observant of you to notice.' His accent was from the West Country. Well-spoken, but with soft edges to his words. He was the most romantic figure I had ever encountered. 'Let's go inside, shall we, children?'

'*Hannah!*' Geoffrey whispered, pulling his arm away from me with a jerk. Behind me, someone flicked my ear.

I flinched, but refused to look. 'What? I was right, wasn't I?'

'You're not supposed to ask people that.'

'How do you know?'

'Mother told me.'

'Well, why didn't she tell me?'

'She did. She told all of us. You weren't listening.'

'But how should we know he was in Egypt if I didn't ask? Anyway, he didn't mind. Adults admire a little spirit. Ask Father.'

We were inside now, nudged in by the tide of children, hanging up our satchels on the hooks by the door with the others. There was only one room in the dark building and it smelled largely of sawdust, overlaid with a whiff of manure from the fields drifting in through the window. The teacher gestured to an empty desk to one side of the room, where the older children sat. Benjamin was quickly settled at the back on a communal table and was soon scribbling with a wax crayon on newspaper. He was beaming at a little girl with blonde curls. Geoffrey was looking around him from the other side of the room, where he was seated next to an enormous farm boy in a hand-knitted pullover. My brother wore a deep scowl. The bigger boy pinched his arm. Geoffrey leaned out from the desk, away from him. I saw myself rising from my chair, walking the breadth of the room in front of an astonished class and teacher, and slapping the giant simpleton, leaving his great jowl to tremble like a slavering bulldog. I would place my hands on my hips and say slowly: 'I imagine it was you who flicked my ear, too, wasn't it, you brute?' I forced my gaze away from Geoffrey to our teacher, who now introduced himself wearily as Mr Bailey, for the benefit of the town children.

Oh, that was a long day in my life. My shoe scuffing the floorboards, the slow intoning of the alphabet by the little ones, a song the children sang at home time, prompted only by Mr Bailey clapping his hands together once, saying, 'Now, ready, children?' I did not know the words of course and so I set my eyes on a row of jam jars filled with hollyhocks on the window ledge behind Mr Bailey. I wondered who had picked them. They trembled in the breeze, their petals shifting from light to dullness as the shadows of clouds drifted across the schoolyard and the children sang:

Summer suns are glowing over land and sea;
Happy light is flowing, bountiful and free;
Everything rejoices in the mellow rays;
Earth's ten thousand voices swell the psalm of praise . . .

I dared a glance at Mr Bailey's face. He was staring out towards the door, beyond our heads. His lower lip creased at its centre briefly. He paused for a moment when they had finished singing, before telling us to collect our things, and that he would see us in the morning, bright and early. He seemed to gather himself before saying the ordinary, hopeful things that adults said to children all the time to jolly them along, to keep them unthinking and obedient. I felt that

I would like to sit in a room with him and ask him questions about himself and his life for hours on end. I would know the story of his troubles, and he would feel better for having talked to me about it. If only I were not a child, I wrote later. Why must childhood go on for so long? I had read many books on all kinds of subjects. I would understand his story too. I had prepared myself for such things.

~

Things livened up a little on our second day in the country. The oafish boy who had pinched Geoffrey, who had pale eyebrows and an Old Testament name like Jonah or Noah, lay in wait for us when we turned down the lane towards the schoolhouse. The first we knew of him was when a sharp-edged rock hit Geoffrey in the back of the head. He yelped and crunched forward, clutching his neck. Then the fat boy was running by us, laughing, soft white flesh rolling at his midriff where his shirt was not properly tucked. I stuck out my foot without more than a second of forethought and he jammed hard against my leg, tripped, went straight down, head smacking into the muddy road, his considerable weight behind it. Unfortunately for him the road was grooved into hard, gravelled ridges by farm vehicles and as he sat up, forlornly surprised, we saw that blood was running from a cut in his forehead and that little stones had embedded themselves like huge freckles in his soft cheeks.

'What happened?' Geoffrey asked me as we watched the boy in the mud, the lane filling with children. 'I didn't touch him.'

'I tripped him,' I said quietly.

'Hannah! You're a holy terror!' Benjamin exclaimed.

'Shhh, Ben,' Geoffrey whispered.

But it was too late. Here came Mr Bailey, getting up speed as he pushed his cane down into the track, vaulting himself along towards us, children parting to let him through. And Jonah/Noah was pointing a finger at me. 'Her!' he said. 'That town girl done it!'

For the entirety of that day I sat at a little desk to the side of Mr Bailey, away from the other children, scarcely believing that this was regarded as punishment. I was on the side of his glass eye and I was at liberty all day—as he spoke to the class, marked exercise books at his desk, gazed sadly out to the fields—to observe the way it sat still in his face as around it muscles twitched minutely in his brow and jaw, and his other eye performed the subtle movements of real, living tissue.

At home time, though, Mrs Walton-Jones came for us. Some message had been transmitted and she gusted into the room as the bell sounded with a hand thrust forward to take hold of mine. 'Thank you, Mr Bailey,' she said loudly. 'I'll manage this from here.'

The boys gathered around her as she pulled me outside. In the yard children lingered, waiting to see what would happen. She leaned down towards my feet, as though she were about to do up my buckles for me, and slapped me on the calf. No such thing had ever happened to me before. It barely hurt, but I found the intimacy of it shocking. Take your hand OFF MY LEG, I wanted to shout. I caught myself, but only enough to ask, 'What on earth are you doing?' as she straightened to her full standing height. Once more we were providing a spectacle for the village children.

'When my boys misbehaved, they were smacked. You are no different. And you must leave that boy alone. It's not his fault, poor thing.'

'But, Mrs Walton-Jones, he threw a stone at Geoffrey. It hit him right in the head!'

'That boy fell flat on his face!' Benjamin said, at her back. 'Whack!' He clapped his hands together. Geoffrey was regarding me sheepishly from under his thick black curls.

She took my hand and Benjamin's, Geoffrey following close behind me, and led us across the yard to the gate, our audience scattering before her heavy stride. 'He's not right, you know. None of them are, those Shipmans.' She dropped her voice. 'Difficult births. Brain damage. She should have stopped at the first.'

I might have stepped into a Victorian novel. I forgave her the smacked leg instantly for this bit of Gothic gossip. She seemed entirely to have forgotten my disgrace, justice having been served. No one threw any more stones at the boys' heads, either.

~

I woke one morning having dreamed of the changing of the guard and smelled charred meat. My stomach flipped with hunger. I dressed quickly and tumbled down the stairs to the kitchen. There was only Mr Walton-Jones there, reading yesterday's paper with a pot of tea and a mug in front of him on the table. I hovered in the doorway, thinking I would retreat until Mrs Walton-Jones was up, but he had lowered his paper and was looking at me with a slightly puzzled expression on his face.

'Good morning—Hannah?'

'Good morning, Mr Walton-Jones. What is that smell? I thought something was cooking.'

'Ah, bit nasty. I'm afraid there's been a fire at the aerodrome. Bomber came in with its tail alight and went down amid the horses. Pilot and several horses perished.'

'You mean, that smell is horses . . . cooking?' And a pilot, I thought, but did not say. I was testing the value of my very occasional capacity to leave a thought unsaid.

'Not to put too fine a point on it.' He picked up the paper again.

At school, there was silence as we sat down at our desks, but Tessa

Donald, a girl whom I had easily vanquished as top of the school in every subject and who loathed me with an intensity I found natural and even comforting, put her hand up immediately after register. 'Oh, Mr Bailey.' He turned his sad gaze upon the girl. 'Father says the injured horses are to be shot this morning.'

I waited with relish for him to set the barbarous little horror straight, but his expression did not change. It rarely did. It was just variations on rueful.

'Yes, of course,' he sighed. 'They must be put out of their misery. It would have been seen to immediately but Mr Emery must be fetched from the fields so he can bring his rifle.'

Benjamin burst into tears across the room. I knew it was him; he snivelled rather a lot when crying, and if he continued he would get the hiccoughs, but I did not turn around. I was waiting to see if there was something else, something I had missed.

'Now, Benjamin. There is no other way. There is no rest home for horses, you know.'

A picture formed in my mind instantly of this thing he had conjured, a rest home for horses, lying in their beds, heads on the pillows, cups of tea on trays in front of them, more of them sitting in easy chairs in a library, hoofs holding books in their laps. What does this man know of rest homes? I wondered. What injuries has he seen? What can happen to a man's body and yet leave him alive? I saw figures on beds with cannon holes where their insides should be, half their heads missing, no one with hands.

Then I remembered what would happen to the remaining horses and clenched my pencil tightly. I said nothing. We were famed for our ignorance of practical matters as it was. And even Mr Bailey was siding with them. You might have thought he would show a little sympathy.

The schoolroom was quiet but for the murmuring of Mr Bailey's voice over a pupil's shoulder every now and again and a fly buzzing near the window, dashing itself against the glass, Mr Bailey too distracted to notice and set it free. When the shots came—crack, crack, crack—my pencil stilled on the page, and we all looked up at him. He was gazing out the window, and though he flinched at the sound, he was lost in some spell that did not break.

Soon the lunch bell sounded and we left our sandwiches in our satchels hanging on the hooks by the door, streaming out into the lane. I do not recall any sign coming for us to move en masse like this. Way up on the road between the hedgerows, villagers were passing in the direction of the aerodrome. Perhaps it was their movement that drew us into the stream. As we reached the house Mrs Walton-Jones was emerging from her rose garden onto the street and fell into step beside us, wiping her hands on her apron.

'Awful, awful business. Eleanor's absolutely distraught. They didn't want the aerodrome next to their field in the first place. Puts the frighteners on the poor horses every time one comes in a bit low. But you do your bit, I suppose. They've lost half in one hit. Not to mention the shock of that poor boy being dragged out of a burning plane in front of the kitchen window.' I saw the Guy from the old days, in Regent's Park, its black shape in the flames.

We drew level with the aerodrome and there was a half-destroyed plane out on the tarmac, men all around it contemplating it gravely, the blackened mid-section and wings and the jagged metal edge where the tail should be. The head of the procession turned down a right of way between the aerodrome field, fenced off with barbed wire, and the horse pasture. We came to a gap in the hedge, a kissing gate, and the horses piled up in the middle of the field. As we climbed over the fence and gathered around the heap the smell of those that had been burned was acrid and there were black, dusty legs and heads, singed-off manes. Others looked perfect, their skins glossy, their muscles curved and smooth. The village, perhaps fifty people with us children, gathered in a circle. One horse had half of its face missing and beneath it there were muscles all twisted together like an anatomy diagram. I looked about for Mr Bailey, but it seemed he had not come.

Perhaps it wouldn't happen now, this gathering towards such an event. Parents would shield the eyes of their children, keep them indoors. But the war had come home to England, and it would have been unthinkable not to go and see what it looked like. No one was frightened, not even the little ones. I saw all the curves of flank and thigh and jaw and could not tell what belonged to which horse. Benjamin's hand slid into mine. The people gazed quietly for a few minutes as more gathered behind us. Flies buzzed. A murmuring rose from the crowd. 'Took Tom twenty years to build up. Gone in a day.' The children whispered to each other about the eyes. Some were missing. Some looked right at you. No one mentioned the burnt pilot or asked at what point he had died.

The smell was a bit much after a while and we all began to drift home and back to school. We passed a man carrying a petrol can going in the opposite direction. In the lane I could again smell the flowers and the grass, and there were birds, bumblebees. Geoffrey and I walked quietly amid the villagers, Benjamin between us, holding our hands.

Emil

MUNICH, 1918

The men's bodies were a horror. They were all the same: thin, bluish, striped with prominent ribs, fading away in their long rows into the shadows. Above them swung kerosene lamps from massive low-hung meat hooks; their delousing shed had once been a slaughterhouse. There were at least fifty men in here, naked, waiting for the orderlies to come along with their great flour sack of powder on a squealing cart, heavy shovel dragging along the stone flags. Emil heard the squeak of the wheel behind him and covered his eyes and mouth, heard the whump of the powder as it hit his head and shoulders, coated his chest and legs. He trudged along behind a crowd of men, his skin alive with sensation: the juddering cold of the old warehouse in November, the heat of the powder, found his scratchy towel and parcel of clothes piled up against the wall.

Here was Müller, dusting himself down, pulling on his shirt. He turned at the sound of Emil's voice and spread his arms out, smiling.

'How do I look?' His civilian clothes were too small for him, the buttons leaving gaps at his chest, the grimy cuffs flapping at his forearms. His trousers skimmed the top of his socks. The peak of his cap was frayed. He always was a slightly odd-looking man, thin as a flagpole with a fleshless head, skeletal, the big eyes of enduring hunger. Laughed frequently though. Filthy mouth.

Emil reached for the string on the nearest parcel, cold fingers fumbling to untie it. 'You look ready for the maids of Munich, friend.'

'Aha! Let's hope they're ready for me! And you, Becker. You look thirsty. I know you saw that beer hall we passed on the way into town.'

'Perhaps we should be getting the men onto trains. Some of them are homesick.' But he was smiling. He had felt an electricity in the streets. Shouting, and banners. Groups of men loitered on corners, nodding as the soldiers moved through. And the news of Ludwig's flight, the King of Bavaria driven out by revolutionaries. There was a feeling abroad; he wanted to mingle with it, merge with the streaming crowds, go with them, be carried forward into a new future that eliminated the past.

'None of them are homesick enough to abandon us after we have brought them back to Germany, safe and sound. They owe us a drink or two. Their mamas can have them back tomorrow.'

~

They had known the border was close when they came upon a queue of a few hundred men, dishevelled and separated from their units, some looking like they had been hiding in the mountains for who knew how much of the war. That was not his business. His squad, the dregs of other squads, had been thrown off the train to demobilise and he simply needed to get them onto another one, preferably on the German side of the border. Emil and Müller led their thirteen men towards a group with horses standing around a fire with black smoke, eating, passing around a bottle of rum. 'What is this?' he said to Müller. Müller shrugged. The men did not answer.

The next hill was a German hill. Beyond it a German town—Munich, he hoped. Someone, somewhere would give him brown clothes or blue or black, and he would light a fire and throw in his grey uniform, say a few words for the families of lice who had travelled home with him. Home in time for Christmas.

He began running past the stagnant stream of soldiers on foot, some leaning on horses, fires lit against the evening cold, playing cards, throwing medals by their ribbons into the pool of cigarettes and notes that would buy nothing in Germany. Müller was at his shoulder, he heard him laugh breathlessly. They were running without fear of being shot, like boys.

The crowd thickened outside two long military tents that lined the road. Four officials sat at tables outside, checking papers by torchlight. The men waiting protested loudly; pushed, jostled. Emil squeezed into a gap at the table with the sparsest crowd. 'Is it just you men here processing our papers?'

The man looked up, gave a hopeful nod, seeking sympathy.

'Just you, for all these men?'

'Just us. We were not expecting so many to arrive without having been properly discharged.'

Emil stepped out of the crowd towards Müller.

'There don't seem to be many of them,' Müller said.

'I know. It's madness.' He jogged over to the first group of soldiers. They looked up, eager for news. 'Come through!' He waved towards the tents. 'Move on!' There were two trucks amid the few hundred men. They grumbled to life, too many men clambering aboard, whooping and whistling. The driver sounded his horn to scatter the men in front. They pressed against the tents as the procession started down the road. Emil ran to a group of horsemen. 'Come on. Keep moving. Everyone through before nightfall. Stay on the road to Munich. We will all arrive together. On, on. They can't shoot us all.'

~

They dressed in the delousing hut, clean, cold, reduced to their habitual condition of fidgeting and shuffling to keep warm.

'You're right,' Emil said. 'They can buy us beer tonight. With luck we can avoid sleep altogether.'

'You're not impressed by our quarters?'

Emil laughed. Next to the delousing hall, in the old cattle pen, where animals once queued to have their throats cut, perhaps a hundred palliasses had been laid on the stone floor. You could see your breath in that room, although it might be better when filled with sleeping men. As Müller had said when they downed their packs and hidden their weapons under the mattresses, it was colder than a trench puddle in there.

~

They had all been drinking with dedication for an hour, packed into a social club, a cramped room hot with bodies, ten tables squeezed in, bread on plates, heavy beer in tall mugs, brewed in the cellar, everything put on free for the soldiers. The proprietor stood behind a short bar at the back wearing a waxed apron as though he were tanning hides, filling their glasses at a tap. 'God bless you,' he said to each of them as he handed them back their glasses, filled but lacking in froth. 'Welcome home to Germany. We are indebted.' The stuff he served was flat, sad puddles of white on its muddy surface, but it hit you fast. Already there was singing, and arguing about the workers' councils, and the surly Schumacher, silent in a corner, as though they'd all been at this for much longer.

Emil raised his glass and attempted to drink his beer down, but finished only a third of it before feeling his gorge rise. He sat watching the movement of the room, the shifting colours, clumsy, thick-headed, glad to relinquish his usual state of sabre-edged alertness for this lazy blur. On the walk home across the slippery frosted cobbles he would be sick, probably, and in the morning he would remember nothing, and he would ride the trains across Germany to Duisburg, and that would be the end of that, if he had any sense.

Except here was Schumacher. Agitated. And so Emil must sharpen up again, watch for trouble. Schumacher sat down too hard in the seat opposite. Its feet scraped a few centimetres across the floor before he steadied himself, leaned on the table until it stilled. 'Let's go to Berlin!' he shouted.

'But you are from Frankfurt,' Müller said jovially, with an edge of warning that Emil heard afterwards like an echo.

'We've missed the action here.' He thrust a finger in Müller's face, tipping his head towards Emil. 'He knows what I mean. Someone just told me they're planning more demonstrations. That's the place to be. I want a say in who runs this country.' His voice snagged on the last few words.

'No one can stop you going wherever you choose,' Emil said quietly.

'Those bastards in Berlin! We need to get up there and set them straight.' Schumacher lifted his glass, spilling a little on the table before standing, staggering away towards the bar.

Müller studied Emil. 'You're not thinking of going, Becker?'

'Not with him, no.'

'You're an officer. There will be rewards for us, in spite of everything, if we are clever. We can be anything we choose now. You don't want to risk that.' Always the glint in his eye, as though he was joking.

'Schumacher is right,' Emil said. 'We put our necks on the block for the glory of those fat old men. There are so many of us, millions. We'll never have this chance again. We'll go back to our lives and be quiet. And they'll come and get us any time they want us.'

Later, some strangers held Schumacher up on a table. He was trying to sing, but mostly moaning. You couldn't bear it if you were sober. A man near the door was sick on his lap when he might easily have stepped outside. Then he lifted his glass and carried on. Emil barely saw these people, just shapes, acting. A woman came in. Oh no, he thought. Arms reached for her as she moved among the tables towards the bar. She moved quickly, batting away clumsy hands, approaching his table. We won't hurt you, he wanted to say. I won't let us. He was too slow. She had passed by. He laid his head on his arm on the table and closed his eyes.

~

The platform at Duisburg was quiet. A few shift workers, a nursemaid with a group of small children. He was late home compared to many, early compared to others, becalmed between the surges from opposite fronts as the soldiers converged on Germany. He stared at the children for a little too long. Snowflakes appeared in the evening air. The nurse gathered the children together and they walked along the platform towards him. The tips of his ears were freezing. There had been no hat in his packet of clothing. He looked at the children. They looked cold to him and the ground, covered in melted snow, looked slippery beneath their feet. He saw as they drew closer their bright scarves and knitted hats pulled down over their ears. They were two boys and a girl, a little older though not very tall, eleven perhaps. He could not tell the ages of children anymore. One of the boys asked his sister questions. She made a show of being tired of it but her cheeks were flushed and she smiled frequently.

The nurse nodded as she passed and said something to the children. The children turned at the stairs, the girl smiling, the boys saluting solemnly. How did they know? What mark was upon him? He was home now. Whatever it was, he hoped it would wear off soon. He returned the salute and followed the group into the dark stairwell. Outside the station snow settled on his cracked lips and in his beard. He felt old, looking out at Königstrasse in the snow. It had not changed at all. He moved out from the shelter of the station and walked across the square, the snow heavier, settling on the shoulders of his greatcoat. It was dark already and his father would be leaving his office soon. In childhood, unless he was ill and his mother confined him to bed, Emil was there every evening in the street below his father's office, waiting to walk home with him to the apartment.

When he reached the union building he stood on the stone flags, looked up at the lit window on the first floor and saw the shape of his father, a little fatter, a little more bent than before. Like a turtle; round back, head thrusting wearily forward. For a moment he didn't know him. He was tidying his desk, opening and closing a drawer, taking his hat from the stand. The movements he knew, could be sure of. After a few moments his father disappeared, the light went out, and his heart pounded as it did when he was a boy for the few moments it took for his father to emerge onto the street.

He saw Emil at once, paused in the dark doorway to stare at the silhouette under the streetlight in the falling snow. He waited for a moment, his hand rising to his chest, and then stepped out into the street towards him without checking for traffic, propelling himself quickly in spite of his roundness. Here he was, Father, his face was still his, a little jowly, though his body had grown older. He put his arms around Emil who took his hands from his pockets and returned his embrace. His father was half a head shorter than him now, though his aroma was the same as it had always been. Tobacco, beer, wool. The men at the front smelled of these too but there was always sharp old sweat, blood, gasoline, excrement. He himself smelled of delousing powder. He hoped Father did not find it repulsive.

He held his father a moment longer, taking in the feeling that it was him, that he had been returned to the days when he was a boy and could embrace his father any time he liked, feel his evening bristles on his cheek. Emil heard words spoken so quietly against his shoulder that he might have imagined them. *It is my boy. The one who comes back*. He straightened eventually and shook his father's hand. They began to walk towards the bridge across the Rhine to their quarter. His father was silent for a while, his voice scratchy when he spoke. 'It's wonderful you're home tonight, Emil. There's a parade tomorrow night to welcome the soldiers. I was sure you'd miss it.'

He peered at his father's face in the dark. 'We'll see. I don't know. I was not intending to wear a uniform again.' His father looked at him sideways but said nothing. 'How is Mother?'

'She's been a bundle of nerves since the soldiers began to return. Superstitious, you know. You'd better get some sleep tonight. She'll be inviting the whole street over to look at you soon enough.' Emil laughed. It was true, she would. 'But listen, I have good news for you. I heard from Manfred in Hamburg last week. He has agreed to take you on to finish your degree. I sent him your records for the polytechnic. It's all arranged. You will be a qualified electrical engineer! Incredible.'

Emil said nothing. They crossed the long bridge, the snow turning the night air white, disappearing into the wide, dark river. Fog spilled from their mouths.

'You're not pleased? It was your dream. A degree, a profession.'

'I planned to go to Berlin, to see what can be done for the revolution. Things are not right yet.'

'This is what I heard! They all turned red out there. Is it so hard to put your weapons away? Getting you home, *that* was the revolution. You can help with the workers' councils here, just to help settle things down. You will be very useful, with your military experience. When everyone is home, things will be fine, and you can go to Hamburg.'

'Workers' councils are all very well, but what has changed? All the same people are in charge of things. They could send us off again tomorrow. It's true I'd be a better-qualified corpse, with a little more money in my pocket.'

They turned into their street. Emil had been walking too quickly for his father, who was panting slightly. He slowed, let him catch his breath.

His father patted him on the back, taking air. 'My boy. Let's celebrate your return. Save the revolution for the morning. Your mother won't believe it's you.'

Emil was quiet. It took the walk down the long street to calm himself, become still enough inside to feel the little fire of shame. Father was right. It could all wait until tomorrow. At the door of the apartment building he took a long cold breath. Mother was up there, and Greta. A meal, however poor—though Father was pretty good at working the black market, you could see it in his girth; that would be all the evidence the police would need if they wanted to make something of it.

His thighs ached as they climbed the stairs. It was he who could not keep up with his father, who was calling up to the apartment for them to come and see what he had brought home with him. Emil heard his mother's voice calling down: 'Klaus? *Emil!*' There were their faces, Mother and Greta, leaning out into the stairwell, peering down into the dark, Greta seeing him, shrieking. If it were not for them, and his growling belly, he would fall into the room and sleep on the rug for days.

~

The following evening Greta clung to his elbow, sitting close to him on the sofa. She told him that his mother had cried in the bedroom after Emil had gone to bed on this sofa where they now sat, and after breakfast had pulled up a floorboard in the kitchen and taken out some money to buy a hat to wear. Greta, thin and tall, her beauty stolen from their mother, went out to the shops with her and bought new stockings from a friend of Father's who kept such things in a secret place at the back of his shop. He saw that there was no question of avoiding the parade.

He shaved in the shared bathroom on the landing and looked at his body in the mirror, which he could see to his waist. He stared at it. He could not see any damage, except that it was thin, and even then not as thin as the men in the delousing shed or some of the civilians he had seen. His body was twenty-two years old and that was all it looked. He practised a smile and stopped. That did not look so good. His teeth were a little frightening and there was something flat in his eyes. But his body and his face were more or less intact, the skin on his chest was smooth, the bullet wounds in his calf and shoulder were not visible and the trench rot in his foot was healed now, mostly, and no longer smelled bad. He could not quite take in the solidity of himself, standing in his bathroom at home. For almost a year—since the last hospital—he had caught only glimpses of his face: a fragment of jaw in a shard of mirror passed between the men. Now he could see his head, his wavy hair, both of his shoulders at once, his muscled arms, his chest. Though it was smooth it had more hair on it than when he went away. Look at that, he thought. There is no sign.

A knock sounded down the hall and he came out onto the landing, pulling on his shirt. There was Thomas's brother Karl, outside the door to the apartment, clean-shaven, his uniform starched and smelling of soap suds, his hair oiled and parted under his helmet. He had returned from the front the week before. Emil could only stare for a moment. He was so like Thomas and yet a different man, with lighter hair, and the features of Thomas minutely different in alignment so that he was not nearly so handsome. Amazing what a few millimetres could do. In return Karl searched his own face, as though looking for the same things in a different form, some similarity of experience to Thomas, some clue to who he might have been by now.

Before Emil could speak Mother was out on the landing and pulling Karl into the kitchen. 'My boy.' She held his face in her hands. 'Your mother has been so worried. Why don't you boys write? You might as well kill us!'

Emil closed the apartment door behind himself, wondering where Greta was, saw she was in the kitchen too, staring at Karl.

'Greta.' Karl nodded. Emil watched his sister's face. She had radiated light whenever Thomas was here, from the earliest days. She too searched Karl's face for him. You are spoken for, Greta, Emil thought. There was an older man, a toolmaker with a polio limp who was not sent away. He saw the pull of memory on her, wondered what would happen.

Father came out of the bedroom, saw Karl and enfolded him in a long embrace. Father was a man for embracing, sentimental, too full of feeling often for those around him. Emil saw that his eyes were wet when he pulled back. Don't, he wanted to say. We are not the boys who went off to the war. And this is not Thomas. But it was not necessary. There had been a moment at dinner when he looked up from his soup to find that they were all pondering him. He was at the bottom of his second bowl, picking it up, drinking the last drop with a slurping sound. He had been readying to lick it when he happened to glance at them. He knew that they had seen it in him, this animal greed. He had left his bowl with thick streaks of soup still on it, enough to fuel a hungry man for another hour, and walked the streets until he was tired enough to think of nothing.

They all walked to the square together, Emil between his parents, his mother's grip on his elbow tight as they slipped a little on the melting snow beneath their feet. Karl and Greta walked ahead, she with her hands in her coat pockets, his loose, as though he were marching. Her pale skin glowed in the cold, under the streetlights. She was a miraculous thing to see. Though thin she was vigorously, abundantly alive. Her movements had an energy he no longer found familiar. They murmured between long silences. She sought news of the gap Thomas had left in the family as though she could touch the shape of the hole he made and so come closer to touching him.

At the square he and Karl left Emil's family and lined up with the other soldiers. The parade was a mess. Many didn't have hats or coats and they were all mixed in together from different companies, ranks muddled. The crowd was thick in spite of the slushy snow on the cobbles and a vicious bite in the air. A band played 'Deutschland über Alles' and Emil stood at attention. The white faces of the crowd sang. He was unable to separate them. It was just eyes and noses and holes where the voices came out. He opened his own mouth but made no sound.

After the parade he was standing with Karl, smoking, when a hand grasped his elbow. He froze, ready for violence, his own: quick, efficient, effective enough to rule out retaliation. He turned and it was just a girl, his age, familiar.

She smiled, baring straight white teeth. 'Emil?' She peered into his eyes.

Karl, next to him, said, 'Hello, Uta! How are you keeping?'

'Karl. Oh, Karl, I was so sorry to hear about Thomas.' She reached out a hand to shake and he took it, nodded, returned his hands to his pockets.

'I'll see you, Emil,' he said, and disappeared into the crowd.

Emil was silent for a moment. He saw now that this was his girlfriend from before. Had she changed something, her hair? Why hadn't he known her? He stepped forward, wrapped her in his arms. 'It's you,' he said. She was so warm, so soft beneath her coat. She smelled astonishing. Her gloved hands were reaching up, leather fingers holding his neck. He led her away from the square and the crowds, his arm around her shoulder. In a cold alley where he could only just hear the crowd he held her close and whispered, 'Take me somewhere quiet.'

'It's quiet here. Tell me how you have been, Emil. There were no letters. I thought—I thought perhaps you had forgotten.'

He heard the catch in her voice. He pulled her tighter to him. 'Uta, Uta, shhh. Is there somewhere warm? I want to hold you as I did before.'

'Well, when you didn't write . . . another came along.'

'Please. I'm here now. Let me be near you.'

'I have an apartment with my sister,' she murmured into his hair. 'She is at the parade. We can go there.'

As they strode along the narrow streets in the dark, passing the occasional couple, faces pressed together as they walked, a sailor urinating in the snow, drunk, a hand against the wall, he knew that he was pulling her along. It was too forceful. He would never have done this before. He was not quite fit for company anymore, he knew it. She had to run a little every now and then to keep up, a little skipping step. He knew but he could not help himself, or slow his pace.

~

He opened his eyes, the discoloured brocade of the sofa beneath his cheek. As his eyes adjusted to the dark he saw that the lintel was piled high with snow. The heat from his mouth warmed his face. He pulled the blanket off his head, reached down to the floor, fingers finding dust and then the metal of his Luger. The apartment was silent but for Father's snores, the boyhood sound of waking on Sundays, or when Father was out of work. He was dressed beneath his blanket, his uniform still, but it would do for now. It would not be noticed at this hour, so long as he wore a civilian coat. He tucked the gun in the pocket of his trousers, took his father's coat from the back of a dining chair, crossed the room and unlocked the door quietly, inching it patiently shut. It was even colder on the landing, where there were no bodies to exchange the icy air for their sleeping breath.

These few mornings since arriving in Germany he woke to a slow-building fury. He had only noticed it since he came home, now there was nothing to be done with it, no requirement to transport his squad safely home, nothing. Irritation jabbed like someone tapping him on the forehead when he was trying to rest. His body recalled the sound of the guns, the rattling of his bones, the slick of grease on hands and the smell of burnt powder. Today it threatened and then went away without trouble. He had something to do. His body was glad to be purposeful, moving towards an act.

On the street, under the lamps, men trudged through the snow, collars up, hats pulled down over eyes, leaving as little of their faces exposed to the world as possible. They drifted towards the station and the factories along the river, those that were still operating. The munitions factories were closed, though some were being reassigned. He followed the men along the river and they were swallowed up in little groups into the vast buildings. Past the factories, an indistinct blue light was appearing over the fields. All he could hear was a crow and his own breath. The guns were silent. The factories had not yet begun their shift. He walked quickly. He wanted to reach the place he knew before the day began, home before light, change into ordinary clothes. It was always the best place, when he and Thomas were boys, and they'd only had their catapults then.

The Luger rubbed against his leg through his pocket. A rifle would have been better, but he had not managed to bring it home: too unwieldy. On the rise beyond the fields a light came on in a farmhouse window. He crouched behind a hedgerow at the edge of a bare cornfield, trained his eye on the furrows, let them adjust to the lines of shadow, watching for movement. Gave himself a moment to appreciate that he was alone. No one could see him, no one had their sights on his head. Last night before he went home she was there. She would always be there now, if he asked her, a warm body, every night. She had dropped the other fellow in an instant. 'I am going to be an electrical engineer,' he had whispered, as though that sealed it, and she had pushed her head into the cave of his neck and jaw. He felt a hollowing out of himself almost immediately. There had been no time to be merely himself, alone. Always the sound of men breathing as he slept and as he woke. And now this girl would be next to him, no freedom even in the dark. Perhaps if he withdrew quietly she could simply carry on with the man she had been with before he returned.

He cocked his pistol. His eyes rested on the field. He must see large areas at once but be ready for the quick movement. He learned to do this with Thomas, here at this field, and there had been plenty of practice since. It would only be a hare, just a hare.

It did not take long before a quickly drawn black line shot across the field, thirty metres ahead of him. He loved these animals, that ran because they liked it. He watched this one's speed to imprint it, get the feel. It was too far to be sure of the Luger's aim in any case. He would probably just warn every hare within earshot to stay clear of this field today.

He waited and breathed, at the corner of his eye another flashing dart from the shrubs, closer. His arm was raised, his hand was ahead of the hare, he waited, took a shot, did not hear the crack, waiting to see, and there it was, the movement stopped. He kept his eye on the point in the field at which he had last seen the hare so that he would not lose it in the furrows. He walked slowly. It was Christmas Eve tomorrow. Mother wanted her sisters to come because he was home. She would have meat to give them now. The apartment would fill through the day with the smell of it cooking. The hare lay slumped over a white ridge as though it was asleep. The bullet wound was a red circle at its shoulder. He took its warm ears, the fur soft against his cold fingers. Its haunch thudded gently against his knee as he carried the animal home.

~

At nine o'clock, the hour of work, Emil stood in the Tiergarten with a million men squeezed into every square metre of the park in a sea that stretched to the Brandenburg Gate a kilometre away, out of sight in the fog. His world was an island of men in an empty bowl inside the mist. A million voices roared 'The Internationale'. His body vibrated like a tuning fork, his own voice at the centre of the sound. The cells of his blood were restored to him. He felt the worn cotton of his shirt against his skin. He was a living being, made up of muscle and organs and power. When this many stood together, made their voices one big instrument, they could not lose. His mouth was open against the fog. The world was changing.

There was a pamphlet in his hand. It read: *Your freedom is at stake! Your future is at stake! The fate of the Revolution is at stake!* This was where he was supposed to be, here in this sea of men. He would never be made to go off to war again. He would never again fight to protect the interests of rich swine who regarded working men as cannon fodder. There had been something valuable in his survival after all. He caught the eye of those in the crowd and they smiled at each other with utter openness, as though they were brothers returned victorious from war. They carried red flags and rifles. His pistol was in his pocket. What force could overcome them now? He was a better shot than any of them. Before he went down he would take ten. And these men would do the same.

By lunchtime he had made his way into the square beneath the police headquarters where he waited with the crowd for word from the leadership inside. Soldiers and sailors and workers crammed into the square beneath the windows. 'We are enough!' a group was shouting. He joined them. 'We are enough!' Still no one came out onto the balcony. He stamped his cold feet, smoked one of his last cigarettes to stave off hunger. He did not want to go off down the lanes to look for a café. He might miss the moment when they emerged onto the balcony and announced the change in government. The fog turned deep blue. No one had eaten since breakfast and there was no word from the leadership in the building. Finally, at the end of the first day, the crowd thinning, he could wait for food no longer, and his bad leg was stiff with the cold. He joined the dispersal out of the city back towards his hostel. He overheard two men behind him.

'They will make a decision tonight, and we will have our orders in the morning,' one said.

'Too late for me. If that wasn't a waste of a day's wages. I'm going back tomorrow. I'll say I was ill.'

Emil's gun was in his pocket. Tomorrow he would rise early and wait near the Reichstag. He would be ready when called. He knew that in the moment when it happened his body would act. There was never time for fear when the moment came.

~

Every day the crowd on the street grew less as the round helmets and rifles of the Freikorps thickened around the edges of the squares and the Tiergarten, their grey uniforms clustering under the Brandenburg Gate and outside the occupied print works and newspaper offices. He was glad he was not holed up in one of them. He'd had an instinct to stay out in the open and he had obeyed it. They must be starving in those buildings; no one could get food in anymore with the government troops everywhere. There was little enough out here. He wandered between factory-floor meetings and gatherings of men debating on the streets. No one could be persuaded to fight the troops. They did the work of a socialist government, these men. They all had brothers, cousins, in uniform. And there were so many of them now, and fewer and fewer who called themselves revolutionaries.

After a week he was down to his last few marks and was frequently dizzy from lack of food. There was nothing to eat anywhere, even if he had money. Sometimes he had the luck to come upon a soup kitchen before they ran out. A woman the age of his mother thrust bread into his hand as he passed a doorway and he kept it in his pocket, made it last a day. He was often lost. The streets looked the same with their groups of workers, hands in pockets, heads bent towards each other, a line of Freikorps on either side of every street now. He was standing in a square that felt familiar. Yes, he had passed this print works on the first day; he recognised its tall black door. The streets seemed quiet, suddenly, oddly quiet. He felt something that reminded him of the front. A change in the air that made you drop, the kind of silence that preceded a rumble. He made himself stay upright: *I am on a Berlin street. This is not the front. Be calm.*

Just then he was almost knocked down by a truck. It braked sharply outside the building and soldiers tumbled out of the back, wheeling a mortar gun down the ramp between four of them. It shone, pristine, as though it had never seen action, had been saved the entire war for this purpose. They positioned it on the cobbles and began immediately to fire on the building. The noise in the square was astonishing, echoing amid the close walls, and then gave way to shouting and boots tramping on stone as those remaining scattered to the lanes. Emil was fixed to the spot behind the truck and the soldiers watching powdery chunks of masonry fall to the street below. A soldier lifted a bullhorn to his mouth. 'You have ten minutes to give yourselves up to government forces. The building is surrounded.'

There was silence in the square and in the building except for a clatter of pans in a kitchen and then, after a moment of silence, a woman's voice calling to her children to come for their meal. Four soldiers had their rifles trained on the black door. There was a flutter of white above Emil's line of sight, a sheet of paper of the kind used for newspapers, but bare of print, tied to a broom. He saw a pair of pale hands wrapped around the handle at the window.

The black door inched open and out came seven men, hands on heads, lining up in front of the building. They looked as tired and thin as men in trenches. When it seemed there were no more, and they stood in a row, dark coats against pale yellow stucco, an ivy pattern spread out behind them that reached up to the roof, one of the soldiers fired, and straightaway before any fell they were all firing. One man had time to start running but was shot in the back. The men lay in front of the building. There was a shout from behind Emil. The crowd was running away down the lanes, no one here now but him, the soldiers and the heap of men. He retreated into the shadows of the nearest lane. Did they care that he saw them? Would they shoot him if they noticed him, or was that the point? That he was there, right behind them, while they shot the men. Was it all for him? he wondered, dizzy, leaning on a wall. He was still looking at the men while the soldiers, Germans, pushed the gun back up the ramp. A patch of blood was spreading from beneath one of the bodies across the flagstones of the neat Berlin square.

At the hostel he picked up his bag and left without a word. All around the dormitory men were doing the same. No one met the others' eyes. On the train he stared out the window as the city became impenetrable forest. He tried to sleep and saw it instantly, the heap of men. He was like a new soldier in the first days of the first battle, mud to his knees, lice crawling inside his collar, guns rattling his brain, in a body that had learned to resist nothing.

Hannah

HAMPSTEAD, 1924

I stood on the wooden platform in my woollen bathing suit above the glassy surface of the pond, early-morning sky reflected, clouds, an oak, and me—little, broad-hipped, bobbed curly hair—flanked by my brothers. Geoffrey was much taller than me by now and Benjamin was about the same. I was seventeen, just, they fifteen and thirteen. The girl I saw in the water was still, arms speared upwards, willing her body towards a smooth, gliding slice. Beneath her skin the cogs turned relentlessly. They never slowed, the little wheels that kept me moving forward, even when my body appeared still.

But their hands were on my back, shoving, they were strong now. And I was tumbling, flailing sideways into the cold water in an inelegant, stinging crash. When I surfaced the water was still settling around me, my skin the length of me tingling with the slap, and they were falling above me, knees hugged to chests, sublime grins. They made an almighty splash and the water, a black, still pond moments before, was once again shattered.

As soon as Geoffrey emerged I dunked him. He surfaced and pushed me down and under water the tiny bubbles clung to our thin chests and limbs, weeds swaying beneath, my legs cycling as I waited for him to leave off. I swam away from the boys, whose splashing and shouting would bring Mother out before long. At the far side of the pond I rested my head on my hands at the edge and felt the warmth of a summer morning on my shoulders. Beyond a little stand of trees that kept this part of the pond quite private Hampstead Heath sloped away towards central London. I always felt that we had moved to the country coming here, but civilised country, where you could still take a tube to do whatever took your fancy.

I contemplated the day, holding up its shape as though it were a gem whose light changed when you moved it. It was my last day at the Camden—I was a grown woman, I would find a job now in the Labour Party or the unions—and my teacher Miss Garnett had promised to take me to Harold Monro's poetry bookshop in Bloomsbury after my French exam, and then to tea. She was convinced I had the makings of a poet and intended to give me something that might inspire me as I stepped out into the world.

'Hannah-Geoffrey-Benjamin!' Mother came out of the French windows calling our names as though they were one exasperating word. Señor Hernandez, the owner of the Spanish school who was just passing by on his daily run, holding his boots in his hand and running in bare feet, looked up at the sound of her voice. It was awful the way she came out onto the heath to call us in.

Señor Hernandez lifted a hand when he saw me lolling at the edge of the pond. '*Hola*, Hannah! *Cómo está?*'

I smiled. I loved Señor Hernandez, as I loved all the regular characters on the heath. He was like one of the flamingos you see now at the heath with his stick-like legs and ball knees. And his lovely habit of carrying his boots, as though they were very precious, but not quite so precious as feeling the grass beneath his feet. I raised an arm. '*Muy bien*, Señor Hernandez.'

He ran into the grove towards the open heath and I turned and swam towards the house where Mother stood at the French windows, her arms heaped with towels.

~

I think that Miss Garnett did not after all meet me that day. It says nothing of it in my diary, only that after school I was lying on my bed in a funk when Father knocked at the door. I had thrown an arm across my eyes, so that there could be no doubt about my mood. And then Father was in the room, looking down at me. I took my arm from my face, but slowly, to ensure my distress was noticeable.

'What it is that you are doing?' He took his gold watch from the pocket of his black waistcoat, made a performance of peering at it, though it was clear he knew the time, had in fact been watching the clock until he had lost patience and burst into my room. 'Come, Hannah. If we leave now they will be speaking still.'

'Must we go tonight?'

'What is this? Yes, of course we go tonight. It is Friday, the night we go. Is this my Hannah that is asking?'

'All right, Papa. Give me a minute. I'll comb my hair.'

'Who cares for your hair? Come, let's go.'

~

It was a Christian on the soapbox. I could tell by the beard and the particular quality of the fervour, even from a distance, through the crowd of men smoking. 'Oh no.'

'Perhaps the gentleman is soon finished. And look who's waiting.'

Behind the Christian was a tiny woman, all her dimensions reduced in perfect proportion from the usual-sized human, sheathed in a long black dress that made her look like a Victorian. Her eyes were lowered and yet she managed to give off a nervous intensity that made the skin on my arms, bare to the elbow with my school blouse sleeves rolled up, prickle in sympathy. 'Oh,' I whispered. 'A suffragist!' They were exquisite, those women, in their fervour—how I imagined Puritans. Not like these large, noisy women you see now with big curly hair and placards who shout a lot. I agree with them of course. They are just rather loud.

'You see now, Hannah. It is always worth the trip, no?' He placed a hand on my back and steered me to the front of the little crowd. The men in their shirt sleeves and woollen vests moved aside to let me through. The Christian *must* be coming to the end, I thought. But then, each time the moment approached when he might stand aside, he stoked himself up again, having just thought of another reason we were all headed for damnation, his face growing redder, his fists clenched by his side. I went into a sort of trance of waiting, listening to the birdsong and the chatter of children, the murmur of the crowd behind me shifting on its feet.

The light was fading though the June twilight would be long. 'Yes, very enjoyable speech, sir. Now we let the lady have her turn.' It was Father. There were mumbles of agreement behind us. The woman in black looked up quickly, first at Father and then at me. I held her gaze for a few seconds but looked back to the Christian before long. It seemed unsisterly to challenge a suffragist. The

Christian spoke more loudly and fervently, spittle gathering at the corners of his bearded mouth, addressing a point somewhere over the tops of our heads. He had made some bargain with God: if he shouted at us for long enough he might be awarded salvation. There were more calls for him to stand down. After a few moments he seemed to return to himself, to where he was, in Hyde Park before a hostile audience. He broke off mid-sentence, stepped down from his box, picked it up and walked away down the path between the trees amid the evening strollers.

The suffragist edged forward, still looking down. She had no box and the crowd shuffled forward like a person bending their head towards a quiet speaker. I glanced behind me. As well as the workers in their vests there were a couple of university students and a tram conductor in his dark uniform and shiny brass buttons. A tramp hovered at the edge of the group, a space clearing around him.

The woman glanced about the crowd and decided to make me her audience. There were no other females. She was older than she had looked from a distance, at least thirty. An old maid, I thought, as I gave her an encouraging smile and nod. No, I corrected myself, an independent woman. As I shall be.

The suffragist began to speak but one would only know because she was moving her lips. The breeze in the summer leaves was enough to drown her out. 'Speak up, love,' came a call. 'It ain't a mothers' meeting.' Father turned and gave the man a glare.

When she spoke again it was much more clearly. She had a strong voice, now she dared use it. I was thrilled, though it was not an unusual speech. I had heard it in substance before, and read it in the pamphlets Father brought me. The woman talked of wartime, of the heavy work the women did in the munitions factories, of how they drove carts around the streets at dawn to hold their husbands' milk rounds, how they toiled in the fields for the nation's food. They were pushed aside without a thought when the men returned. Some resorted to prostitution to survive. A man at my shoulder let out a piercing whistle, throwing the woman off her stride and making me jump. She looked away from me, blushed a little. 'And still no vote for women under thirty,' she pushed on. 'As though after all we have done, we are but children.' Here she fixed her eye on me very definitely and I returned her confidence with a clear nod.

She did not speak for more than ten minutes, put off by the response to the Christian perhaps. Some of the men, including Father, cheered and clapped but a good number jeered. I applauded until my hands stung. The woman looked at the ground, unsure how long to stay, and then quite suddenly walked past the crowd, within a foot of me, disappearing behind us into the evening.

We stayed for another, a miner from Derbyshire whom the men loved, but I had lost concentration. My earlier dark mood had receded. Finely dressed ladies with prams or beaux walked along the pathways, glancing out from under their hats to see who was watching. It was wonderful: the presence of men all around me, their working-day scents, mysterious and lovely, Father at my shoulder, always close, separating me from the crowd and yet offering me the licence to be here. If I had the power to reclaim a moment, perhaps it would be this one.

'So, Hannah, we put a stop to your mother's worry?' Father said as the light faded and the men began to disperse. 'Time for our supper, I think.' On our walk through the park to the tube the flat light of the Serpentine flickered beyond the trees; Father said, 'Democracy, Hannah. This is what it is. The people speak directly to each other. Here, with the police walking by! And you know my Hannah—you are ready now. You are ready to take the stage!'

'Do you really think so, Father?'

'Yes, what are we waiting for? You practise at home for me and Mama. What is it you talk about after last Labour meeting? Birth control? Excellent topic. Too many poor children running round streets for lone mothers to feed. Begin to study—tonight!'

Birth control! Was I up to that? But if Father said I was, then why on earth not. I had come home from the meeting ranting, lifting chunks of the speaker's stump speech verbatim, afire with the passion that women's lives must be improved. Well, I could just do it again, and no matter that I had no life experience of anything at all that might lead to a requirement for birth control.

I held Father's hand as we walked. Oh, he could be a wonderful father. He would always be a foreigner, with his anachronistic manner of trimming his moustache, as though it would be a betrayal to change it after thirty years in England. And he boomed every word, wherever you were, so that no conversation was ever truly private. But I felt a stab of love for him, walking in the park on that long summer evening. He had no affection for the Labour Party, but if that was my training for a life of opinions and argument, then he would allow it. I did not mind who saw me, an almost grown woman, holding his hand. Here we were at the green centre of London, in the heart of England. I was flooded with newness and sensation. Father, still a wide-eyed foreigner, was right. Anyone could speak here. *I* could speak.

~

Later that summer, I was put under a curfew, which I ignored. Youth Labour meetings went on until late. Young socialists are world-class gabbers, and so here I was inching along a stone wall in the last of the evening light, shoes in one hand, the other gripping the ivy-covered bricks of the house, when I came to our tenants the Gasks' window, and was forced to pause. Small things rustled in the black leaves. I bent carefully so as not to fall backwards into the damp grass and inched my feet side to side along the ledge. The maisonettes were split-level; the Gasks' study was next to my bedroom although their sitting room was upstairs. I had to pass a wide expanse of glass looking directly into the study to reach safety. The Gasks were the sort who still regarded the absence of blackouts as the ultimate freedom and never drew curtains that could be left open. I hoped neither of them had pressing deadlines that might keep them at the desk tonight.

The window was tall and as I crept along the ledge, leaning in a little to grip the upper frame, I was stretched as far as my small body could manage. My heart thudded. Though it was dark in the room but for a light spilling from the landing I dreaded being discovered like this by our wonderful neighbours, spread out like a butterfly under a pin as I took each wide careful step towards my own window. Hurrying a little, I lost my footing for an instant and righted myself, paused, looked properly inside the Gasks' study where there was, I knew, a little black desk. It was scratched and old and not quite level, and on it sat a glossy black typewriter, the thrilling clatter of whose silver-edged keys I often heard from my own room next door as I fell asleep at night and woke in the morning. I could see the typewriter and the desk, a lumpy shadow on top of a flat surface, as my eyes adjusted. Then I could see them very well; the room was brightening. The door next to the desk swung towards me and I took two long reckless steps towards my own window.

I made it, but I could not help lingering at the very edge of the Gasks' window, peering in from the side, a strange night-time creature of the heath clinging to the frame, as Mrs Gask, in a daring trouser suit with a silk scarf tied around her cropped hair and knotted at her bare neck, sat down at the typewriter and turned on a bright chrome lamp. She peered myopically for a moment at the sheet of paper then began to type quickly with two fingers, pausing now and then to read what she had written, nod, continue. I committed the image to memory, a grown-up woman typing by lamplight late at night, and took the last step to my own window.

On the sash of my locked window was a nail file. I jimmied it gently between the frames and flicked the lock open, the window instantly slipping down an inch with a thunk. I drew up the lower frame very slowly and stepped through onto my bed, which gave out a tiny squeak. My window rattled as I closed it and hurried under the covers, trying to silence my breathing, just as Mother opened the door. 'Hannah?' I concentrated upon each breath, letting it in and out in increments, slow and quiet like a sleeper, though my heart was quick, my brow damp against the pillow.

~

After the following week's meeting, as I sailed down from the window to the bed, leg outstretched, Mother flung the door open, observed me bounce for a moment on the mattress, hot-faced in the light from the hall. 'Hannah! We agreed. Ten o'clock! It is not *safe*. How many children must be murdered for you to be home by dark?'

I remained on the bed, where I was the taller for once. 'But I am *not* a child. And I cannot simply leave the meeting halfway through. I have been elected secretary of the branch and I shall do my job!'

'No, Hannah. You will be home at ten or you shan't leave the house at all.'

'How dare you! I shall speak to Father about this.'

Mother closed the door, leaving me standing on the bed in the dark, the window open to the late summer night. Where is Father?

I stormed silently. Listening in the sitting room, newspaper in his lap? He would never ask me to give up my position. After weeks of lobbying I had managed to oust the elderly and entirely ineffectual membership secretary and I could not abandon my duties now. This was where I was supposed to be. It was what I was supposed to do.

It was hours before I slept. I gave up believing that I would manage it. I could not, before I had hauled Father out of bed to demand he state his own position. He! He was the one who had just last week accompanied me to Speakers' Corner, carried a crate from the shop for me, hushed anyone who dared to interrupt as I gave my first rather haranguing attempt at a stump speech on, as he had suggested, birth control. But I slipped under, eventually, my reading light still shining on the book open on my stomach. The next I knew there was daylight on my eyelids, a light hand on my shoulder, Mother leaving the room, turning off the lamp on my bookshelf as she went. By the time she reached the doorway the viciousness was fully awake in me. 'It is because you have no intellectual life of your own, isn't it? *That's* why you torture me.'

Mother's hand reached behind her for the doorknob. She hesitated for a narrow instant and was gone, the knob unwinding, the latch clicking gently into its groove.

~

At dinner the following night I sat, chewing my beef slowly, saying nothing, as the boys enthused about a new footballer whose exploits had captured the hearts of boys and men the length and breadth of the land. I waited for Father to speak. He and Mother remained silent throughout the meal though the boys did not notice. They were wild about their new hero. Geoffrey, somehow, had got hold of a hand press some time before and printed a weekly rag made up largely of gossip about the people who lived on our street. Though his portraits were thinly disguised, they were clearly recognisable, and Father had told him never to let copies circulate among our neighbours. The sketches were a little cruel but rather funny. He was stashing the money under a floorboard for Lord knew what venture. After bolting down his food, he hauled Benjamin upstairs to help him write a special feature, to be entitled: 'The Most Skilful and Modest Footballer England Has Ever Seen' or some such. I pushed my own chair back.

'Not you, Hannah,' Father said.

I sat heavily, sighing, as I heard the boys dragging the press along the floor above. It was just about the longest day of the year. Outside the window the oak was dark green and voices drifted in from the heath.

Well then, I thought. I will set this straight. I will make Father understand.

Mother stacked the dishes, not looking at me, and took them out to the kitchen, leaving me alone with him at the table.

'You will come home from the meetings at nine o'clock.'

'What? No, Father, no. They never finish before ten. How can I?'

'Then you leave early.'

'I will lose my position! I worked so hard—'

'You must have safety, Hannah! This precious Labour Party needs the blood of young girls now?'

'You have gone mad. There has been one murder—in Stepney, mind you—and the whole of London has lost its head.'

'She was the same as you. Young girl walking around the city alone. Thinking what could happen? Then dead. Like that. You must not be stubborn. Not attractive, Hannah.'

'Attractive? What do I care about that? Father, really.'

'There is a solution. You know it.'

'No.' I would not look at him. Mother was in the kitchen, washing the dishes. I heard the clink and slosh intermittently, between the volleys of our argument.

'Hannah, it is so simple. I wait outside for you. You finish when you like. I will be there. No matter if it's eleven, twelve. I may get cold, yes. Boring. Daughter busy turning into Bolshevik. But Mother can sleep tonight. I can sleep tonight.'

'I cannot, Father. I *cannot*. I do not require the protection of a man.'

'This thing is not because you are a woman. This is because you are a child. My responsibility. My daughter.'

'Father!'

'Then you are home at nine. That is all. We agree.'

The sound of Mother at the sink had stopped, though she had not come out of the kitchen. 'Happy, Mother?' I called as I thundered out of the dining room and into my bedroom.

~

When I returned from work the next day everyone was out. I opened the door to my room and stared. The bed had been moved away from the window to accommodate a table. It was the little black desk of the Gasks, on which thousands of words of newsprint had been produced. I ran across the room and laid my hands on its surface, nicked and scuffed as though each story written atop it were the result of some violent struggle. If I did not have my hands here lying on its cool surface, could not see the light falling from the window reflected in its shiny black paint, I would not believe it. Was this some trick of my parents to make me amenable? A sharp pain knocked at my ribs.

I took a soft leather notebook from under my pillow and a fountain pen from the bookshelf, knowing even as I did it that it was a bad idea, placed them carefully at the centre of the desk, beneath the large white-framed windows open to the trees of the heath and the summer sky. A writer's desk, here, in my room.

On the street a motor vehicle rumbled for a second or two before cutting out. Mrs Gask was out there, calling to the driver. I ran down the stairs, out of the open front door and onto the street where Mrs Gask was standing next to a van with its back doors open. 'Mrs Gask,' I called out to her. 'Your desk. It is in my room!'

Mrs Gask turned and took my hands in her own. 'Yes, Hannah dear. It is a gift from William and me.'

'But why don't you need it? You are not—giving up journalism?'

'Oh, Hannah. Your face. We would not disappoint you so. We are going to Paris for a while, and all about. The *Daily News* wants stories from the Continent, peacetime dispatches from our neighbours, that sort of thing.'

'It is the most wonderful present. And you and Mr Gask will have such a time! I am almost eaten alive with envy.'

'One day it will be you, Hannah dear. You are a much cleverer young woman than I ever was. Do you know, my French is appalling, in spite of all you've tried to teach me.'

I thought I would cry right here on the street with the removalist looking on. 'I shall miss you, Mrs Gask. We could never have such nice tenants as you and Mr Gask again.'

'And we will never again have such kind landlords. What a joy you are, dear Hannah. What a clever, determined young lady. Goodbye and good luck.'

Mrs Gask thrust forth a hand for me to shake. I offered my own briefly and ran inside before I could disgrace myself. In my room the desk was as I left it in its perfect position beneath the window. The pages of the journal flapped against one another in the breeze.

~

The next morning, when Mother came in to wake me, I groaned under the covers.

'What's wrong, little one?'

'Don't feel well.'

Mother laid the back of her hand across my forehead. Her long pale fingers, always cool. 'Goodness. You are burning up. Stay in bed. I'll bring you tea.'

When she had gone I pulled the hot-water bottle from under the covers and threw it under the bed.

As I drank my tea, Geoffrey appeared at the door in his school uniform, glowering. 'What's supposed to be the matter with you?'

'Spanish flu. Go to school.'

'Do you want to buy a copy of the *Heath Herald* to read in bed? Special edition.'

'I don't like football.'

'There's a fairly devastating exposé of the goings-on at number twelve.'

'Oh, all right then. There's tuppence on the dresser.'

He took the coin, left a thin newssheet in its place.

'Geoffrey?'

'Yes.'

'Where's Benjamin?'

'Playing out on the heath.'

'Oh.'

I looked at him, made an effort to fix his face in my memory—not the scowling version, rather how he looked when he too was playing on the heath, running, smiling, curls pulled back by the wind. Or now, that look of grim satisfaction when he had just made a sale.

As he went out I put the picture aside and thought through my morning.

After an age the house fell silent. Father left early to visit his shops, of which there were now three. Mother called in Benjamin and the boys went off next after the usual whining and scuffle with Mother over combing hair, brushing teeth. There had been a commotion when Benjamin thought he'd twisted his ankle after sliding down the banister but he was all right after Mother made him sit with ice on it for a while. He had actually broken his arm once sliding down the banister but he never would stop. I wanted to go out for a look at him but it would seem odd when I was supposed to be bedridden. Then at last Mother, who came in quietly with the basket over her arm, told me she was going to walk across the heath to the market at Golders Green and asked if there was anything special I would like her to bring back.

'No, thank you, Mother,' I said quietly as she kissed my brow. I could not look at her as she left, even to remember later.

I listened for a moment to the quiet of the house. When you listened it was never so quiet as you thought. There was the water gurgling in the hot-water system, the loud tick of the clock in the hall, a schoolmaster shouting at a class of boys cross-country running on the heath. Come on then, Hannah, I told myself. I pushed off the covers, beneath which I was fully dressed, and reached under the bed for my brown leather case. It was heavy. On top of it was yesterday's edition of the *Ham and High*. There was the address circled in red. A Mrs Windsor in Willow Road. I unclasped my case, laid the *Ham and High* and Geoffrey's *Heath Herald* on my clothes and refastened it.

I stood before the desk for a moment, case in hand, the high-stacked clouds billowing over the pond, and leaned forward, rested my head on its cool painted surface. Go, Hannah. The case was heavy.

It banged against my legs on the stairs. At the door I snapped my key quietly onto the bureau and stepped outside.

As I lugged my case along the empty street under scudding clouds, the work of carrying it warming me in spite of a chill breeze, I must have been sad, mustn't I? I was not an entirely heartless young woman. But that is not the feeling I remember as I walked away from our lovely house that accommodated everybody I loved. I felt a pure, sweet burst of energy, to be moving, to be out in the world, to be on my way.

Part II

Emil

THE NORTH SEA, 1929

Strange to ride as a passenger aboard this empty steamer. No shift to prepare for, hours to kill to Bremen, shuffling about the ship like a wealthy old tycoon deprived of the cabarets and pretty waitresses and cool heavy linen.

Emil sat on a stool he had brought up onto the first-class deck from his cabin, sliding around a little in the spray, the only furniture on the broad gleaming road of decking that stretched away fore and aft. His body was cold inside his coat but his face was warm in the morning sun that had dropped a silver blanket over the sea as they ploughed east towards Germany. A dark figure appeared against the glare, rounding the prow, growing larger along the shining road. There was something in the walk he knew: the little bob after impact. A roundish man, bouncing towards him. A cheerful walk. It was Meier, a young engineer he had met in Ireland when he went over with Siemens for the hydro-electric scheme at Ardnacrusha. The sight of his walk, the round stomach and face, fat-lipped smile, took him back to that place before the years at sea, the solitary weeks, the rough chaos of furloughs at port. His marriage to Ava was new then. He carried the knowledge of his fine, bright-haired wife across the sea like a medal in his pocket. The secret of how he had discovered her at a dance in Düsseldorf and talked her into marriage within a week. And Ireland, a wonder, that light after the night voyage falling on his new-feeling skin, dawn on the dock at Dún Laoghaire, the ride into Dublin and the streets filled with musicians, beggars and priests from some unfolding story—even Ireland just a place in the big world now, just another he had seen.

He stood, held out his hand. 'Meier!'

'Ah, Becker. It *is* you! I saw your name on the roster when I boarded in England but did not believe it. You look well.'

'And you, Meier. Where have you been all this time? Did you stay on in Ireland?'

'I did. I saw the opening, and the lights going on in the towns. It was a true marvel. And now, since August, I work on the ships. It is a quieter life than we're used to, Becker.'

'Until you reach port. But you're right. I have never read so much in my life.'

'You always were the intellectual. Let me guess. Kant? Nietzsche?'

'The fellow before me left a lot of murder mysteries, in several languages. I am now able to commit the perfect crime in Paris, Berlin or London.'

Meier leaned over the rail, his face rosy in the autumn sun, his thinning hair trailing shipwards in the wind. He drew a hipflask from the pocket of his greatcoat, offered it to Emil, who took a draught. 'Irish whiskey. That takes me back.'

'What else is a man to drink? I am ruined for schnapps forever. It doesn't warm you in the same way. You know, Becker, I'm remembering the last time I saw you, you devil. Wasn't it that night . . . ?'

Emil smiled at the sea. He knew what Meier was talking about. It was the night they had crept through the workers' camp, between huge tents that emitted the sounds of men sleeping and talking, down to the project. He and Meier had climbed across the scaffolding onto one of the massive pipes set out over the dam, sat astride it, drinking whiskey for perhaps an hour, this man talking about Irish girls, the exact and detailed ways in which they differed from Germans. He remembered that Meier's enthusiasm seemed untempered by actual experience. Then the boy had dropped the bottle. It fell into the blackness beneath them for long seconds before shattering on the stony bank below. The guard dogs went off and they had scrambled along the slippery pipes with splayed legs and outstretched arms, snagging on bolts, giggling, uncoordinated, suddenly frightened of falling—that bottle had taken a long time to hit the bottom—then scurrying through camp, chests on fire, to the engineers' barracks. The chains of the dogs clattered behind them; the Alsatians were wild for a catch.

Emil was on a train across the green country to Dún Laoghaire the next day. He'd been offered a position in Finland, setting up a smaller power plant, and since then he had tested equipment on the ships. He had never known what came of that night, but here was Meier, none the worse. Everyone a little older and wiser. He felt a pang for youth and stupidity. It seemed to him he was not a man to do such things now.

'I almost got my head kicked for that one.' Meier smiled. 'And you, you were the ringleader! And then you were away, scot-free.'

'We did no harm. They didn't discipline you, did they?'

'They could not prove it was me. And since you were gone, they let it go after a few days. But you know, I would do it again. I shall never forget it.'

'No.' Emil laughed. 'Me neither.'

'I remember,' said Meier, offering him another draught, 'there was a baby . . .'

'Yes, Hans. He's three now. I'll see him tomorrow.'

Meier clapped him on the shoulder. 'That's right. A boy! And your beautiful wife? She's well?'

'I think so. I've not seen either of them for several months. It's not always easy to tell, from letters.'

'No, that's true. Still, they'll put on a fine homecoming for you. You're lucky to have a family to welcome you. I'm returning for some training. Then back to sea.'

'You are a young man still. Did you never find an Irish girl?'

'Irish girls don't want to go to Germany. They prefer America. I should know. I asked enough of them.'

'Spend your leave with us. You can stay at my apartment. It's no good coming home with nothing to do.'

Meier took a drink. 'That's all right, Emil. I won't be staying in Germany for long. I find I like the sea.'

Emil felt the whiskey burn close to his heart. In his coat pocket he had a picture of the boy, an old one. He was not much more than a baby, sitting on his mother's lap for his portrait. Emil had taken them to the studio on his visit before last. It had cost a fortune, but he was paid and fed well, and liked to spend his money on them.

In the distance was the dark green line of the shore. In his gut spread a small fear. That he did not know his wife. That the boy would look at him as if he were a stranger, after this long separation. And the town might be too much changed to recognise. Father wrote that he was not worried about these Nazis. Or the communists with their little bombs. Each time he detailed something he was not worried about, Emil felt his anxiety drifting up off the page.

He was a lucky man next to this Meier. Mostly, he felt warm, a heat coming from the green horizon, pulling him towards it, guiding him into the gap in the land at the Elbe, on down into his country, the land not yet frozen for winter, to his town and his woman and his boy, who would launch himself into his arms, then hang off his neck and chatter until the cavernous spaces the sea wind had cleared in his head were blown away entirely.

~

A seal barked, bringing him into blackness after the bright confusion of dreams. His eyes were open, his heart quick. His wife's hand clenched his forearm. There it was again—not a seal, Hans. It was his boy, making this animal sound in the black room. He sat up. Ava was already striking a match for the kerosene lantern.

'Papa,' the boy rasped from his stretcher on Ava's side of the bed. She caught a flame on the third attempt and his face was illuminated: slick, white, frightened. The flame trembled as she touched it to the wick of the lamp and Emil skirted the bed in a second, lifted the boy from his stretcher. He was heavier than he looked, and burning, though the room was cold. Emil sat on the bed, clutching Hans's limp shoulder with one hand, dragging off the blankets with the other. He looked at his wife, close up against him, holding the boy's long fringe out of his eye, kissing his forehead, murmuring. Again came the barking cough. 'What is it?' he asked her.

'The croup. It's a curse in winter. Early this year.'

'What do we do for him?'

'I'll boil water. He needs the steam. He'll be all right.'

How do you know? he thought, watching her move purposefully into the kitchen. How do you know what to do? He placed a hand lightly on the boy's labouring ribs, felt the breath grazing the inside of his chest.

'Sit me,' Hans whispered.

'What?'

'Sit him up more,' Ava called from the kitchen, where she was filling the kettle for the stove. 'It helps him to breathe. And please distract him. He mustn't cry.'

Emil stared into the boy's face in the flickering circle of light, his body hot against Emil's arm. He let out the cough again, but fainter. His lids were heavy.

'We haven't had a chance to discuss my travels, have we, boy? You are always so busy, with your drawing and your ball. Anyway, it may interest you to know I rode the biggest ship ever made in Germany across the Atlantic Ocean. The waves were as tall as three men. Underneath us were sharks and jellyfish. All around, especially after sunset, were pirate ships.'

The boy smiled sleepily. 'I like pirates. They've got swords. And black hats.'

'Precisely. I saw them through my telescope, and they were watching *us* through *their* telescopes, making sure we weren't coming for their treasure. When they saw me looking at them, they waved their swords in the air.'

'Were you, Papa? Were you after their treasure?'

'Of course. Everybody wants the pirates' treasure. It's the most valuable treasure of all. But I had no sword of my own, unfortunately.'

The boy coughed. It sounded almost like a normal cough. 'What did you do?'

'I watched them through my telescope. If they came too close, I fired a warning shot with my musket.'

'What's a musket?'

'The kind of gun you need to warn pirates with.'

'Where'd you get that?'

'Standard issue.'

Ava appeared at the door with a basin of steaming water, a towel over her arm. 'Come, Hans.' She placed the basin carefully on the floor. The boy slipped from Emil's lap and kneeled before it, breathing in the steam, coughing. She draped the towel over his head. 'Not too low,' she said softly. 'Don't scald your nose.'

'The cough sounded better then,' Emil said as she sat down next to him.

She nodded. 'It passes quickly. So long as he doesn't panic. He has learned what to do.'

'Even so, I'll run and fetch the doctor.'

'Hush, no. The doctor charges a fortune if you wake him.'

'That doesn't matter,' he whispered. 'I have the money. I'll go now.'

She put a hand on his. 'No, Emil. Look, he's all right. It passes quickly.'

The boy in his pyjamas kneeled under the tent silently. His shoulders were thin. There were the knobs of his spine. After a moment he sat back, pushed the towel onto his neck, took deep breaths from the air in the room, then pulled the towel back over his head. The room was quiet but for the sound of him taking in the vapour. His draped shadow flickered large on the wall.

'Come to bed now, Hans,' Ava said, after a few minutes. She stood, took the towel, kissed the boy, then picked up the bowl and carried the things out to the kitchen. Hans began to gather his blankets from the floor. Emil stood, leaned down, took them from him.

'Come up to the big bed. You sleep with Mama. I'll take your bed.'

Hans regarded him, his arms wrapped around the bundle of blankets, giggling. 'You're too big!'

'I can shrink myself. It's a skill we learn at sea. To hide from pirates.'

The boy laughed, coughed a little, climbed onto the big bed. 'Show me!'

Emil curled up on the stretcher, making himself small, and pulled the blankets over his head, peeking from a gap. The enclosed space smelled of boy: soap, honey cake, earth. Hans was grinning, quilt tucked up under his arms.

'What's this?' Ava said from the doorway. She climbed in on the other side of the boy, leaned across him to turn off the light. Her hair fell across his face, concealing him at the last moment before darkness.

The stretcher was tiny, and creaked as Emil tried to settle himself. His legs had to stay pulled towards his chest to fit, and he could not shift for fear of disturbing them. He listened for every breath in the dark, until his limbs were cramped from enforced stillness. Hans began to snore lightly, a rhythmic whistle and light rasp. Emil stretched his legs a few centimetres, bedsprings whining, stilled himself again. So he went until morning, listening for Hans's breath, daring to move only occasionally. When the darkness at the window began to lift, and Ava stirred, he slipped down into the dark, still listening for the sound of the boy's breathing.

~

Emil needed new boots and he took Hans with him to buy them. The boy chose the most expensive pair for him, and he did not have the heart to say no. Walking home, Hans clutching the package of boots to his chest, he wondered what Ava would say. Rather, he knew.

She would say nothing, but the counting of the coins for his daily beer would be a fraction slower and there would be harder bread for breakfast, warmed over until it was gone, mould cut out in little snipped corners. It did not matter that he had work. She saw those without it and worried that it would catch. But he had not seen the boy for months, and they were fine boots. They would last longer than the cheap kind, and so were really a sensible purchase.

It was mild at home after the North Sea. Every dawn had been a blue fog, the ship's horn lost in a world with no edges. Walking on deck alone before the dark lifted he felt that the edges of himself too were becoming indistinct. The boy was wrapped in scarf and mittens though Emil felt warm, almost hot in his sweater. But then he had been carrying Hans on his shoulders, a boy thin but dense, all his intent latent in his strong little body. Now the boy shed clothing as he struggled valiantly along the pavement with the large package.

At the door to the apartment building Emil paused for a second but Hans hurled himself against the wood and was off up the stairs. Inside he smelled sausages cooking, stirring the juices of his stomach.

'Mama!' he heard from above. 'Look at Papa's boots!' and the crackling of thick paper as the boy tore open the package. Ava's murmur. You never knew what she was saying to him. The boy declaimed, always—'I am happy!' 'You are sleeping!' (each dawn)—and in response there came the continual murmur of his wife. He wondered whether the words were important or whether it was just an instinctive hushing noise she made, another form of her responses to his own occasional exuberance when drinking or happy. 'Shhh, Emil, not so loudly now.' 'Please, dear. The boy is tired. Let him settle.'

There was Ava's murmur but then, this time, an audible sharpness, clear words: 'Enough, Hans. Play in the bedroom now.'

There came a protest as Emil grew closer to the second-floor apartment: 'But, Mama, the boots!' He heard the thud of them—one, two—hitting the wooden floor above and a slammed door. Hans had been banished and was outraged. So far as Emil knew, such a thing had never happened before. The boy was spoiled by everyone who knew him.

She was waiting on the landing when he reached it, holding out a card, the light in the kitchen spilling into the stairwell around her. The boots were in the doorway, awry, like the feet of a cripple. Their champion was throwing a football at a wall repeatedly inside the apartment.

Her arm was thrust at him, rigid, straight. He took the card. Rage filled the close space of the landing. The card, he saw, was a telegram. He held it up to the light coming from behind her.

> *Herr Becker. Owing to cancellation of orders, the company will reduce test voyages forthwith. Testing on all remaining missions will be carried out by the chief engineer. Please attend the office in Düsseldorf at your earliest convenience for severance conditions. Thanking you for your service. Herr Faber. Employment office.*

He picked up the boots and entered the apartment, placed them on the small square table that filled most of the space in the kitchen.

'You should have joined the NSDAP,' she whispered, quickly, as though she'd been waiting to say it, saving it.

'What in God's name are you talking about?'

'They still have jobs. They find them for you when you are a member.'

'You have lost your mind. I'm sorry about the job. Father will put me on to something in the factories for now. At least I'll be here, with you and Hans.'

'If you go over to the party, you won't be out of work again. We cannot manage if you're unemployed. We have no savings. Johanna's husband was out of work and they got him a permanent position, high up in the party.'

'As a hired thug, Ava. Johanna's husband will be kicking the heads of Jews in his permanent position. Is that what you're asking me to do to put bread on the table?'

'Shhh,' she said, and tilted her head towards the wall. 'She'll hear you. She has contacts.'

'Christ! Goddamn her contacts!' Her hands flew to her ears and she closed her eyes. The repetitive thump of the ball against the bedroom wall had stopped. He spoke more quietly, a finger pointed towards her: 'Do not believe their filth. I forbid you.'

She looked down. He did not know himself, like this. But she must see. She was not a stupid woman, not like Johanna, an ignorant peasant who crossed herself when the Jewish schoolteacher passed her on the street. He had been away so much in these last years, since Hans was born. He looked at her face. She had brought her hands down by her side. She was still so beautiful, hair so fair, skin clear and taut across her cheekbones, eyes round and grey and unreadable. He wanted to ask her: 'And you, what do you think of Jews?'

This was his own madness now. She was frightened of having no money, and that was all. But he knew how to find work. He had never been unemployed, never, even in hard times.

After a few moments she went in to the boy and started up with that murmuring. He must go to Father's office. Father knew—always—where the jobs were. He had a map in his head dotted with factories with little red pins for each body required. No doubt it was easier to hold the map in place in his mind since the American crash, particularly as he did not include Nazi jobs in his inventory. He must go, and yet he did not relish telling his father. He would worry, and it was not his job to worry about a grown man and how he fed his family. On the stairs he heard a wail from above. Emil had left without saying goodbye. Hans was screeching. Ava would have the devil of a time making him quiet again.

~

He woke at midday to the alarm, unsure for a couple of seconds why he had been sleeping with brightness bleeding at the borders of the windows. His body was on the brink of sweating beneath the pile of heavy blankets though the air in the room was cool on his face. Hans's bed was empty and the apartment was quiet.

He remembered: he was on the late shift. Ava had left bread, cheese, sausage and an apple on the table for him. She would be at her sister's in Krefeld with the boy. They took the train there on Tuesdays. After he had washed in the bathroom on the landing, he checked the clock and took his satchel. His boots smelled of polish when he pulled them on, and he saw the smudges of Hans's thumbprints from where it hung on the doorknob.

It was a decent walk to the factory, he could have taken the streetcar, but he didn't mind. He had agreed to walk, and Ava saved the pfennigs in a tall glass jar in the pantry between the oats and the sugar against the day when this job too would disappear. The walk took him away from the high street, the women's domain in the daytime until recently. Now, boys he had known at school hung about, carrying their placards, shouting over each other, occasionally landing a punch on an opponent's head in a territorial scuffle. He walked away from all that along the banks of the cold brown river, lined with factories and warehouses, the fields of childhood gone as the town had spread. Many of the buildings were quiet now, their flat grey faces silently recalling industry and bustle, hourly deliveries, men shouting, the roar and rhythm of machines.

His factory was known to him from earlier days. He had watched it go up the summer before he started school. Thomas was a presence that he felt as soon as he was in the building's shadow. In his body, not his mind. He was just there, the memory of his boyhood friend, in the space between the walls, and on the banks of the river, and the little space beyond the building where there was still a narrow strip of pasture and the hummock behind which they had built their den.

The factory made tools—hammers, screwdrivers, spanners—and nuts, screws, bolts. It was work. Father told him he didn't have to take it but he couldn't be fussy. He supervised the shift, checked the machines, signed the men in and out. It left his mind to work over what his eyes had seen since he came home. As thousands of tiny pieces of metal passed before his eyes, the workers' fingers sorting, pushing, their bodies moving around the machines in synchronicity, he saw men marching in brown shirts with banners, shouting.

He was free to let his memory pass through the days at sea, and in the countries of the world. He remembered Freetown. There were women on the streets in brightly coloured dresses with dazzling teeth. Children running in the laneways, at the markets, with the smell of smoke and cooking food and bodies and spices making the air thick. And in Ireland everyone moved slowly as though they were as old as time and their eyes had seen it all. The adults, that is. The children were as quick and bad as children everywhere. Stole from building sites. Learned filthy words in German and shouted them over and over again.

There was a barmaid in the village pub when he worked on the Shannon. She had white skin and black, wild hair. Even her eyes looked at you as though you were one of those she'd seen before a thousand times. You might be foreign, the boss around here. So what.

He brought his attention back to the men, the machines. A sound or rather a dimming of sound pulled him back into the vast space beneath the long glass wall of the manager's office above. Usually there was a river of voices that he did not habitually separate from the rhythm of machines. The men had stopped talking and were glancing up towards the office, trying not to make it apparent that they were doing so. But when fifty men looked up, you could not help but follow their gaze. Behind the glass were uniformed men, a row of four policemen, peering down at them with the manager and his deputy. Emil, like the workers, lifted his eyes without moving his head. From above he might be watching the conveyor belt, as he should be. He focused on the policeman at the end of the row, the one nearest to him. The man looked straight at Emil, and raised a hand. God, that gesture. It was him, Thomas. But it was not, of course. His brother, Karl, he had grown so like him, and like their father. He had been working somewhere else, Hanover? Father had not told him he was back, or that he was a policeman. Emil nodded, just a little dip of the chin.

A worker, Bern, standing close to Emil, asked, 'Know him?'

Emil looked at Bern. He had him down as a communist. Something in his brand of tobacco, the quality of his sneer. 'No.' He paused. 'Used to. Well, his brother.'

'He knows you, that's for sure. Been watching you since he came in.'

'Back to work.'

Bern hesitated, not quite long enough for it to be a direct challenge, and shuffled back to the belt.

What did it matter, who knew whom? There were few in this town of whom he did not know something. He looked at the men on his shift. Several glanced quickly away.

~

At the end of the shift he took the card with the men's names up to the office to give to the manager. The deputy stood in front of his desk in a little anteroom putting on his coat. He stared at Emil for a moment, nodded, then jogged down the stairs, his boots clattering on the steel grilles. Emil knocked at the door and waited. Herr Peters was on the telephone, speaking in harsh bursts, low and urgent. The phone clicked and Emil heard: 'Come!' Emil stood in front of the desk and looked out through the glass as the new shift started up below, the men fresher, smiling after a day of freedom: errands for their wives, sleep, sex, beer. Their shoulders were not yet stiff with repeated movements and exhaustion.

Peters watched him for a moment. He seemed almost elderly, tired, irritated from the phone call, or this job. Emil knew from his father that Peters used to teach engineering in Düsseldorf but lost his job after some sort of disgrace, blown up or entirely manufactured by a Nazi in the polytechnic administration. 'Well?'

'Oh, excuse me, Herr Peters. The timesheet for my shift.'

'Call me Colleague,' he muttered as he took the card, slotting it into an index on his desk. 'I am in the union, like you. I suppose you're wondering what the visit from the police was about.'

Emil shrugged, hands in pockets. On the factory floor his replacement for the night shift, a boy of no more than twenty-two, was trying to keep his eyes open, slumped against the wall, his mouth falling open, closing, swallowing, slipping open again. 'They are all stirred up about the latest election. They think there will be more strikes.'

'What do they care about a strike here?'

'When the men are out they fight, they say. They say we have communists here.'

'There are communists everywhere. And Nazis. Did they say anything about Nazis fighting?'

'They did not.'

Emil had been watching the factory floor. Now he chanced a direct look at the manager's face. Peters must have been aware that Emil knew his history. Emil's father was notorious for his uncanny knowledge of affairs and his fondness for gossip.

Peters held his gaze for a moment before turning his head towards the factory floor. 'We'll lose a shift soon,' he said. 'But don't worry. That joker down there will be first to go. Look, there he is, napping through the shift again. And there are his men, laughing at him, slacking off.'

Emil saw that the men were chatting, paying less attention to the parts on the belt than they should. Only the machine operators were attentive to the task of not losing a finger or an eye. Irritation flared. He was their union representative. He did not want to put himself out for lazy men. He reminded himself that the men did not choose their foreman.

Peters held out a hand to shake. Emil took it quickly, shook it firmly as he said goodbye, held it for a moment longer than was usual. Peters looked Emil once more in the eye.

Something in him these days looked for a spark. An ignition. In every encounter, in every face and touch of the hand, he was alive to the meaning of a dozen tiny gestures. He stored the information carefully for the day he might need it.

~

On the dark river, the factories were quiet apart from the one or two running a night shift. A match flare warmed his face briefly as he lit his cigarette. An owl called from across the wide water. There were oars splashing, voices, laughter, some illicit escapade. He was not going home. He was joining the guard for a Social Democrat and free trade union rally at the beer hall. He always attended the meetings, when home, but now something extra was required. Last week in Düsseldorf a trade union official was injured when a brown shirt threw a chair at him before he had opened his mouth to speak. He heard from his father that the police hung back when there was trouble from the storm-troopers. They still turned up to rallies, but did less and less. Above the sounds of the river at night he heard a different kind of noise. He knew it; it was the voice of a crowd singing. The sound crept across his skin. He knew the words they sang, even though they were indistinct. *Clear the streets for the brown battalions. Clear the streets for the storm-troopers! Already millions look with hope to the swastika. The day of freedom and bread is dawning!*

This will blow over, Father told him. The workers were solid, unswayed by fanatics. But nothing blew over. You lay on your back in a gas-filled crater with a mask on your head and a knife in your hand waiting for someone to fall on top of you. When the shadow crossed the crater, you thrust out your hand and let him fall on your blade, or he would get you with his. Every second you were ready.

He had his knife. The handle was smooth in his pocket. The blade in its sheath was always sharp. He honed it in the night when everyone slept, long dark silences between rasping strikes, trying not to disturb his wife and son, hoping they would not come out and find him like this, a stranger at the table, sharpening a knife. He walked into the streets away from the river, towards the sound of the voices.

The police should worry less about the striking. It was the singing that always ended with spilled blood.

By the time he reached the beer hall, the crowd was mostly inside the building and the singing had given way to noisy chatter. He joined the men and women bustling through the double doors from the street. Inside it was warm and fuggy and he was amid a jostle of bodies making their way into the rows of wooden chairs. The long tables had been stacked against the walls. There was laughter and shouting and one shirt in two was brown. He caught the eye of one, head shorn but for a floppy fringe, shining eyes, a smile of anticipation, a little drunken stumble. There were too many free unionists in this town for them to be locals. They had been bussed in, in those trucks of theirs. He cast about between their heads for the speakers, glimpsed a movement from beyond the side curtain at the edge of the stage. It was the secretary of the local branch of the SPD, peering into the crowd. Moisture reflected light on his brow. Emil shoved through to the stairs at the side of the stage. A couple of men pushed back with elbows and fists but most stood aside.

Behind the curtain was a small group of men gathered in a knot. He knew them all, his father and his colleagues. They looked doddery though none was older than his father at fifty-five, hunched together like children abandoned unexpectedly in a strange place. Martin, his father's friend since their childhood in Dülken, saw Emil first. The man's shoulders dipped with relief as though with the arrival of this man he'd known since he was a baby everything would be all right.

Emil's father turned, beamed, shook his hand, clapped his shoulder. 'I knew you would come. I told them to stop worrying. Old women!' He turned to the others, who eyed Emil from the shadows. 'Didn't I tell you, boys?' They nodded warily. 'Emil is our man.'

'But, Father,' Emil said quietly, not for the others, 'where are the other Reichsbanner? Your guard? Where are the rest?'

'Well, in the end it was just Martin's boy and Helmut's and you, and some police, but it seems no one has come.'

'I saw police on my way in. I'll talk to them.'

'No, they have agreed to stay, but they won't come onstage. They don't want to antagonise the brown shirts by appearing to take sides.'

'Father, don't go out. There are hundreds of them. It's a set-up.'

'Oh no,' he sighed. 'We must go out. All the more reason. You see—' he smiled, caught his breath '—we won't be intimidated.' His eyes shone beneath a film of water.

Oh God, thought Emil. He looked at the others. They would rather have been anywhere but here. They were elected officials, not soldiers. They had all been too old for the war; the men back in the hall mostly too young. 'Who is speaking tonight?'

They shrugged, looked at Klaus.

'We've decided just me tonight, Emil,' his father said. 'We must demonstrate the support of the metalworkers' union for the SPD. Reassure people that they needn't be frightened of voting with their conscience.'

Emil stared at the men. 'You're sending him out there alone? Let's go and ask for a gun from one of these thugs. You can shoot Father yourselves and save them the trouble.'

'Now, Emil . . .' His father laid a hand on his shoulder.

A party official puffed up his chest a little. 'We will all be with him onstage—'

Martin interrupted him. 'I will speak too, Emil. You're right. We cannot let him speak alone.'

Emil remembered the moment this morning when he took his satchel off the hook on the door in the bright kitchen. He had thought of his Luger, beneath the floorboard under Hans's fold-out bed. No, he had told himself. You can't go back from a gunshot. With a knife, there are choices, degrees of harm. He turned and looked past the curtain into the writhing hall. The front rows were filled with fat-chested brown shirts, staring at the empty chairs on the stage. They'd put the hefty ones up front to intimidate the speakers. As he came through the hall he'd seen plenty of scrawny types the SA had probably picked up off the street last week. They began to stamp, at first chaotically then in a slow coordinated rhythm.

'Okay.' He nodded to his father and Martin. 'Who's first?'

Martin took a step towards him.

One of the men lifted a placard from against the wall and thrust it at Emil. 'You lead us in with this.' The men looked at each other. Emil could not see what the placard said in the dark but took it, moving towards the curtain.

'Let's go. Before they start gnawing at the furniture.'

They followed him towards the stage. Emil could hear his father wheezing behind him. He stepped out into the dim electric light, still dazzling after the shadows backstage. At first there was absolute silence as they walked across the stage. He heard the footfalls of his new boots and the shuffle of the men behind him across the floorboards. A bottle smashed somewhere towards the back of the hall. There was laughter among the rows of brown shirts. Emil stepped forward to the podium while the others took their seats to his side. He opened his mouth and booing and whistling filled the hall. He took a breath and sent his voice out into the room. His body remembered how to make itself heard over mortar fire, bombing, screaming. 'Ladies and gentlemen, the undersecretary of the Duisburg-Hamborn branch, Herr Lang.'

He took his placard to the end of the row of chairs and stood next to the one vacated by Martin as he took the podium. Out in the crowd he saw faces he knew, over and over again: from the army, from school, from work. It seemed possible he might be imagining it. No one gave any sign of recognising him. The booing and stamping filled his chest, hollowing out his muscles. He glanced down at his banner. THE NATIONAL SOCIALISTS ARE THE ENEMY OF THE WORKER. VOTE SPD. VOTE FOR FREEDOM FROM TYRANNY.

As he read it, a beer bottle smashed against the letters. He felt the jolt against his hand and his face was sprayed with beer. He scanned the faces in the crowd as though he could find his man, drag him up here, show him what happened to those who tried such tricks. He glanced sideways. Father mopped his brow with a handkerchief. Martin was beginning words, faltering, raising a hand. Something flew past the speaker's head, heavy and fast, so close he shrank against the podium, shuffled into his chair, folded his arms, face hot. The room was filled with a roaring of voices, scraping chairs, every man on his feet. Women, too, he saw them scattered about, faces contorted like the rest, shouting. Emil looked behind the podium to see what the missile was: a plank of wood with a row of three nails sticking out. He needed to get the men offstage but they were stunned, staring out at the room as though it would all stop in a moment, if they were just patient. They were casting glances at him as though he, somehow, had the power to quell a room of lunatics in the grip of a bloodlust. All this in seconds.

His father was standing. The official at the far end of the row of chairs was making for the curtain. A bottle missed him and flew directly into Father's face. His hand was on his nose and then coming away, dark liquid gushing. He reached his slick, blackened hand towards Emil, who was in the air, flying off the stage, jumping into the crowd, placard raised, without a thought other than smashing these SA thugs, inserting himself into the mad throng, inflicting damage. He landed on hard bodies, bounced off, skidded on beer-wet floor into the meaty thicket of the front row. The placard was wrenched from his hands, splinters jagging his palms, and he was down in the dark, his head pitching forward into a foul-smelling crotch and then a chair, the top of a boot. He grabbed a thin calf and pulled it towards his chest. He felt the man topple over his body, heard the swearing of a brown shirt as his colleague landed on him. They stamped on Emil's fingers, then his head. He reached for the knife in his pocket as they turned him over. Way above, their faces formed a ring. Was that Max from his polytechnic class? It could not be. There was a circle of light above their heads. A metal blow beneath his chin and a tear, a slick rupture at his stomach, and the circle closed to black.

~

He woke shivering, his belly and crotch wet. His cheek throbbed against the icy curve of a cobblestone. He swallowed, took down something little and hard like a peanut. He found the gap in his back teeth with his tongue. Throughout the war he had kept his teeth and now some Nazi had knocked one out. He opened his eyes. He knew all the streets of this town but he did not know this one for a moment. But those blue doors were familiar, they were the doors of the beer hall. Someone had taken the trouble to drag him outside. He could see past the building to the square, where a few people were still about. It must be late. The street was empty, the beer hall doors closed, the building silent, as though nothing had happened there. He clenched his muscles, feeling for damage. His ribs were bruised, his jaw was throbbing and beneath the sharpness of these injuries there was something deeper, something that was making his whole body shiver. He brought a hand slowly to his stomach, found congealed wetness, lifted his fingers to his face in the lamplight. Black-stained, glistening. He must reach the square, get help, or he would lose too much blood. The inside of a man was wet and glittering, dark. Rhythmic, pulsing, a soft machine. This knowledge was no help to him. He must think only of what he needed to do first, and then what he needed to do after that.

He pulled himself up against the wall. His arms and legs were all right though his body was gripped by spasms. It was as though he had been knocked out in October but had woken to a February freeze. He could walk, slowly, one hand on the wall, one on his stomach, holding his shirt to the wound to slow the bleeding. His hand was soon covered but that was not what he would think about. It was twenty metres to the square, forty of his halting paces. He counted them as he moved. It took five minutes of concentration, of telling himself *now, step*, to reach the end of the street. There was no one in the square by the time he reached it. He would use his last few steps to reach a lamp, so that when someone came they would not pass him by in the dark. What if it were one of them who came? His mind threw up the question without warning. He did not allow the next thought. He must only cross the road that lined the square without a wall to help him. One step. And another. Three more. For the last step it felt that his stomach was opening up. He knew what came out of men when they were opened. He must reach the lamp before he fell. Push forward. His fingers slipped on the cold surface, squeezed tighter. He let himself down towards the ground, inched down the pole, sat against it, sweating, shivering, concentrating on staying upright, staying awake. Where was Father? His stomach clenched, pain tore through the wound. He was on the stage, with the men. They would have helped him. The blood on his face, in his white hair. They would have helped him, if they did not run.

Shapes appeared at the far side of the square. People, they had seen him, stopped. He called, hoarse. 'Help me!' Again, a little louder. 'I'm injured.' The shapes receded. He heard a woman's heels on the cobbles. Shadows swallowed by a side street.

He looked at his watch in the lamplight. One o'clock. He allowed himself to wonder what the chances were of being found, of the people who found him helping him to a doctor, or at least bandaging him and keeping him warm until morning. For a moment he hoped. This is my hometown. Someone may come who knows it is me: Emil Becker.

A thirst overwhelmed him. His right hand was not bloody. He traced a finger in the frost on the lamppost until it melted and then put his finger in his mouth. It was a tiny droplet on his vast arid tongue so he did it again and again until eventually some reached his throat. All the concentration of his body gathered towards the moisture at the tip of his finger, pressing upon his tongue.

His eyes were closing. Steel caps clicked across the icy cobbles. He could not open his eyes. The rhythm of the heels did not change. Quick, purposeful, someone was coming, for better or worse. He slipped down the pole towards whatever approached.

~

It was dark but changing. There was light against his lids and breath falling on his face. It took a moment to ungum his eyes. There was the boy, standing over him in the kitchen while he lay on the little sofa. Everything hurt. It seemed at first like an indiscriminate throbbing, but then he could identify gradations, places where it was worse. The boy studied him. There was a bandage, he felt it on his head as he shifted, another on his stomach, beneath his pyjamas. The boy's face hovered against the indigo window. They looked at each other for many seconds without speaking, the boy's long face making serious appraisal. He noticed after a while that Ava was at the bedroom door, watching them. 'Hans,' she whispered. 'Let Papa sleep.'

The boy reached out a finger slowly and touched a cut above Emil's eyebrow. His little nail hit new, soft scab. There came a momentary concentration of soreness around the boy's fingertip where the pain gathered as though the finger was a magnet and the pain made up of filings. The boy removed his finger and the pain resettled in various pockets of his body.

He closed his eyes. When he opened them the boy had gone. It was daylight, a dull day outside, seeping in between the apartment blocks, and Ava was scrubbing the kitchen floor on her knees. 'What are you doing?' he said quietly, afraid to move anything.

'Getting the blood out of the floorboards before the landlady sees it. She keeps dropping in unannounced.'

'Come here,' he said. She left the pink rag at the sink, washed her hands, leaned on the bench. 'How did I get home?'

'Someone knocked on the door and left you there. A man. I smelled his cologne after he had gone.' She stood before the window, flushed from work, her apron pulled tight across her stomach, her dark figure a neat shape cut out of the grey light. She was a clean fresh thing. She did not want to come too close to his body, its smells and seepage, and yet it must have been she who dressed his wounds.

'Ava. Sit with me.' She bowed her head, remained in place, the table between them. 'You're angry with me.'

She was silent for a moment. 'Why did you go? You cannot fight them! You should not be encouraging your father. He is not a young man.'

'Father will always fight for workers.'

'They are workers too. And they will win!'

'No. They will only win if everyone gives up so easily. You fight them now, before they are too powerful. *We* will win. I know it. Please, come here. Everything hurts. Sit with me.'

She drew close, kneeled beside the sofa, looked him in the eye, the line of her lips straight, determined. She smelled of oranges and nutmeg. Where did she find these things? He leaned his head gingerly against her hair. 'What did you tell Hans?'

She eyed the bedroom door, behind which the boy was supposed to be taking his nap, though he had been known to sit silently for an hour, sorting his marbles on his bed, making patterns in the dust on the window pane.

'That you fell into a machine at the factory.'

'My God. He'll think his father is an imbecile!'

'Better that,' she murmured.

He closed his eyes, felt her weight shift from the sofa beside him, heard the rhythmic wiping of her rag across the floor.

~

He had been off work for a week when Peters came by at the end of the afternoon shift. The flat was empty but for Emil and he answered the door himself. He could move around so long as he took it slowly. Emil knew why the manager had come as soon as he saw him and so they did not discuss the matter of his job. He took a bottle of beer from the shelf, unstoppered it, poured out two glasses. They sat at the table. '*Prost!*' Emil drank it back. Peters did the same, though only drank half the glass. Emil topped them up.

'I hear it was brown shirts.'

Emil nodded, sipping the second glass more slowly. The pain was receding.

'They will get theirs,' Peters said so quietly he might not have said it at all.

Emil nodded again.

'You were an officer, weren't you, Becker? And decorated. Iron Cross?'

'Second class. Two a penny.'

'Not quite. In any case, you can organise men, can't you? I have seen it.'

Emil laughed. 'And yet I'm unemployed, with all my talents.'

'There is other work to be done in times like these.' The man's voice faded as he forced out the words. 'Don't you think?'

'Perhaps. But you know, I have a young son. My wife is already angry that I got myself beaten up.'

'Then you have a future to fight for.'

'Easy to say.'

Peters let out a nervous laugh. 'Perhaps not so easy.' He was sweating, though the kitchen was cold, the window running with droplets of condensation from the heat of their bodies.

Emil looked at him. He was Klaus's age, more or less, but of a different class. He had no local accent. A neatly trimmed beard. He saw again the blood pouring from his father's face, his eyes it seemed. He had no more recent image with which to replace this one, neither of them having permission from their wives to leave their flats. 'No, not so easy to say.'

'I know others.'

'Yes, of course, there are the unions. The SPD. The communists even. And the Reichsbanner. They're not taking it lying down.'

The man eyed him. 'There are others,' he said. 'And other ways. There are soldiers, like you. Not everyone gave back their pistols.'

No one gave them back, Emil thought. But you need bullets. And something with a longer range.

Peters could see him thinking. 'Thank you for the beer, Becker.' He stood. 'I'm sorry about the job. Perhaps your father can put you in touch with something else, something that fits your qualifications better.'

Emil pulled himself to his feet carefully, held out his hand. 'Where can I find you?'

Peters handed him a piece of paper. 'I play cards on a Friday night. Many people come and go. It's a good place to chat.'

Emil opened the door, watched the bald circle on top of the man's head weave a spiral down the stairs.

Hannah

PARIS, 1930

In Paris I slept in a narrow bed under the sloping roof of a tall apartment building in rue du Sommerard. The bed had springs that were coming through the ticking and by May it was sweltering under the eaves. I lay perspiring at night with the window open, listening to the voices and traffic spilling off the Boulevard Saint-Michel. The room was so small that the two-hob stove could be reached even when sitting on the bed. My neighbour Marie in the next room on the landing, a pale beauty with Chinese-black hair, also a teacher at the school, came in every afternoon and we sat on the bed playing cards on my counterpane and boiling eggs in the kettle without having to do more than stretch an arm out to the sink and the stove. When we let the whistle blow for the full three minutes it took the eggs to cook our landlady would tramp upstairs and rap on the door with her cane. But boiling eggs for tea, like living in these tiny rooms, was how we managed to live on our meagre wage, and so when she came to my door I feigned ignorance of French, one more stupid Englishwoman in Paris, and smiled haplessly over Marie's shoulder like a simpleton.

One warm night, in my airless room *sous les toits*, after our tea of eggs and game of whist, Marie announced that she was going out. It was Friday and we only had Saturday morning left of the week's teaching. That morning after class we had gone along to the office and been handed our little brown envelopes of francs, and so, I had hoped, we might go to the Russian restaurant on Saint-Michel as we often did and eat blintzes and drink Russian tea. Or I would eat a blintz and she would watch me wipe chocolate sauce from my mouth. She was careful of her figure. I hardly saw the point. Paris was a city where one walked and walked, tireless with wonder, and living in our rooms imposed a stringent exercise regime. When one came home at night and turned on the light in the foyer, it was then necessary to run up five flights of stairs before it turned itself off only a very few minutes later. I have never been so fit before or since.

The appeal of the Russian restaurant however was not merely in the desserts, or the borscht, which I found comfortingly similar to Mother's; rather it was in the characters one found there. The proprietor was a fantastically ancient man with two silent middle-aged daughters with necks like swans and crumpling décolletages. They sat at the corner table and the father crammed food into his cavernous mouth, or did his accounts, or drank with fat criminal-looking men with shiny collars and the women sat, staring into space, remembering, we imagined, the beautiful rooms of their palaces.

Marie trounced me with a casually flung down card and a little shrug. 'There,' she said. 'I win, Anglaise. Now, I must prepare to go out.'

'But where are you going? It's Friday! What about Misha's?'

'Oh,' she said. 'We can go next week. Jean-Paul is coming soon.' She was already standing, my end of the bed sinking disconcertingly.

Then she was gone with a little shake of her slippery black hair, as if to shrug off obligations to plain girls with no other way to spend a Friday evening than fantasising about Russian émigrés and eating wickedly fattening food.

A little later, as I sat on the narrow balcony in search of a breeze, the sky growing pale in the long evening, I saw her, five flights down on the street. A tall young student bent forward to kiss her cheeks. Four kisses, delivered slowly, his hands holding her elbows as though they were saucers. They strode out across the street and disappeared into a lane, his hand on her back, and I in a little funk jumped down from my post and pulled a comb through my tangled hair, preparing to go and see the Russians alone.

Later still, lying in the dark after midnight, I heard her return. The light fizzed on outside my room as she entered the foyer below, and her footsteps came slowly up the stairs. You won't make it, I thought. *Hurry.* I had heard her complete only two sets of stairs when the light clicked off again. She continued at the same pace: step, step, step, no rush. In the dark room, the narrow bed, I imagined myself into her body, hand gliding along the wooden rail, stepping slowly in the dark, skin remembering the tall student, unable to quicken my pace. She was still climbing those stairs as I fell asleep.

The morning found me back on the balcony, shutters open to the city, the stone cooling the underside of my legs while the sun warmed my knees. A window box below was filled with red and white flowers and down on Sommerard there was a boulangerie on the opposite corner. Amid the flow of bicycles, carts and motorcars driving on the wrong side of the road Parisians stepped out from the shade of the trees and crossed the street for their bread. As customers emerged from the shop you could see whether they lived alone or in a house of hungry children by the number of baguettes and bags of croissants tucked under their arm or in a basket. The smells of Paris for me: those eggs boiling in my hot little room, geraniums and cooking butter.

The sun, slanting between the buildings onto my legs between the railings, slipped above the roofs and my hair and neck were emblazoned. This was a part of waking up to the world on these mornings. To sit and wait for the sun to warm my skin, listening to the sounds down in the streets, then reach back and boil the kettle for coffee. This morning I sat there for a little longer than usual. There was no sound from next door. Marie was sleeping off her late night while I let the sun warm me like an embrace.

All through college in Oxford I had dreamed of being abroad. I had got into Ruskin on a scholarship. It was not part of the university, but a college for the children of workers—I met half the future Labour Party among the teachers and students. It was a wonderful time in my life, filled with young people with all sorts of passionate ideas about the world, but even then, I longed to travel, to begin the grand adventure I felt was waiting. Anyway, when, after exams, a friend had told me that a new mixed school in Paris needed an English tutor, I had sat up all night while the others celebrated freedom from study and written a letter to the headmistress in perfect French, the wastepaper basket at my feet filling with discarded efforts. Ruskin College had lent me the passage and I had come to Paris the previous autumn, surviving a winter of feet-numbing cold, staying on alone in the apartment over a solitary Christmas, to bring me here to this May day, the trees full, my skin warm.

My friends had all by the end of exams found positions with Labour MPs or the trade unions and though I admired them I could not help thinking it a bit dreary to be moving to Leeds or Sunderland and pressing on immediately with the business of Labour politics. I had a more glamorous route towards social equality in mind. I would learn languages, live among the working classes of Europe and write about their lives, their writing and their education. I wanted to leave England, to speak in other languages, to transform myself from a well-brought-up English girl into a citizen of Europe, at home in a dozen countries. I had in mind days of toiling over a typewriter until the whorls of my fingers were coated in ink and evenings of attending parties for poor but brilliant intellectuals in worn jackets who smoked themselves half to death and drank wine in enamel mugs. If I had only known of the real writers milling about the place at the time! I would have stalked them in their cafés in every spare moment.

A knock came at the door. I was dreaming in the window, waiting for the kettle to boil, and jumped down quickly to pull on my robe. Our landlady, a woman who I imagined slept in her pressed Parisian clothes as I never saw her in anything more casual than a suit and high-laced boots, solemnly handed me a yellow piece of paper, a telegram. I wanted to refuse it. No, I thought immediately. This is where I belong. I have earned the right. But the piece of paper, as I knew that it would, possessed a higher authority. Geoffrey was the only one to whom I wrote. For him to splash out on a telegram augured badly.

Father v. ill, it read. *Home straight away. Otherwise, regret. G.*

The paper shook in my hand. It was still a month until summer holidays. I could not keep this job, nor spend the summer in Paris as an au pair as I had planned, if I left now. It had been six years, I realised, since I had seen Father. Outrage and shame did battle inside me, and I'm glad to say that shame won, though perhaps not by as much as it might have.

I poured my coffee while in the hallway Marie drifted along to the bathroom barely awake. Eventually she knocked quietly on my door and our shoes echoed on those interminable stairs for almost the last time. I waited out on the street beside her, bag in hand, looking out of the shade at the bright Paris street. Along came our carriage, the horses clopping slowly to a standstill under the low pale leaves. We bumped in our high seat down the avenues towards the school, all about us lucky people who were permitted to stay on these streets: to work, dream, plan, write. Beside me Marie dozed against the worn leather seat as we slowed on the gravel driveway. I shook her arm gently as we came to a stop in front of the steps of the grand old building, reclaimed for the children of workers, its plaster flaking, and the coachman climbed up and opened our door, held up a gloved hand to help us down. Our shoes crunched on the stones as we approached the steps. I felt the point of a little rock lodge in a hole in my shoe. I had to tread lightly on the step. It tapped, giving me away, as I went along the hall with its parquetry floor towards the English room, where the children greeted me with their ''Ello, 'Annah!' for the last time.

~

Geoffrey was there to meet me off the tube. He stooped down to take my case as we met on the platform. He was tall now, implacable. His thoughts were his own, like other adults. Somewhere in this young man's face was the boy I had known. My anger dissipated as I took in his shabby trousers and worn jacket, his unwashed hair, his shoes as disgraceful as my own, his eyes distant, his fingernails bitten. To look at the distraction upon my brother's face was to enter instantly a world of illness and imminent death. My separation from it, my life in Paris and before, at Ruskin, seemed artificial, dreamed.

We walked straight to the hospital at Hampstead. I had never in my life entered such a place. We were robustly healthy children, and if my parents had periods of illness, they kept them quiet. The long corridor smelled of school: disinfectant and a kitchen somewhere producing vats of unappetising stew by the gallon. Our shoes squeaked down the empty hallway as we went along to his ward.

At the end of a row of beds in a dim room lay a tiny man in a long white bed with a little head adrift at the centre of a large white pillow. Occupying the other beds was an array of unfortunate souls coughing and hawking. I looked back at the little man and saw that it was my father. Even his hand, wrinkled and small on the white counterpane, seemed shrunken. My dear father, the grand Russian merchant of my youth, whose desperate boyhood poverty was ever the fuel of his compassion and energy, had been miniaturised. It was as though he had been reduced to some earlier moment, had been brought back to a time when he had nothing and was nobody.

Geoffrey shook his hand. Father lifted his other slowly from the bed and laid it on top of Geoffrey's long pink fingers. 'Now, my Geoffrey. What did you bring me here?' he whispered. This was followed by such a bout of coughing that a nurse hurried to his bed, giving me a stern look, and sat him up by wedging her bottom in beside him, arm around his shoulders. Father shook his head, shooed her away, beckoning me closer. His big wet eyes did not leave my face. 'Is it you, my Hannah? Look. You are a woman now.'

I sat next to him on the bed. He took my hands. His were as small as mine. He has been ancient in my memory but he was younger than I am now. How long has he been like this, I wondered, and no one thought to fetch me? I looked at Geoffrey looking at his father, recalled my desertion, and retracted the thought before it was expressed.

'Now, Hannah. No tears. Not my bravest girl.' He patted my hand, turned to Geoffrey, who was peering now with a slightly appalled expression at the other patients, who were, if sentient, watching our little tableau unfold. 'Do you see this, Geoffrey? My Hannah has come home.'

Geoffrey brought his attention back to us, nodded vaguely. He gave me a quizzical glance, as though to say, what will you do now?

'Papa,' I said. 'I did not know—'

'Hush, Hannah.' His voice was so soft, where it had always boomed, too loud, too foreign. 'You think I would prevent my Hannah and her grand career? The child of mine at Oxford!'

'It was not the university.'

'Hush, hush. You are living the life, my little. Speak to me something in French. I will remember.'

I took a quick look at Geoffrey. So far as I knew he did not understand French. '*Mon cher Papa,*' I whispered. '*Je suis désolée que j'ai vous départis. Vous et Maman.*'

A little smile in his grey face, another cough.

'*N'oubli jamais ta mére, ma petite,*' he said, and it was so strange to hear him speak in this language, though he had several. It was as though we were new people.

'Now,' he said to Geoffrey, 'take my little one home to see her mother. It is time for my nap.'

His eyes were closed before I was on my feet. I touched his sleeve, and Geoffrey stooped to pick up my case, and we walked past the row of beds, the men with their big harried eyes watching us depart.

We walked across the lovely heath, through its solemn corridors, a hundred shades of living green, towards our pond. As we approached it I broke our silence to say, 'Do you remember the strike?' He nodded. 'I was here,' I said. 'By the pond. I heard the miners' choir sing to raise money for the families of the striking men. It was just before I went away to college. I saw you looking out from your window.'

He nodded again.

'Did you see me, Geoffrey?'

'Yes, Hannah. I did.'

'Then why did you not come down to talk to me?'

'You looked as though you were crying. I thought it—private.'

'Oh. It was the choir. Did you hear them singing "Bread of Heaven"? I had never heard anything like it. It was—I can't explain. It was being poor, and I heard Wales, somehow, in the men's voices. And I was standing beneath our house and not able to come in. Did you hear them?'

'Yes. I wrote about them for my paper.'

I laughed. 'The *Hampstead Herald*? Did it take on a political bent?'

'I worked for the real *Herald* by then.'

I looked at him. 'No!' I put a hand to my heart. We were just reaching the foreshore. I stopped before the little gap in the hedge that took us through to our French windows. 'You work for the *Daily Herald*? You are a *writer*?' I realised that I had assumed he was a student without having bothered to ask.

'Why so surprised?'

'For the Labour Party?'

'I do some pieces for Pankhurst's commie rag too, under a pseudonym. Don't tell anyone. I'd lose my job.'

'I am astounded.'

He laughed, and we went in, and Benjamin was tearing down the stairs, all his baby fat gone, as lean and eager still as a puppy, and wearing, quite miraculously, an RAF uniform. What a handsome young man he was. I was, again, astonished by a brother of mine. His black hair *gleamed.*

~

I did not see Mother until the next day, when she returned from the hospital at dawn. I was in my old bed, my room just the same as it always was, except Geoffrey had stolen my desk, and when I woke she was sitting beside me in the chair in the horrible void the desk had left. She did not say a word, but as my eyes lit upon her face, older now, everyone older, her chin crumpled for a moment and I knew that Father had gone, and I wept on her chest until the boys came in, and we all sat together on my bed holding hands until the sun came into my room. I had wasted time so irretrievably, the last of Father's years, and yet neither my mother nor my brothers, not at that moment nor any after, ever uttered a word of reproach.

~

I slipped back into my London life of Labour Party meetings and haunting the bookshop at South Hill, wishing I had a source of income that would allow me to buy everything I laid my hands on. Some evenings I lounged on Geoffrey's bed while he sat at my little black desk over a shiny typewriter with silver keys. He curled himself around it, as though he were drawing it into the workings of his body. His shoulder blades stretched the fabric of his tweed jacket and he smoked, peered out the window or fixed his gaze on me, without I think really seeing me, pecking out words furiously, reading them back to me after a couple of paragraphs. He wrote about the rising unemployed, the Wobblies in America, fascism in Germany and Italy. He had friends in these places, but he also travelled widely. He referred to Pankhurst by her first name: *Emmeline.* He had become something quite incredible while I had been looking in a different direction. I coughed in the smoke from his endless cigarettes and said, 'Yes, bravo. Very stirring!' at intervals. Occasionally I might add a suggestion of my own, which he would accept and include, nodding seriously, and I had to still the little leap in my chest.

Benjamin came home from base some weekends and everything was cheerier when he was about the place. He palmed me the odd shilling—to buy hats, he said, but I bought books and eventually a pair of shoes. I was aware of preparation, of stocking provisions for my next adventure. One Saturday I went with them both to the pub. At the southern corner of the heath was a smoky, dark little tavern filled with working men and a couple of tarted-up women who looked glamorous from a distance but old and heavily set, mannish, up close. We sat with half-pints of ale in front of us and told stories about Father, did his voice—Benjamin was spot on: *Children! There are Christians at the door! Come, come! Convert them!*—and banged the table until eventually we looked up to find the landlord standing over us. 'You oughtn't to have this young lady here. Is she even twenty-one?'

'She's no lady,' Benjamin snorted. 'She's our sister!'

Geoffrey stood, took my elbow.

'You're a rude man,' I said, shaking my gloves at the landlord. 'For your information, I am twenty-three and a woman of the world!' I slipped a little on the stair on the way out. I should not have begun on that second glass of beer.

I was desperate to be away again. I felt I had been snapped back like a piece of rubber from the life that beckoned me. I wrote letters constantly to old friends from Ruskin, to my contacts in the Labour Party who had begun to spread about the country, to anyone I could think of that might know of an opportunity for me to travel and work, to restart my faltered career. It was thrilling to watch Geoffrey at his life of the newspaperman, but searing too, to witness him pounding out his stories at my very own desk.

One morning in August I received a letter from a friend still in Oxford, a lovely Scot, Annabel McCloud. Mother brought it into my room with my cup of tea. I had attended economics lectures with Annabel, we girls sitting to one side, away from the young men, but nevertheless in the theatre, allowed to listen, and to notate, and to learn. Here is her letter, in schoolgirl handwriting, tucked in my journal for the ninth of August, 1930. *Dearest Hannah*, it begins. *You have been much on my mind lately. I have a proposition to put to you . . .*

It seemed that she had won a travelling scholarship from Ruskin which presented the princely sum of fifteen pounds to a woman for the purposes of travel and study 'with a particular focus on the education of working people'. Oh, I thought. Such a thing was made for *me*! Her mother was ill, she went on to explain, and Annabel could not now take it up. The college would be happy to give it to me, as its purposes were so close to my own frequently expressed wishes. The scholarship must be for travel to Berlin, as Annabel had already made arrangements there. They would house me with workers, and I must attend classes at a workers' college for a period when I arrived, and after that I was free to fulfil the terms of the scholarship as I saw fit. Annabel could not know the course she set me on. I am very glad I still have her letter, and indeed that her mother was ill, though I hope of course that she recovered quickly and completely and carried on robustly into old age.

I ran into Geoffrey's room, letter clutched in hand. He was asleep, having worked late on a piece, laid out fully clothed atop the blankets. I shook the letter over his face. 'I am to go to Berlin! I am to attend a workers' college there! Geoffrey, wake up!'

He peered blearily at me. 'Well, write to me then,' he said. 'I'll do a piece on it.'

All there was for me to do now was to learn German, which I set about doing over the next month with some assistance from Geoffrey and a dictionary I found at the library. I confess here to the only theft of my life. When it was time to travel, I did not return that dictionary, packing it in my case with my new shoes, and it fell apart, thumbed to death, before the 1930s were half finished. Later, in 1940, when I returned briefly to Mother's house for the most desperate of reasons, something possessed me to set aside two shillings of my sorry little heap of savings, place them in an envelope and slip it into the returned-books slot.

But I am running ahead. My grand departure. As my train pulled out of Liverpool Street, Benjamin waving me off in his uniform, a plump girl opposite me eyeing me with clear envy, my notebook was already open on my lap. I caught sight of my pulse, visible and strong. I watched the miniature heart beat at my wrist, my secret hope: that the nib of my pen would break open the skin of the world.

~

I rolled into Berlin as the bright morning spread across the fields and forests. I had travelled so far east it seemed that if I continued just a little further I would reach the land of Father and all my grandparents. I peered into the dark pine trees gathered at the edge of the track, unnerved by the black space between them, so unlike the welcoming shade of an English wood.

I changed trains for Wedding, and as I stepped onto the train I saw a trio of girls not yet twenty sitting opposite, leaning back in their seats, surreptitiously eying off a cluster of SA at the other end of the carriage. I took a seat close by and watched them murmur to one another. One offered me a shy smile. I beamed in return, happy to be acknowledged by a Berliner. The girls wore blouses open at the neck and their décolletages were tanned and shining in the late summer heat. They all wore bobs, loose locks artfully veiling their eyes.

I followed their gaze to the five or so young men, who were affecting not to notice their admirers, talking a little too loudly, one giving another a playful punch. There was a ban on political uniforms at the time, but they all wore identical white shirts and grey trousers with highly polished boots and shaven hair, and looked around themselves with that confidence of men in a gang. They stood without holding onto the leather straps above them as the train juddered and sped around bends and halted jerkily at the stations. Their muscular legs, outlined in their fitted trousers, held their shifting ground while all around them women struggled with prams, men made their way uncomplainingly by them with briefcases and children gambolled down the aisle, treating them as a large piece of furniture or a wall around which you must unthinkingly make your way.

After a time one of them nodded at his companions, separated from the pack and approached the girls, walking towards me down the aisle. I stared, invisible, his attention firmly elsewhere. As he drew level with me I smelled his cologne, saw how his eyebrows almost met at the centre of his brow, heard the quick sigh as he screwed up his courage to talk to the girls. He was very close to me. If he were to sit down here, in this spare seat before me, I believed I might with enough time persuade him to change his mind about what he was, about the purpose of his life. That was my view of politics in those days: that if one only had the chance to explain things all sorts of progress would be made. It has hardened somewhat since then.

As he reached the girls the door opened and I saw that it was Wedding station and jumped to my feet, lugging my case past the girls as they gazed up at the boy, waiting to see what he would say, to whom he would say it. I alighted, case bumping my legs. The platform was filled with men who looked at the ground, dressed in old blue shirts, frayed trousers, washed-out caps. There were women, as poorly dressed as the men and old before their time. Young mothers behind prams missing teeth, no colour in their clothes or in their hair. As I passed out of the station there were a few men shuffling about, and as I drew closer a thin, stooped man with a matted beard stopped in front of me and stretched cupped, shaking fingers towards my chin as though he were going to stroke it.

'*Entschuldigung*,' I said, as clearly as I could. '*Ich habe keine*.'

He passed by, very close, his breath rotten, his coat giving off the reek of old tobacco. I thought at once of the reichsmarks pinned to the lining of my case and blushed, walking quickly on.

I found the address without trouble, a tired-looking tenement with strips of fabric strung up inside the windows. I set down my case and looked up at the building. The street was empty, the sun hot on my back. I was wearing my coat, as it would not fit in my case with the books I had accumulated over the summer. It was very still in this narrow street, the air close with drains and refuse. For a moment I considered returning home to my pleasant room and Mother's cooking and the teasing of my brothers. I could find work as the secretary to an MP. An image of Geoffrey at my desk appeared to me: belting away at the keys, shoving the return, a cigarette hanging from the corner of his mouth. I lifted a hand and pressed the doorbell. I heard it ring loudly inside and wondered whom I might be disturbing, whether the family was actually expecting me. I knew they were to be paid a little by Ruskin for my board and wondered whether I might already be a source of resentment, a difficult necessity, in a struggling household.

It was too late to worry about it now, the door was being drawn away from me and a head appeared low, as low as mine, and then there was a woman as small as me with a lovely oval face, hair scraped back, smiling warmly. She was in her thirties, with a wide mouth, bright teeth, green eyes with kind wrinkles at the corners. What a thing it is to be in another country, reliant on strangers, and for one of them to be pleased to see you. And what might have become of such people? Those apartments are not standing now. The entire street was demolished by British bombs during the war.

The woman reached a hand around the door and took my wrist, gave it a little tug. 'Fräulein Jacob?'

'*Meinen Koffer*,' I said. Extricating myself from her gentle grip, I retreated onto the bright step for my suitcase. She waited for me, smiling in the dim light, hands folded in front of her apron. '*Kommen sie bitte*.' She led me down half a flight of stone stairs where it was darker still and the cold of the stone even in summer pressed itself against the soles of my shoes.

She unlocked the door before us, took my case from me, and stood aside to let me enter. I was in a gloomy room about the size of our kitchen at home with one high, small window, barely illuminating a space crammed with a narrow bed, a cot across its foot, a tiny kitchen bench with a stove and cupboard, a bathing stand, a laundry rack hanging from the ceiling and a dining table which, though small, was too big for the area allotted to it. A man and toddler of indeterminate gender sat at the table, plates in front of them, looking at me, or at least the dark shape I made in the doorway. After a few long seconds I gathered myself to say hello, and to move forward into the room to allow my hostess to come in behind me, though this meant pressing myself up against a dining chair and looming over the room's inhabitants.

The toddler, who it seemed was a girl, laughed at me as soon as I spoke. My accent was suspect even to an infant. It must be remembered I had taught myself German quickly, and largely from a dictionary. And then the woman was settling me down at the table and asking me about my journey, and the man was standing to offer me food from the bench, and I did my best to smile at the baby.

Scraps of bread and a jug of milk were pushed towards me. The woman, who had by now introduced herself as Frau Gunther—Anna—offered me a plate and a mug. I drew them towards me uncertainly.

My stomach was threatening to growl. I shifted position in my seat to quell it. I had packed no food for the last part of the train journey, not having the experience to plan ahead, but there was so little here that I wondered what this child would have for lunch if I took this bread now. They watched me, waiting, and so I took a small slice and bit it, nodded, smiling: my first taste of sourdough. It had a chewy, tasty rind.

The man stood from the table. He was more serious than his wife but similarly handsome and, like her, little. He was thin but straight-backed, with a head of thick black hair, greying at the temples. It was cool in this room cut out of the earth but the smell of bodies made me feel hot and I thought that perhaps the child was sitting in a wet nappy.

Herr Gunther smiled shyly as I chewed my bread as slowly as I could manage, and moved to the end of the table, turning his back to me. Frau Gunther fed the child some sort of mush from a wooden spoon scraped around a cooking pot. A movement beyond her caught my horrified attention for a second. The man was removing his shirt. I fixed my eyes upon my food, the baby, the woman, who did not act as though anything was amiss. I looked at my last square of bread, which I had been trying to eat slowly but which had somehow almost disappeared, and put it into my mouth.

The man was washing at the stand, sluicing water under his arms, over his shoulders, through his hair. He shook his head, whinnied quietly at the cold. The woman leaned over the child, intent on packing in the last few spoonfuls. I swallowed down my food and glanced very quickly towards the other end of the table. I had not after all seen the back of a male adult before. The men in shirt sleeves rowing at Oxford, forearms pink and shining in the sun, backs pressed against thin cotton, sunbathers at Brighton in their bathing suits, but never the naked spine, its ripples, the shipwreck of the ribcage, the muscles of the shoulder blades, together in a man's body. All this I absorbed in a brief moment. A crumb caught in my throat and I tried not to cough. My plate clear, I smiled at the woman fearfully, as she was looking at me, waiting perhaps for me to speak, to talk of my plans.

I was desperate to be out of the room, up on the sunny street. The man was taking his shirt from where he had hung it carefully on his chair and was pulling it on over his shoulders with little tugs of the fabric where it had stuck to his damp shoulders. What is the German? I was thinking furiously and then it came out of my mouth without the embellishments that bring courtesy to language. 'I intend to look at Berlin. I am meeting a friend. I will return this afternoon.'

It was true. I did have an appointment. A member of the SPD was to take me around a factory and on another day a hostel to see how the people lived. It was always their aim that I might report to someone who mattered the difficulties the German working people and unemployed faced, the constant intimidation by Nazis, the hardships imposed on the country by foreign debt from the last war. They were desperate or hopeful enough to think someone like me could help and I was happy to believe them.

I unpinned a note from my case while they fussed over the baby and left my belongings tucked under my chair. 'I will pack you some food,' Frau Gunther said.

'No,' I said quickly. 'I am meeting my friend for lunch.'

~

The factory made buttons and was staffed by long tables of women embroidering, painting, sorting under low-hanging lights. The work was gruelling—it was heart-rending to see how closely they held the buttons to their faces, and how long the queue at the door of women looking for work, the most hopelessly countenanced those with little children at their side. I silently thanked Father for providing me with an education and went off to lunch with my associate, fatigued and feeling far from home.

After an afternoon nodding at the back of a class for workers on the subject of Goethe, very little of which I understood, I decided it was time to break into my note at a street café on Unter den Linden. Soon a feast appeared before me: coffee, piles of bread, ham, pickles, cheese and, not slowing to think of all the hungry people I had seen that day, I demolished the lot. I ordered another coffee, while I watched the flux of traffic, the workers gradually replaced by the various gangs you saw in those times. Somehow one knew what group they belonged to in spite of the ban on uniforms. The Nazis went about in the largest packs and all had hair that was shaven either at the back or all over. The communists went in for a lot of shouting and the SPD were relatively respectable and watchful. A table of them sat at the next table along to me, men and women, talking conspiratorially, looking about them.

A tide of people passed my table as the sky grew pale and the sun slipped behind the buildings. Most of them would not see as much food in the next two days as I had just put away in fifteen minutes. As I came to the end of my coffee I was aware that I should be getting home, that my hosts might worry, that it was rude to stay away too long. Oh, but I did not want to be in that room, much as I liked the Gunthers. How would one spend the evening in such a small space? Where on earth were they planning to put me to sleep? Just as I was resigning myself to the fact that however it was all going to be managed I would just have to make the best of it, a man with a blue cotton jacket and a bright red beard sat down at my table. He said in English, 'Welcome to Berlin, Fräulein.'

I hesitated. In France I might have bluffed it out. My accent in Paris was passable. 'But how did you know I was English? You have not heard me speak.'

He tapped his nose. 'I know some things.' He held out a hand across my plate of debris. 'Viktor. Pleased to meet you.' At the same time he waved his other hand in the air for the waiter. 'Two beers, please. The lady looks thirsty.'

I shook his hand. 'I don't really drink beer,' I said.

'You are in Berlin now.'

Well, I thought. Here is an excuse to put off going back to my digs for half an hour, in any case. 'It is my turn to make an assumption about you,' I said. I had to speak loudly as an accordion player had started up at the next café along the pavement. The civilised crowd at the neighbouring table were casting glances in our direction. 'I am imagining that you are a communist. Am I right?'

The glasses of beer had arrived at our table. He lifted his, smiled and drank. He spread a hand, gesturing at the people passing by on the street, of whom there were now many. The pavements were jostling with groups of men and a few women, talking among themselves, looking at the other groups as they went by. 'One in three of these people are communists,' he said with a smile. 'But I will tell you something, Fräulein. They will all go over to the Nazis before long.'

'And what makes you so certain of that?'

'I love my brothers, but they are a rabble. They really have things worked out over there. Have you seen the parades?'

'But surely what you believe comes into this? Either you believe in a fair share for all, to a greater or lesser extent, or you believe in that rot they come out with.' I was drinking a little fast out of nerves. 'Surely you see that they are mad?'

'Oh yes, you and I know that, but I am not so sure about my comrades.' Our neighbours were staring at him openly now. Presumably at least one of them understood English. One of the young women was murmuring to the others as we spoke. 'But do not worry.' He leaned forward. '*I* will not go over to those brutes.'

'Where did you learn to speak English? You're very fluent.'

'In London. I am a traveller.'

I smiled. 'Yes, me too.' And we talked about London for a while, where he had been a German tutor, and our friends lost interest in us. After a little time I found myself paying for the beers, of which he had by now had two, along with my dinner. I would have to be more careful with money. If I threw it about like this I would quickly go through my travel funds and as yet I had no way to make more. The college had told me they might be able to put me in touch with the unions, who might have some translation work available, but for now my German was nowhere near up to scratch, and here I was chatting away in English. 'Listen, Viktor. I am here to learn German. You must let me try at least.' He agreed, and our conversation instantly became rather more basic.

I stood to leave, thinking now I really must get back to the Gunthers before dark fell. The wide avenue was filled with people and voices and a number of clashing accordions. 'I must go to the station,' I said carefully. 'My people are waiting.' I felt that old impatience with being a stranger to a language. I was not myself when I could not say everything I meant. When we had spoken English, there had been an undercurrent to the conversation. There was as much meaning beneath the surface of our words as above it. Now I was reduced to a dull simplicity.

'I will escort you. These streets can be a little lively at night.' And so I found myself bustled along the Unter den Linden, arm linked with a red-bearded communist whom I half feared might transmogrify into a Nazi at any moment. Just then there came the blaring of horns along the street, and a lot of shouting, and the crowds began to push back onto the pavement as a procession of motorbuses filled with SA, brown shirts replaced by white, went by. They were singing loudly while the accordion players stood motionless, fingers resting on the keys, upstaged by the parade.

'Aren't political songs forbidden?' I asked my companion.

'They have changed the words. Listen. No mention of the swastika. It is all blue skies and green fields, as though they are farmers.'

'Where are they going?'

'To a rally.' He stopped on the pavement for a moment amid the crowd, looked me in the eye. 'Hey,' he said, 'what do you say? Let's go along too.'

'To a Nazi Party rally?'

'Yes, naturally. I think you will find it interesting.'

'Would they let us in?'

'Perhaps we are fine young Nazis. What do they know?'

Gracious, I thought, as a queasy thrill surged within me. 'All right. How do we find it?'

'We follow the procession. Look.'

I saw that in fact a good portion of the crowd was following the parade along, as the motorbuses were travelling at walking pace, and so we joined the flow, which was actually much easier than trying to stand still amid all the movement. We followed the procession down a side street to a hall and simply floated along with the crowd passing into the dimness of the building, my friend smiling all the time. He seemed to find the whole thing quite a caper.

He guided me, a hand on my back, into a little knot of merry-looking types to the left of the stage. They nodded as we joined them and I had the impression they were here to make a noise. But, then, was there anyone here who was not? At the very front of the auditorium a row of the white-shirted brown shirts were filing out, forming a barrier between the audience and the stage. Then three men walked onto the platform and the audience began to settle. The large wooden doors slammed shut and the first of the men nodded towards the back of the room and launched immediately into a harangue, most of the words of which were lost on me. Had I better German, I would still have had trouble following. It was incredible—he simply began shouting the moment he opened his mouth, and the audience began shouting along with him. Repeatedly he shouted the words '*Juden raus*,' which of course I knew, and the little gang around me began to brandish fists in the air and to boo and hiss at him and at the other audience members, who were cheering and stamping their feet. It was electrifying, to hear human voices make such sounds. To my amazement I quickly joined in and we were like cats in the night, bristling and hissing at those around us. The row behind us was pushing forward and the row in front could not move at all as they were buttressed by the line of SA in front of the stage, and so we were pressed more and more tightly, and the man on the stage shouted with ever more fervour and we booed so loudly that nothing anyone said could be made out. Viktor was by now jumping in the air, throwing himself forward, his formerly cheerful face contorted and ugly. It was by no means clear which side he was on.

I had to stop making any kind of noise at all after a few moments because I was in danger of being crushed, and was trying to remain upright, steadying myself with a hand on the back in front. Then the members of our little cluster were suddenly shot sideways as the rows in front and behind converged, convulsed from the crowd into an area at the side where one could not see the stage, and so was almost empty, but for two SA, one either side of an open exit into the evening air. One lurched towards me, grabbed my arm and shoved me out of the door onto the metal fire stairs. I turned to protest and was met by the body of the next protestor to be ejected, followed by two more, Viktor left behind in the heaving mass inside the auditorium. The others were trying to push their way back in but the door slammed and we found ourselves on the relatively quiet street, listening to the muffled ruckus beyond the door. They began at once to bang their fists on the door but the fresh air had brought me to my senses and I stepped quickly down the stairs and away up the street in search of the nearest U-Bahn station.

As I walked amid the people on the street I caught my breath. What on earth had just happened? It was a revelation how quickly a room full of people shouting could lead one to become heedless of safety, to shout and catcall with the ferocity of a picket. Now that it was over I felt the excitement drain from my body, leaving me utterly exhausted. Fortunately I came upon a station quickly and trudged down the stairs, feet aching, feeling in my pocket for change for my ticket. I was relieved to discover that my money was still there. It was as though I had lived through a flood, or a fire, and expected everything to be different now, to have to begin over with nothing.

By the time I arrived back at the tenement I was past caring how I was to be accommodated. It was dark and the poor had surged towards me on the platform at Wedding station and so I felt compelled to walk quickly in spite of my sore legs and drained spirit.

Mrs Gunther answered my knock so quickly it was as though she had waited behind the door all day. Once more she took hold of my wrist and pulled me inside. Her hand was cool and soft in spite of the hard work it no doubt undertook on a daily basis. 'Fräulein Jacob, come inside. You must be very tired. Come in, have some warm milk with Trudel.'

I stopped in the corridor, lit by a weak bulb. I mustered my last ounce of energy to find the words I needed, her hand still encircled about my wrist. 'Frau Gunther, where will I sleep? There is no room.'

She smiled shyly. 'It's all right. We have prepared for you. You are welcome here. You will see.'

We stepped once more into the little apartment. I did not understand at first what I was seeing. The room was dimmer even than before, the window black with the night, though its ledge held a row of church candles in empty glass jars. I heard the little girl's giggle. In front of me the table had been upturned, the cavity stuffed with blankets and cushions, and the girl sat in it, tucked in her father's lap, drinking milk. I could just make out their faces in the candlelight, the girl leaning on her father's chest.

'Ernst is about to go out on his shift,' Frau Gunther said quietly behind me. 'We hope that this will be all right for you. It is really very comfortable. But if you are not happy on the floor, you are welcome to my own bed.'

'Oh, no—it's perfect,' I said, as Herr Gunther stood, handing the little girl gently to his wife, kissing her on the forehead. I sat down myself in the warm space they had vacated, while Frau Gunther poured me some milk from the jug on the stove. They talked quietly on the other side of the door, and then her husband was away up the stairs, and she returned with the child and I did my best before I lost consciousness to tell her a little of my day.

Emil

DUISBURG, 1932

It was the hottest day of summer so far, like a day from boyhood, though it was late in the season. Emil stood outside the factory in his shirt sleeves watching the peeling wooden boat judder along to the dock. There was Christian with his old blue cap and round spectacles, smoking his pipe as he brought her in. Emil dropped his own cigarette in the river. The water closed over it, a flat blue sheet of steel dimpling briefly.

Schulman the funeral director fed his horses up in the yard. They snorted quietly. Good horses, he'd noticed as they came in, calm. Another time he'd see about the boy riding one, if the man didn't mind the contact with Emil. Some were nervous of being seen with him since the election.

Christian did not have a winch on his boat. He tied it to the pier and dropped the gangplank at the back. Emil saw the long crates straightaway, amid a pile of smaller boxes containing who knew what, and took an end of one while Christian took the other. He talked away in Flemish and lifted crates and tightened the rope, all the while puffing at the pipe. Emil had known him since his days with Siemens and had never seen him without it. He had smoked in the engine room and during inspections, when they were lined up in uniform for the company officials to look over a new ship. They'd shared a cabin. Every night the man packed a last fill before climbing into his bunk and fell asleep when it was almost done. He timed it beautifully even when they'd been into the schnapps.

They loaded the long boxes one by one onto a flat trolley on the high bank and began to steer it carefully over the grass, past the factory, up to the yard where Schulman waited with the horses. He acknowledged Emil and Christian as they loaded his covered dray but did not move to jump down and help. As Emil shook hands with Christian, the pipe still glued to his lip, Emil glanced up behind him, saw the venetians part in the window set high in the wall, gave a nod.

Emil climbed in behind the boxes, pulled the flap up after him and bolted it, saw an old blanket in a corner and rolled it up to sit on it. He saw through the gap the boat reversing out into the river, engine labouring, and then all he saw was the plough of its wake, the river flattening again as the horses strained against the harness.

He continued to peer over the low wall at the back of the dray as they bumped into town. It was busy now. Men hung around the streets, waiting for a spark, whatever they could turn into something. Schulman ploughed the horses through a crowd as though it was market day, except it was all men, men who should be in work, and they were doing nothing but talking and eyeing one another. As they came to the crossroads that marked the boundary of the Jewish quarter, he saw a cluster of men he knew to be SA. A rabbinical student drew close to them, tall, pale, inward. One of them said something, lurching towards him, as though giving a child a sudden fright. The man stepped quickly into the gutter before hurrying into the quarter. The men were laughing as the dray passed by.

At the back of the funeral parlour they unloaded the crates into the workshop. Schulman left the cart at the entrance to his courtyard, horses tethered, blocking the entrance. He took two hammers from a shelf behind him, handed one to Emil, and they began to prise nails from the crates with the claws. Emil opened the first crate and they stood over it. There was the coffin, pine, plain. He laid his hands on it, opened the lid, held it open with one hand while the other foraged about in the sawdust. Nothing. Schulman began another. They went through three more. 'You think we have been swindled?' Schulman laughed nervously.

'No,' Emil replied. 'These are good people. If there was a problem, word would have got through. Christian would have known.'

Then Schulman, his arms up to the elbows in sawdust, let out a sigh. Emil looked up from his own crate and waited. Schulman brought forth a long cloth bag, tied securely at one end, something long and hard in it, rolled up in a cloth. He reached inside and pulled out a rifle. 'Emil, you are a miracle worker.' Schulman balanced it for a moment across his hand and forearm. It was a Mauser. Emil knew how the butt would sit against his shoulder, the strength of the kick when it fired.

Later, when they'd found everything they had asked for, they stood in the yard while Schulman fed the horses.

'Are you an optimist, Becker?'

Emil thought for a moment. 'Only an optimist would get himself mixed up in a foolish scheme like this one, friend.'

Schulman smiled, patted the horse, dipped his head.

Emil left by the backyard, squeezing out past the horses into the alley, avoiding the main street until he'd weaved his way out of the Jewish quarter. It was close in the lanes. There were the smells of life in the apartments and yards: a ginger cake baking, basement toilets, the comforting tang of animals, pungent in the heat. He heard shouting on the street, cheering, a peal of laughter. A person had just been humiliated in some pointless, brutal way.

After twenty minutes, he was at the door to his apartment building. As he reached for the handle, he saw again the rifle lying across Schulman's hand above the open coffin in the backroom of the funeral parlour. He remembered something a Turk had said as he cleaned his rifle in the trenches, taking out the bullets, checking the mechanism of the safety catch, then cleaning and checking it again: 'Trust in God, but tie your horse first.'

~

'No, Emil, you're mad, I won't let you do it. It's snowing. He'll catch his death.'

'We'll be walking. It'll be warm enough. He can wear the coat my father gave him for his last birthday.'

'It is too small.'

'It will do for the job.'

He could hear the boy in the bedroom, opening cupboard doors, pushing hangers to one side, looking for the coat from the winter before. 'Found it, Papa,' came his voice.

'Okay,' Emil called back. 'Put it on. We're going.'

The boy appeared in the room, squeezed into his old coat, buttons ready to burst, a serious look on his face.

'Wait,' Ava said. 'Take my scarf, if you must go.'

'Mama!'

'If you don't wear it you're not going and that's the truth.'

Hans gave his father a look. Emil shrugged. She came back with a long pink scarf in her hand and made to tie it around the boy's neck. 'No, Mama. It's pink!' He looked again at Emil.

'Give me the scarf, Ava. He can have mine.'

Mother and boy stared at him.

'Who cares? It's pink. What does it matter?' He unravelled his grey scarf, handed it to the boy and took Ava's scarf from her, opened the door, took the box of pamphlets from the dining table. 'We'll see you in an hour or so.'

The boy was behind him on the stairs. 'Don't you mind, really?'

Emil laughed. 'It's the warmest scarf I have ever worn.'

'Tell me, Papa. What's on the pamphlets?'

'They explain what we think about the Nazis, why we need another election.'

'Georg's brother has joined the Hitler Youth. They go marching. And next year they will learn to shoot a rifle.'

'They are thugs, boy. They will learn to shoot their rifles and they will go around pointing them at people who never did anything to them.'

'Won't I be allowed to join the Hitler Youth?'

'My God, no. Never.'

'Well, then, what can I join?'

'You don't need to join anything. I'll teach you how to shoot a rifle.'

'Really? You mean, you know how it's done?'

Emil reached forward to open the door onto the street at the bottom of the stairs. Hans was looking at him, waiting. 'Yes,' he said eventually. 'I can show you, when you're older.'

The boy seemed happy with this as he stepped out into the snow, swirling around his face. He stuck out his tongue immediately to catch the flakes. Emil reached inside the box and handed him a pile of leaflets. 'Hold them to your chest. Tuck your hand inside your coat, like this. Otherwise you won't be able to feel them in five minutes. Now, you're doing this side of the street, I'll do the other. Don't go racing off. I'm an old man, remember. Don't make me look slow. I have my pride.'

Hans nodded, made for the first door. Emil called after him as he began to cross the street, 'Go up into the apartment buildings and put one under each door. If anyone says anything to you, say I'm coming up right behind you.'

They worked their way along the dark street. It was Emil who had to wait for his son, because he had given himself the houses to do and Hans the apartments, with all their stairs. His leg was bad in the cold. He had got himself some shifts for Peters, sorting nuts and bolts and bits of pipe, and he had to stand all day. It was all that was available. With his leg he would have struggled to get up the stairs of more than a few blocks without needing to rest. The boy would be tired but he would eat and sleep well when they were done.

The street was quiet. He could smell his neighbours' meals cooking. Those men in work were home from their shifts and the children had long since been called in from the streets, leaving half-finished snowmen and heaps of snowballs behind them on the pavement.

They had done their street in about twenty minutes. Emil's feet were going numb because he had to wait for Hans, snow seeping into the open seams in his boots. Emil waited on the corner for his son to finish the last building. He came out, panting. 'We don't have to go so fast,' Emil said. 'Do you want me to do the apartments?'

Hans shook his head, leaning on his knees, a few crumpled pamphlets left in his hand. After a moment he caught his breath and spoke. 'There was a scary old woman. I had to run down the stairs.'

'How did she scare you?'

'She shouted at me when I put the pamphlet under the door.'

'What did she say?'

'She called me a dirty communist. Are we dirty communists?'

Emil laughed. 'No. And they wash the same as anyone, when there's water. Come on. Let's do another street. Or are you too tired?'

Hans stood up straight. 'No, Papa.' He smiled, forcing his breath back to normal. 'I'm not tired at all. Let's do some more.'

~

The snow had stopped by the time they were back outside their apartment building. Hans leaned forward on Emil's hip, eyes closed. Emil took his shoulders, set him upright. 'Go up, Hans. Mother will have soup for you. And here, I have something for afterwards.' From his pocket he drew a paper bag of chocolate cat's tongues. Hans peered into the bag in the dim light spilling from the apartments and smiled.

'Aren't you coming up, Papa?'

'I've got something to do. I'll be back when you're asleep.'

'Mama won't let you go if you come up, will she?'

'Perhaps not. In any case, I don't want to drag my bad leg up the stairs only to come down again straight afterwards.'

'I did every one. I didn't skip any at all.'

'I know. I never doubted it.'

Hans smiled sleepily and went in. Emil followed him inside and stood in the vestibule listening to his footsteps tread slowly up the four flights. The rap at the door, a creak, Ava's voice, the floorboards shifting as she stepped to the balustrade to look over. He stayed in the shadows, heard her move back and the door close.

He stepped back out into the cold and made for the river. He could have walked across it, if he had had business on the other side. This afternoon it had been busy with skaters, but he took his usual path alongside it, careful not to stray off the path in the snow and onto the ice. He had seen it split under the weight of a child more than once, and then the scurry to haul them out, not always successfully. Eventually, he reached the factory, quiet at night now. It had not run a night shift for two years. Many around it were closed altogether.

On the far side of the factory, where no light spilled from the town, he felt around him in the snow for a stone with the toe of his boot. He felt only slimy grass beneath the thick snow. In his pocket was a little change. He took a coin and threw it at the high window, heard the chink, went back around to the front of the building. After a moment, the door opened a crack and he stepped into the dark. He could smell the man who had let him in, and the metal of the machines, the grease that kept them working. It was slightly less cold away from the iced-over river.

'Emil,' came Karl's voice softly, and he made out the shape of him as they moved towards the stairs, where a faint light crept from under the office doorway above and at the edges of the blinds.

'Karl.'

They stepped quietly on the metal stairs, hands on the cold brick walls. Emil's leg was very stiff now. He needed to sit for a while.

Karl put his mouth to the door when they reached the top. 'It's Becker,' he said quietly.

The light went off for a moment and the door opened. They stepped inside. He could feel the presence of several men in the office. Emil closed the door behind him and stood in the dark, men breathing all around. 'We meet in the dark now?' he said and the light went on, dazzling after the night and the dark factory. He put his hand over his eyes to make out the features of the dark shapes in the room. There was Schulman, of course, three unionists and SPD men who had done some work for the Reichsbanner, and an addition to the usual gathering, the communist Fischer. He was related to Emil's mother in some distant fashion. Cousin of a cousin? He'd been involved with the workers' and soldiers' councils after the war, Emil remembered.

He could trust them, as far as he knew—as far as they felt they could trust him, probably. Behind the secretary's desk sat Herr Peters. There was no longer a secretary employed by the firm, and so the desk was bare but for the steel flasks of the men, filled with schnapps. 'You're late, Emil,' he said. 'We were worried.' He looked closely at him. 'That's a fine scarf.'

Emil glanced down at the scarf, took the empty seat, brought out his own flask. 'Father brought me some leaflets at the last minute. I wanted to get started on them.'

'You still think pamphlets will do it?' the man next to him said with a bitter laugh.

'There's always hope. We did better in this election. We should work with that, if we can. Keep at it.'

Peters nodded. He seemed to think Emil had information that others did not, seemed to trust him more than these others. But trust was all or nothing, not more or less, thought Emil. There might come a time when any of them could denounce any one of the others and that would be the end of him. It might already be here.

'Karl has been waiting for you in order to give us news, Emil,' Peters said.

They all sat forward, waiting for Karl to speak. He looked at Emil and began. He was unanimated, hard to read, a member of the party and yet here with them. His information to date had been good, and the police still officially supported the SPD government.

Emil wondered where Thomas would be now. Perhaps that was the source of Karl's confusion. 'I think that the pamphlets will not do you much good now, Emil.'

'Why do you say that?'

'It's a feeling. They say that Hitler is impatient with elections.'

'What can he do without being elected? He has already refused to be part of a coalition. His influence is fading, surely?' Peters said.

'People are saying he has the force, with the SA and now the Steel Helmets. He will find some other way.'

'You must join a strike,' the communist interjected.

Peters looked at Emil.

'There are too many unemployed,' Emil said. 'Who would notice?'

'They say he will stop at nothing,' Karl went on. His voice was quiet but they were listening. 'My feeling is—I feel that this is true.'

Peters was still looking at Emil. He leaned across his desk. 'It's possible you're wrong, of course.'

Karl shrugged.

Fischer said, 'We must act now. You must join with us.'

Emil found that they were all looking at him. He wondered whether it was the scarf.

Karl went on: 'They want lists of enemies.' They waited for him to continue. 'They will start with the politicals, then the foreigners.'

'You mean Jews,' Peters said.

Karl reddened for a moment, avoided Schulman's eye. 'Yes, that's what they called them. They mean also gypsies and Slavs. Some of them are very keen. They have started making lists of their neighbours without being asked.'

'Who do they have down as their politicals?' Emil asked.

'Unionists. SPD. Not the communists. They want to bring them over. They have weapons, they say.'

Father's name is on a list in some grubby thug's drawer, Emil thought. 'Where are our weapons now? Are they clean? Has anyone checked them recently?'

Peters glanced at Schulman. 'They are safe. But it is not time to think about that.'

'There's no point in having them if they're not ready to use. If we're not ready. Do all of you know how to use them?' A few of them looked down. 'Come on, I'll show you. It's simple.' Emil was standing. Fischer was also on his feet.

The others looked at Peters. 'Listen, Emil. First we must discuss what we plan to do. The Reichsbanner has helped at the rallies of course, and the elections. But can we really arm ourselves? It's not policy.'

'Then why did I send for them?'

'It was worse then—the July election, it looked bad.'

'They're making lists. They're preparing. Shall we wait to be arrested?'

'How do you plan to stop them?'

'We should all take a rifle, or pistol, whatever you're able to use, and when the time comes, we must hide. If there is a list, everyone here is on it.' He looked at Fischer. 'You may make your own decision about which way things are going. But you're right. It's better if we join together. We can sort out our disagreements later.' He addressed the others. 'If they come for you, you will defend yourself. I will send a sign, and we'll find each other. We'll meet the other units in the other towns. We'll have our own list. We'll work through it until they cannot function, and we shall have a proper election. Fischer's right. We must join together.'

An SPD man who had not spoken to now said, 'You expect us to murder them?'

'You can wait for them to get you first, if you choose,' Emil said. 'Only don't give me away—' he pointed a finger at him, '—or I shall come even sooner.'

Karl stood by the door still, hands in his coat pockets, looking at the floor.

'Karl,' Peters said, 'you know them. You must give us your honest appraisal now. Is it time? Are we going to need these weapons?'

When Karl looked at him Emil felt his stomach shift. He would always be the brother of Thomas, he would always bring Emil's childhood into the room with him. It was dangerous, this feeling. He could not make a proper assessment of the man. Who was to say whose side he was really on? And yet it was not in him to exclude him or go against him. 'I think, somehow, we will win.' He was looking at the floor, the circle formed by their dilapidated shoes in the lantern light. He does not mean us, Emil thought.

'And the police,' Peters went on. 'Your colleagues. Which way will they go?'

'They will defend the law.'

'Whoever makes it?'

'Yes. Perhaps. Yes.'

'Okay,' Emil said. 'I say we meet in the New Year. I'll show you how to use the guns. If anyone does not want one, he should not come.'

'We must continue our usual work with the Reichsbanner,' Peters said. 'We must protect the unions and the SPD, and agitate for a new election. Another may be decisive. Everything may still turn out for the best.' He raised his glass. 'And then we may all forget we ever knew one another. Spend our evenings with our lovely wives again.'

The men gave out a mumble of assent, drank from their flasks. Fischer leaned back into the shadows, his body straight in spite of the chair, his hands in the pockets of his overalls.

'I have to go,' Emil said. 'I'm out too late already.'

'Me too,' Karl said. 'I must go as well.'

They nodded, drank gravely, raised hands as Emil and Karl left the room and descended the dark stairs into the factory. Halfway down, Emil felt a hand on his shoulder and stopped. 'Emil,' Karl whispered, his voice carrying even so in the cavernous dark above the machines. 'I will not be coming again.'

Emil shook Karl's hand in the dark. 'Goodbye, Karl. Good luck. Be careful with yourself.' He could not see Karl's face. He continued down the stairs. There was silence behind him. He let himself out onto the path and made his way along the icy river towards home.

~

In Father's office, the secretary was taking down Christmas decorations at the window, standing on a desk. One of her stocking seams was not straight. It was distracting. Klaus was writing down the times and places of the next few rallies agitating for another election for Emil to pass on to the Reichsbanner. Zelma turned in the window. 'Did Hans enjoy the holiday, Emil?' She stepped down onto the chair, arms full of ornaments. He stood to help her. 'I'm all right,' she said. 'Don't worry.'

'Yes, too much. He doesn't want to go back to school. Too much fun to be had at home.'

'That's the danger. It's your father. He spoils him.'

'I blame him too. He receives only exemplary discipline from me.'

She laughed. 'I can imagine.' She addressed his father now, 'Herr Becker, can you manage? I told Michael I'd be home in time to cook for his parents. They're coming on the train from Düsseldorf.'

'Yes, yes, Zelma.' He waved at her. 'Go. And don't hurry in tomorrow. Stay and have breakfast with them. They will want to spend time with you.'

She smiled at Emil. 'Thank you, Herr Becker. I'll see you in the morning.'

Emil watched his father, listening to Zelma's heels on the stairs. The building was otherwise quiet and outside the traffic was picking up as the day ended. He looked at the strands of pale hair combed back from Klaus's forehead and wondered how much longer his father would work. The union was supposed to pay him a pension from the age of sixty, only a few years away now, but funds were low, with so many unemployed, and his father liked coming here. What would he do at home, in the apartment? Drive Mother to distraction, probably. And how would he keep on top of all the gossip?

'I hear a rumour,' his father said without looking up from the piece of paper onto which he was copying addresses. Oh yes, thought Emil. That's unusual. 'I hear you have brought weapons into town.'

Emil froze. 'Father, who told you? Who knows?'

'That is not the point,' he said, looking up. He leaned forward, his paunch pressing against the desk, lowered his voice. 'Have you lost your mind? What do you think you are going to do with them?'

'Defend ourselves. And, Father, it is the point. If someone has told you, then someone's talking. I need to know who it is.'

'Don't worry. He told only me.'

'Father, forgive me. You are the biggest gossip in town. If someone is telling you, they're not being as discreet as I would hope.'

'Well then.' He threw a hand in the air. 'I will tell you, before you go holding an inquisition. Herr Peters is concerned. He thinks you are pushing things along too quickly. He told me only so that I would talk to you.'

'It was his idea. He brought me in on it.'

'He wanted only to be prepared. But now he says you are talking about going after the bosses.'

'Not yet. Not if we don't have to. For now I'm working to help us win the election. We brought them in when things looked bad, after the July election.'

Klaus was satisfied with this, for a moment. 'This is still a democracy. We still have elections. Their success is waning. These other methods—you will go too far. And there will be no way back.'

'You have seen what they do.'

'But that is not what we do, Emil.' He finished writing, handed Emil the piece of paper. 'Now, Mother wants you all round for dinner this weekend.'

'We can feed ourselves, you know.'

'I know, yes, you have been working. Greta has news.'

'Has she broken down his defences at last?'

'Good God, I hope so. Mother cannot sleep for worrying about her. Says she will die an old maid if she wastes much more time on this ditherer.'

'You want me to go and see him?'

'Have you become a mobster since I last saw you, Emil?' But there was a glint in his eye. 'Come on, walk down with me. There is time for a beer with an old man before you go back to your life of crime, surely.'

~

Klaus was not at his desk. The other union functionaries were rushing through the corridors cradling files, hair awry. Zelma was again at the window, looking down onto the street. She wore a dark green suit. It gave her a smart silhouette at the bright window. 'Zelma,' Emil said. She started.

'Oh, Emil.' She stopped, peered at him. 'I'm not sure you should be wandering about.'

'You spend too much time listening to Father.'

'Still, they're out for blood down there.'

'Where is he? Have you seen him?'

'Not yet. He comes in late sometimes now. I believe he's getting a little old for this game.' Emil cast a look over his father's desk. There were piles of paper everywhere, an ashtray, a cup with a coffee mark at the rim. 'He won't let me touch it. He insists he can't find anything when I do.'

'If he comes in, would you tell him I was looking for him? There's talk of a strike. I need to know what he wants to do.'

'Bit late for that, don't you think? Haven't you heard the news?'

'Of course. I need to know what action he wants to take.'

She lifted her hands, gestured at the desks, the furniture, the photographs of labour leaders on the walls. 'Emil, it's over for us, for now. You should spend your time with your family until things settle.'

'Hans is fine. He's at school, where he belongs.' He backed into the corridor, pushed himself quickly down the stairs.

Since he had entered the building not ten minutes before, the pavement had begun to fill with men and women in their working clothes who had come to a halt, chatting in little groups with a look about them of mild elation, though he knew many of them had come to SPD rallies at one time or another. On the other side of the wide road, beyond the carts and buses and tramlines and bare trees, the pavement was crowded with SA. Some looked drunk, tilting cheerfully into the road, though it was barely eight in the morning.

A man stood just in front of him on the step of an office building entrance, shouting. A group thickened across the path to listen, blocking Emil's way. 'Excuse me,' he said, several times, but no one budged. He could not make himself understood above the man's shouts and the crowd's rowdy gossiping.

'These are great times, friends!' the man was shouting.

Emil looked at him. He was one of them, his face lit with it, the alcohol of fervour. Panic fluttered—he must find Father.

'How do you make that out, Ostler?' Next to Emil a man with hands jammed in the pockets of paint-spattered overalls, cap pulled low, scowled at the speaker.

Ostler beamed at his audience. 'Germany will finally be great again. We shall throw off the boot of the French from our necks. The money will flow, and our wages will restore this town to glory. And then—'

'You are a warmonger.' The painter thrust a finger towards him. 'You dodged the last one, and now look at you.'

'This town dies without the renewal of war. Our factories are quiet, we cannot feed our children when they cry for food. Imagine . . .' He held a hand in the air, brought it down, fingers fluttering. The heads of the crowd followed its progress. 'Money will rain on these streets once more. You will hear the sound of the men's feet marching to work! The factories and the docks will be humming with industry!'

Emil, without knowing it, had stepped forward. 'Your sons will die of cold in a trench and working people will shred their fingers making shells and machine guns. The money will rain only on the capitalists and profiteers.' He cast a hand across the people around him. 'None of us were given a vote.' The crowd had turned to look at him, their expressions unreadable. 'You—' he held a finger above the man's head, as though to strike him with lightning '—you will allow this tyrant to finish Germany once and for all. I'm ashamed to call myself German.'

He felt his fists clenched at his thighs. The people around him were quiet. For a moment he could hear breathing, jeers drifting over from the other side of the street, the tram bell ringing for people to move aside.

'I know you,' this man Ostler said quietly. 'You are the socialist Becker. You run with that rabble, the Reichsbanner.' He smiled to himself. 'It is you who are finished, friend. All you scum who stabbed us in the back at our moment of glory. You would rather strike than make this country great. You *should* be ashamed. I hope they line you up with your friends and put a bullet through your treacherous skull.'

Emil was at the step, had felt the softness of a woman's upper arm beneath her woollen coat as he jostled her aside. His fingers closed on the man's lapels. He pulled him forward, onto the pavement. 'There is not a thing between your ears if you believe Hitler will do this town or any other a scrap of good.'

'Oh, yes.' The man spoke to the crowd over Emil's shoulder. 'Just what I would expect of a thug like you. Solve your disagreements with your fists. Charming.'

He felt others at his back, a firm, gentle hand pressing on his elbow, and released the man, who made a fussy show of dusting his lapels where Emil's fingers had been.

'Some of us have jobs to go to.'

Emil's cheeks were hot. He pushed his way through the crowd. The men at Emil's back were Schilling and Klein. He had last seen them at the meeting in Peters' office. 'That Ostler is a notorious fool,' Schilling said loudly. 'He has grand ideas. They say he wants to run for mayor as a Nazi.'

Emil attempted a laugh. 'Is no one going to work today?' His blood was slowing, the tightness leaving his neck and shoulders. The mass of people was so thick now that it spilled into the road. He would never find Father. The driver of a blocked car leaned on his horn. A rock bounced on its bonnet and into the crowd, raising a disapproving gasp from several bystanders.

'Those who do have jobs will hardly get into trouble,' Klein said.

'I suppose not.'

From the corner of his eye he caught a sudden movement in the crowd. The mass on the other side had spread across the road and a current was pushing against those around him. There were shouts of annoyance as a wedge of SA thrust themselves through the surge, in front of a tram, onto this side of the street. A fist knocked Klein's head sideways. Emil reached forward, wrapping his arm around the neck of a shaved-headed man, not young, knotty and lean in the shoulders and arms. The man stamped on his boot with steel-capped heels. Emil swore, released him, felt sharp knuckles burn his cheekbone. As his head snapped back it seemed there were brown shirts everywhere. Their faces intent, thrilled. A ten-metre stretch of pavement broke out in punching and kicking. Beneath his feet was a Nazi. Emil stepped on his big thigh as he tried to break through into the road to find Schilling and Klein.

He pushed down off the pavement and saw them, already here in the road, leaning forward, arms dangling like baboons, a long rake of a brown shirt in front making quick swipes at them with the ragged-looking blade of a hunting knife. This man had not seen Emil at his side. Emil punched him in the head and he staggered, dropped the knife. Emil kicked it into the forest of legs. The man swung round and managed to land a heavy fist on Emil's ear before stumbling into his chest. Emil grabbed his shoulders, pushed him upright. The man made a prong of two fingers and jabbed Emil in the eyes. Pain roared inside his head. He shouted, reaching forward blindly, grabbing cotton, a sinewy shoulder, squeezed, pushed the man down. When he managed to open his eyes he saw over the man's head the streets emptying. Police ran along the tramline with batons. One stopped at two SA slapping a man's face, stepped around them and hauled the man by his shirt towards a police van.

Emil reached down and grabbed his opponent's ankle, pulled it out from under him, dragged the stunned body towards the pavement, felt the skull bump against the kerb. All around him people fled. Somewhere behind him was the dark gap of an alley. The man's body seemed to grip the ground, kept catching and bouncing as Emil pulled him away from the street.

A child's voice cut through the throbbing and sirens. 'Papa!' Emil froze, skin shrinking, dropped the man's leg. He turned slowly and they were there: his father, hair in damp ropes, face red and moist, the boy in his arms, head held against his chest, dangling legs, too big to be carried, pushing against him, straining towards Emil. Hans loosed himself from his grandfather's grasp. The man at Emil's feet bumped against his shins on all fours as he pulled himself to his feet, staggered off into the street. The boy flung his arms around Emil's thighs and squeezed, as though to restrain him. 'What are you doing? What are you doing? You pulled that man. His head bumped on the ground!'

Emil could not take in enough air. He put a hand on his knee and the other on Hans's head. The dense cool silk of it sent a shock through him. His father too was heaving from the effort of carrying the boy through the melee. He stared at Emil, mouth agape. Eventually he placed a hand on Hans's shoulder and pulled him upright. 'Come, boy. We will go inside now. Come, Emil, up to the office. Zelma will make us coffee.'

By the time they had trudged up the stairs and into the office, the street below was as quiet as the Sabbath. Zelma stood from her desk by the window and rushed to them as they entered the room. 'Hans!' She looked at the men. 'God in heaven, what will your mother say?'

She fussed him onto her chair, spinning him around, which he usually found thrilling. Today he peered sullenly into his lap, before abruptly being sick in it. 'My darling! Oh, I am an imbecile.' She hurried him into the corridor, a hand on his back, peering briefly at Klaus and Emil, silently flanking Klaus's desk. The boy's head was bowed, his trousers ruined.

The room empty, the street silent, Klaus leaned forward, gripped the edge of the desk. Emil felt a trickle of blood begin to move down his cheek. 'What were you going to do to that man?'

'Nothing. I don't know. Nothing.'

'I saw you from down the street. You were dragging him into the alley.'

Yes, he remembered. He had felt the dark gap of the alley open up behind him. It had been part of some plan. There came the sound from the corridor of a child shouting: 'It was a Nazi. A Nazi man! You don't know anything about my papa!' And then something between a roar and a scream: a small creature attempting to scare off something bigger.

Emil covered his face with his hand and closed his eyes. Whatever had changed in the world would not soon be returning to the way it was.

~

When the knock came at the apartment door he was awake instantly, sitting up, but Ava was faster still. She was at the bedroom door, tying her robe. The boy slept and shifted in his bed.

'Don't let them in, and say I am away.'

He sensed her turn in the darkness but she said nothing. The knock had been soft, polite. That was something. Then he heard her in the kitchen. 'Who is it?' she said quietly. He heard a muffled murmur. 'He's not here,' she replied. Then, at the bedroom door, she whispered quickly, 'It's Karl Bremmer.'

'Okay,' Emil said. 'Talk to him in the kitchen. But I am still not here.' The boy laughed in his sleep.

She was opening the kitchen door to the landing and there were footsteps on the boards in the next room. At first, still, he could not hear him when he spoke.

'No,' she said. 'That is not correct.'

Karl raised his voice, loudly enough for Emil to hear. He sounded agitated, but also as though he was speaking for an audience beyond the kitchen door. 'He's on a list. They believe he has guns. Tell him. Tell him there's no doubt about this.'

Ava said something inaudible and Karl murmured in response.

He sat in the dark, trying to keep his breathing quiet. There was silence in the kitchen for several moments. They were not speaking at all, he would hear them. Ava and Karl, standing in the dark kitchen. After a while he heard the door open and close, footsteps receding on the stairs.

~

He stepped aboard the train amid the squeeze of workers just after dusk. These men might happily sniff out his presence among them, turn him over to the nearest SS. Close among them, men of his town, he might see a face he knew at any moment.

He took a seat next to an older woman, nodded from beneath his cap as he took the empty place, newly vacated, warm from another. The sky was a deep blue outside the window. They passed through a black stand of pines just before Krefeld and then he glimpsed a tree-lined avenue of grand old houses and densely turfed lawns under tall lamps. A couple, identical bulky shapes in their winter clothes, held each other's hands as they walked down the middle of the empty road.

It was cold still but would not be for much longer. He thought of the night he had made a hole in the ice on the river with a welding torch and watched the rifles slide into the black water. Even as the water closed over them he felt it was the wrong decision, a bad mistake with no possible remedy, but he had promised Father. He wondered how far the river had taken them before they sank to the bottom, ruined from the moment they had slid beneath the surface.

The train slowed further as it reached the platform. He tugged his cap low, pulled his scarf up over his mouth and joined the huddle at the door. There was old mutton fat and smoke in the fibres of their coats. At the end of the platform, slick with early frost and glittering in the light from the train windows, were two SS with dogs. A man just off the train shot his arm out in the air. 'Heil Hitler!' he barked. The men, who had been smiling over some joke, looked at him and then returned his greeting, expressions resolute. There welled up in Emil's gut an awful urge to laugh. He tucked his chin still further into his collar and passed by them, through the station, onto the road.

His shoulders loosened as he walked the quiet streets amid the straggle of homecomers. He knew this town but was unlikely to see anyone he knew on the street after dark. He walked quickly, it was very cold, though spring was close.

Soon he was standing in the hall of an apartment building at the edge of dark fields. The building had a large garden with chickens, he heard them fussing and chucking in the cold. Ava's sister opened the door to a blast of heat and colour—bright curtains, a reddish tapestry in the hallway, a yellow rug on the wooden floor. And the woman, like her sister, tall, slender, white-blonde, and yet a stranger. In Magdalena's face, Ava's unreadability became a blankness. He removed his cap, held it in front of him. 'Magdalena?'

She smiled slowly. 'Come in, Emil. Hans has nodded off on the sofa, but we were about to wake him for supper.'

She stood aside and he went in, stamping the feeling into his feet on the mat. In the sitting room, next to a bright fire in a large square fireplace, Ava sat on a long low sofa, Hans's face on her leg, features obscured by pale hair. She looked at Emil, waited for him to speak.

He sat next to her. Her body transmitted heat along his arm and leg but he had the feeling that he did not know her, that he had been mistaken in believing he did. Yet here was a part of them both, snoring lightly on her lap, long legs hanging off the edge of the sofa, feet almost toasting in the fire.

'Where are you staying?' she whispered. Magdalena scraped a metal spoon in a pan behind them somewhere in the apartment. He could smell meat roasting, spiced vegetables.

He took the long fingers of her hand from the boy's head, drew a long breath. After a moment she laid down his hand, eased the boy's head off her lap. 'I will help Magda in the kitchen.'

Hans's head lay against his hip. The boy stirred at the sound of his mother's heels on the wooden floor, clipping down the hall. Emil laid a hand on his shoulder as he opened his eyes. The boy pushed himself up, stared at him, wriggled into his lap, held him fast, head against his chest. These people, his wife and now his child, their bodies were filled with heat, but he could not get himself warm. It was as though he had already left them to wander some foggy land where he was still permitted to feel enough to know that he was as cold as the grave. 'You are shivering, Papa.' The boy held him, thin arms binding him in threads of fire. Then Ava's voice came, calling them into the kitchen for supper.

~

Emil woke later than usual in his tiny, borrowed apartment, heat radiating from the window. The May Day celebrations had kept him up late the night before, drunken SA shouting in the street below until well after midnight. Now the sound of a truck braking suddenly, a man giving orders outside brought him back to life. He was across the room in a moment, behind the edge of the window, watching through the gap at the edge of the curtain as uniformed men poured out of their trucks and into the offices of the metalworkers' union in the morning sunshine. Because he had overslept, he did not know whether his father was inside yet this morning. Picking up his keys, watching to make sure there were none left out there, he turned to go down, to run to Father's apartment and warn him. He had not been out in daylight for weeks but today he'd risk it. They'd been harassing the unionists for a while, but this, such numbers occupying the offices, was new. Best for Father to avoid it if he could.

He had watched Klaus's progress along the street from the bridge every day since he'd found this place. Puffing, red-faced, later and later to work. Even later today, Emil hoped. And he watched every evening to see Father come out, his old body labouring as he breathed, tired after the stairs. It was not until after that, until dark, that Emil could leave the apartment, or he would be seen.

Something red, unfurling, caught his eye as he emerged from behind the curtain and back into the dark part of the flat away from the window. A swastika fell from a pole jutting through his father's office window, so large it seemed it would drape down to the street. A figure below, the flag catching his eye, flinched, looked up at it.

Him, his shape, his wheezing walk, his face the colour of a tomato. 'No, Father,' Emil breathed against the glass. But there was, he saw, a policeman immediately behind him and they were at the door already, going inside.

The building was full of those men. From here he could see through the windows that they were going continually up and down the stairs and in and out of the offices, overturning filing cabinets and desk drawers. He saw a flurry of paper at a window explode upwards and float down out of sight.

He tried to see Father at the stair windows but there were too many others passing up and down. Some came out and left in their trucks. More arrived and left again. A dozen times as he stood at the window he told himself: You must go in. If they must have someone, you will take his place. But then he thought of Hans and made himself still. They had no reason to do any more than intimidate Father and the other unionists, as they had before. If Emil entered the building they would arrest him, and more. Still he waited, watching them come in and out and dark swathes of them pass one window and then another. *Father, come out, come out.* But no one came out except storm-troopers and SS. And more always went back in.

After perhaps an hour he heard the quick papery slide of an object on the floor. He moved across the bedroom silently on socked feet. There was someone in the building, perhaps still only two metres away, on the landing. Emil crouched, his knee popping, slipped a thumbnail under the closest corner, then the fleshy part of his thumb and he had it, carried it quietly away from the door, listening for boots on the stairs.

Back behind the curtain he moved as close as he could to the window, saw a policeman walking quickly away from the building, towards the river. Karl had a policeman's walk: with purpose but not hurry, long strides that covered the ground as quickly as was required. He let the folded paper fall open. 'Don't go into the union offices. It's a trap. Take the train for Aachen. There will be police, not many. Take it in any case. Tomorrow there will be no chance.'

He glanced again up the street. Karl's back had disappeared. He wanted to call him back, to ask what was happening in the building. There had been harassment of the unions before. A few broken windows. This business with the swastikas.

All day he stood, weakening with hunger at the window. In the afternoon he saw Zelma come out onto the street followed by the other secretaries. She was crying. *I will go down now. She can tell me.* But after the women came a knot of storm-troopers, fanning out along the street as the women left, holding their rubber coshes at their thighs. And then an SS officer in his dark suit, a pistol in his hand. He swayed a little, stepped too heavily off the stair.

The workers came along the pavement from the other offices, going home at the end of the day. They peered up at the swastika and went around the trucks, a river of people, an unfaltering tide that met again beyond the vehicles, flowing on towards the river. Could he get word to Ava? Could he send something? Something to say that he was still here in the world, that the boy must not be allowed to forget. And Mother. But what could he tell her? He must wait. Wait and see.

As it grew dark there was movement at the door onto the street. They began to spill out beneath the streetlight, the union secretaries, ties loose, collars wrong, a balding man's last strands of hair sticking straight up from his head instead of combed flat. Perhaps ten came out, reluctant to move into the street, but more bunched up behind them and the SA men hit their legs with the coshes until they spread out in the road. Another pressed an object to their foreheads and with each press the man anointed would scream, arms flying up to his head, and stumble after the others into the street. The SA shone torches on their faces and Emil cast about furiously for his father. He was not there. He knew all of these men. He knew the shape of his father, every detail of the way he moved his body. None of these were him. Good news, surely. He was being spared this humiliation. Could Emil have missed him, escorted out a back door, sent home, sacked?

Emil leaned, head against the cold window, saw his father's colleagues march along the street, flanked by SA. He caught the movement of others at their windows above the street and edged back behind the curtain. Then the street was empty. He took a packet of papers from the open case on the bare bed and slid it into his jacket's inner pocket, crossed the room to the door and slipped out to the dark stairwell, moving silently, a finger tracing around the walls for guidance as he went down, step after step to the street.

He emerged from the back door and had to move slowly along the side alley so as not to breathe audibly. There was a guard, he saw from the shadows, on either side of the door to the union offices. There were streetlights, enough to see him by if he came out of the alley. He edged back into the darkness. He could hear the march returning, their boots—they made them march in time—the SA laughing and calling, a man crying out. Another sound that made his hair stand up on his neck. The unionists were singing 'The Internationale' in thin, frightened voices. At the back of the building was a wall. He climbed, knees first, onto the metal lid of a rubbish bin, caps of his boots scraping, up onto the wall and down, knees jarring. Another alley, another wall until he smelled the river. A dog in a frenzy somewhere, leaping against its chain.

At the bank he felt the river surge along, close by him, without seeing it. His breath ripped his chest as he followed the path beyond the houses, away from the factories, towards the station.

Part III

Hannah

BRUSSELS, 1933

Brussels, after Berlin, was quiet and civilised, to an almost unsettling degree. I remember quiet evenings walking home through the narrow cobbled streets from my interpreting work at the Maison du Peuple thinking: Where is everybody? Are they not worried about what is happening on their doorstep?

Life in Brussels had its own excitements, of a professional nature. I had here my first full-time job as an interpreter and translator, from French and German into English, for the trade unions of Belgium and further afield. Many days were spent relaying messages and attending meetings between visiting delegates at headquarters. I spent much of my time at international conferences, concentrating as furiously as I ever have done in my life. I always came away with a headache but also the feeling that I wished Father and my brothers could see me now. I thought too of Mrs Reznik, who had in her way trained me in this strange practice of listening in one language and transmitting another.

One day in May I had spent the morning in a miner's cage, of all places. I had been crammed in with a Belgian union leader for the miners and his British counterpart. It was very frightening, the descent into the dark earth, away from people and light and air, but they chatted away, old hands, and I concentrated, terrified, on helping them to understand one another.

Now, on this extraordinary morning, back at the office, the dirt brushed off my stockings, I was to present the wife of the Belgian Prime Minister, a Walloon woman interested in workers' conditions. She spoke in French for her audience, pausing decorously for me to translate for delegates, and I had the chance to settle back into my skin, to become once again a capable young woman about her business rather than a trembling, tiny creature trapped beneath the earth.

As our visitor began to thank her hosts, and the inhabitants of the room shifted in their seats, I saw a man seated beneath the tall window at the back of the room, not gazing at our visitor, politely enraptured like the rest, nor even appearing to notice her presence. He sat in the shade beneath the huge rectangle of sunlight, legs crossed, body folded forward from the base of his spine, hands in the pockets of his trousers, peering outside towards the rooftops and spires of the city. It seemed as though he did not see what was in front of him. His clothes did not match. He wore the navy blue twill trousers of a worker, not quite long enough, exposing socks and a couple of inches of calf on the crossed leg, and the shirt and grey plaid jacket of a union functionary.

There started up beneath the window the sudden ruckus of a marching band. His hand shot to his eyes. He wiped them and looked again out the window, briefly bewildered. Rupert, the Flemish translator, appeared beside him and pulled down the window. I almost missed my cue as I witnessed my colleague place a hand briefly on the man's shoulder. His head moved minutely towards Rupert but then he looked away again, out above the roofs.

'Hannah,' came a sharp whisper from my superior, a ferociously clever Belgian woman who went on to be a diplomat, and I realised our guest was smiling down at me from the lectern. I smiled back, hot-cheeked, and stood. I thanked her for her speech and ushered her towards the buffet tables in the next room.

As the chairs scraped on the wooden floor and the delegates formed around our guest and me in a moving phalanx, drawn towards the food, my eye caught in the gaps between the bodies glimpses of the man at the window. Why, I wondered, do you not pay the slightest bit of attention to the wife of the Prime Minister? Why do you wear mismatched clothes? And why does Rupert touch your shoulder so gently, as though you are an invalid?

Perhaps he was some sort of unfortunate, a simpleton, a worker involved in an industrial accident that had left him damaged in mind or body. I remained close by our guest. She glanced towards the window once, shook her head kindly, continued to answer questions, nod, smile down at us like a willowy fairy. The set of the man's body though, the readiness in his shoulders—he seemed ready to act: stand, turn, work—persuaded me against any assessment of damage or deficiency.

Later, in the afternoon, when the place had settled into its usual rhythms of meetings, the comings and goings of union delegates, the laughter of secretaries in the kitchenette, I came into the meeting room to look for my notebook, which I had misplaced in the morning's excitement. There he was, sitting on a wooden chair in his old position under the window, his form now rendered in the light of afternoon, his clothes and skin the pale soft texture of a certain kind of Dutch painting, his body as still as though he had in fact been painted.

He was leaning towards the room, elbows on his knees, looking at the space between his feet. Next to him stood Rupert, writing in a little notebook. The seated man spoke intermittently. Rupert nodded gravely, though I knew him to be the playful, mocking type, from whom every word has at least two meanings, even when dealing with only one language at a time. Then he jotted something down, waited silently for the man to speak once more. I resolved to ask him before the end of the day who this was, and what sort of details he was taking down about him. I tidied some papers quietly at the other end of the room, watching. They were not, it seemed, aware of my presence.

Once Rupert paused, looked sideways at the man, pencil suspended above his notebook, leaned in, said something, as though making absolutely certain of a detail. The man shrugged, passed one hand over the other, lifted his head and stared for a moment into the room, directly at me. A shiver went through me, as I thought I had been caught spying, but I did not look away. I was too curious for that. Before, I had only caught him in profile, in the morning shadows, or just now, the curly black thicket of the top of his head as he stared at the floor. Here was his face, held to the light. It was beautiful, and there was something else: a little shock, travelling instantly through my entire body. A recognition, a sense that we were somehow of the same kind.

In those few moments, his face presented to the room, I could not have said whether he saw me as he stared across the room for longer than anyone would call polite. Then it seemed he did, quite definitely, for an instant. His gaze caught upon mine. Something firmed in his focus, and his expression became weary, rather than simply lost. He let his chin dip back towards the floor, and answered whatever it was Rupert had asked him. Then he coughed for a while, and Rupert once more laid a hand upon his shoulder.

As I think of Rupert, cadaverous and intent, though warm-hearted as I knew him to be, and I see him again leaning on the sill, hunched over his work of drawing forth this man's story, my memory narrows in on that notebook in his hands, that held on its pages the pieces of Emil that I did not know, that he barely spoke of to me. Rupert, I fear, must have been killed in the camps, though even now my body rejects such knowledge. In a shoebox, in an attic, is his little black book with its cream pages covered with close handwriting from the days when we were all young. If I found that book, it would tell the words that came from Emil's mouth fresh from exile. It is buried in the obscure archive of some family that never knew him, when by rights it should be mine.

~

I stood at the door, bag hooked over gloved wrist, hair combed, ready to step out into the spring afternoon and find some supper before the union rally at seven o'clock. The others had already gone, but I liked to tidy up before I left. This was the closest thing I had to a home, and I was house-proud: I always gave one last look over my shoulder at the straightened desks cleared of coffee cups and ashtrays, chairs tucked neatly around the long horseshoe of the conference table, covers on the typewriters of the translators and secretaries, grey metal filing drawers closed, heavy white blinds drawn down against the golden sun towards the end of the day. My hand on the doorknob, I heard the low intermittent rumble of male voices from the kitchenette, away off the hall leading to the private offices. As my heels clicked across the wooden floor the voices ceased. Reaching the little kitchen I saw it was them, Rupert and the man who I'd come to think of over the course of the day as the Lost Worker.

Rupert, with his scalded-milk skin and pink-rimmed eyes from long hours of work and drink and debate, smiled his wry smile and began to speak in German, while the man leaned against the sideboard, hands gripping the countertop behind him, elbows pointed back to the wall, chin low. I had assumed the man was Flemish, as it was Rupert who had been assigned to him, but greater than these surprises was the condition of the man's boots, to which his own gaze led me. They were caked with dried mud on the uppers, encrusted laces flaking on the black and white tiles, a pink flash of foot visible at the open seam at the side—no socks. I glanced at my own shoes. I had recently done my best to polish over the dull stretched leather and had recently used a small part of my precious wages to have them re-heeled.

A few things happened within the space of a moment. Rupert reached the end of his introduction, to which I had barely listened, though I did hear for the first time in my life this man's name: Emil Becker. As though startled by the sound of it, the man looked up to see that I was comparing our shoes and appeared to do the same. A smile passed over his lips so briefly it might never have happened. It had vanished by the time he reached a hand towards me. 'You are translator,' he said in English, his voice cracking, as I took his hand. I wondered that he had taken the trouble to find out my position and nationality at the same time as I experienced the warm, dry touch of his fingers, the attention directed upon me from within the fine wreckage of his exhausted face.

'Herr Becker,' I said, my first words to him, 'we must find you some shoes, and then supper.'

~

You are older than I, I decided as I stole glances at him smoking and eating in a dim café. Beneath the table were his feet, close enough to mine to tap against them with each shifting of position, and encased now in a brand-new pair of shoes. The sales clerk had offered to dispose of the ruined boots, holding them away from him, making tweezers of finger and thumb, trying to suppress his horror. Emil had assented.

I wanted to know how old he was. He seemed not quite of this century, just a little too old-fashioned for the gaudiness of the 1920s to have made an impression. There was something in his look, beneath the window, and in the kitchenette in his tragic shoes, that put a damper on my usual boldness. Still, I found questions to put that might be regarded only as friendly, unintrusive. He was careful with his answers, perhaps because he insisted on speaking in English. I discovered that he was from the Ruhr, that before the crash he had been an electrical engineer on the Shannon hydro-electric project and then testing the equipment on ocean liners. I watched his hands as he ate, drank, smoke. Practical square hands with strong fingers, nails that needed trimming. 'And how do you like Brussels?' I asked him, as though he were a sojourner and not a ragged refugee. Around him the walls of the café were lined with framed photographs of actresses and singers all affecting that smouldering look of the nightclub stars of Berlin. He looked about him as though to say: Is that where I find myself?

I had run down a bricked-off lane. What I really wanted to ask him was: What on earth happened to your shoes? Instead, I picked over my omelette, and wondered what could with decorum be extracted from Rupert tomorrow.

From the other side of the table there was a repeated, rapid movement. I cast my eyes at his plate for a moment. His fork was going like the shovel of a navvy at a ditch that was filling with mud even as he dug. He had just about cleared his plate, while my own was still more or less full. He laid down his fork and pulled a packet of cigarettes from his shirt pocket. I pretended not to notice that he had eaten his meal like a starving wretch and continued with my own.

There was money in my pocket. Rupert had pressed a note into my palm as we left the office and there was plenty left from the shoes. Emil had chosen the cheapest, though I had told him that he should choose according to comfort. The clerk had also provided socks. I busied myself with some gloves by the window then. In any case, I had money for our meal, so I paid, and we left our table ready to make our way to the demonstration.

As I weaved my way through the other diners I sensed him behind me, and did my best not to hurry—or as Mother might have put it, charge like a baby elephant—or stumble, or to appear ruffled in any way. He was quite close; once I felt his cool breath on my neck where the skin was bare beneath my clipped bob.

In the streets around the Grand Place workers were gathering. The narrow cobbled lanes were filling with men and women and banners floated overhead, the red silk billowing in the spring breeze. Emil scowled a little into the faces of those around us. It was quite crowded in the lane and as we edged towards the square his elbow brushed frequently against my arm.

The mild chaos, the cheery jostling as the crowd squeezed towards the square, seemed nothing more than a slightly boisterous market night in comparison to my time in Berlin. The barely contained fever of that city lurched in me every time I heard a cheer or the sound of a motor revving. These medieval lanes, filled with the smell of melting chocolate and ladies' perfume, occupied a world in which there was no such person as Adolf Hitler, or the dark-uniformed SS in their sleek motorcars, or burly SA forever hanging about the streets, searching out some commotion.

We shuffled into the back of the square. It was my French-speaking mining delegate at the podium, as I had known it would be. He was speaking about the dreadful conditions in which the men worked, to which I now felt I could enthusiastically attest. I peered sideways to see what Herr Becker made of this. Perhaps the never-ending horror of the miners' working conditions seemed beside the point to this German, whom I was beginning to believe had experienced equivalent horrors. Yet he stood patiently, keeping close. The Flemish speaker took the stage and the crowd crumbled at its edges. Air moved among us again. Now his attention seemed to harden. I saw that he understood this language, whereas the speech in French had merely washed over him. Eventually I felt his hand grip my upper arm lightly, his breath pass across my ear: 'Come, he repeats himself.' I did not know Flemish, and was happy enough to move on, though I feared this might be the end of our evening.

We edged free of the mass at the back of the square. Out here, beyond the press of demonstrators, a breeze passed over my bare arms. There had been no time to go home and fetch a cardigan before dinner. I could not help but smile. It was one of those moments in which you are fully aware of where you are, and where you have come from, and for a second or two take full possession of the delicious improbability of your life.

'Excuse me,' he said, a finger on my forearm. 'I have no currency, Miss Jacob. But I will take you to a café, please. Perhaps we can drink one brandy for an hour.'

'We'll make it last,' I said with a laugh. Even my laugh, I remember, was circumspect, as though I should not frighten him with extreme emotions. 'It would be my pleasure.'

'One day, I will repay you.'

We found a round metal table whose legs creaked against the sloping cobblestones every time one set down a drink too firmly, which he did every few seconds, between sips, for all his talk of one brandy in an hour. He was nearing the end of his third, while I was still on my first, letting its fire warm me as my arms grew cool in the dusk and the cheerful demonstrators disappeared from the steep lane. We talked of the novels of Conrad, whom he had read at sea. He did not once lapse into German, though I offered to speak it several times, and so when he attempted to explain what he liked about Conrad he had to say it simply, in his limited vocabulary. 'He is always the foreigner.'

'Stranger?' I ventured.

'Yes, that's right, stranger also. Foreigner.'

As I came to the end of my brandy, swishing the last viscous drop in my glass, I found the nerve once more to regard his handsome face without looking away. His features had relaxed. I saw that I had distracted him from his troubles and dreaded the moment that he would notice it was dark, that I was shivering, and that inside the café the tables were stacked and the gloomy, ancient proprietor was sweeping the floor with long melancholy strokes of his broom, leaning on it occasionally to peer out the doors to the street, where we were the only remaining customers.

He clanked down his glass on the table and raised a hand in the air. Our friend was with us in an instant with our tally scribbled on a little square of paper. I paid, with a small tip, and for a moment felt as old as my companion, his equal.

'I will walk with you to the house.'

I slipped my arm through his, sensing him freeze for an instant within his jacket. Then his chest loosened and we walked through the maze around the Grand Place to my pension. We reached it in moments, walking in silence. Our bodies connected, I felt something that I had not seen; he had a very slight limp, a little pause before placing down his left foot that was so brief as to be invisible. I thought: I will see him tomorrow, surely, at the union offices, but how can I make certain of this? I could not contemplate the possibility of a night cooped up in my stuffy room, in my narrow bed, worrying myself for hours about it.

I relinquished his elbow and fished in my bag for the key. 'This is my building, Herr Becker. Will I see you tomorrow at the Maison du Peuple?'

I found he had taken my hand with both of his, the one over which my bag was hooked. 'I will make a strange proposal. I will stay with you. For only a few hours.'

My other hand closed on the cold metal of my key at the bottom of my bag. A hundred questions forced their way into my head. I had become a confident traveller, a capable linguist. I was at home in the world, never more so than in a new country. Yet this thing he was asking, I knew nothing, practically, of what it might be. 'Yes,' I said, and smiled at him in the weak light of the street lantern. I could make out only enough to see that he breathed out, his brow smoothing momentarily, and that he took a small step forward, uncurling his fingers towards me for the silver key.

It was not what I imagined, what happened next. I asked him to come up the stairs quietly. My landlady made a habit of appearing in her white gown like a phantom at her door as I passed on the middle landing in the dead of night, gabbling in Flemish at my retreating back. He did not make a sound, stepping lightly as a bride in his new shoes. And I, with every step on the stairs and down the long creaking landing with this German close behind, wondered what on earth I thought I was doing. Every woman passes this way once, I told myself. Now it is my turn, at the grand age of twenty-six.

Finally, I opened the trapdoor above our heads. There was almost no light here, the one lantern on the corridor below casting very little our way. I felt his arm reach past me to hold the trapdoor open and I climbed the last stairs into my room. I went forward carefully in the dark the few steps from one end of the bed to the other to switch on the lantern on my nightstand. He was in the room now, the trapdoor closed behind him. If we were to sit, it was to be on the bed, or my packing case, piled high with dictionaries and papers.

He sat on the bed, the springs creaking quietly. 'Come.' He placed a hand next to him. He was not looking at my face. I felt it was my shoes he was studying again. 'I will not hurt you, I promise.' I sat down a little heavily, the bed shifting, tipping me towards him. He whispered, in German, still not looking at my face. Now that he could use his own words, he changed, became himself, fluent. I concentrated all my experience on catching the precise meaning of every word, spoken so softly, in a voice already made low by cigarettes. 'I mean nothing by being here. Just for tonight, it is very difficult to be alone. I shall lie on the floor while you sleep. I will not touch a hair on your head. You are a kind young woman. Just allow me to lie here on the floor until it is light, and I will leave in the morning, before anyone in the house awakes.'

I stared at him for a moment. He looked up at last. 'I speak too quickly?' he said in English, fearful.

'Emil, I can make room for you. We will lie here together until morning. I feel—' I switched to German. 'It is not I who must be made to feel safe, but you. You are safe here. Please, sleep in the bed. Leave when you have rested.'

I pulled back the counterpane. He studied his hands for a moment, then my face, and nodded. We removed our shoes in silence, placing them softly on the rug in a row: his shiny cheap shoes, hard, smelling of new leather, my old worn things, shaped to my feet, a hole appearing in the sole as I removed my foot. We lay, creaking, stiff, back on the bed, side by side, on our backs, like bodies in the crypt. After a moment, I gathered the courage to take his hand.

'I had a wife, a son,' he said in German. 'And Father. I saw the men come, they went into the building in the morning. There were so many. I stayed in the apartment. I stayed all day. They brought them out, marched them with torches. He was not among them. I searched every face. He is easy to find, Father, he is a fat man these days. He was not among them.'

I was afraid to move, to alter the pressure in my fingers, to breathe. He was silent. I waited for more but there was nothing but his breath and his beating heart. We lay for hours, into the night, towards morning. It seemed then I dreamed and stirred. There were church bells. And then I must have slept again, because I woke briefly to a thing entirely new to me: I was lying on my side, with a man's knees tucked up behind mine, his body repeating the shape of my own, the weight of his hand resting on my waist, the light breath of his sleep rushing softly past my ear.

Emil

HAMPSTEAD, 1936

He did not expect to sleep a full night anymore. He was used to some sort of disturbance in his dreams, in his body, and then an hour or more of watching the edge of the windows for dawn. His days in England were spent in a light-headed confusion, a slippage between worlds. The language seemed like something from another planet. On the building sites and production lines perfectly normal-looking people opened their mouths and emitted the sounds of aliens. He had to shake off this feeling, concentrate. Only then did he find he knew the language, understood what they were saying.

Sleep was easier when Hannah was beside him. At least he was able to drop off again, when he had assured himself that she was there, placed a hand on her leg. Then he closed his eyes and sank down. But he had run out of work in the towns of the north. Now they stayed at her mother's house in Hampstead, and they did not sleep in the same bed here.

Night after night as he drifted in and out of sleep he found himself standing outside a room, watching, as two fat wolves crammed through the door and leaped with sickening agility onto a table. He saw only their backs, hunkering over something on the ground. The same dream for two years, since his mother's letter. Walkers had found Father's body in the woods with those of three of his colleagues. In the months between his disappearance and the day he was found, Nazi officials had written Father letters, insisting he report for work. After he had been dug up, they sent Mother a bill for gloves and cleaning fluid, and arrested the unionists who attended the funeral.

He opened his eyes. The walls of Benjamin's childhood room were growing pale. On the shelf by the window his trophies for football and archery caught the early sun. Birds had started up in the trees on the heath. Emil's first thought was to wish sickness, some permanent affliction, upon the perfect body of his boy so that when the day came for the young men to leave town on an endless train he would remain behind with his mother, baking the bread, teaching the schoolchildren.

He slept a little more, lightly, and then Hannah was speaking in her room. 'Yes, Mother. You know he likes tea. You can go in.' Shy footsteps pressed the boards in the hall. He pulled the blanket over his chest as the door opened slowly towards the bed.

~

He sat on a bench out of sight in the trees at the top of Parliament Hill, away from the paths any of them might use to go up to Golders Green or the tube. Though he was hidden by the deep shade of a group of oaks, from up here on the hill he saw way down across the green parklands to St Paul's and the taller buildings of the city. One could place the whole of the centre of Duisburg on top of this park. He closed his eyes and imagined for a moment that just down there, where a woman with a red hat leaned over a child, was his first school, Hans's school now, and that further down where the ponds began was the river and the docks.

He had never expected London to have such places. Though you could be in the midst of a heaving crowd descending into the tube or surging onto a bus, in a minute or two it was open, green and a little wild, that tamed wildness the English liked to make around their country houses, and from his bench he could see a few of those. You could shoot rabbits, if you were up early, and if the sight of a German with a rifle were not likely to have the bobbies hurtling across the park, holding onto their ridiculous hats. And then he'd be on the front page of the *Ham and High* as a warning against letting in any more Fifth Columnists from the Continent.

He checked his watch, given to him by Benjamin, who had just bought a new one, he claimed. 'Here,' he said, catching sight of Emil's bare wrist over dinner, 'you must have this, until your things arrive.' Before he could refuse it Hannah was buckling it onto his wrist and kissing her brother.

It was just after three. In an hour he could respectably return to the house. The truth was he had barely looked for work today. At the window of a building site cabin by Camden Lock a mottle-nosed foreman batted him away without bothering to speak, like a man tired of shooing the cat off the dining table. That wasn't so bad; there were those thrilled at the chance to unleash something waiting within them, calling him a filthy kraut, spitting, deliberately or otherwise.

Still, it was enough to put him off, tired as he was and with his latest chest ailment giving him trouble. He rarely got work unless it was through Hannah's long-tentacled network of Labour friends from college and her work in the party. He went out looking because a man could not stay in an old woman's house, or let his lover work, without at least trying. Once he'd managed to get himself a week in a pub, a job he'd liked: the instant fug of warmth, beer smells and smoke in the narrow rooms, the grand emotions of the British after a couple of pints, but then the landlord gave the job to a friend in need. Emil, stateless as he was, paid from a paper bag hidden beneath the cash drawer, was sacked on the spot with a shrug and the offer of a free pint.

Today his body had rebelled, brought him up here, sitting until his back had grown stiff against the metal of the bench. Hannah had given him Orwell's *Down and Out in Paris and London*. The author, whose real name was Blair, worked in the local bookshop and had advised Hannah on her reading once or twice, let her borrow books without paying. She seemed almost in love with the man, talked about him at dinner while her mother cast worried glances at Emil. Hannah told him later, when they found a moment to speak alone in the kitchen, 'Mother thinks that you are too handsome for me as it is, and that it is just tempting fate to rattle on about famous authors all through a meal.'

He read the book slowly, smiling at this middle-class Englishman's eccentric love of poverty. Ah, if Hannah were only here to help with the vocabulary. From time to time he took his little notebook from his pocket and wrote down words that looked interesting: *leprous, pawnable, grimy, verminous.*

He wished she were just here, beside him, for any reason, talking herself into a red face about something or other. It had been weeks since they had even slept in the same bed. When they stayed with friends in the north, they slept on a narrow trundle or lumpy sofa. There were never enough blankets for those cold houses in their wet streets. He did not care, so long as her small plump body was there when he fell asleep and when he woke. Now he slept in Benjamin's room, stared out into the dark over the pond until late, wondering whether she was awake or asleep.

Eventually he tired of wrestling with English sentences and snoozed, head lolling against the back of the bench, the afternoon sun creeping across his face. He was woken by a nanny calling some children away from him. He opened his eyes to a pair of crop-headed boys, and it seemed to him he saw the same green-eyed boy in two heads, one ten centimetres higher than the other. The little one let out a rude snigger and they ran off. He checked his watch. He could go home now.

He walked a little faster than he intended, glad to be moving. The sun in the open was warmer than it had been yet this year and you could smell flowers in the park beds and gardens. He headed down into the cool avenues near the ponds. He wondered whether she would come out for a walk before dinner. He always felt at his best walking, but it was hard to get her away from her desk. Every job she was offered she must take, and she did so without complaint, though he saw that she wore her glasses more and more, that she stifled yawns at dinner, that her mother found her asleep, head on her papers.

Before long he reached the furthest edge of the pond from the house. The boats gathered at the corner, water slapping between them. No one was out this afternoon. It was only April, the water very cold, the breeze off the pond chilly. Everyone was over on the sunny plains of the heath, not here in the shade by the water. He gazed across its surface towards her house and saw that she was out at the French windows. There was her little shape, in a pale blouse and skirt, hand over her eyes, peering out over the pond. He stepped out of the shade, raised a hand. Her body leaned forward, froze for a moment, then she began to run around the rim of the water towards him. Her curly bobbed hair lurched and streamed. She never cared how she looked. Something white and stiff, not a handkerchief—paper, flapped in her hand and then she disappeared behind the trees.

He walked quickly to save her running all the way around the pond. What news could there be that would make her charge through the grass like this? He had never seen her break out of her perpetually brisk walk in the three years since he had met her. He could not yet tell whether the news was good or bad, but then, after a minute, her face emerged from the shade of the trees and he saw that though she was breathing hard, she was beaming.

When she reached him she leaned like a schoolboy on her bare knees, which bore bright scratches from the undergrowth. She smiled up at him, trying to catch her breath. 'What is it?' he asked, her smile infectious.

She thrust the letter towards him. He peered at it, making out at first only a few words. It took him several passes over an English sentence to reorder the verbs into a sequence that made sense, and her eagerness distracted him. His eye picked out: *Winchester, hostel, straightaway.* He felt her hand on his wrist. 'I have been offered the position of warden at the Winchester youth hostel. Though of course it is really you who has it. My friends in the party have arranged it. It is work, Emil. Proper, steady work, and a home, and meals, and safety. Can you believe it?' she whispered, glancing back towards the house. 'We will have our own room. Our own house!'

He took her in his arms. Her eyes were wet against the skin where his shirt opened at the throat. He held her as tight as he dared. 'You are a miracle. You make magic. How do you do these things?'

Hannah stepped back, her heel splashing at the edge of the pond, laughing. 'I have very kind and clever friends.' She smiled. 'They have sent a photograph, too. It is the most beautiful place. The old city mill, on a little bridge, right over the river. It *is* like magic. And we are to start as soon as we can pack up and move. The warden is quite ill, and they have bookings for next month and throughout the summer.'

He studied the letter again. This time he saw the words: *twenty beds*. All this time he had waited only for one for themselves, and one, somehow, one to spare. Now this, written on headed paper, with a signature beneath: *twenty*.

She took his hand, pulling him towards the heath. 'Come on,' she said. 'I cannot sit still. Let's walk up the hill and make our plans. Oh, Emil. I cannot believe what has fallen into our lap.'

No, he thought. You did it: with your letters and your telegrams and your unsleeping will.

The sun slanted across the heath, shooting out long shadows from the feet of the afternoon walkers. The smell of cut grass burst from every footfall. It was dangerous to hope, to cast his thoughts too far ahead, stupid and dangerous. He watched her back, her neck as she pulled him out into the open. She looked like something fey, enchanted, in her white clothes against the spring-green grass. His legs felt strong, his chest quiet. He found he could keep up with her easily.

~

Emil let himself into the courtyard through the high gate off the bridge. As he opened the door to the kitchen the voice of Robeson filled the air above the narrow river. She had set up the gramophone, unpacked her records. He hung his satchel on the kitchen door, went through to the common room with its vaulted ceiling and oak beams, and found her sitting at the far end of one of the long trestle tables he'd put together from old church doors last week.

She had not noticed him, reading her book as she was, smiling, at Robeson or the story. Her body looked tired reclining against the wooden chair, legs straight under the table. This afternoon she had washed and polished the window frames and floors in time for their first guests, due in the morning. He had planed the rough beams in the ceiling and now the air was thick with the smells of sawdust and linseed, in spite of the doors and windows being open to the spring afternoon. Always there was the sound of rushing water beneath the building. He felt constantly cool and wet.

In ten days they had unpacked the few things they had accumulated after two and a half years of shifting in and out of her mother's flat to friends' back rooms and hostels. The same friends—unionists, party secretaries—donated linen and books. In the corner of their room, under the eaves, she had asked him to place her black desk, and the typewriter she had bought with her Belgian earnings.

He watched her tuck her hair behind her ear. There was a little colour in her face from working outside, on the windows. The surface of her was calm, but underneath there was movement, always. Her brain was a bright and noisy place. Even in her sleep, she chattered away in her various languages, asking questions usually. 'And how do you manage the children in your little house?' 'Where will he go for work if they shut down the colliery?' 'Is this sweet? I have not seen this kind of bread before.'

She put a finger on the page to mark her place and looked up, thinking, saw him, smiled. After the work of the day, of the past years, she had found a moment of peace, and he was sorry to break it. He crossed the floor, sat next to her, the music in his ears, water beneath their feet, put a hand on hers. Her face when she saw him up close—he must look a fright. 'Where did you go?' she said after a moment, her voice small.

'Past the college and the *Dom*, out into the fields.'

'Cathedral.'

'Hannah, I must ask you . . .'

'What?'

He pushed on. 'I want to bring them here. We have some room now.'

'Who?'

'Hans. Ava.'

She took her hand from under his, with her other placed her book on the table on its open pages, firmly. '*Here?*' He nodded. She had told him more than once that she would love to meet his boy. 'But you can't be serious.' He waited, watching her face. He had learned. You had to let her think and wear herself out. 'She is your ex-wife. Am I supposed to feed her and wash her smalls?'

What was this 'smalls'? But he could imagine. 'She will not permit him to come alone. Hannah—'

'*Hannah* what? Damn you!'

She stamped out through the kitchen. He registered the slammed door through his feet, rather than hearing it. He went to the gramophone, lifted the needle. Robeson was too much at this moment. If I just wait a little longer, he told himself. She is a person with a kind heart and a short temper. She will walk along the river and argue with herself until she is tired. He had only one idea, one plan with poorly worked out details, and he had taken the first step.

~

Emil watched Hans sleep against the red seat of the train, England rolling past him at the window. The boy opened his eyes and Emil said, 'When I first laid eyes on you, your ear was the size of a grape.'

'*Papa*,' the boy sighed.

Ava, thinner, with a few more lines at her eyes, gazed out at the English countryside. He saw again the strangeness of the bright fields, the sparsity of trees. She had never before left Germany. The boy sat next to her, knee to knee with Emil, long and thin now, all the fat of early childhood gone entirely. His calves were almost as long as Emil's—his legs seemed to have shot out from under his body, waiting for the rest of him to catch up. His hair was still as pale as Ava's. The pair of them sat against the red leather seat, foreigners with outlandish white heads, cool blue eyes, smooth tanned skin, among the pale faces and muddy blond and brown hair of the English.

'Do you remember, Papa, when you and Opa took me to the foundry? And you put a big mask on me, and we watched them making pipes?'

Emil cast his mind back across the borders to his town. 'Yes, I do remember that. I'm amazed that you do. You were only small then.'

'He never stops talking of it,' Ava said quietly, still looking out the window.

After a time Hans too seemed to notice he was in a foreign country, and watched the fields and little towns pass by outside the window until he fell asleep once more against his mother. 'He didn't sleep on the boat at all,' she said. 'I should tell you,' she went on quietly, still looking outside, 'I am going to be married.'

'Oh?' He watched her face. 'To whom?'

'You know him. Karl Bremmer.'

He closed his eyes for a moment. His sense of the world, of what he had known about it, shifted a little. The night Karl came to the apartment, his wife had stood silently in the dark kitchen with him. He put it to one side. He saw her hair the day they married, braids like corn rows against her head, a giddy smile he could not imagine returning. She danced with everyone in the room: the children, the old men. 'Do you trust him?'

Finally, she turned to him. 'Everything has changed. You don't know anything.' She lifted a hand towards the window. 'Now that you are English. Yes, I trust him. I trust everyone. Everyone is the same.'

He recalled what Greta had said in her last letter: *There is no fighting. They have all made themselves quiet. Me too. We are all quiet.*

The boy slipped against his mother as the train leaned into a turn. His white hair fell over his eyes. 'I am not English,' Emil said. 'I am not anything.'

~

The sun was high as they approached the bridge. 'How long have you been walking with a stick?' Ava asked as they walked slowly through the town.

'Some days it's worse than others. This town has many hills.'

The boy ran ahead and returned, like a puppy, running twice as far as they walked in order to cover the same distance. When they reached the bridge, he had to call him back from the far side. He pushed open the gate to find Hannah in the courtyard, down in the new herb bed, watering plants, pulling out what it seemed she had decided were weeds, but was actually new parsley.

She turned in her crouch, peering into the sun at them, red in the face, perspiring. This morning she had said, several times: 'She will take me as she finds me.' Having wiped her hands on her apron she offered one up to Ava, who was regarding her silently. Then the boy was bowling into the little courtyard, a streak of white-blond hair, skipping across the flagstones, thrusting down a hand to her where she crouched in the garden beds. She shook his hand and he pulled her to her feet, laughing. He was taller than she was, already.

'Das ist Ava,' Emil introduced her, careful not to touch his former wife. Hannah scowled into the light, and then smiled. *'Und Hans.'*

'Speak English, please.' Ava smiled, turning to him. 'Hans wishes to learn.'

Hannah once more held a hand out. 'Welcome, Ava. Please come and have some tea. It's a long journey. I have made it many times. How was the crossing?'

Ava looked uncertain. Emil translated. 'Very calm,' she told Hannah eventually. And England is pretty. It is a surprise.'

Inside, Hans ran straight up the wooden staircase and Emil followed him while the women chatted in the kitchen. He showed him the dormitory, with the guests' rucksacks leaning against the walls—torches, watches and penknives on the wooden crates he'd painted for bedside tables—and then the little room under the eaves Hans was to share with Ava. The boy immediately jumped on his bed and bounced in the air, coming within millimetres of bumping his head on the sloping ceiling.

Down in the courtyard he heard their German guests, a youth hiking group, filling the courtyard, back from their walk, singing, laughing. German voices in the English countryside. He peered down at them through the open window as the boy jumped. Loud, tanned boys. White shirts, long shorts, bony knees. The quantity of food they put away reminded him of army days, when the cook dished up everything he had and it disappeared in seconds. The last three through the gate bellowed a song he remembered, a Christian folksong about the glory of spring. The boys stamped the mud off their boots on the paving stones. The leaves hanging over them were pale green and the cherry blossoms cast a pink light on their faces.

'Deutsche!' Hans yelped and jumped off the bed, tumbled downstairs. Emil followed him down, heard him in the kitchen.

'*Kuchen!*' he said. Hannah must have tea out for the German boys. '*Kann ich?*'

'*In einem moment*,' he heard Hannah say, her voice stern. Please, don't annoy Ava, he thought. But then, more gently, in English: 'Come, Hans, join the others at the table. The cake is for everyone.'

~

The following morning Hans rode on Emil's shoulders as they walked up through the narrow streets on the edge of town and into the countryside. The sun was hot and Ava had pinned a cloth around the boy's shoulders when he refused to wear a shirt. He had decided that he was a pirate on his bridge, commanding his vessel. Behind them Hannah walked with Ava. In the shady lanes the foliage grew dark and thick and the boy skimmed the leaves with his outstretched hands, shouting orders. Emil heard Hannah ask Ava about Duisburg, and the health of Emil's mother. He did not hear her answers over Hans's nonsense. Emil's chest wheezed with the weight of the boy on his shoulders, but he didn't put him down. He'd have all the time in the world to rest, later.

They emerged into sunlight at the end of a row of beeches, the fields spread out below them, yellow and green amid the farmhouses and the nearby village, and Ava took a camera from her leather satchel. 'Be still, everyone. I will take your photograph.' Hannah stood close to him, squinting in the morning sun, while Ava adjusted the lens. He felt her grip his shirt at his hip with her strong little fingers. Ava, the bright fields behind her white hair, long brown legs, was at ease with the camera, relaxed with the little box between her and what she saw. She took the picture and then held out the camera to Hannah. 'You can take one of us?' Hannah approached dutifully. 'The settings are correct if you stand here,' Ava told her, pointing at the patch of ground under her own feet. Hannah's body radiated ill temper.

Pictures taken, the boy slithered down his back and ran off into a pea field with his arms in the air and his hair and clothes soon just little flashes in the green. Emil went in after him, amid the tall pea plants, listening for his voice. It was dark and cool and smelled fresh. If he could maintain the walls encircling him, he could preserve this happiness.

He heard the women at the edge of the field, beyond the hedgerow. He waited for a moment, Hans calling from further and further into the field. 'He is a beautiful boy, Ava,' Hannah was saying. He listened to the tone of her voice. It sounded friendly. That was good. 'You've done well with him. How does he manage, without a father?'

There was silence. He imagined Ava's coolness, her lids heavy. 'Thank you, Hannah.' So strange to hear her speak English. 'He is bad boy sometimes but he will have new father soon.'

'Oh?'

'Emil has not told you. But that is normal. I will marry again.'

The boy called, muffled, distant. Emil waited still. 'Papa! Papa! You cannot find me!'

Hannah's voice: 'He doesn't mind you coming here?'

'He knows Hans must say goodbye.'

He stood among the bright greenery, unable to move. The boy's call sounded as though it was in another field now.

'Perhaps I should not ask, but Emil can tell you I will always say what I am thinking. Is he a member of the party?'

'I don't know this word, "Party".'

'The Nazis. The Nazi Party.'

Silence. Emil tried to breathe quietly.

'And does Emil know this, Ava?'

'He knows Karl. Everybody is a member now.'

'Well, *you* must know, Emil never was.'

Ava sighed quickly. 'No, of course not. He left.' After a few moments: 'You wear no ring.'

'No, I don't. We are not married.'

'Not—*verlobt*?'

'Oh well, yes, after a fashion. But Emil is stateless. I would become stateless too if we were to marry, and we should have no home at all.'

Be calm, Hannah, he thought. There was a rustling crash and it seemed the boy had made a loop and tumbled through a hedge and out of the field at the women's feet. Ava was hushing him, that cool disapproval at low frequency. Emil returned to himself, thrashed his way out of the field, found a gap in the hedgerow. He was breathing heavily. 'Emil,' Hannah said. 'You must stop running about like a mad thing. You will kill yourself.' There was an edge to her voice. He tried to catch her eye, but she was watching the boy race off again, a scowl making her seem older than she was, still not thirty.

When they had caught up with Hans they sat under a broad-spreading oak in a field which lay fallow and grassy, and Ava conjured and unstoppered two bottles of lemonade she had made with her son that morning. All around them were the smells of the country: grass, cow manure, earth. Clouds of little insects floated around them. The boy climbed the tree, hanging like a monkey upside down above their heads. Ava lay in the shaded grass, eyes closed, forehead smooth, eyelashes resting on her cheeks without a tremor as the boy swung back and forth above her head calling: 'Mama, Mama!' Her hands lay on her flat stomach. Hannah was watching her. Her temper had not lifted. She caught Emil's eye, reddened and turned away, steadying her gaze on the blurred horizon.

~

The boy was sleeping, as he used to, in a stretcher beside his mother's bed. Ava sat next to Emil, closer than necessary, on the bigger bed. The window in the roof was open to the warm night. The river ran beneath them. They spoke in German now that Hannah was not present, though the air was filled with the possibility of her listening on the other side of the wall. 'You told me she was your wife. You insisted I divorce you so that you could marry her.'

'That's what I want, but we cannot marry. She would lose her citizenship.' He looked at the sleeping boy, smiling at something in his dreams. He looked again at Ava. He had never been able to tell what thoughts lay beyond her eyes. 'Ava, you cannot go back. You must stay. There is room here for you. You are safe.'

She laughed briefly, gestured at the wall. 'And she would tolerate this?'

He paused. 'Yes. She would. She knows what will happen when you go back.'

'Does she? Perhaps she could tell me.'

'Germany will go to war, you know this. And if the war lasts long enough, he will go. Before that, they will make him a Nazi. They will poison his mind. He will become—'

'We are German. We live in Germany. If we stay here, we are stateless, like you. You think your girlfriend will support us all forever?'

'Hannah would surprise you. You don't know her. You can help with the hostel. Hannah cannot cook or sew. She does her translations. You would be useful, practical. It's perfect—we have so much room.'

If he knew what to say, he would say it, though he could only imagine the difficulty it would bring. If he could just keep Hans here, everything else could be arranged.

She spoke loudly, not quite shouting. 'If you are not married, then you can come back. You could prevent me from marrying Karl. It is right, it is decent, for the parents of a child to remain together.' She dropped her voice, glancing at the boy. 'We could be a family, live in the country, if this is what you like, the quiet life.'

He looked down. Her hand was on his thigh. He stared at it for a moment. 'You're mad. How can you say this?'

'She is a clever little woman. They are like that. You like her brains. But you will tire of that. I think perhaps you already do.'

'*Who* is like that? I will not believe you mean such things. I would marry her in a heartbeat. If I return to Germany, they'll shoot me on sight. Have you forgotten?'

'That was a mistake, what happened to your father. Karl knows people. He said they were no good, those men. They were drunk. It was a tragedy. They have been disciplined. Life is much more orderly now. Those early days, it's true they were chaotic.'

He removed her hand from his leg. 'Ava, please. Please. If you return, there's nothing I can do for him. And Karl, he has decency I know, but he will do what he needs to do.'

Her eyes dulled. She looked away. 'I think it's time to sleep. Perhaps you shouldn't be in here, so late at night.' She gestured towards the wall with her chin. There were lines at the edge of her mouth he had not seen before. He brought his hands to his face, rubbed his forehead, his cheeks. He could not look at the boy, sleeping in the lamplight. He left without another word, descended the stairs, and the second set, down to the millrace, sat beside the dark rushing water, letting the sound flood every corner of his mind.

~

A deep bounce at the foot of the bed woke him. He could not open his eyes straightaway. The image of the wolves on the table, ready to descend on something below—it took a moment to shake off. In the bright room the boy was jumping, grinning, watching their faces for the moment they would at last acknowledge him. He laughed as Emil stirred. The sun cast small squares of light on the bouncing boy, the white bed, Hannah, sighing. He smiled, closed his eyes again on the twitching pillow, the mattress reverberating with the weight of the boy flinging himself towards the low, sloping ceiling. 'Good Lord,' Hannah murmured, eyes still closed. 'It's like living with a chimpanzee.'

Emil reached up and grabbed the boy, bringing him down mid-jump. The boy giggled and snorted with the effort of trying to contain his laughter. Hot limbs flailed. Hannah edged out of bed. 'I'll make tea,' she said, tying her dressing gown over her nightdress, patched at the elbows. She was off, heavily, down the stairs with the boy careering after her. Emil was left in the quiet on the sunlit pillows. His heart beat quickly, as though he were the one who had been jumping up and down on the bed.

Down in the common room, he saw that two of the German boys had risen early and filled the enormous china pot with tea. The day before, they had asked Hannah to show them how to do it, having never drunk tea before. 'Really,' she said, 'what could there be to learn? You put in the tea, and then you put in the water.' She went through the ritual with them. The warming of the pot, the proportion of tea to water, the length of time needed for it to brew. You would have thought she had been packing an opium pipe for the attention they paid, but he saw that their interest charmed her, and now they had repaid her attention by making the tea for her before she came down.

As he reached the bottom stair the boys were pulling out chairs, whispering to Ava, '*Setzen Sie sich bitte*,' gesturing for the women and the boy to sit down with exaggerated gallantry, gleeful. Emil had insisted no one speak German at meals and the boys spoke almost no English, so there was this charade of no one being able to communicate in speech. He nodded on his way through to the kitchen. The German group at this hour, in their pyjamas, smelled of milk and biscuits and laundered sheets. He heard from the galley the boys discussing the walk they planned to take this morning and Ava and Hans murmuring to each other in their secret way.

Hannah followed him into the kitchen and began to bring out the cheese and ham and cold eggs from the day before. She cut up bread, two entire loaves of it. He watched her piling up food onto boards and platters, her hands rough with food, handling bricks of cheese as though she were going to build a wall with them.

'They will not stay,' he said.

She paused, ready to take the first platter. 'Did you really think they would?'

'I think if I can get them here, maybe . . .'

'Is there nothing we can do?' she said. 'It is unbearable.' She left the platter, laid buttery fingers on his forearm. 'He is a wonderful boy.'

'I asked her. She says no.'

She studied his face for a moment. 'Whatever you manage to arrange with her, you have my support. I like him so much. I can get used to anything else, I imagine.'

'Yes. He is a good boy.'

~

When everyone had eaten, Emil stood at the door to the kitchen observing in action the precise drill he had taught the boys. On the first evening they were assigned roles, and performed them twice daily with joyful solemnity. He watched as two from each long table cleared the plates, moving down either side of the table and staggering to the kitchen with piles as long as their skinny arms. A scraper at the bin. A washer. A wiper. Two to put away. Two to sweep the floor. Hans played the clown, pretending he was about to drop great piles of plates, but the youths would not be put off course, though they laughed as they swept his feet, put foam from the sink in his hair. At some point in the proceedings Hans tired of the games and wandered into the courtyard. He was often drawn out there by the arrival of the milkman with his dray and immense Shire horse, blinkered and docile in spite of its mass. Or a butterfly, or the unpredictable tide of his blood, carrying him off on some secret errand.

When the floor was clean, the tables and kitchen sideboards spotless, the boys began to assemble in a row along the wall, trying not to smile as they stood to attention. Lined up like this the differences in their size and physical maturity were stark, though they were all thirteen or fourteen. The tallest was as tall as Emil and much wider around the girth. Next to him, the smallest was only a little taller than Hans and just as thin. There was a little dark boy at one end of the row who held himself apart. How did you slip in with these? Emil wondered as he waited for the boys to still themselves.

'Hans!' he called. 'Attention!' He took his position at the centre of the floor beside the rope that hung from the great beam bracing the building.

The boy burst through the kitchen doorway, realising from the configuration of the room that his moment had arrived. 'Me first!' he cried, flinging himself at his father. Emil managed to peel the boy off long enough to pull up a trapdoor at his feet and Hans was immediately yanking off his shirt in such a hurry that he left his cuffs buttoned and his hands became stuck in the sleeves. Undeterred he pulled his shorts down with his shirt still hanging inside out from his wrists. The boys in their row were holding in laughter. Emil bent forward to help him with the last buttons and handed him the rope silently.

Hans positioned himself at the edge of the square hole in the floor and looked up at Emil, his face open, full of trust. Emil wanted to reach for him, gather him in, and then they would run together, across the fields, until they found some warm, dark barn that smelled of hay and animals. He nodded and the boy jumped, disappearing through the floor. In the same moment came the splash, the whoop, the cheering of the older boys. Through the little square window, black water surged over the dappled marble of the boy's body, and he gulped and choked and laughed for perhaps a minute before Emil signalled the first two boys forward to haul him up, dripping, laughing, onto the floor of the common room. Hannah had fetched a pile of towels from the line in the courtyard and Ava took one for Hans, came forward to wrap up the shivering boy, kissing his wet forehead as he beamed at her.

The rest took it in turns, peeling down to their underwear, leaving a little pile of clothes in their place in the line. Hans stayed to watch them all, towel around his shoulders. Some were nervous, but all were more nervous still of being shown to lack the courage to jump. At the end, when the boys had gone off to dry themselves and dress for their hike, and Ava too had slipped away, Emil began to unbutton his shirt. With the others gone he stripped naked.

'You look like you're wearing a white bathing suit!' Hans said. Hannah laughed. He looked down. His body was white to his elbows and his knees where it had been covered by clothes on his long walks through the fields or along the towpath. He laughed and stepped out over nothing, hands grazed by the rough rope as his weight threw him downwards. The plunge into icy water, as though his blood was transformed into a cold gas. He might be a boy himself. The lake on

Sundays, the river that summer when he was very young. He had simply wanted to swim and so he did. He still remembered Thomas's face. Later, crossing the Dutch canals, his clothes piled on a tray stolen from the windowsill of a farm kitchen and pushed ahead of him across the water. The water still smelling of the ice of winter, not long thawed, flowing around his body like a tide of chilled fear.

The cold black water enclosed his face. He let his body run horizontal with the stream. When he opened his eyes, lifted his head, in the square of light above was the dark shape of the boy's head, glinting in the room. He was looking down at him, his chin resting on crossed wrists on the floor. He saw too that Hannah's legs hung into the dark space beneath the building. He could make out the fleshy balls of her bare feet, the faint wet sheen of her calves flashing as she swung her legs in the spray.

He could stay here, flowing in the river, seeing them above whenever he opened his eyes. But when he opened them again the boy had gone. For Hans, to be awake was to be moving. Emil let the water run over his head one last time and began to pull himself up into the sunlit room, the rope scratching between his thighs, boards warm beneath his feet, Hannah bringing a thin dry towel. There were strands of red in her curly dark hair. He pulled her towards him.

'You're getting me wet.'

'So you will get wet.' But he released her, began to pull on his clothes from their heap on the floor. She fastened his shirt buttons, having to stretch to reach his collar.

'What will you do? What can I do? Shall *I* talk to her?'

'Oh no.' God, no, Hannah. You poke like a child at a clam. It will snap shut on you. 'No, I walk and think. It is impossible to talk to Ava.'

~

The clouds had settled low over the fields by the time he was free of town. The air felt damp but the striking of his boots on the bumpy road made his body feel better, not so restless as in the hostel. He liked these English days where the air wet your skin slowly over the course of a long walk. It was a waste of his hours, to spend them without Hans, but in any case Ava had heard the boy cough after his dip, and would not let him out on this damp day.

On his walks his brain had always solved his puzzles for him, told him which way to go. Whatever decision had revealed itself to him by the time he returned to the river, the little bridge, would be the one he followed, no matter the difficulties it scattered in its path. Without a plan of one kind or another, you were a strand of a dandelion, drifting across the fields, fetching up wherever the breeze set you down.

At the far edge of the field beneath the road he caught a streak of white, the German boys in a line at the edge of the pasture, white shirts catching the weak light against the dark green hedge. What must the English make of them in their matching shirts and neckerchiefs? Strange boy scouts perhaps. He remembered being one of such a group, before the war. That feeling of the world opening up to the touch. Their bodies were filled with the near uncontainable urge towards whatever they would do, whatever they would be. They would feel like this, with this degree of purity, until they reached some gore-strewn front. Then never again except as flashes, brief, thrilling urges borne out of the past and quickly lost. If he were king, he'd have them all stay.

They went through a gap in the hedge he could not see from here. Disappearing one by one, hidden on the other side by an orchard, wandering into the circle of a witch's spell. A cloud of those leggy flying insects the English called daddy long-legs flew up in his face from the grassy verge beneath his feet. When they cleared he saw the shining rail of the train tracks catch a shaft of sun. Next week he would take Ava and Hans on the train to London and then to Harwich for their ship. It did not seem possible. Some event must intervene. The boy's room already smelled of the soap with which Ava had always washed him. It was his room now.

The hiking group reappeared at the top of the field, near the rail lines. He had told them to keep away from the tracks. There were a few spots where you could get stuck at the bottom of a steep cutting and had to go through a blind tunnel to get out. He had found that out the hard way, jogging, chest burning, through a dank blackness towards the arch of light, hoping that was not a train he heard above his ragged breath.

Having reached the top of a rise he sat on the gnarled roots of a tree and took his water flask from his satchel. He traced the line of the boys, growing smaller along the cutting, the head of the group stopping at a bridge where one rail line passed over another. Emil delved in his satchel for his birdwatching binoculars, lifted them to his eyes. It took a moment to find them, blurred white shapes in the fields. They were gathering in a blob by the bridge. He focused the lenses until they became individual shapes. A couple leaned over a map, rested on another's back. One handed the other something and he struck it against the map: a pencil, a mark. He stood, keeping his binoculars on them, packed his flask, began to walk quickly down the road, which would meet the bridge half a mile down.

When he reached the bridge, several minutes later, out of breath, they had gone. He leaned on an oak, resting in its shadow. He took out his binoculars again and scanned the railway line further on. He found them, gathering again, but they had left the train tracks. Now they had climbed the embankment to the A road that led in one direction to London and in the other to the coast, to Southampton. He refocused the lenses. Again they had grouped on a bridge, this time across the Itchen. He cursed. His soldier's mind was awake. He knew what they were looking for: the bridges, the places where rails and roads crossed. The most efficient positions for explosives, the places you could approach unseen, where interruptions would cost the most.

He turned, retracing his steps towards Winchester. He was in no hurry now. He would go to the police and what would happen would happen. It was not about these boys that he thought. There was nothing to be done for them, about them. His mind was a white iron sheet, cooling into shape. The plan he needed was revealing itself in the only form possible.

~

The women were not speaking at dinner. In fact they were sitting at different tables, and it would be possible to miss their antagonism amid the noise of the Germans eating except that the mood had spread. The boy sat at the head of a long table staring into his stew, taking a resentful mouthful every now and then as though his mother were standing at his shoulder, threatening the loss of some privilege if he did not eat the food he had been given. She was at the other table, making a point of speaking in German to the three or four boys around her. She glanced across at Emil every now and then, delivering a blank-faced challenge. Hannah sat beside him, fury evident in each scrape of her spoon against china.

Before dinner, in the kitchen, she had told him: 'She as good as called me a Jew.'

'What did she say, truly?' He took the wooden spoon from the pot and licked it. Dinner was ready.

'She said I was a *traveller.* That I did not understand her because I had no homeland.' She slammed down a pile of plates on the sideboard. 'I was born in this country. You should have heard the way she said it! Oh, she is a Nazi. Why did you ever marry her?'

'Because of course she was not a Nazi. She was a nice girl who liked to dance. She is not a Nazi now. You have been to Germany. You have heard the way they talk. It's a disease.'

'Oh, I know! I know. Why did I even try to speak to her? I have made it all worse.'

'It makes no difference at all. If you are an angel, she will not listen. This is what I tell you.'

Now Hannah busied herself by studying the boys who were passing down bowls for dessert, laughing and thrusting their spoons into their food. Emil had just finished making it, rhubarb crumble with custard—a recipe learned from Hannah's mother—and the common room was filled with the smell of stewing fruit and cinnamon. He finished in moments, like the boys, and watched their faces. They were grimacing at each other, thinking the adults did not notice. For once the boy did not try to get himself included in their games.

When almost everyone had eaten their dessert but Hannah, who had not touched it, the boys pushed their bowls away, made a show of clutching their stomachs. Then a tall boy, Albert, with high cheekbones but soft, dreamy eyes, stood up, striking his knife on his tin mug. Emil saw that he looked at Hannah. Perhaps they meant to thank their hosts, on their last night. He hoped they would make it brief. It was possible the police would come. They had made agreeable noises when he told them about the maps, but he caught their smirks. He was not expecting much.

Albert continued to regard Hannah, and she summoned up a smile. From the demeanour of the other boys, smiling, waiting, it was clear he was about to sing. Emil had noticed this one enjoyed his own voice. He sang loudly on their hikes, often as they came into the courtyard, so he had an audience beyond his friends. The others stood, ready to join him, and Hannah held the boy's gaze as they began. Their voices together made the hair on the back of his neck rise. The room was filled, every corner, with this unearthly clarity and volume. Then the words became clear, the song known to him. '*Yes, when the Jewish blood splashes from the knives, things will go twice as well.*' Emil saw the gooseflesh on Hannah's arms. She seemed frozen, as he was, for a moment. Then he was standing, his scraping chair cutting across their voices. He addressed himself to the boy, Albert, in English. 'You will not sing those songs here. Clear the table, please.'

The voices petered out until there was only the sound of the water beneath the floor. The boy was standing stiff and straight. It took a moment for his mouth to close. He had turned to Emil but could not hold his gaze for more than a moment. His chin trembled minutely. The others began to pass their bowls to him in silence.

'No,' said Emil. 'He will get them himself.' Albert walked along the table, stacking them. Hans stood to help him. 'Sit.' Emil pointed at his chair and Hans sat down, staring at him. It took several minutes for Albert to clear the long tables. The boys shifted in their seats and kicked their chair legs. The hall was filled with china clinking, Albert's footsteps creaking, no voices. Ava was staring openly at Hannah, her expression unreadable. Hannah herself kept her eyes fixed on the boy as he walked the length of the room to the kitchen and back, over and over again.

Eventually, Hans, unable to sit still any longer, ran upstairs. The other boys took this as a sign to leave the table, and traipsed silently up after him, delivering little pinches and shoves on the narrow stairwell. Ava followed them with a nod goodnight. Hannah did not wait for Emil to speak, but went out into the evening, closing the door very carefully behind her, as though she would not give them the satisfaction of slamming it.

~

With this many sleeping in the house, could he really be the only one awake? Hannah had come into their room late, where he sat trying to read, and changed into her nightgown without speaking or looking at him. He put down his book but she turned out the lamp and in the light from the moon he saw her turn away. He listened to her breathing. She fell asleep quickly. He had never known her angered into silence and he sat for a while at the edge of the bed, the bright moon at the window, watching her shape under the sheet. This light was like the light at sea some nights. It felt, sitting here, accompanying her sleeping shape, that all his anchors to the world were drifting quietly over sand. He lay down on top of the counterpane, clothed, waiting for the sounds in the house to settle.

His socks brushed the boards as he crossed the floor, took the three steps to the stairs. One of the boys snored, a bed creaked. As he descended, their sounds were replaced by running water. You could never quite believe as you stepped onto the floor of the common room that it would be dry. He made his way between the tables. No one would hear the creak of his steps above the water, but neither would he hear anyone approach.

In the kitchen, in the dark cupboard, ziggurats of coins were piled behind an empty box of soap flakes. They were not sorted into pounds, shillings and pence, but according to which account Hannah meant them for. This was the only money in the house, except for a little he was allowed for cigarettes and beer that he had already put in his satchel. There would be none to spare until Hannah was paid for her last translation job, and the unions were slow these days. He took a few coins from each heap, thinking, Hannah, I am sorry. He unhooked his satchel from the kitchen door and went down towards the millrace.

Under the house, moving slowly so that the money in his pockets did not chink, he felt very cold. The water hit the mossy walls and sprayed his legs on the stairs. He opened the laundry door and reached towards the bench to his right for the torch, assaulted by the smell of a room that was never completely dry. He shone his light over the lines of white shirts and grey shorts to a row across the corner of the same clothes, slightly miniaturised. He had put them through the mangle this morning but when he took the fabric between his fingers now it was damp. They always needed an hour in the courtyard in the sun but there was no way to manage it that he could see. He folded the clothes carefully, placed them in the satchel, left the flap open to keep them from mildewing, and put the satchel where it would not be seen immediately, on the hook on the back of the door.

Back in bed she shifted, her leg grazing his. 'You are wet and cold,' she murmured.

He said nothing. Perhaps she was not truly awake.

'Those boys,' she said. 'Do you know what makes me so cross? Their dreadful manners. I have made their sandwiches and washed their sheets.'

'I think it was not meant at you. They believe everyone loves to hear such songs. Their parents would applaud them.'

'I have never felt like this in Germany. I know what to expect. And my friends are wonderful. So brave. Now I'm surrounded.'

'Not Hans. Not me.'

'Oh no.' She found his hand, lying on the covers. 'Of course not. That is not what I meant at all.'

'I could kill them all in their beds.'

Her hand was still. 'I cannot see your face. You are not serious.'

'No, Hannah.'

'Your humour is certainly dry.'

He squeezed her hand. 'They will all die soon enough.'

'Oh, you must stop. It is not even remotely funny.'

'I know.' He closed his eyes. He imagined them returning to their homes, their mothers taking them in their arms at the doors of their houses and apartments. Their fathers would come in from work and shake their hands. Not all fathers needed to embrace you, force the air out of your chest. They would return to gentle families. Some favoured soul would catch Hitler right in the eye with a lovely silver bullet. He would like to see that bullet, flat at one end, through the glass of a museum case one day. Then they'd hang the others in a row outside the Reichstag, and the boys sleeping next door would be free to go quietly through life, with women, with their own boys, working, drinking, walking in the fields. Long, insignificant lives in which they harmed no one.

~

When he woke she was already at her desk in the corner where the roof sloped low. He opened his eyes, knowing instantly what he had to do today.

'Tell me,' she said, letting her thick dictionary fall on the desk in exasperation. 'What is the word for the person who makes the moulds into which the hot metal is poured? I don't even know the English. I am getting nowhere with this.'

'What are you doing?'

'I have the union conference in three weeks. Metalworkers and miners. Miners I can manage, but the vocabulary is impossible when you barely know the English in the first place. You must go through all this with me when you have the time. If I know what people do I know what the unions are likely to discuss.'

'Former.'

'Former?'

'The word for moulder. The one who makes the mould.' Father was a moulder, that was his trade.

'Oh, goodness. So simple. Thank you.'

She had not looked up once. Her concentration made her beautiful, the more so because he doubted another would see it, that a seriousness of purpose could make a person lovely. He heard the boys calling to each other in the common room below, clattering the plates, shovelling coal into the stove in the kitchen. 'The boys were marking maps. I saw them yesterday.'

She did not answer.

'They were marking the places where you put the bombs. The best places, the most effective.'

She dropped her pencil on the page in front of her. Now she turned in her chair. 'No!'

'Yes, I followed them. I saw it.'

'You must go to the police,' she whispered.

'I did. But they are—*unschuldig.* What is it?'

'Innocent. Or stupid, rather. Well, we must get the maps off them before they leave.'

'You think so? How?'

'Take them out of their bags. They're going today. We must get on with it.' He regarded her for a moment. 'Well of course we must,' she insisted. 'Or else the blood of the people killed by those bombs shall be on our hands. It might even be us. They've been busy packing, ready to go after breakfast. I'll go down and get them all eating. You do it then.'

'Yes, all right.' He felt light for a moment. He pulled on his clothes as she scribbled something down, stood, smoothed her shorts and made for the door. He took her hand and kissed her on top of the head. 'You must be normal.'

She laughed. 'I shall try my best. And you must be quick. Imagine if they caught us!'

'You are talking about embarrassment? It does not matter.'

'No, I suppose not. Mustn't be so British about it.' And she was off down the stairs, and greeting Ava and the boys as though no one had called her a traveller or sung those songs in her house.

Food would keep them busy for perhaps fifteen minutes. The door to the dormitory was ajar. He stood on the landing, peering in. The rucksacks were lined up against the wall, their satchels leaning on the bigger bags. Each boy had folded his sheets and blankets and placed them at the foot of the bed. The window was open to air the room. There were twelve sets of bags; he could allow himself no more than a minute for each. Perhaps all the maps were in one bag. He went in, along through the bunks, read the name tags sewn into the lip of the packs, found Albert's, unbuckled the straps, reached down into the bag. He felt clothes, soft, probably unwashed. It did not smell good in there. A glass bottle. Alcohol perhaps. They had masked it well. A soap box, toothbrush, paste. Nothing that felt like a map. He heard one of the boys downstairs, laughing. It might be Albert. It was one of those who liked to draw attention to himself, who laughed too loudly. He refastened the rucksack, felt about in the satchel, did the same for the others. Penknives, compasses. His fingers searched for paper. He went through them all. It was hot up here, under the eaves. He lined the rucksacks neatly against the wall and began to straighten the satchels. He heard footsteps on the stairs, ran his hand over the remaining satchels and rucksacks quickly to set them straight, and slipped into his own room. The door opened as he stood beside the bed, a light sweat over him. It was Hannah.

'Anything?'

'No.'

'Nothing?' she said quietly. 'You couldn't be mistaken about what you saw?'

'No. They must keep the maps in their clothes.'

'Well, we cannot search them. It's not even as though we are enemies. Do you think they might have posted them home already?'

'There has been no time since I saw them. I have done my best. The English don't deserve to be warned, I think.'

'Don't say that. If they knew what was happening . . .'

'They choose not to know. It might put them off their pudding. Go down. I will think for a moment. Perhaps there is something.'

~

Hans giggled at the end of the row of boys lined up along the towpath. Emil swung his cane under his arm as he walked one way along the line, and then the other. 'Attention!' The boys smirked and trembled. He saw Hannah watching at the bedroom window, below her a group of children on the bridge pointing down at the spectacle on the towpath. 'Important English tradition!' he shouted as he paraded before the boys, hiking stick tucked under his arm. Every now and then he tapped a boy's leg or arm with it to make him stand straighter. Hans at the far end of the row, smaller than the others, blonder, laughed until he was bent over. 'All men to leave English shores must begin the journey by water!'

He had reached Hans. He handed him his stick, looked into his eyes until the boy stopped giggling, and stepped backwards into the river, fully clothed. He felt his clothes cling in the cold water, opened his eyes and a curled-up body shot down past him in a stream of bubbles, then more of them, the water a blur of bubbles and boys' peaceful faces, eyes closed, drifting back to the top. He surfaced to their shrieks and saw Hans, alone on the bank, waiting with the cane. He called up to him. 'Come, Hans. The water is lovely.' The boy laid the cane carefully on the grass and jumped into the air, knees gathered up in his arms, his face open to the sky, enraptured. As Hans came splashing down almost on top of him, Emil moved to one side, the boy missing his head by a centimetre or two.

He trod water, Hans paddling furiously in front of him, watched the others shout and dunk each other, dark, sleek heads like otters, racing to the other bank while he bobbed in a private orbit around the head of his son, paler, catching the light. Hans filled his cheeks with river water and floated on his back, spouted like a whale. The Germans' shirts ballooned behind them. There would be no time now to put their clothes through the mangle before they caught their train. He thought of the damp, mildewy parcels they would hand their mothers at the other end of their journey. The ruined papers in the pockets. How they would disintegrate along the folds, come apart in the women's hands.

~

The boy was quiet, in a mood Emil did not recognise. Perhaps he was overwhelmed by the crowd at Waterloo, on the tube. He was not used to large cities, though they had changed trains in London before, when he first arrived in England. Emil took hold of his hand as they hurried down the long escalator, the wind rushing up from the tunnel as a train approached. The boy withdrew it. 'I'm not six anymore, Papa.' Emil looked at him, but his face was set on his destination below.

Walking through the quiet streets of Hampstead, Hans said at last: 'Mama did not mention this.'

'I asked her not to ruin the surprise.' He felt for the key in his pocket. He knew that Hannah's mother was away in Wales, but hoped that Benjamin or Geoffrey were home. He would rather surprise them on their doorstep than have them come home late and find a boy asleep in one of their beds.

He thought he would take him through the heath and go in the back door. It was like something from a story, that house, in its row of different-sized English terraced houses all looking over the pond.

'Where are we going?' the boy asked as they set off into the long grass that led around the water. It was midsummer and there were children rowing, splashing their oars.

'Shhh. Surprise.'

'Can we go out in one of those boats tomorrow?'

'We can go tonight, when everyone's asleep.'

'Really?'

'Why not?'

They pushed through the overgrown path. As Emil stepped over the low wall into the garden, Hans took his hand and pulled him back. 'Papa!'

He turned and smiled. 'What?'

'You cannot go into the rich people's garden.'

'Ah . . . but we know these people, and they're not really rich.'

At the French windows, Emil cupped a hand over his eyes and peered into the dining room. Geoffrey was there at the table, his long back hunched over some papers. Emil fished in his pocket for a coin and rapped on the glass.

Geoffrey peered at him, saw the boy, came towards them and opened the door. 'Bloody hell, Emil. Last person I expected to see.'

Hans loitered at Emil's back. 'Come on, Hans. Have a guess who this is.' Hans stared solemnly. 'Can't you guess?'

Geoffrey thrust down a hand. 'Pleased to meet you. Geoffrey Jacob, at your service.'

Hans looked up at his father. 'Jacob?'

'Yes, it is Hannah's little brother, believe it or not. Can we come in?'

Geoffrey took a lunge backwards. 'Of course, of course. Is my sister not with you?' Emil gave a slight shake of his head, caught his eye. 'Do you want to have a look around the house?' Geoffrey asked Hans. 'There were fairies in the attic last time I looked.'

Emil translated for him.

'Only little girls believe in fairies,' he told his father.

Geoffrey laughed, answered in German. 'You are too quick for me. See if you can find my brother's flying trophies. We'll hide them. It makes him crazy.'

'Your brother is a pilot?'

'He'll be back soon. He'll tell you all about it, for hours and hours.'

'Better find them before he gets here,' Emil said. 'Go on, see where they are. He hides them in a new place every time.'

He went along the corridor to the stairs. They heard his shoes going up slowly. 'What's going on?' Geoffrey said, in English now, because Emil had always insisted. 'Where's Hannah?'

'She doesn't know we're here.'

'Jesus H. Why not?'

'We left without telling anyone. His mother's taking him back to Germany next week. Nothing I say can change her mind. I just need time to think. Somewhere safe.'

'Mother's back Monday. And Benjamin's around this weekend. He could go either way.'

'If you could just keep it all quiet, until we've gone, help Hans not to worry.'

'You're going to have to tell him what you're doing at some point.' Emil watched his face for a sign of what he would do. The landing creaked above them. Geoffrey put his fingers through his hair. 'I do have friends though. People who might sympathise with your situation. Let me think about it. We can talk about it in the morning.'

'Thank you, Geoffrey. I know this is a strange thing. I have to make a plan. Then I will tell Hannah, and Ava. I need to make a plan first.'

~

He stood at the window in Hannah's room, the layers of the park—the water, the rows of trees, the hills—shades of deep blue. In another ten minutes it would be dark and it would all disappear. Down on the pond in a rowing boat was Hans, laughing as though he would hurt himself. Facing away from him was Benjamin, in his uniform, his hat on the boy's head. He could not hear what Benjamin was saying but his head was moving around, as though he were pulling faces. He was glad Hans liked him. He was still a little wary of Geoffrey, with his big, gloomy eyes and worried mouth. The telephone rang in the downstairs hall. The ring went through him like the sounding of a raid. Don't pick it up, he thought. I need time to think.

The ringing stopped and he heard Geoffrey's voice, quiet, muffled by the door between them. 'Yes they are, but you mustn't tell her yet.'

He heard her voice, tinny in the receiver, from the top of the stairs. She must be shouting.

'I am only telling you so you don't call the police. If you must tell her something, tell her only that he has been in touch with friends, that they are safe. I don't want her beating my door down.' Another pause. He cut her off. 'You say this as though I had something to do with it. Keep her calm until morning. I'll see if he'll ring you then.' He replaced the receiver, looked up the stairs, gave Emil a weary shake of the head, and went out.

~

In the night he woke, rose stiffly from the sofa and went upstairs to check on the boy, asleep in Hannah's room. It took a few seconds for his eyes to adjust to the dark as he stood at the door, and he felt that his heart had stopped as he saw that the bed was empty. He made himself move forward into the room to put his hand on the bed, to be sure, and tripped against something on the floor, a bony leg. 'Hans?'

'Yes, Papa.' He had not been asleep.

'What are you doing on the floor? Why are you not in the bed?'

'I thought—it might not be clean.'

Emil was kneeling next to him, finding his shoulder with his hand. 'What do you mean?' He was still confused from sleep, from the dream. Is that what he had said? That the bed would not be clean?

'I saw some things, in the old woman's room.'

'In Hannah's mother's room? What do you mean? When were you in there?' He felt ill, short of breath.

'When Geoffrey sent me to look for the trophies. There was a funny bible. And photographs of old people. There was one of those rabbis.'

'What of it, Hans? Why are you sleeping on the floor instead of in a perfectly good bed?'

'Father,' he whispered, shifting against him on the floor, 'they are really Jews! We should not even be here.'

He reached forward, thrust his hands into Hans's armpits, lifted him clear of the blankets, set him heavily on the bed. He could just about see his face, big-eyed, staring at him. 'There is nothing wrong with being Jewish,' he made himself say in a harsh whisper. He wanted to strike the boy across the face, hard enough for him to remember. 'These are people, good people, that is all. Don't ever listen to anyone say those things. You are much too clever for this. Any one of these people would do anything to help you. Anything you needed they would give to you in a second. That is what you must always remember. Promise me. Always.'

There was silence. His hands were still under the boy's arms. He lifted him a little, let him bounce on the bed. 'Promise me!'

'Yes, yes, all right, Papa. I liked Benjamin. I didn't want to believe it.'

'There is no reason not to like Benjamin.' Emil took him in his arms. He wanted to apologise for the urge to strike him as he pressed his little head to his neck. 'I like him as much as I've liked anyone.'

'Me too, Papa. He gave me his compass, and I thought I would not be able to keep it.' The boy was crying, but trying not to show it. Emil felt him will his shoulders to be still, shifting his face onto his father's shirt so that he would not feel his tears.

~

The telephone rang again at six. He was at the hall table from the sofa in seconds. He stared at it for a short moment, lifted it to his ear. 'Becker,' he said.

There was a sound he did not know, a wailing, and then Hannah, speaking loudly to make herself heard. 'Oh Lord, you must come back. I cannot do anything with her. She slept for a little while but when she woke she was worse.'

Then she was talking to someone else, in German. 'No, it is not him. No, please, Ava, please calm down. We will sort it all out.'

That sound grew close suddenly. Ava had the phone now. It was terrible, but he had to listen. Eventually she spoke, her voice without any control, only just making words. 'Bring him back or I will go to the police. And then I will tell the German police. When they find you they will kill you. I know who to speak to, to make it happen.'

Hannah's voice returned. 'This isn't going to work, Emil. There isn't any way for this to work. I thought perhaps you might be able to find a way, but you can't.'

'All right.'

'You will bring him back today?'

'When he wakes.'

He replaced the receiver. He could hear Ava's wail until it clicked in the cradle. He hoped it had not woken the boy.

When he spoke the words, he had still been thinking perhaps, perhaps there is a way. By the time he was through the hallway and the kitchen and out in the wet grass, striding up towards the heath, wet hems whipping his ankles, he knew that there was not. He imagined making that sound that he had just heard, but it was not possible for him. He would instruct his body. He had done it before. It must simply be made to let go of one more thing that was too much to live without.

Part IV

Hannah

WINCHESTER, 1940

I appear to have lost a large part of the 1930s. There is little in my notebooks and the gaps between entries are dark hollows in my memory. It was difficult to write at all in that period. The first years in England were terribly insecure financially. We were continually moving about the country at the scent of work, and then there was the absolute windfall of our hostel in Winchester: a secure home and income. I was a refugee in my own country until we lived there. Still, those years were laid end to end with long days, rising at six to feed the young people, falling into bed after supper for sixteen had been eaten and the remains cleared away. I was too busy, too steamrolled by exhaustion to keep up my journals through that later part of the 1930s and so those years have tipped into the dark sea, irretrievable. I see too as I go on with this that writing came with movement, that when I was still, so was my pen.

There are a couple of bits and bobs clinging to the slippery deck. I remember disturbing and somehow comical news from Spain via

Geoffrey, who ran a news agency in London dealing with information from the front. I do wonder whether it is Orwell's book whose details I have retained though. I read passages to Emil from it I remember, following him about the place as he made the dinner or put a screw into a wobbly chair. Then there was the dire news on the wireless. We never knew what to feel. Poor Czechoslovakia, poor Poland. But perhaps, perhaps it could be over quickly, now that it had started. Wars make one selfish. Our main wish was that it would be finished before Emil's boy had any part in it. He was still very young when the war began. There was time. The thought of it not going well for Britain we did not discuss. Neither of us would be treated well in the event of invasion.

Emil's pale-headed boy is like silver panned from dust. I see him. He carried all our hopes with him as he dashed about amid our legs. One's heart ached to look at him. Then there was the mother, the image of a pale reed trembling at the edge of any room that contained her son. *Ava*. I have not heard that name mentioned in thirty years and yet for a moment just now she was standing before me, here in the sitting room, with that look she used to give me. It said, 'Whatever it is he sees in you, I assure you that it will soon wear off.' I was very young, and did my best to be polite. It was not her fault Emil had had to leave Germany, and there was great sensitivity about the child. We had to take care not to upset her. Emil was trying to convince her to stay. After they returned to Germany she sent her photos of us all together that summer, and that was the last we heard from her.

And the water. I could not forget that. It rushed beneath us unceasingly, day and night, the last sound one heard at night, the first in the morning. One felt cool, always, and a little damp, which was lovely in summer and oppressive in winter, when the aim was always to be warmer and drier.

The one blessing granted by the onset of war was that we occasionally had some time to ourselves, and I was free to restart my journal. I began it by fuming at Chamberlain's spinelessness while Hitler marched into Czechoslovakia, and then, when we finally declared war, began to worry about almost everything: how Benjamin would fare in the RAF (though his job was to train other pilots now, thank God), whether we would be able to stay open and in employment and shelter, what the outcome of the categorisation of 'enemy aliens' might be. As it turned out they had Emil down as 'B' category, which seemed to mean they weren't quite sure about him, but did not definitely view him as a fascist. In any case, we had both applied to work for intelligence, translating German intercepts or some such, but were rejected soon after his placement in the B category. Presumably they had fluent German speakers coming out of their ears, that they could leave two to waste.

Our guests were mostly London children after war was declared. Many parents were glad to have them out of the city, in case the bombing began without warning one night. But there were those who worried about our proximity to the coast, and vulnerability to invasion, and so the groups were neither large nor frequent.

That was not the only reason for the silence that dropped over the mill like snow in that first winter of the war. Emil could no longer make any kind of contact with those he had left behind in Germany. Though the boy's mother had not been in touch, Emil's mother and sister had gone to great lengths to keep him supplied with news of the boy. Now there was nothing at all. I remember the Itchen frozen beneath us, the mill silent, and he padding quietly through the house, down the stairs to the millrace, standing on the icy boards to pour water on the frozen pipes, or walking out into the snow without hat or scarf to fetch the groceries, with never a word. I was afraid, for myself as well as for his relatives. It felt as though I too were unreachably distant from him, across some impenetrable border.

In England we were both apart now from those around us. It had been possible to explain to people before the war that he was a refugee, even though he was not Jewish. Now we were adrift on a little island, separate from the townspeople, and not married, still. It was more important than ever that I not risk my citizenship. Apart from anything else, the youth hostel was run in my name. Here we were, with a home, a living: safety. My being British was our anchor, keeping us in place while all around us bodies were simply picked up and carried along with the surge.

When spring came, it was lovely, as it always is. It was as though we had some presentiment that the war could not remain such a timid, polite affair for much longer, that every English lane lined with wildflowers and sprouting hedgerows was old and precious, that this pretty little town with its students and cathedral could not remain as it was for much longer and so must be treasured in each moment of its continuing existence.

On the ninth of May, 1940 they extended conscription to include those up to the age of thirty-six. This meant Geoffrey joining up but he was given a special role with intelligence, reporting back to the government on conditions in the forces, and though it would be dangerous, at least he did not have to fight, or cross enemy lines. Mother rang to tell me about it, in tears. I suspected Geoffrey would love it. I imagined his long form in uniform doubled up with his notebook on a bouncing army truck or on the deck of a troop ship.

On the twelfth of May I woke to country noises, birds, a cow in a field, and one of those sparkling early summer days that England produces every now and then. I knew before I opened my eyes that Emil was awake. He always woke before me. This morning, something had lifted in him. He laid a hand on my stomach. For a brief moment, he did not carry his losses so heavily. It was the morning itself I think. I could hear a pigeon cooing above the rushing of water beneath the building. The scent of wildflowers in a little jam jar on the window ledge I had picked on my walk along the river the day before filled the room. When I opened my eyes, the sky was pale blue through the open window. The hostel was empty, silent but for the water below. I placed a hand on his shoulder, kissed the skin there, near the scar of an old bullet. He was older than I was, but still young.

It was unusual for us to be alone in the building, surrounded by quiet. You could hear for once the sounds of the town above the river: the milkman's horse clopping over the bridge, the bells of the cathedral. We were alone for now, and we took a moment for ourselves, in that private, silent moment of the war.

Afterwards, as we lay in our small, quiet room, he took my hand and pulled me up from the bed. He smiled, the possessor of a secret. He led me down the narrow creaking stairs to the common room. We were naked, still. I was and am a small, round woman, but I have never felt self-conscious about nakedness. Perhaps that is something only the beautiful suffer. The sound of the water gave me gooseflesh. We stopped at the trapdoor over the millrace. He pulled it up by its rope, the water rushing beneath us.

He was smiling as he released my hand. 'Don't do it today,' I said. 'I'll wash you. I'll boil water for a tub.' He laughed again, brought up the rope that hung down through the trapdoor and steadied his feet on the lip of the wooden floor. 'One day you'll hit your head and that will be the end of it.'

Then I was falling, the iron of his forearm crushing me into his body. The water seemed thick with the cold, as though we were submerged in a jellied ice. I couldn't breathe. When my head surfaced

I screamed, my lungs bursting. I have not used my voice in that way before or since. I was as alive in that moment as I ever have been. My legs and arms thrashed about, resisting the cold. And yet the stripe of his arm across my stomach and the press of his chest on my back were hot in the water.

He was laughing, one arm in the air, holding the rope. I made myself still. Our bodies flowed in the rapid water. It was dark under the building. Light crept beneath in little shoots, illuminating an inch of water here and there.

'I read about a boy who had a heart attack jumping into a cold river.' My teeth chattered as I spoke. I could not see his face. He kissed the top of my head.

'Hold onto me, Hannah,' he said. I twisted around. The curve beneath his chin was just visible in the darkness. He let go of me and reached a hand towards the stone stairs. 'Here, climb up.'

My scrambling onto stone was a graceless thing, but he managed not to laugh. He followed me up, and fetched towels from the linen cupboard, and I sat naked and dripping and warm at the mess table while he made tea.

~

At ten they came. The knock on the door was gentle and courteous. He looked at me. We were peeling potatoes at the bench, and though I had not known before, I knew now. 'Don't answer it, Emil.'

'What difference does it make?'

I wiped my hands on my apron and walked the length of the common room, all the chairs empty where our young people ate and sang, and the knock came again, a little sharper, more business-like.

On the steps in the courtyard were two policemen. Navy blue uniforms, bobby helmets. I knew them—we knew everybody in

Winchester, running the hostel—and yet suddenly I did not know them. The younger, PC McIlray, coloured to his ears. 'Mrs Becker,' said his partner, PC Baldwin. Baldwin, according to Emil, was as often as not in The White Lion in the evening before dinner; he generally left late, the worse for wear. You could see the evidence of it here in the spring light: a mottled nose, pink threads in the whites of his eyes.

'It's Miss Jacob, actually,' I replied. It really was a beautiful day. The blue of the sky above the rooftops was deepening and the wisteria that spilled over the brick walls of the courtyard was just beginning to open its lilac blooms. The stream glistened in the sunlight. Everything was fresh. I felt as though my heart had stopped.

He looked puzzled. McIlray gazed at his shoes. Emil appeared at my shoulder. 'Mr Becker,' Baldwin said, glad, I think, to be past the moment of dealing with the woman. 'There's time to collect a few necessaries, but you must come with us now.'

Emil stepped out from behind me. He was carrying my suitcase, the one I used for work. He did not have his own at that time in his life. He possessed almost nothing. He sighed deeply as he set down the case on the street and took me in his arms.

'How long is this for?' I asked Emil, as though he were the one in charge.

'Just a few days, Mrs—' Baldwin said. 'It's for his own good, with the way things are just now.'

I found myself shouting. 'And how will they be different on Friday? Will Hitler have seen sense by then?'

'Write to your friends,' Emil whispered into my hair, and released me. And they were opening the car doors on the little bridge, and guiding him into the back seat, and driving away from the river towards the guildhall, around the corner, gone. I stood on the steps in the sunlight for several moments, dazzled, thinking nothing just for a moment, before my mind began its frantic whirring.

~

I wrote, I wrote to everybody, of course, and one thing about wartime: there's no time to wallow. The day after he was taken away, twenty Land Girls arrived to dig for victory for the rest of the summer. And so I worked from the second I woke until I fell into bed exhausted, legs aching, to feed them, clean up after them, shop, do the accounts, help the laundrywoman who was now spending most of her time on her husband's farm where they too were growing wartime supplies. It was as well the girls were here, nevertheless. The last of my translation work had dried up and the Home Office had not yet replied to my second application to do translation work for Intelligence, which I had, I confess, sent accompanied by a long and rather angry letter. If the hostel closed I should be destitute.

If I found a moment, I wrote yet another letter, or occasionally the odd note in my journal, feeling that I must keep a record of the injustice unfolding in our lives. If I sat idle, I would think about the conditions in which they kept the men, whether there was ill treatment of the Germans, with Hitler's armies sweeping through the Low Countries. And if I thought about that, I would imagine those soldiers landing at Southampton, coming over the bridge in their trucks, requisitioning the hostel, and what would happen to me then? I mostly forced myself to stop my imaginings when they had been allowed to reach this point. What good would it do Emil? England had not been invaded. The only people being rounded up were refugees, a situation I must set myself against with any weapon at my disposal.

At my desk, the paper blank in the typewriter, shoulders aching from my hours at the laundry mangle, I heard the door slam downstairs, the girls' thunderous boots on the kitchen tiles, their cacophony of accents. They were the noisiest, most vigorous young women I had ever come across. I could hear them now, teasing each other about their beaux, soldiers at the nearby barracks, idle since Dunkirk, creating havoc in the town in the evenings. 'You don't mind them big, do you, Lorna?' a girl called Evelyn was shouting from below. 'I thought you were going to jump on him right there and then!' Most of the ribbing was kind. I could not help but like them, though they seemed slightly intimidated, in spite of towering over me. I think they thought me a little posh, intellectual. The knowledge of my German 'fiancé', gleaned in the town, made them additionally wary, and so when I was in the room there was among them a slightly remote respect, a thoughtful watching. It was quite clear that when I was not in the room I was the frequent subject of their tireless gossip.

At first they had been more forthcoming with me, more inclusive, but soon after they arrived there had been a procession of the evacuated soldiers from France through the town. One morning in late May as I waited for news, and began to give up hope of hearing anything amid the frenzy of the evacuation, a gaggle of the Land Girls returned at about eleven, banging the front door, hurtling into the kitchen to find me. 'Miss JACOB! You must come now or you'll miss them! The boys are coming!' I took off my apron and stepped outside with them. Out on the bridge I could hear the tooting of horns and cheers from up around the bend, coming down towards the town. And then there they were, truck after truck filled with khaki-garbed men, shyly grinning, waving to the swarm of girls risking life and limb to run among the vehicles. My girls could not help themselves. They too ran after the lorries, cheering and shrieking. The streets were filling with the townspeople, come out from the shops and houses. The young men's faces, in the weak sunlight of southern England, looked tired, slightly disbelieving.

I stood at the side of the road with a couple of the shyer girls as the men passed. The girls waved and smiled and I, deeply glad that these soldiers were safe, wished that I could see that Emil was too, with the evidence of my own eyes, as I saw these men now, solid and real, out of danger, at least for now. Jostled by the crowd, I felt a wet drop on my face though the sky was clear and blue. I looked to my left, where it had come from, and there was a tall, thin woman staring at me, hands on hips. I sensed from this woman's demeanour, and from the gasps of the Land Girls beside me, that she had spat on me. I drew my handkerchief from my pocket and wiped my face, waiting for an explanation. 'You've got a nerve,' the woman said. I did not know how to defend myself, not knowing what I had done, though a twisting in my stomach gave me a clue. There had been hints of this even before the arrest—sudden silences in the post office when I entered, an abrupt cessation of invitations to the Women's Institute meetings, not that I'd ever attended them.

'Here!' piped up one of my girls. 'What'd you do that for? That's filthy, that is!'

'She's a German's tart,' said the woman. 'And that's what we think of that sort of thing round here. She ought to be strung up.'

'Now just listen,' I began, and faltered. It was no use. The throng around us were all looking at me now. The Land Girls were waiting for me to say it wasn't true. The faces of people I recognised, all around me, had become the faces of strangers. I tried again. I had been taught to stand up for myself, not to be bullied by the mob. I knew how to speak to a heckling crowd. You remembered that they were human, that individually each had a heart, and conscience. 'Emil is a refugee. If you knew what he has suffered—'

'She goes to Germany all the time!' the woman told her audience. 'Wouldn't surprise me one bit if they were spies.'

There was general assent in the grumbles of the crowd. Everyone was standing very close. I feared that if I tried to speak further, I would go to pieces, and I refused to do that in front of these people. I knew that they were ignorant before they were hateful, but what was the difference when you were at the centre of a pack of them, having the air squeezed out of you? I stepped onto the road and walked alongside the procession, chin up, until I reached the bridge and home. It is their experience of the last war, I told myself. It is their lack of education. But you could not say that for the vicar's wife, Mrs Bantree. She had been to Cambridge. I was not used to being actively disliked, and it set the tone for the months to follow while I waited for news of Emil. I felt something settle around my shoulders and over my head, like a widow's shawl, that cast me into a dim silence.

~

The weeks passed with no news, only the drudgery and occasional amusement of caring for the Land Girls. My past began to feel unreal. Sometimes I had to find a quiet moment to go upstairs to look at his medal, his clothes, the pair of work boots, the packet of letters from Germany he had left behind, to furnish myself with proof. His clothes were losing the smell of him, his tobacco and cologne. The streets were quiet as everyone waited to see what would happen when the war began properly. No one looked at me, and I knew that it was brave and decent of the laundrywoman to keep coming. One day, battling along the high street in the rain with umbrella and shopping bags because the grocer would no longer deliver, I saw a woman, the wife of a refugee, Mrs Schlindwein. It seemed that she had already seen me and was eyeing me warily from beneath her rain bonnet. Surely *you're* going to give me the time of day, I thought. And then: Well, I will give her no choice. 'Hello, Dora,' I said loudly as the woman approached. 'Any news of Isaac?'

She stopped and looked into my face wordlessly for a moment. Then she said, 'Hannah, they are going to send them away.'

'What on earth do you mean? They are already sent away.'

'Away from England. Away from Europe. To other continents.'

'How do you know this? What have you heard?' My hand I realised, because she looked at it, was gripping her forearm.

She shook her head, looking away from me. She had some source she would not reveal. 'You must see,' she said. 'It is so unfair for us. How can they trust the other Germans? I'm sure your Emil is decent, but how would anyone know? But the Jewish men . . . Isaac was in a camp. This will kill him.'

I said no more but bustled away down the hill towards the river with my umbrella and baggage. I had never felt more alone, though the hostel was filled with noisy young women taking a day off in the rain. I could not walk down the street without people staring at me, not giving a damn now, apparently, whether I noticed them doing it or not.

That night I sat at my desk, back aching, staring at a piece of writing paper—on the desk, not in the typewriter—on which at some point I had written *Dear Mother* and nothing else. It was smudged. A cold mug of coffee sat before me. I must have dozed off with my hand on the paper. One of the girls was singing. The sound of her voice, and of the other girls' sudden silence, was what had woken me. I did not know the song and could not make out many of the words but it sounded like an old folk lament for a faraway love. One of those heartbreaking things where the woman is left with a baby on the shore waiting for the fishermen to find his body at sea. I undressed as quietly as I could so as not to miss any of the song, but she was soon finished, her voice replaced by the rush of water beneath the building. But not for long. The girls started up singing all those songs they drag out in wartime, songs from my childhood.

As I laid my head on the pillow I remembered the singing of the German boys from before the war, their pure voices, wide smiles. There were several groups of them in the first year or so of the hostel. They were all now old enough to fight and die, those hundred or so boys we had looked after. Hans was still just fourteen, though more than old enough for the Hitler Youth. I could not bear these thoughts that came at night. I pushed them away from me and fell into sleep.

~

The next day, there was a knock at the door in the middle of the afternoon, just as the girls were returning from the farms. I was trying to get tea onto the table, huge plates of jam sandwiches and tea in the big pot. I asked one of the girls, Milly, a flighty girl with two or three soldiers on the go from the base, to finish up while I answered the door. She was a pretty girl. She gave me a slightly cow-like stare before scurrying off into the kitchen and I wondered if that was her appeal to the soldiers: that sensual, stupid slowness, followed by an eagerness to please.

At the door was a man I had not seen for years, Kenneth Timms. I knew him at Ruskin, and he had visited us before the war, but since then had become a Labour MP for a Midlands electorate and rarely came this far south, into dense Tory territory. He was one of the men to whom I had written trying to find news of Emil. He had aged, as they all had, but Kenneth wore the years heavily. His face held a pinched expression and the wild curls of which he was always a little proud at Ruskin had gone now. He was almost completely bald. For a moment I didn't recognise him. When I did he seemed to be in disguise. I remembered I used to have something of a crush on him at college. 'Kenneth!' I said eventually. 'Please come in. How are you?'

He seemed bewildered by the kinetic force and volume of the Land Girls tearing about the place, stealing each other's sandwiches, shrieking at one another, sloshing tea all over the table.

'Come through,' I said. 'Where it's quiet.'

I tried not to rush him, sitting him down next to me at the desk in the back office. 'You are a long way from home, Ken. What brings you down here?'

'A Labour conference in Southampton.'

I knew that I should ask about it, and how his daughters were, but I could not wait. 'Do you have news of Emil?'

It seemed he had been waiting for permission to speak, as it tumbled out now in a rush in his Derbyshire accent. 'Hannah, I do have something, and it is rather worrying. I am not sure if it concerns Emil or not. It is very difficult to obtain accurate information. You see, a ship was sunk in the Irish Sea last Tuesday. The *Arandora Star*.'

I stared at him for several seconds, motionless.

'What seems to have happened is that they sent a shipload for Canada. They were Italians and Germans. I am told that they were all fascists, category A, the ones interned in thirty-nine. Emil would not be in that category, but it is all so confusing. We receive a different memo every day.'

I forced myself to speak. 'What happened to the men on board?'

He looked at me, stricken. 'They were lost, my dear. Only a few hundred saved.'

'Of course,' I said after a few moments, 'Emil is not a fascist. They know that.'

'No, no.' He put his hand on mine. It was a little moist. 'They have always been clear about the categories. But still . . .'

'What Kenneth? What is it?'

'My constituent, Mrs Singer—her husband was category C, classed unequivocally as a refugee. He was on it. He was lost.'

In the other room the girls grew rowdier. 'Don't be such a little tramp!' one shrieked. If those girls started off the war with morals, by God they were gone now. I began to chew a nail. Usually I managed to control this habit, which I regarded as revolting, in company. In private, Emil always told me to stop. I find I am doing it even now, when I pause typing to remember.

I placed my hands in my lap and looked him in the eye. 'Kenneth, thank you for coming all this way. I have not received a letter. I will not believe he was on board until I see a letter. If you could get an actual list—in any case, I feel that I would know, somehow.'

'They won't give out a list. They will only say yes or no if next of kin gives them a name. That is what I came to tell you. Here is who you write to.' He handed me a scrap of paper. 'You should contact them yourself.'

At the door, I could tell he wanted to say that he was sorry, but I would not have it. I hurried him out to his car, shook his hand, thanked him for coming, slipped the ragged triangle of paper in my apron pocket and returned to the house.

When he had gone, I began to peel the carrots for dinner. We had an enviable supply of fresh vegetables with the girls doing the work they did. For once, I did not ask the girls to help in the kitchen. After they had cleared the tea things, I sent them out to walk in the fields. It was so beautifully fresh, after rain the day before.

As I prepared the stew, I told myself, many times: I am peeling carrots. I am peeling potatoes, and occasionally: There is no letter.

He is not on the list. The thought hovered. I batted it away. There had been no letter about anything at all. They are not in touch with you, I went on at myself. For one thing, you are not his wife.

When the stew was done, and there were no pressing tasks for the moment, I sat down at the table and examined my poor fingernails. Even then, as my stiff body at last unfolded, I could not allow myself to believe he was lost. I simply refused to do it. I sat very still, and quiet, waiting for the girls to return.

~

A week later, I scolded one of the girls for attempting to malinger as the others trooped off to their work blearily in the cool early morning. She was another one of those with rather a complicated love life. She said she had a cold, and her eyes and nose were red, but I had heard one of them crying in the night. I was unsympathetic, giving her a little speech about her duty to serve with the troops at their lowest ebb. Eventually the wretched girl sloped off after the others, ready to sob anew. I had simply wanted the place to myself for a few hours and, it seemed, was prepared to act the bully to ensure that I had my way. After the girl had finally gone, I sat down with a cup of tea and a saucer of biscuits in a square of sunlight at the long trestle before an empty sheet of paper, with the address Kenneth gave me in my hand. I might as well know once and for all, I was thinking when I heard the slither of the mail falling to the mat. As always I told myself to expect nothing, either good or bad.

I made myself wait for as much as five seconds and then walked quickly to the door. I saw it immediately, a blue envelope, a handwritten address, a letter that looked different, personal, precious, poking out from amid the official guff. I knew even before I picked it up, leaving the others where they lay on the mat; it was his handwriting, addressed to me at Mother's, crossed out and sent on to me here. I ripped it open as I returned to my seat, tearing straight through the address printed on the back. The letter would mean nothing until I saw its date. The delays with the censors meant it might have been sent at any time. It was dated the fourth of July. *After* the sinking of the *Arandora Star.* I held the pieces together with jittery fingers. I was suddenly ravenously hungry and crammed a biscuit in my mouth, feeling I had not eaten properly for weeks.

Douglas Camp
Isle of Man
4th July, 1940

My dearest Hannah,

I hope you have received the previous letters which I sent to you. I have received nothing from you, but I believe that you do not know where I am. They have offered to send us to —— and said that wives can follow. I have told you this before. If you have received my previous letters, I am sorry to repeat the information.

Everyone knows that you are my darling wife. You should use my name now. Write to the Home Office. Ask your friends to help you. There might not be time to wait for arrangements. Organise yourself, in case.

There followed a long passage almost entirely blacked out by the censor. I believed that it expressed his love and loneliness. Some words had been left alone: *fondness, missing, empty.* It was as though the censor on the one hand believed Emil's words of love to contain some kind of forbidden, dangerous message, but on the other wanted me to know the tone of them, just in case they were what they seemed to be. The British for you.

I could not believe I held something so precious in my hands, my dusty hands that had scrubbed and peeled and washed all morning. I shall do *whatever* he requires of me, I told myself. More. I will not falter. I had a week left of the young women. I would write to the Youth Hostel Association and ask them to find another warden for the next billet. I began to calculate what my few possessions were worth. I had a friend from college whom I had already bothered endlessly but whom I must now ask to help me get permission to travel to the country beneath the censor's ink, whatever it might be. He would probably be glad to do this, to be rid of me at last. I knew that this was how persistence worked, how you received eventual consent for what you asked. You went on until that moment when they just wanted it to be done with, for them to be shot of you. I've seen that look on some official's face many times. The one that says: Oh dear Lord, not you again. And then you know you have them.

I held the letter up to the light, trying in vain to see some mark beneath the blackout that might give me a clue to the name of the country. I believed it must be Canada, after the news of the *Arandora Star.* Fine then. I spoke French if it was to be required. I would happily go to Canada, if we could only be together there. Would the men be released? So far from Europe and the war? Or perhaps I would be expected to be interned in a camp with him. I knew nothing about the future, not the smallest detail, and yet somehow I had to prepare for it.

I fell asleep that night in our bed with the letter in my hand, tucked in its taped-together envelope. My dreams were filled with the sea, great ships, emerging submarines, bright flashes over grey waters. I did not even know if it were possible for a civilian to go to sea in such times. Then, too, I was quite afraid of the ocean, spent many sleepless nights before every short trip to Europe, and this journey was likely to be much longer. But he had asked me to go. And I would apply all of my intellect to every last administrative detail; I would find the right person to beg, make my case, pluck the requisite money out of the ether, and we would be refugees together.

Emil

THE ISLE OF MAN, 1940

The men had been at sea for only a few hours, below decks in dank dormitories, when Emil heard the motors grinding, felt the hull shift sideways against the sea, their speed drop away. They were ordered up on deck and saw a long beach lined with a high wire fence, boarding houses, the dark shapes of people wandering along the promenade. Have we even left England? he wondered. There were no signs on the dock. 'Isle of Man,' an officer told them as he hurried them across the gangway. 'Douglas Camp. Fresh air. Decent food. You're lucky.' The air *was* wonderful. The tangy sea, the cold wind. They had been in a new housing estate on the fringes of Liverpool for weeks. Their overcrowded rooms and tents had quickly become close and rank and food was so scarce that some had taken to rummaging through dustbins. His spirits lifted a little.

Low grey skies sat over the town, casting the red brick of the boarding houses in a dull light. Seagulls cried as they wheeled about the docks in a gang, looking for holidaymakers to bully for food. Slim pickings these days. They marched with their cases along the dock to a high metal gate in the wire fence. Passed through, rifles on them, along the seafront to yet another man with a list on a board. The British army must have a whole regiment of these, with an aircraft hangar full of boards and pencils.

He was assigned to a room in a house a few hundred metres along the promenade. He and two others let themselves in. The red patterned carpet, the smell in it of ancient meals of meat and potatoes and green beans, the long wooden banister—he had stayed in houses like this when they came ashore with Siemens. At any moment a landlady might appear from some back office with a smile and a glass of sherry, a widow not yet dyeing her hair. He found his room upstairs while the others found theirs. Only two beds: one made neatly, a suitcase beneath it, the other bare, with blankets and sheets folded at its foot. The window was open and the smell of the sea came in on the breeze, curtains billowing. A crate, turned on its side so its divider made a shelf, sat between the beds. There were books, miraculously, some in German. He sat on the low bed to read the spines. Thomas Mann, Kafka, Shakespeare plays, poetry: Yeats, Auden. He wished he had paper. He wanted to write to Hannah at once. She would be thrilled at this piece of good fortune. And yet another marvel: next to the books, wedged in as a bookend, an exquisite little globe of hand-painted wood, Germany small enough to fit easily beneath the tip of his forefinger, Britain not the length of a staple and yet all its intricate coastline beautifully drawn. The Isle of Man was barely a dot, though; even this expert hand could do no more for this tiny, forgotten place.

~

He met the owner of the books and the marvellous globe walking along the promenade at dusk. On a bench in the strange pink light from the sea and sky sat a man with a well-cut waistcoat, thick, just-combed brown hair and round gold-rimmed glasses. He was holding a paperback in one hand and a handmade cigarette in the other. Emil sat next to him. The man did not appear to notice. 'I wonder if you are my roommate,' Emil said, looking out at the shifting surface of the ocean that touched all the continents of the world.

The man turned, holding his page open, cigarette away from his face. 'What makes you say that?'

'Well, he has so far been absent from our room, though he has left behind him plenty of books. I have wanted to ask him all day if I could borrow one, but so far, no luck. I have been quite bored.'

'Did you come over from Liverpool with the others?'

Emil nodded. This man was smaller and more perfectly made than most. There was a liveliness behind his eyes that made Emil like him instantly. A neat, crisp man. And, it seemed, happy in his skin, incredibly. He set the book upside down on his knee and held out a hand. 'Solomon Lek. Take any book you like. Then I might have someone to talk to about them.'

'Emil Becker. You find the energy to discuss literature?'

'Oh yes. There are not many situations where a discussion about books can't cheer me up. Those poor characters always have it so much worse than us. Read the Russians. Marvellous! And look, we have been sent to a holiday camp.'

They looked together at the high rolls of wire above their heads and laughed. 'My wife would like you,' Emil said.

'Then you must keep her away from me at all costs. I am greedy for the affection of intelligent women.'

'Well, she is not really my wife. I could not prevent you from liking her as much as I do. Or her you.'

'You're a man who carries his stories within him,' Lek said thoughtfully. 'I'm surprised you have any need for books at all. Have a cigarette. Tell me as much as a perfect stranger is allowed to know.'

And so he did, talking mostly of Hannah and the countries he had seen travelling on the ships. Emil had a quarter-bottle of whiskey for which he had given up a good pen in Liverpool. They drank and smoked and watched the sky lose its colour. They might have been free. Travellers in a port, exchanging stories before the next voyage. Solomon told him a little too. He came from Berlin. He was born there, went to the university and became a literature professor, until in 1933 he had his books burned and was forced out of his job. Emil's books too had ended up on a bonfire on the street, Greta had written. Solomon came to England and became a teacher. His family—a mother, aunt and cousins—had not wanted to accompany him. He did not say why.

Solomon was arrested at the school, in front of his English class, at the beginning of the British round-up. The event was familiar to him from when they had come for him in Berlin; although then the head of his department had been accompanied by a posse of eager young henchmen.

'I'm happy to be among German speakers again, Becker. I could talk like a drunkard, as you have learned, regrettably. But I miss my books. I was proud of my library. In Berlin, I used to give books away to my students. I think about it every time I pick up one of these old things.' He showed Emil his book, its torn cover, pages coming unglued. 'I can see them, all the pristine books I threw about freely. Can you imagine? Insanity!' Then, as night fell and the curfew siren sounded, and they stood to walk along to the house, Lek offered him a piece of information he had come by the day before. 'They are going to ask for volunteers for Canada.'

'Where did you hear that?'

Solomon tapped his nose. 'I am considering my options.'

'You would go all that way? You might be there for the whole war.'

'Who would miss me? I'm not a good traveller, but I will do my best to be courageous. And you, you strike me as an adventurer, a man who likes to do things in the world. Perhaps a long journey would suit you.'

Emil could not imagine he looked like anything of the sort, but he liked this man, who made conversation a series of thoughtful gifts, offered happily.

'And, Emil, in addition—' Solomon's eyes were sparkling '—they say that wives will follow.'

'Really? You're married?'

'I was thinking of your excellent fiancée, who would find me so appealing were we to meet.'

The next day, leaflets were pasted on all the lampposts, asking for volunteers for Canada. It promised that wives and children would follow, work would be found, return passage would be paid when England was made secure. This Lek was clearly a good man to know.

~

July turned cold. If they left the window open at night a freezing blast roared off the sea and into the room. When they closed it the glass rattled in the old frames. Emil dreamed he was away at sea and awoke ravenous, the sea air gusting emptiness through him night after night.

Large numbers of the men went along to the office to put their names on the list for Canada. Some of them had been in German camps. Some, like him, had other experiences of the Nazis. Lately you could not look at the surface of the sea without wondering about submarines, torpedoes. As he signed the paper, he wondered whether Hannah had remained in Winchester, not twenty miles from the coast. How well would the British defend their island? The soldiers who guarded them did not inspire hope. They seemed a mix of arbitrary discipline—no elbows on the table at meals, make your bed every morning—and bewildering softness, expecting the men to be excited about treacle cake once a week, becoming hysterical on the sidelines of internee football games.

The men heard nothing for several days, and then one windy night, the room filled with salty, wet air, soldiers entered the houses along the promenade shouting names and orders. A soldier came, stood over Emil. 'Lek?'

Solomon sighed, put his feet on the floor.

'What is this?' Emil said. 'What is happening?'

The man had turned to Solomon. 'Downstairs, with your case, five minutes.' Then he was thumping down the stairs, opening another door, barking out another name.

'This can't be right,' Emil said. 'We volunteered together.'

'Perhaps you'll come later. Perhaps there's more than one boat.'

'I'll come too. They never keep track. They're hopeless.'

'I'm not sure, Emil.'

'Don't worry. We'll just stick together.'

Solomon shrugged and scooped his books into his bag. He paused. 'Do you want to take half the books, in case we get split up?'

'If you wish.'

'Yes. They will travel like kings and queens. Safest apart.'

Emil fastened his case, three of Solomon's books inside. 'Come on, we'll mix in with the others.'

On the street there were soldiers with lists, checking men off and directing them to join a line along the wire fence. Emil tried to duck through amid the crowd. A hand grabbed the back of his collar. 'Name?' It was the soldier who had woken them.

He plucked a common surname from the air. 'Schlösser.'

'Not here. You've made a mistake. Back to bed, Schlösser.'

When the soldier moved along, he tried it again, was stopped again. This time the soldier jabbed him back to the house with his bayonet, tearing his jacket. 'Come out again and I'll shoot you.'

He went upstairs, watched them from the window, looking for Solomon. The day was breaking over the sea. They were all lined up now with their cases. He peered at the faces in the half-light. Quite a few were known fascists. What might that mean? At the tail of the line, there he was, a pale flash of sickness and worry, casting about for his friend. Emil raised a hand at the window. Solomon glanced up. They exchanged a look. Emil knew there was no use in shouting over the hectoring of the guards. He wanted to tell Solomon: I will see you again, you will be all right, but then they were moving, and he saw only the back of him, moving along the seafront towards the dock, where a troop carrier was waiting.

~

He spent that day walking up and down the promenade. Why round Solomon up with the Nazis? But he knew the answer. Because they didn't know what they were doing. Because whenever someone wanted to round people up, they would rather catch extras than miss one.

At breakfast the next day, after Emil had spent the previous twenty-four hours trying to tap officers for information and walking himself into an exhaustion that allowed him to sleep, the commander of the camp came into breakfast mess and made an announcement. At seven o'clock yesterday morning the *Arandora Star*, bound for Canada and carrying several hundred men who had been sitting at these almost empty tables two days before, was torpedoed by a German submarine off the coast of Ireland. Most of the twelve hundred or so on board, including a large number of Italians, were lost at sea.

He left the mess hall, a mildewy church room, as quickly as he could move between the long tables of men all doing the same. It was a bright clear morning. He stood at the fence looking out to sea for a long time. The sun made a sheen on the waves. He had no place to put the information he had received and so he thought of the models of ships he used to make for his boy, the thoughtless pleasure in chiselling and in the smell of wood shavings.

~

A week later at dawn, as he lay sleeping badly on the bed, the other still empty, a hand landed on his shoulder. He took hold of the wrist before his eyes were open. He was not surprised, as he looked into the boy guard's face, which wore a look of mild terror, or perhaps embarrassment. He was not sure he had even been asleep, so ready was he to stand up, pull his already-packed case from under the bed, shuffle down the stairs with the others, join the throng outside. The waves were loud, it was a wild sea. This was his last dawn in England, he was certain.

They marched silently along the promenade to the dock. There had been rumours that the *Arandora Star* did not have a convoy. The men around him were silently ashen as they lugged their cases towards the troop carrier. No one, now, wanted to go to Canada.

It was a rough crossing to Liverpool. Some of the younger ones tried to talk about where they might be going, but were quickly hushed. Soon enough they came down the gangway at the dock, where a huge ship occupied most of the quay. Alongside it was a line of trucks, soldiers shouting at their occupants, spilling from the vehicles in their hundreds. As those from the Isle of Man stepped down onto the quay the soldiers ran to the gangway and began shouting at them too, holding up the jagged blades of their bayonets. The refugees, huddled together, looked into one another's faces uncomprehendingly. Emil wondered whether he had underestimated the English. They did not look like overenthusiastic football supporters now. He remembered the men he fought in Turkey and Palestine, their faces as they charged, the darkness in their throats.

Out on the dock, as the men tried to hold onto their suitcases, the soldiers immediately began to push and harangue them towards a large group gathered under guard at the gangway to the ship. Many, Emil included, were forced to abandon their cases on the dock in the surge as they were jostled forward with the others. He saw with a lurch in his chest the back of a head he recognised, that thick hair now lank and awry, the glasses, his silk scarf crumpled, and put his hand in the air. It took him a few more moments to believe it. 'Solomon!' he shouted, men crushing him on all sides, the soldiers pushing and shouting. Solomon did not hear him in the madness. One of the soldiers smacked him across the shoulders with the flank of his rifle. 'Shut it, you filthy kraut.' Emil grasped the butt of the weapon, but a German behind pushed him forward up the gangway, away from the soldier. 'Are you crazy? These men are rabid.'

As they approached the high grey walls of the ship, the crowd seethed in boiling hotspots. Beyond the turmoil, Emil saw the name of the ship painted on its military grey metal: *Dunera*. He was soon close enough to the melee to see what was happening among the men. Fights were breaking out over luggage. Up on the gangplank an elderly Jewish man was struggling to hold onto an instrument case—for a tuba, Emil thought; it was very large—as a fat soldier pulled it, jabbing with his bayonet at the elderly man, who would not let go. The case eventually slipped free of their grasps and fell the depth of the exposed hull to the dark water below. There was a momentary silence among those closest by as they watched the descent of the instrument, and then the fighting over luggage began again with more violence and energy.

Eventually, the captain, down on the docks amid the round-up, fired a rifle into the air and the crowd stilled. Emil was close enough now to Solomon to reach out and touch him. Beneath his hand he felt the rough wool of his friend's heavy winter coat and saw that his neck was moist with sweat. Somehow he had hung onto his coat, or found another. Solomon's face turned and broke into a brief, warm smile. 'Herr Becker! Welcome to hell!'

'What's happening here?' Emil asked.

'Perhaps they're expecting trouble, because of the *Arandora*. I choose to hope they will calm down when we're on board.'

The captain spoke into a loudhailer, with military emphasis on every fourth or fifth word. 'These are your orders, Fritz. Hand over your luggage to my men as you approach the gangplank. We will return it later. You cannot take it to your quarters, there is no room. Obey all orders. I will not ask twice. We do not like spies, so do not give us any excuses. And speak English, not kraut. Proceed.'

The men began to shuffle on board more quietly, murmuring questions to one another. Emil drew level with a guard. 'I need the receipt for my suitcase!' Emil told him, but was shoved along by the crowd. It was Hannah's case. She had it when he met her. She was using it as a bedside table in her bedsit in Brussels. It was next to his face that morning when he woke. He could not just give it over to these brutes. He felt a hand on his wrist. Before he could get his other hand to it in the crush, he glimpsed another soldier, a few feet away, holding up Emil's watch to a colleague with delight. 'That's my watch!' he shouted, but already he was being herded onto the gangplank, three abreast with men and sagging in the middle, forced to keep moving away from his watch—Benjamin's watch—and its new owner by the mass of bodies behind. He grasped Solomon's wrist, their arms stretching as men crammed between them. Someone thrust a heel into Emil's bad leg and water sprang to his eyes. Behind him a boy was crying. Ahead of him there was a sudden slowdown that threatened to topple those around him off the gangplank. Emil looked down. The strip of water between the quay and the ship was a long way beneath, dark, oily. Solomon turned back towards him from up ahead. 'Slow down,' he addressed the surge of men. 'The rabbi is frail. Slow down, please!'

But still they came, swarming up towards the ship, harassed by the soldiers below. Emil and Solomon reached a lower deck and were herded aft, feeling the sudden loss of air as they went down, past rolled wire, below decks, into a low-ceilinged space crowded with hammocks and tables. Soldiers were shouting at them. 'Find a bed. Sit on it. Shut up!'

As the men descended into the bowels of the ship, hundreds pushing in behind them, it quickly became apparent that there would not be enough hammocks for even half the men. 'Here,' Solomon said to Emil. 'Between us, we'll take a hammock and a table, and we'll swap, every night. He who sleeps on the table can have my coat as a mattress. That way we need never sleep on the floor.'

The hold filled quickly around them, and when it was full, more crowded in, until they were huddled on the floor and in the hammocks, muttering to each other in the dark in disbelief. Emil sat on the table to reserve it while Solomon lay curled on his side in the hammock, his head balanced on the taut edge so that he could talk to Emil. 'You were on the *Arandora*?' Emil asked. A thrum of complaint rose around them, intermittently silenced by the yap of a guard.

Solomon nodded. 'I was near the lifeboats. The captain told me to get on one. Some of them broke as the ship went down. Ours was all right, but there was hardly anyone on it. We got some people out of the sea. Not many.'

'Listen,' Emil said, 'you must take the hammock for the voyage. I'll manage on the table.'

'No, your cough is worse than ever. I'm fine. Not a scratch on me.'

'But you must rest. It was only a few days ago. I cannot believe they have you on another ship so soon.'

'Perhaps I'm their lucky charm. Me and the others who did not drown.'

'Then I'm glad you're with me. Perhaps this time the ship will make it to Canada.'

'Emil, we can go to Timbuktu for all I care. So long as we get there in one piece.'

~

They lay in the crowded hold all day without food, restless and sweating. There was a latrine at the rear, soon blocked and overflowing. The guards would not let them move about the ship to use another. The portholes were covered over with boards but there were gaps and they sensed nightfall, just as the engines rumbled into life and they began to move off. As soon as they left the shelter of the port they felt immediately that they were heading into rough waters. The men grew rowdy, talking loudly, excitedly, groaning, some of the boys crying, some old salts singing. Eventually, when it became clear that no food was coming, and that they must make it through the night however they chose, the men withdrew from each other in their hammocks, curled on tables, some on the floor, trying to stay away from the sloshing latrine as the ship pitched and tumbled away from England.

Emil's table was close to the latrine and it slid around in the slick of foul water from the overflowing buckets. The air was black and fetid. Solomon's shape lay above him in the hammock, so close he almost touched him when he turned on his side. He dared not speak, in case Solomon had fallen asleep. He did not have the heart to wake a man who against all odds had found some rest.

Emil stared into the thick black air above the men's heads, these prisoners pitched into their darkest moments by the lurching of the ship. The hold was peopled with all of their nightmares: violent men, shattering glass, speechless farewells on railway platforms. He slipped eventually into a sleep more like illness than rest, a place of inescapable lucidity and repetition, of loss that filled his body like a sweet, poisonous gas.

In the first moments as he sank under he immediately began a strange circular journey around the streets of his childhood. He rode the bicycle that his father built for him from scraps around the ten blocks that spread out from the apartment, the perimeter prescribed by his mother, past the school, the bakery with its wonderful morning aromas, the train station where the commuters swarmed onto the platform for trains to Düsseldorf in the morning and swarmed out again in the evening, the church, the police station. Along the river, the new warehouses and factories. As his table moved around the rolling deck it came into his dream that he could not remember which was closest to his home: the school or the shops. He became furious with himself. It was his job to remember exactly where everything was. Someone would come whom he would be charged with telling about the town, about what happened where, in precise detail, and there could be no question of simply forgetting.

He was a grown man, hiding in an apartment across the street from the trade union building. He did not know what he was hiding from, but then he saw them. It was early, and as the day's work was due to begin and workers filled the streets on the way to their offices, two lorries drew alongside the union building and disgorged what seemed to be thousands of men, all in dark, crisp uniforms. They streamed into the building while around them the workers on the street kept their heads down, even as they came to a halt to allow the men to pass. They came without end, like a plague of insects, so numerous and close together that they were a black swarm rather than a group of individuals.

Emil watched them from the window of the apartment, frozen as he saw through the windows of the trade union building the stairs and the offices filling with the black figures. Then, as the workers outside began once more to surge along the street towards their workplaces, there was his father, elderly, portly, running from the river against the tide of people on the street towards his offices. Emil remained immobile in the window as his father drew closer to the swarm, growing closer to being absorbed with every passing instant. The moment went on and on as Emil skated around the deck. The men still swarming from the lorries, his father running towards them, Emil frozen in the window. Inside his body there was a box of flickering light and dark, in which his father was running perpetually towards the building, and he was always watching, unmoving. For the rest of the night in that little box the scene did not end, only repeated, an inescapable loop.

Eventually, as the weakest chink of light crept through the boarded-up portholes and the storm eased, he finally began to leave the darkness, coming up through the layers towards his life as it was now. Solomon's voice came quietly from above. 'How many nights would you say it takes to reach Canada?'

Emil pulled his compass from his pocket, glad that it had not been stolen from him in the night. Hans had left it behind. It had been in his pocket the years since then. He would not put it past these Neanderthals to swipe it from him while he slept. 'They're not taking us to Canada,' he said, studying it by the weak light from the edge of the porthole. Solomon leaned over the edge of the hammock and Emil held the compass up to show him. Its arrow pointed south, not west.

~

By their third day at sea, rumours rippled and skirmished among the men in their hammocks and tables. Though the sky was overcast it was possible for all to see from the light at morning exercise that they were not going west. During their twenty-minute jog around the deck in which the weaker, slower men were insulted and hectored, an older man with shoulders like a wrestler's, a Nazi, said to Emil: 'They tell me you have a compass.' Emil pretended not to hear. The Nazi pushed him. Emil punched him in the nose, blood appearing straightaway at his nostrils. The English guard beside them, Cook, a man who seemed to be of subnormal intelligence, perhaps even brain-damaged, and who took great pleasure in violence of any sort, let out a whoop. 'That's it, Jerry. Show him what you're made of!' The officer at the bow ordered the men to keep moving and jabbed a boy close to him with the butt of his rifle.

That night, Emil lay in the hammock, trembling. He felt Solomon stand from the table and loom over him in the light from the dim lantern tied to the crossbeams above. 'You're shaking,' he was saying. 'Your shirt is wet. I'll take you to the infirmary.'

Emil stared past him, seeing not the men in the shadowy bowels of the ship but Papa, thin, young, running away from him on the ice, pulling a pale-headed boy on a sled. Solomon took hold of Emil's arm and pulled him gently to his feet.

Emil was aware intermittently that someone was trying to bear him along the gangways and up and down stairs. He was confused by the darkness, the soldiers that reared up out of the shadows. I am a prisoner of the British, he thought. They will put my head on a stick. Each time he attempted to take his own weight both men fell on the floor, and it took minutes for Solomon to get him back on his feet, sliding him up against the metal wall to manage it. When they finally reached the infirmary the twenty or so beds were filled with men with dysentery, bayonet wounds and one suicide attempt, his wrists bandaged. Emil stared at the man's soiled bandages as he lay there with his eyes closed and Solomon moved him on to where several men sat on wooden foldaway chairs at the end of the room. One of them noticed Solomon and Emil and stood. Solomon slipped Emil's arm from round his neck and dropped him into the chair. 'Where are the medical officers?' Emil heard him say. He looked like he was shouting. And then he looked like Thomas. So, they were both prisoners. He couldn't help but feel relieved.

The man nodded towards one of the beds where there was a man in uniform, as dishevelled and forlorn in sleep as the men around him. His friend, it was Solomon now, said something to Emil's neighbour who put out a hand to keep Emil upright in his chair while Solomon approached the sleeping medical officer. Emil saw one man stand over another, could not establish who they were. It was a ship, with soldiers. But one of those men was a friend, trying to help him. Without his help he would die. Something had gone wrong inside his body. His blood was poison. He recognised the feeling, but he did not know from where.

The man Solomon was shaking jolted, sat upright immediately, and Emil lurched forward, thinking to save his friend from a blow. He was falling forward. The man with his hand on his arm pulled him back onto the chair.

His friend was talking to the man he had woken and was pointing to Emil. They approached him together. The man placed his hand on his forehead. The hand was very cool and dry. How was this man so cool in this furnace?

'Could it be malaria?' Solomon asked the man in English. 'I think he was in Palestine, and Turkey.'

The man nodded thoughtfully and said something from deep underwater and they began to manoeuvre themselves under his arms, to take him somewhere. The man in the chair next to them began to grumble. He was upset about something. 'Hours,' he said. 'Hours and hours.'

No one had a chance to answer him because just then a thump hit the ship low down behind them and several of the men fell off their beds and started screaming. Emil was wrenched from the grasp of Solomon and the doctor and fell to the floor. It smelled of ammonia but it was cold. A nice cold, hard surface under his cheek. A second strike shook the floor and he saw the blur of feet rushing towards the door. Solomon and the doctor steadied themselves and pulled Emil to his feet. There was an English voice in the corridor. 'Stay below! Stay below!'

When they had grappled Emil back onto a bed, the doctor went out to the stairway. 'What's going on? Are we under attack?' he called up to the guard. 'Shouldn't we get ready to evacuate?'

'Orders are to stay below! Just do as you're told.'

Then there was a soldier in the room, hurtling from the stairwell into the infirmary. A big man like a stupid bull, pushing patients from their beds onto the floor. The soldier crashed through the beds towards Emil, face red, and then he was pulling him onto the floor and kicking him in the head, once, twice, screaming at him. Do I know this man? was all Emil could manage to think. There was a feeling amid the assault that some old trouble was surfacing, something he'd believed himself done with.

His head flashed with bright light, as though something had detonated inside it. He heard someone scream as the explosions in his head came one upon the other. 'Filthy German swine have torpedoed us. We will all die, you filthy kraut.' He felt liquid in his ear. Saw nothing. Then there were men on every side, German voices, gathering around his attacker, bearing him away.

He felt his friend help him onto the bed. He recognised his voice and when he opened his eyes he saw him, knew him. It was Solomon Lek, the man with the books, the man who didn't drown. If this man stayed with him, he would be all right. He was lucky. Solomon pulled a chair alongside the bed and rested on Emil's legs, arms and head, pinning them down, so that he would not fall off. Solomon fell asleep instantly. At some point the medical officer returned and gave him quinine, he knew the smell as it came towards his face. Ah yes.

Emil closed his eyes and felt the doctor touch his ear, pat the dried blood with something that stung. When he had gone Emil slipped inside himself into a place where the man kicked him until he could not see. For the rest of the night Emil understood that the screaming man was a Nazi, that the British army was run by them now, and that none of them would ever see land, nor even daylight, again.

~

Emil mended, slowly, and was transferred back into the cavernous hold with the other men, still shaky, with the cleared-out lightness of recovery. He suffered their jokes about his holiday in the infirmary without comment, not sharp enough to offer a response. He slept one night a little better than the other, rocked in the hammock, enclosed within his cocoon. Several days into the voyage, they were called on deck at dawn. It took two hours for two and a half thousand men to shuffle out, blinking under a pink sky, onto the deck. Everyone could clearly see from the position of the great red orb breaking free of the ocean that they were heading south. Emil looked at the men around him, their faces lined and hairy in the pink light, and wondered where in God's name they would all end up.

'Men,' came the voice of the captain through a loudhailer from way up ahead, 'now that we have left Europe behind us, I can inform you of our destination. It is Australia, where you will remain for the duration of this war, and will pose no more threat to the security of the British Isles. Dismissed.'

As the men shuffled and mumbled to each other, a word, repeated over and over in an incredulous whisper, hovered above the crowd: *Australia!* Emil watched the sun at the horizon finally lift free of the water with a viscous drop and absorbed the information. They had all included Australia on their list of possible destinations but now that it was a certainty it was an incredible thing to take in. But so then would be Shanghai, or India. He tried not to think of the number of mines laid across the vast spread of the Atlantic and Indian oceans.

He had heard the voices of Australians in the trenches at night, had taken plenty with his rifle. The Australians had been brown, dirty, scared, mad and vicious, just like them. They looked the same inside when their intestines were spilling out into the mud. Their faces looked the same when they lay in a shell crater, wounded, as good as dead. And there had been a group of them at the hostel once. Louder than the English. Taller. More energetic. They had given the impression they ate a lot of beef and lamb, and spent their spare time swimming and playing cricket. No doubt there was more to it.

It seemed beyond belief that they would reach the other side of the world intact. Even if he did, Hannah could not reach him. For the duration of the war, the captain had said. Hitler and Churchill might fight forever. They seemed to have an appetite for it. He drank in the acres of ocean knowing that at any moment they would be ordered below. He could not see what was coming and he could not think of what was past. He was still light with illness. Too much thought would knock him off his feet.

Solomon squeezed through to him as they reached the stairs. 'What do you think?' He was smiling. He looked young. 'I have a cousin in Melbourne. I should not say it out loud—' he dropped his voice low among the babbling of the other men '—but I *do* feel lucky! To survive two torpedo attacks, and now this!'

Emil saw in Solomon's face his own response as a younger man when he discovered the destination of his next voyage with Siemens. He rarely knew a thing about the place printed on the paper, it was the names that were exciting. Reykjavik. Caracas. 'Do you think letters can be sent from Australia, in wartime?'

Solomon turned to him. They were being sucked into the door with the crowd. They would not see each other's faces clearly again for a long time. 'Oh yes, I had one from my cousin. She said I should come.'

Emil felt a hand on his arm, a soft pressure, as they went back into the darkness, and the stench of themselves.

~

At Freetown they smelled the sharp barbecue cooking and the sweetly rotten tropical plants. The place was lit up like a tree at Christmas after their months of blackout in England and at sea but they glimpsed the lights only through the gaps in the porthole or on the gangway, through wire. They took extra trips across to the putrid latrines to breathe in Africa and see the black silhouettes of the immense palm trees stirring in the breeze before the collective odour of their own insides overwhelmed them. Emil had been here before, was free then to roam the alleyways and marketplaces and bars, scramble up the red slopes behind the town for a view of the pale ocean, and did not know whether he was luckier than the younger men, who were desperate to see it, or worse off, knowing the strangeness and wonder they were missing, right there on the shore, close enough to smell, to feel. As they departed the coast of Sierra Leone, the men who ruled this floating kingdom, for a reason known only to them, opened the cases they had not thrown overboard and distributed clothes and towels at random. Perhaps the stink of the internees had become too much for them. Or perhaps they had already taken everything they wanted.

At first the men would not use them, not wanting to sully each other's possessions, but the soldiers refused to make any attempt to assign items to their true owners, and so the men at last took the supplies and changed their clothes for the first time in three weeks. And then they were all briefly cleaner, their shirts and underclothes whiter and still smelling of the laundries of their landladies, wives and mothers, but they became an odd collection of souls whose clothes did not fit them, worrying constantly that they would chance upon their owner at exercise or dinner and cause irredeemable offence. They were ordered to throw their discarded, lice-infested clothing overboard, and so behind their ship, strewn back towards the lush, mountainous coast of Africa, they left a wide wake of trousers, shirts and hats that drifted momentarily on the foamy green surface before sinking to the bottom of the Atlantic to create an exotic garden for the creatures that lived there. Emil watched as his group returned from their dumping expedition on deck, wondering which of the litter stranded behind them was his, how much of Hannah's translation fees it had cost.

He spent the rest of his journey in the trousers of a man with legs a couple of inches shorter and the shirt of a man with broad shoulders, a thick neck and long arms, hoping particularly not to meet the owner of this shirt, giant that he must be. Only a very few razors were distributed, and no shaving cream or mirrors, and so hardly any men attempted to shave. Emil wore his ill-fitting clothes and itchy, lice-ridden beard through another five weeks of dry biscuits, thin soup and no fresh fruit or vegetables, three rounds of dysentery and the loss of a stone in weight. He had just enough energy to feel sorry for the kosher Jews who appeared to live on little more than the occasional dash of lime juice in their black tea. His hair, still for the most part black when his journey began, was almost entirely grey by the time they reached Fremantle. He knew this because Solomon commented on it one morning when the angle of the ship allowed a sliver of morning light to fall upon his head in the hammock. His teeth ached with the intensity of a nail lodged in his brain that someone occasionally moved around a little for good measure.

To pass the time he listened to Solomon's talks on literature and helped whittle the bottom of table legs into tiny, match-like sticks for one of the boys who was building a steamer with real matches and scraps of wood gathered from the men and one or two of the kinder guards. He ran a book on how many days Solomon could go without being sick. His record was three. The internees owed him fifty-seven pounds, fifteen shillings and fourpence, which he promised to split with Solomon, if he ever received it.

After they rounded the southern tip of Western Australia, glimpsing from the gangways the grey-green scrub and red dirt, they sailed off into nothing again, until they reached Adelaide, its dry hills in the distance beyond the flat dusty suburbs. These places, these far-flung outposts of Englishness with corrugated tin roofs. It was bewildering to see such domesticity perched on the edge of the desert with dust skimming along the streets in the warm, dry wind.

Of Melbourne they saw nothing. Most of the men were not allowed to disembark, or to move about, though some were taken off, including a group of Nazis, offloaded for God knew where. The others cheered as the Nazis were ordered on deck. 'May that be the last we see of your kind!' the man in the hammock next to Emil shouted, a usually quiet chemist who had given his own daily lectures from his table for the past two months. But you always saw Nazis again, Emil thought. More rose up to replace them. Here they were, on the other side of the world, and still there were Nazis.

For the last few days at sea, as they steamed north along the coast of New South Wales, the air on the ship was thick with rumour and anxiety. Even the men who had slipped into lethargy and sickness for most of the passage, who had ignored the maths and physics and literature lectures and avoided the chess games played with sets made of matchsticks on squares etched into a table top, even these seemed to wake up, talk late into the night like the rest, ask their neighbour what they knew of Australia, of Aborigines, of kangaroos, of the food.

Early on a September morning, no one quite knew which anymore, the ship's engines ground as it slowed to a halt. Emil lay awake in his hammock, listening for the approach of the tug. There it was, distant at first, then unmistakable, and then they were moving again. He climbed down from the hammock and gestured to Solomon, who was lying with his arms behind his head, listening as well to the growl of the tug coming alongside.

Solomon, on the table for this last night at sea, watched Emil slip down from his hammock and land softly on the floor beside him before climbing onto a table where another man lay sleeping under a porthole. Balanced astride the sleeping man's legs, he leaned against the porthole, one of the few that had been uncovered during the journey. The man woke. 'Hey! What are you doing?' he said, but in the light from the porthole it was clear that all around the hold men were jumping on their neighbours' tables to do the same. The man beneath Emil was quickly up beside him. Men crowded around the circles of light. They came into Sydney Harbour jostling around the portholes, ten to a window, absorbing unstable flashes of pink sky and sandstone and eucalyptus trunks, blue harbour, dark forests, fields. Emil saw fishing trawlers, naval ships, ferries, lone fishermen on tiny dinghies. Wharfs, mansions, windows flashing like jewels, the curved steel bridge, of which he had seen photographs, soaring above the next hill. All in glimpses of a second or two pressed by odorous flesh, rancid breath on all sides, the others telling him to get down and give the others a go.

Soon the broad waters of the main harbour narrowed to a long inlet amid a crowding of wharfs and smokestacks and railway lines and the ship was shunted alongside a dock. They were kept below decks until evening. Through the long day the men returned at intervals to the portholes. All that changed was the position of the flotillas of working boats docking at the wharfs with their stinking fish and crates of cargo, that and the deepening of blue as the sun rose higher in the sky. The men cursed and fidgeted and prayed. There was some laughter. Today, tomorrow, they would walk on land again. They had not, astonishingly, been blown to smithereens.

Emil and Solomon sat on the table and tried to imagine the country outside. 'Have you read *Kangaroo*?' Solomon asked Emil. 'There are wonderful descriptions of the country, and the feel of the country to a European. Fascists too, believe it or not.'

'No,' said Emil. 'I have met Australians but I don't know much about them. It seems hot already, and this is only spring.'

'Perhaps it's not so hot everywhere. Remember the pastor said that we're destined for a pleasant camp, with gardens?'

'He also told us that God was guiding us across the sea in his gentle hands.'

'I suppose we shall find out soon enough, when they let us off this ship. I shall not miss the sea.'

'One swim would be nice, wouldn't it? Before they take us away. Did you see the water of the harbour? There were little beaches all along the shores. One could swim in a different place every day.'

Solomon laughed. 'I cannot swim, Emil. It's a miracle I have survived the ocean all this time.'

'Then for God's sake, I'll teach you! You'll go home from Australia swimming like a fish. And then we will both learn to ride a surfboard!'

At dusk the order came to file up on deck with their belongings. What could they mean but the shirts on their backs? Instantly there was a sense of others on the ship, for whom an effort must be made, for whom it must be made to seem that there was a proper relationship between these men and their luggage.

As they emerged from the hours of slowly shuffling bodies on the stairways onto the deck above the harbour, their impatience erupting in little shoves and falls, they peered around themselves, ignoring the carping of the soldiers. The sky was the same pale grey as the water and the chimneys had ceased belching black smoke into the low cloud gathered at the end of the day. Factory and warehouse workers filed out of huge dark buildings, little black creatures swarming across the docks and into the streets above the harbour. A long train sat in sidings beneath them. The men watched it, after they had taken in all else, as though it would change, or tell them something about their fate.

A crowd had gathered below, held back by a line of Australian soldiers with their lopsided hats. In front of the soldiers was a row of police, all along the quay, staring up at the men on the ship. Emil wondered what these people had been told about them.

There was movement at the other end of the deck, and the taller men saw and called back that they were beginning to disembark, and there started up pushing and surging. Solomon kept hold of Emil's shirt sleeve. All were pressed together and the evening was still warm though a little breeze was lifting off the harbour, bringing up to them the smell of the sea and the petrol fumes of the boats. A soldier nearby shouted some orders and the men settled. After what seemed an age of imprisonment in the crowd, men close to them began to move, and then it was them shuffling unsteadily towards the gangplank. They came across the narrow gap, dark water below, onto the ungiving land, the deadness of solid earth reverberating through knees and spine. As they stepped down, Solomon whispered: 'Australia!'

The police and soldiers watched them as they moved forward, straggling towards the train. Some of the police were sweating. Workers had gathered behind the lines of uniformed men and stared frankly. Emil looked around him at his fellows. The men were starving thin with fat beards and wild hair. They looked as though they were dangerous prisoners, locked up on some notorious rock for years. A woman pushed up behind the police guard as they walked by. 'Dirty

Jews!' she called. He looked at her face. She was the first woman he had seen for two months. Not bad beneath the scowl; well-turned-out, dark hair waved about her face, luscious red lipstick. An office worker. Respectable. If she could be made to smile . . . But he knew any woman, of any description, would be appealing. All around him the men were staring at her and the other women gathered behind the guard. No one else cared what they were saying either. Each thought of the same things. Clean hair that smelled like flowers. Long, plump limbs. Soft, giving skin. They did not seem like nice women, these Australians, but no one just now was as discerning as he might be.

When they reached the train, they were ordered to space themselves out along the carriages. There was endless counting. The men had over the weeks taken to murmuring numbers quietly to put them off. Whether or not it was their doing, the soldiers always came up with a different number. Finally Emil and Solomon, still miraculously together, boarded an old train with leather seats that smelled of the old life, of travel with family, of summers across nearby borders. Then they filled the train with their terrible stench and the soldiers came among them and opened the windows. You could jump right out of one, if you had a mind to it. The soldiers were mostly overweight and old, not the tall bronzed figures they had imagined and talked about. Perhaps these men were tall and bronzed in the last war.

Emil took a seat next to Solomon, who was looking about himself, smiling, and they faced forward as the train finally shunted out into Sydney, the men chattering too loudly, as though they were off to war and must bolster their courage by showing off. The light fell away over the roofs of the little terraced houses. They saw in the dusk warehouses, scrubby cuttings. Occasionally a child on a bike down a little side street. They were all fascinated by the children, as though they had not seen a child before. Such little hands and feet.

Some tramps around a fire in the wasteland beyond a suburban train station. The soldiers brought around sandwiches, fruit and tea, passing them out with cheery voices, though it was hard to understand what they said. It was the best meal Emil had ever tasted. The orange was incredible, the apple unbelievably sweet and crisp. They laughed as the juice spurted across their shirt bibs.

After their meal, they fell asleep to the rocking motion of the train on the rails. Emil dreamed of nothing; he was simply at rest for seven hours, and then he opened his eyes to the country lit with the colours of the sunrise outside the window. The others were opening their eyes too and they watched in silence, smiling occasionally as birds—small parrots, big black and white crow-like creatures—swooped amid the glowing trunks of eucalyptus. As the morning grew full and bright Emil noticed that opposite him an old Australian soldier snored, clutching his rifle between his knees. The three Germans surrounding him looked at each other and laughed. Emil watched the country unfold outside the wide window like a cinema screen, leaning back in his seat, eyes on the horizon. He could do this for days.

Late in the afternoon they came to a standstill. He pulled up the window next to him. The air outside was warm and still. A cluster of dry-looking eucalypts swept the dirt road, which was somewhere between orange and red. 'Sheep on the track!' they heard someone call from the end of the carriage, and the men laughed again. The train started up soon afterwards.

Too quickly, after a day of cards with the soldiers and the green of the land growing sparser and sparser, little towns appearing out of nothing and then a few moments later gone, they were pulling into a town. Then there was the endless process of the engine coupling and uncoupling rows of carriages to pull them into parallel lines along the station. 'Get your bags!' came an order from the ground. 'They like to joke, these Australians,' someone said. They stood, stretched legs, jumped down off the carriage onto the ground below, hardly anyone carrying more than a coat or hat.

Then they were back in the awful endless drudgery of two thousand men being shifted from one place to another as they were corralled into rows. Emil looked around him at the flat, rusty plains and low, tin-roofed houses, wondering where it was they planned to put them. When they were finally gathered at one end of the station, the first of the men already having moved off, they saw it, the high barbed wire of the camp beyond the town, the long, low huts, the guard towers, the barren spaces between. Behind the guards, townspeople had gathered on the platform to look at them. Emil caught the eye of a boy no more than five, hiding behind his father, a serious-faced farmer. Beside the station house, a mounted gun was pointed at the men. The platform was lined with soldiers with rifles. Some pointed them at the men, some didn't seem to have their heart in it, and their rifles hung from their shoulder straps somewhere between the ground and the soldiers' knees as their owners watched the internees shuffle by in their hundreds.

The earth all around them was flat—there was a parade ground across the tracks—the sky grey. Ahead of them the long thin straggle of emaciated men, ragged clothes hanging off their bones, marched from the station towards the camp. Emil and Solomon carried nothing. Their riches were in their pockets. Emil had a cigarette from a soldier on the train. Solomon had a toilet roll, on which he had written his shipboard diary, rolled and tucked into his loose waistband. It helped keep his trousers up.

'Cheer up,' said the soldier behind them. 'Tea's on. Mutton tonight.'

They walked silently along the dirt road, the houses and the station behind them, scratching at lice and peering into the afternoon haze at the flat red pasture all around them. There were cows—chewing on what, one could scarcely imagine. Thin sheep. You could see their ribs. Lone trees, white branches reaching out into the blue. Emil, trudging forward amid the stinking bodies, stared at the blurred line where the reddish brown scrub met the sky.

'Whatever next?' said Solomon.

Finally, they approached the high gates in the barbed wire, guarded on each side by a soldier with a fixed bayonet, hundreds of men before them filling the space between the half-built huts, hundreds still to come behind. Emil moved on without time to hesitate, pushed inside, beyond the wire.

Hannah

LIVERPOOL, 1940

Mother and I spent many nights in the cellar that September as the German bombers droned over London. In bed in the dark, when the floor trembled, I thought I was at sea. She called at my bedroom door before the air-raid siren had finished, flask of tea in one hand, torch in the other. I reached for my dressing gown on the door, and down we went, away from the house with its lamps and smells of living, and into the coal-dusty cellar stairwell. The walls were damp at the bottom, so close to the pond, and I peered at the gaps in the mortar in the light of the single hanging bulb, returned to childhood fears of drowning underground. Mother must have taken clean enamel mugs down there in the day, because they were always there on a little table ready, with magazines and a tin of fresh biscuits. There were two wicker chairs on a round rag rug, each with a blanket folded over the arm. Mother sang quietly in Welsh when the ground shook while I chewed my nails and sent up messages to the bomber pilots: Do not drop your bombs on me. I love your country, and your language, your music and your books. Some of us shall be friends again one day. Keep going, over the fields, and the sea.

Now I stood at the rail of the *Largs Bay* at Liverpool, the crowd of tiny people on the dock beneath dreary in their winter coats. The north was not the England I knew, but I took it into my body: the grey sky, the seagulls wheeling above the shipping containers, the smell of sand and salt. There was a sudden beauty in the squat red buildings and the wide port of Liverpool—it came with the nightly bombings, the threat of imminent destruction. When I left London the day before, the train running through the backs of the flats, gashes had been taken out of the streets and fires still smouldered. Until then, the rubble of the East End on the front of the *Evening Standard* was almost too much to believe.

My nail-bitten fingers gripped the cold, rough rail. My travelling companions were beside me: Jill Baum, wife of another refugee at the Hay camp, and her two children, Polly and Henry. We had only just met, peering at one another with frank unease in an awful café behind the dock, exchanging little snippets—of trepidation about the ship's food, of our mutual shock upon learning Australia was the men's destination.

We were silent at the rail, all of us, she towering at my side. As the ship let out its horn and pulled away from the dock my heart longed for land while his body drew mine across the wet rim of the world.

Barrage balloons floated above the buildings, the skyline still intact. The balloons made the world strange and fantastic, a place I did not quite know, a memory, a vision. I watched them and gripped the rail. In my mind I was a traveller, I loved always to be away, but my body was a landlubber's, easily frightened, unsteady.

We reached open waters and the wind tore through my coat and beneath my clothes. The other passengers drifted indoors and I watched the wide wake spreading at the stern, beyond it the long ships of the rear convoy, our companions until Africa, a reminder of the silent vessels beneath the grey water, surfacing at night, unseen. The line of England disappeared into the sea and the curfew sounded. We were to be inside at dusk for the blackout.

That dark ship, the juddering of the torch as I staggered towards the bathroom, slapping about for the wall. Jill had a cast-iron stomach, a flinty, unwavering humour, but her children were as mortal and queasy as I was. One night I woke, stomach turning over, eyes wide open. On the bunk opposite me Henry peered out of the darkness of his fringe, an eye glinting. His hand reached to the edge of the bunk and I was out of bed in an instant, feet knowing their way to the door. As I stepped inside the bathroom I heard him behind me, unsealing the heavy metal door of the cabin. He must wait now. I had no choice.

Those first nights at sea were wretched and long. I leaned against the wall in the foul bathroom. I thought of Mother in the cellar with her flask of tea, wondered whether she had removed the extra chair and mug now. I imagined her in the torchlight, the blanket over her knees, singing, though perhaps, I saw now, she had done that only for my benefit.

~

Our cases were packed and fastened, sitting neatly under our bunks. The night before we were to arrive in Sydney, I lay with my face to the metal wall of the cabin, listening to those who did not intend to sleep that night. There was a timbre to the calls of drunken people. Even the women released deep lowing sounds that might have come out of the jungle, monkey-like cackles.

My hand on the metal, I thought: This is what we must do today. As soon as our shoes touch Australian soil we must find some means of transport—be it bicycle, train or horse and cart—and reach the camp as soon as possible. I had a vision of a desert, with sand dunes, a barbed-wire fence and army huts at the end of a long, straight road. In the scheme of things, the wild place of my imaginings was tantalisingly close now. These last few hundred miles must be erased like the rest.

The sea rocked me to sleep as the calls on deck grew sparse and half-hearted. I did not feel that I had slept. A moment later, it seemed, an announcement on the ship's public address system was waking me again and the children were tumbling out of their beds, high-pitched and excitable, Polly wanting to find a friend she had made up on deck. Jill shushed them sharply, removing her night shades. The voice on the tannoy was the captain's; we were level with Botany Bay. I thought of convict gangs in chains in a half-made colony.

Along with the rest of the ship, we rushed up onto the deck, buttoning our clothes as we went. The children stuck with me, surging up the stairs, bobbing along with the crowd. Out onto the deck we all poured. After eight weeks at sea we were to walk on land again. I saw it through the crowd amassing at the rail: the dark forests above the cliffs. Cast myself through the thicket and beyond to the desert, to this place, Hay, where Emil was held. How did they treat Germans? Did they beat them or degrade them? I saw his body, thin and unloved. Ribs and shoulder blades, shirt hanging.

I made my way through to the rail with the children, Jill arriving beside us, hair combed and pinned, lipstick done. My arms were brown in the pink light, hair grown to my shoulders. A man lifted a pyjama-clad boy above the railing to see the distant houses clustered around the wide basin of Botany Bay, and then the long sun-bright strips of sandstone cliff and beach as we steamed north for the harbour. A refugee family nudged each other and laughed forlornly.

There was a shining white lighthouse perched high on a long finger of land, its lantern a small halo in the early sun, and then we were rounding the headland into the arms of the town, an English town, somehow, with solid houses, grassed slopes, fields. I recognised it, after the foreignness of Africa and Asia. But yet it was so far, so bright and blue and yellow and grey-green. It gleamed, Sydney, even in the dawn. The light hit water and windows and the tree trunks were pink beneath the dark foliage. And London, far behind us in another life, seemed a place of squeezed-together streets, red brick, dark roofs. The buses and hackney cabs inching through in the rain, the people huddled beneath the awnings of the markets in the squares, the whole country crouching beneath a low sky.

The crowd on deck looked quietly at its new home, wondering. The refugees, the homecomers. A pelican flew along beside us for a moment, its great wings casting a shadow that rippled over the surface of the water below. The sac under its beak was something prehistoric. Polly laughed. I stared at the valleys of bungalows, the occasional white mansion perching on the slopes above the glossy water, tried to see into the dense, shady bush, those trees with mad limbs and dripping leaves. *He has been here.*

We rounded one more of the thin promontories. A shout from the bow and a rush forward. That immense bridge, spanning the halves of the city, beyond it the water glinting amid dark tentacles of wooded land, trailing into the water. Jill said loudly, 'These colonials certainly know how to build a bridge!' A couple of Australian women eyed her for a moment, took in her moneyed glamour. Her height and figure. We slowed, nudged to the left by the little grey tug below, ground noisily past the main quay, under the incredible bridge, and around to the chaos of work and commerce of a smaller side harbour. A crowd gathered at the dock, looking as though they would fall in amid the fishing boats. The sun as we turned fell heavy on our faces. We slowed and the breeze stilled and the moisture in the air penetrated our clothes at once.

Beyond the spectators a group of men prepared for our arrival, waiting by the side of a line of open-doored trucks with their arms folded: meaty, unflappable wharfies, huge shoulders shining. I gripped the rail and breathed in the warm, steamy air above Sydney—petrol, sweet-smelling plants—burning to be down among the people and getting on with our journey. Even in my eagerness I had that sensation at the back of my neck of encountering a new city: the bustle of the seafront, the horn of the ship, the work that happens around boats and places where they meet the land. The incredible light, the deep gullies of the streets going away from the water.

A feeling rushed up in me. I wanted to lay my fingers on Emil's arm and talk to him. But these things must be put aside if I were to keep on. Instead I reminded myself: he has led the way here, prepared the ground. If he has stepped on this earth it is ready and safe.

We waited for the signal to collect our luggage. Still the gangplank was not down. Along the dock a butcher climbed into a van with a headless pig draped over his shoulder, its forelegs trailing down his back.

Then the messy, hot business of disembarkation, the filling-in of forms, the crowds about us doing the same, irritable, flustered, the children hungry. A very quietly spoken bureaucrat agreed to telephone the train station for me to ask about the train for Hay, and he murmured so quietly into the mouthpiece amid the mayhem and bustle that it seemed like a dream. Still, he was writing down numbers, and he replaced the receiver very gently as he turned the piece of paper around so that I could read it. The train would leave in the evening and arrive the following afternoon. Whatever would we do all day with our luggage, and the heat, and these fractious children? I found Jill waiting outside the gents' for Henry. 'Well, Jill,' I sighed, 'we must find some way to amuse the children until this evening. The train doesn't leave until after six.'

'You mean to go *today*?' She towered above me in that dusty hall, her hands on her hips, her thin arms triangles glued to a stick.

'Indeed I do. Surely you are not thinking of delaying? You won't sleep before you see him, you know.'

She let out a sigh, never one to conceal ill temper, a characteristic I found almost relaxing. An excess of courtesy leaves me all at sea about a person's intentions. I made myself stay still and silent for a second rather than push forward or surrender, Jill squinting over my head at the bustling dock. 'I feel sure I would sleep until Christmas, given the chance. But all right, Hannah. It's a ghastly town.'

We made arrangements to leave our cases and headed out into the tropical heat. I had never known anything like it, so wet, so heavy, as though one were deep in a rainforest, and yet the miraculous blue sky was endless. As we stepped out onto the street a couple of scruffy boys tore past us, nearly knocking Jill to the ground. Laughing, lusty little tearaways, their skin as tanned as aged wood, their heads shaved for lice, the city their garden. A passing wharfie took in a voluptuous gulp of Jill as she smoothed her dress and hair. We decided on a walk around the streets above the harbour, hoping to find a shady café. Perhaps we thought we were in Spain or Italy.

We pushed our stiff limbs, still clad in ship clothes, up towards the span of the great steel bridge, amid the sandstone buildings and palm trees, numb with exhaustion. The children skipped and laughed, whispered and ducked down side streets. My God, I thought. If you get lost, how should we ever find you? The glinting harbour flashed down an alleyway between two rows of lovely but peeling terraced houses, jacarandas bursting from the tiny gardens. Three children, then five then four, dashed in and out of a cobbled yard through a pair of wide, propped-open wooden shutters. Their mother, picking lemons, wore a loose button-through dress covered in tiny pale yellow flowers. Her hair greyed prematurely at her smooth temple. I remember her so clearly, there she is, that astonishing sky above the lemon tree, the chaos of her children doing nothing to interrupt her calm. Perhaps I remember her because the sight of her soothed me. This ordinary woman was entirely at home here, even if we were not. I felt compelled to ask her if we could buy lemonade from her, and she smiled, and her children sprang into action, while Jill whispered my name crossly at my back. The woman sat us down on an iron bench beneath what I later learned was a passionfruit vine, and the children produced lemonade in a huge tin jug. Polly and Henry hung back, staring at them from behind the meagre covering of their own mother, but guzzling the lemonade that was handed to them, their hot little faces wide-eyed and stern. The drink was sweet and fresh. My mind was crammed with colour. Oh, I thought, in spite of everything, as the cool liquid slipped down. I could live here.

We were all briefly in better moods afterwards. We wandered out into the alley, the woman having refused our money, and saw the sparkling blue of the harbour at the bottom of the hill. Fantastic birds swooped and warbled among the palm trees, frangipanis, jacarandas and eucalypts spilling over the walls of the courtyards. Could Jill really find this town ghastly? It was true that smoke belched from unseen chimneys below and gave off a bitter smell, and the harbour was rowdy with foghorns and traffic clattering over the bridge, but it was all so bright and chaotically gorgeous: a new world, far from the troubles of Europe on the face of things. The light as the day swelled into itself, filled its sails. And these people, working people, living among this loveliness.

Whatever Jill might say, she and the children were as curious as I was. That first day in Australia, we could not stop moving, after our months at sea. We walked, and walked, and even indulged the children with a tram ride. Afterwards, they jumped back down onto the hot road; it was the first time I had seen them laugh in weeks. We peered carefully at everything, under this incredible light. You could almost imagine released convicts living in the sandstone cottages, but then on Pitt Street the lunchtime crowd of office workers, stepping on and off the trams and into their offices, were smart and modern, especially the women. They looked quite American, with tilted hats and long sharply cut skirts. The men dressed exactly alike; suit trousers and no jacket, white shirt open at the collar, dark hat, many smoking, pushing steadily towards their destination. There was constant movement about us but no hurry.

We turned a corner and all was quiet, the streets wide and empty, a lone slow elderly lady hauling shopping baskets over a crossroads in such a stretched-out instant that it seemed one had to be part of a different order of time to see her move, like watching a sunflower open in the morning or turn its head in a field with a thousand others through the day. We stopped at the corner for a moment, deciding where to head next, and as we did I experienced one of those alterations in sense that one has with little sleep in a new place—just as I felt when I stepped out of the station in a new city: Cologne, Stockholm, Lyon—where the world was a performance playing out in front of me against a painted set. The sandstone offices and the town hall, the stray figures on the street, etched in light and shade, delivering some meaning that I could not grasp, forcing me against myself, to be still, to wait, and then we were off again, the streetscape moving by, and I at last felt dizzy with tiredness and hunger.

Somehow, eventually, we had passed our first day on Australian soil. Finally, we collapsed into a taxi, collected our cases and made our way to the train station. Hauling my luggage up onto the train, the sky at last losing its blinding colour, I gazed out at the fan of train tracks, the long shelters, the sober faces on the platforms. I had the strength left only to notice that there was still salt on my lips, as though I stood at the prow of the *Largs Bay*, spray wetting my face. It took a moment to realise that it was not sea water but the salt of my own skin, gathered there from my first day in the Australian heat.

~

On the reddish-brown horizon, a road shimmering into eternity, there appeared a line of trees like a city skyline, how one imagined New York or Chicago, such a vision incompatible with this wild place. We passed farm buildings, ancient and mysterious open rusting barns with roofs set upon iron poles so that, beyond the silhouette of farming machinery, one could see yet more of the red plain. Then we were passing a tiny town and its single broad baking street, awnings covering shade that would swallow you whole. A couple of sombre men in dark hats emerged from the shade, slowly crossing the road as though to the reading of a will. A farm lorry passed by after them, children on the back waving from the flatbed, a dog barking, dust flying. They were all freckles and pale red hair. I thought of Steinbeck novels and bone-crushing poverty, though the children were plump and laughing, as well-fed and lively as any I had seen.

I leaned back against the hot seat and closed my eyes. My coolest memory drank me up: the plunge into the millrace on the morning he went away. I dwelled for as long as possible in the cool water, his arm across my back, the warmth of our bodies where they pressed against one another. I was drawing ever closer to his face, his body, his strong square hands.

There was yet more though of the plains, the vast upside-down bowl of the sky. And then we came at last past the town with its silver rod of briefly metalled road, the dreary grid of clapboard houses on short stilts, whole dusty blocks of empty lots.

We eased our stiff bodies out of the train and onto the platform. Beyond the station, out where the road disintegrated to red earth once more, at the hazy, liquid edge of vision, high guard towers loomed. A barrier fell like a guillotine between the road and the buildings: a wall of barbed wire. We stopped where we were on the empty platform. 'That's it, isn't it?' Jill said quietly.

For once I could not speak.

Jill and the children, a mother and her ducks, made for the cool gloom of the waiting room. She was asking the stationmaster about a hotel. I interrupted her. 'What are you doing?' I said. I would have shouted it, but for the children.

'Finding a bed, and then lying down on it.'

'But, Jill, they're right there! We could walk it in minutes. We have come so far.'

'Hannah dear, you should see yourself.'

'Good grief! Who on earth cares? After all this time, we are *here*.' I took a breath. I was close to tears with tiredness and confusion. 'But of course—the children. You're right. We'll get settled first.'

The stationmaster made a telephone call and a few minutes later a van came down the desolate street and threw up dust outside the station. The proprietor of the Commercial Hotel drove us into town, and I tried not to look behind me at the guard towers above the roofs.

Jill was conciliatory in the room. 'You may use the bathroom first, Hannah. We shall take all day.'

I stood in the bath letting brown water pummel my shoulders from a wide metal showerhead, grinding my teeth. Startling, that my body could do this ugly thing of its own volition. As I turned off the shower I heard from the next room the insistent rhythmic squeak of the children jumping on the bed, mad with freedom and sugar, having bolted down a powdery-looking chocolate bar thrust on them by the landlord's wife.

My skin was shining in the heat before I had even left the bathroom. One might as well not bother bathing. No matter, I thought. If Jill still does not consider herself presentable I shall walk across town. If I arrive wearing a coating of dust so be it.

Emil

HAY, 1940

Emil sat at the small desk he had made from milk crates beneath the window of the hut, which blasted heat like the open door of a bread oven. The window gave on to a square of corrugated tin, the wall of the hut next door. He was filling in yet another form. They had, it seemed, found a category for men like him, unionists and social democrats, those known to have opposed the Nazis. It was an agony, all these forms—for compensation for their things, of qualifications and experience that might be put to use—with nothing ever to show for it but a stone-cold bureaucratic silence. Hopes raised, hopes dashed. And the talk all the time of what might be possible, rumours that sprang up in the camp like the willy-willies in the dust, whipping around the place, stirring everything up. He couldn't bear it. He went for walks around the perimeter, scratching his ankles in the scrub, hearing the sounds of the town as he put some distance between himself and the huts: church bells, the daily train. Every now and then the breeze brought him schoolchildren in a yard somewhere amid the houses near the station, the gentle clamour of them speaking all at once. He could not walk for long. The journey had weakened his leg and his chest.

He had taken to seeking out a game of chess in a dormitory hut or in the mess. It was understood you did not talk while your opponent was thinking. He had become much better at chess than he ever had been before. Solomon would no longer play him, preferring the odds with the younger men, whom Emil tried to avoid. They could not hold more than a move or two at a time in their heads for dreaming about girls, sporting triumphs and escape to the British army. At night they talked of Mother's *pfeffernüsse*, a childhood dive into the Danube, the smell of German trains. 'You are too young to be this nostalgic,' he told them. Really, he just wanted them to stop, to let him be quiet, and save themselves the disturbance of those hours and hours of wanting.

His pencil hovered above the form. His father's voice came to him, as clearly as if he stood behind him in the hut: *One foot after the other, Emil. That's the only way to get where you are going.* Yes, he thought, what else is there to be done? He wrote down what he could, tried to find the English in his memory for the names: brown shirts, rallies, secret police, murder. He had written these things before, exposed himself to the bureaucracy, put down the words assigned the job of describing what was perpetrated, what was lost. He could do it quickly and then think of other matters, like the chess game he had left in train last night at curfew. He wrote what he needed to write: *SA and SS occupied the building and beat and shot the union secretaries.* Wrote quickly, and did not think. Signed the thing, walked it over to the administration block, the men crammed into the strips of shade along the sides of the huts, smoking, arguing about Hegel, betting camp currency on a game of cards.

When he returned to the hut, hoping to sleep away the hottest hours while the others were driven out from beneath the tin roofs, he found Solomon lying on his palliasse, next to Emil's, hands behind his head, gazing up at a pair of lizards scurrying across the ceiling.

'Not too hot for you in here?'

'Thinking cool thoughts, Emil. I am remembering the Wannsee frozen over and a girl I used to take skating. Her scarf used to fly out behind her very fetchingly. I think she knew it too. I could never get her off the ice once she started.'

'I filled out the form.'

Solomon turned on his side, leaning on his elbow. 'Good for you. Perhaps you'll be back in time to see some snow.'

'I try not to get my hopes up, but you know how it is.'

'Well, you do have some very useful friends. They'll put in a word for you.'

He lay down on his own bed and felt the sweat begin immediately between his body and the woollen blanket. 'Tell me again about these cool thoughts.'

'When you fell over on the ice, you didn't feel it at first, as you skated about, keeping warm. But then walking home your trousers would be wet and cold against your leg, and you felt your skin was beginning to freeze.'

'Then, when you thawed yourself out, your feet ached,' Emil added.

'What I wouldn't give now for chilblains.'

Emil closed his eyes. After helping to build the hydro-electric station in Ireland he had been sent to Finland to supervise the construction of a water power plant to run sawmills and plywood and pulp factories. Before they could begin they had to transport the pieces of the vast machines across thirty miles of ice and snow without cranes or snow trucks. He had sat in the freezing hut at the port drawing sketches of sledges, floats and hoists in the dim light of early afternoon. Then every day for a month he and the men stood out on the dock in the dark mornings sawing and hammering until they were ready. They sent for the dogs and the drivers and carted the pieces of machinery across the white country to the pine forests, the air freezing his beard. The dogs barked at first, ready to run. They moved off and there was nothing, just the sound of the snow beneath the treads, a black smudge of trees coming into view in the midst of the snowy land and sky.

He was amazed to find that it worked. For a moment before he slept he felt cold, reached for his blanket to pull it up, felt droplets of ice in his beard, a stinging wind slice into his slitted eyes. Then he slept and saw the dogs squabbling over fish, growling in their throats, jumping straight into the air, barking madly.

~

After dinner, a fine lamb stew from the internee-run camp kitchen, one of the diggers caught his eye across the mess, held a piece of paper in the air. 'Telegram,' he mouthed, an encouraging look on his face. The men at his table watched him as he read it. Meckel, opposite, one of those who never seemed to have absorbed the concept of privacy, stared at the piece of paper with open-mouthed lust.

'Good news?' Solomon asked above the scraping of plates with hungry spoons, the din of insects.

'It's my release. The tribunal accepted me onto their list.'

'And yet you are still here among us,' Meckel leered.

Emil looked at his face, a little slipped on one side. 'Yes, Meckel. Still here with you.'

'Will they return you to England?' Solomon said.

'It says I'm free to apply for a transport.'

Solomon laid a hand on his shoulder. 'My God, that's wonderful news. You must get word to Hannah.'

Emil nodded, looking at the telegram, saw himself in her mother's garden, throwing a stone at her window like a boy.

All around them chairs were scraping, and the men, having got their morsel of news, were sighing and picking up plates to take to the kitchen.

'Come, Emil,' Solomon said. 'Let's go and blow our wages on a Viennese coffee. We'll hunt down Schiff. I hear he has cigars.'

'I can't help thinking, I asked her to follow me.'

'But you have had no word that she has.'

'I have had no word of anything.'

'But haven't you said it all along? They would never have let her near a ship with all those U-boats infesting the waters.'

'Of course. I become too used to gloomy thoughts.'

When the others were asleep, or at least lying still, existing inside themselves as they had learned to do, he slipped out of the hut and went over to the parade ground. The floodlights shone over the camp. He raised a hand to his friend O'Mara in the guard tower. Not a bad chess player, for a beginner. The digger raised a hand in return. All right, he told himself. I will go back to England. We'll forget this stupidity. I will work in a munitions factory. Make the bombs they need.

He imagined his body into an office above a factory floor, the great riveted cylinders of bombs suspended before him. They will see me, how I make them work, and think of the thousands of us, German engineers above factory floors all over Germany. It will be all they need to build their bombs as hard and fast as their minds and fingers can go.

Hannah

In the end, I waited for Jill. It was just too fiercely hot to walk across town, and she had arranged to borrow the proprietor's van. The children strained away from their mother on the verandah as she tugged at Polly's hem to straighten it and passed a licked finger over Henry's fringe, sorely in need of a trim. I feared for Polly's white dress in the dust. Henry scratched his leg beneath his woollen shorts. Their faces were bright with scrubbing, mine I imagine dark and murderous with the wait. Finally, we reinterred ourselves in the stifling heat of the van and drove the five minutes out beyond the back blocks towards the guard towers, drawing quickly closer to the high rows of barbed wire, the long rows of military huts. Dark figures moved among them, shadows long in the late afternoon sun. Jill looked ghastly for once, absolutely sick beneath her powder and lipstick.

As we approached the high wire gates of the compound a soldier with a rifle slung across his shoulder emerged from the small wooden building on stilts that presided over the road. Here was a famous Australian digger in the road before us. We in England had always been enamoured of the pictures of them in Turkey and North Africa with their suntanned skin and slouch hats. They seemed to be of a larger, more physically able race than we Europeans, somehow. I wondered if this one here, not quite what I had previously imagined, with his ruddy cheeks and paunch, knew Emil, was decent to him. I sprang out of the car, feeling Jill's consternation at my back as she bundled the children out. 'Sir,' I shouted as the man stared and I arrived at his shadow. 'We have come all the way from England to see our men. Please, we must be allowed to visit.'

It took a long time for him to speak. These people were rich with time, they were dripping with it. He considered at unendurable length what manner of object had fetched up before him. 'Visits have to be arranged in advance, ma'am. Camp rules.'

'We arrived in Sydney yesterday after eight weeks at sea. We have since travelled overnight on the train with small children. How long would you have us wait?'

Again, the pause, the endless bovine consideration. He leaned his gun against the doorway and scratched his stomach. 'Take your names now. Come back in the morning.'

'Pah!'

I heard Polly whisper a long 'Oooh' and then Jill spoke from behind me. There was something in her hand, which she offered up to the soldier. 'Here,' she said. 'Take your young lady out somewhere nice.'

He looked at her hand now, as did I. There was a pound note rolled up in it. 'This is the *Australian army*, love.' He drew out his words, as though we were foreigners. 'We don't take backhanders. Now what's your name? We'll find your men. Bring 'em at eleven tomorrow. And we'll pretend I didn't see the other thing.'

We sheepishly gave him our names, and those of the men, and climbed back into the hot car in silence. After the short drive back to the hotel, Jill announced that she would lie down before dinner while the children had ice creams. I could not face the thought of trying to sleep myself, Emil so close, and told Jill that I would explore the town, though I held out little hope for places of interest.

I walked away from the high street towards the shimmering plains beyond the river, tiny cows and black trees blurring in the haze. The space here was like nothing I'd experienced. The sky seemed infinite. The heat blasted off the earth, late as it was in the day, a rush of it up my legs. My hair clung to my neck.

As I traipsed forlornly back along the main street towards the hotel I noticed a fairly grand old building with its door ajar. I thought I would step out of the sun for a moment and so I pulled back the large creaking door and found myself in a dusty, cavernous room with only small, high windows casting squares of light on the wooden floor. I could see no inhabitants but the relief of shade was so intense I was not willing to leave straightaway. Along the opposite wall I saw in the gloom a few low shelves of books. I wandered over to them and found a selection of school readers, bibles, trade manuals and some novels: Dickens, Austen, Hardy. I was surprised to find some books about Hitler and the European situation among the others.

I picked one up to leaf through it, wondering vaguely what it might make of things from this distance, but then I saw that in any case it was printed in London. I did not take in many of the words on the page before me, only the strangeness of standing still, of letting time pass, my shoes planted on wooden boards an inch or two above the solid, dry earth, which I could smell, continually. I realised then that there were voices, women's voices, conversing gently within the walls of this dour, dark building. But of course they were not within the walls, the women. The slightly echoing timbre suggested to me that they were in a kitchen somewhere. The past opened up in my head and I thought for a moment that if I could open a hatch into that kitchen I would see Mother at the bench making tea.

I waited, eyes smarting, for the owners of the voices to appear and eject me into the furnace of the day. They went on, murmuring, and I studied the book intently—the descriptions of the SS and the brown shirts flooding the towns, the talk of the brainwashing of the ordinary German people—and began to feel as though I were teetering on some slippery ledge.

I coughed at last and the voices ceased suddenly. Polite, quick footsteps on tiles, more than one pair of feet. Then I saw from the corner of my eye that they were emerging from a door that I had not noticed at the far end of the long hall. Two women in loose floral-print dresses. Deeply tanned faces and arms, the creases at their elbows white inside. Tall women, one stick thin with strong shoulders, the other doughy and pretty in a well-worn, motherly way. I forced myself to look up as they approached. It seemed that I was swaying, that they were walking the length of a ballroom on a ship towards me, that they had their sea legs and I did not.

'Hello, miss?' said the thin woman. Her friend smiled, an open-hearted smile without reserve. 'Can we help you with something?'

'Well,' I began, my English accent seeming overdone suddenly, 'I wanted to step out of the sun for a moment. And then I became interested in your library.'

'Library!' The larger one laughed. 'Well I doubt it's been called that before. Are you staying at the hotel?'

I nodded, catching my voice. 'My fiancé is in the camp. I have not been allowed to see him yet.'

'Oh, Mrs Stuart, he's one of those poor souls.'

Mrs Stuart eyed me seriously. 'When did your ship arrive, dear?'

'Yesterday,' I said. The vastness of my journey seemed to yawn at the heel of my shoes. 'Could I trouble you for a glass of water?' The one who was not Mrs Stuart disappeared through the door from which she had emerged at speed.

Mrs Stuart leaned down towards me. 'They're good people at the hotel but you'll run up a shocking bill.'

There are people who seem to intuit your deepest worries at a glance. I had reached the end of my journey with my pockets all but empty, had been skipping meals wherever possible, counting my pennies while Jill was busy with the children. Now I feared that my stomach would rumble and expose me.

'If you like, you may stay with me. I run the store in town, and my boys are in Africa. You can have their room.'

'Oh, no. We have only just met and here you are rearranging your home for me.'

'It's not much, dear, but you're welcome.' She did not smile. I found later that her smiles were rare bursts of sunshine breaking through the clouds of a serious existence, her husband long dead, the business of the store and of worrying about her sons, away in Egypt, hers alone to manage.

I accepted her offer, leaving Jill a note at the hotel for when she woke, thanking her for everything and asking her whether she would mind coming to fetch me in the morning for the drive to the camp. She was a wealthy woman, in spite of the circumstances, and I was not concerned about her shouldering the bill alone. I insisted Mrs Stuart must not take the trouble to clear out the boys' room, which was filled with boxes and baffling bits of machinery. So she and Mrs Kelly, her friend, made me up a bed in the sleep-out, Mrs Kelly fussing over my decision to sleep 'in the wilds'. 'But this is perfect!' I said and meant it. For all my travelling, sleeping on a verandah with only an insect screen between myself and the elements was something quite new.

That night, I lay on a comfortable ticking mattress, between freshly laundered sheets that gave up a eucalyptus smell as I sank into them. Stars were visible through the insect meshing and the crickets emitted their astonishing synchronised thrumming. On one side of us was the ugly red Anglican church and in front were the empty blocks stretching towards the camp and the plains. The land was lit by an eerie glow from the floodlights at the camp and so Mrs Stuart had pegged a sheet across the wire mesh for me to pull across when I wanted to sleep.

I lay in serendipitous luxury, wondering if the soldiers had, truly, told him I was here. I allowed myself to believe it, that he was awake in his bed among the beds of the other men, a mile left of the twelve thousand, thinking of me.

~

I slept more soundly that night than I expected to after my months of sharing confined spaces with Jill and her snuffling children. My body enjoyed the luxury of being alone, even as I slept. I woke on the long verandah to a cacophony of excitable birds. The racket of the creatures here was fantastic. I pulled back the curtain and lay back in bed, took in the pale blue dawn, the pepper trees in the yard, the shape of Mrs Stuart's mangy black dog lying next to the outhouse. Let the certainty fill and warm me that this morning, in a very few hours' time, that my hand, this one here, would touch Emil's. I allowed myself one short moment to marvel at myself, that I had accomplished this feat of following him to Australia.

I smelled bacon cooking while I washed at the outhouse sink alongside the house, made barely private by a corrugated tin wall that did not reach to the ground, and wondered how Mrs Stuart remained so thin. Dinner the night before had been immense, and followed by cake. My journey had hollowed me out beneath my ribs, skimmed off the softness of my limbs, but Mrs Stuart's cooking would soon put paid to that.

After washing I ventured into the kitchen, well slept, briefly cool and clean, tidy and contained. My host was serving up a stack of bacon, eggs, mushrooms, tomatoes and potatoes left over from dinner the night before at the enormous table. Her kitchen was on a larger scale than any you would see in England, and was furnished with all sorts of delightful curiosities, like wooden cupboards with mesh sides for keeping meat from the flies and an enamel teapot large enough for at least ten visitors. All the benches in this kitchen for giants appeared to have been fitted to suit her impressive height. As she served up breakfast on an enormous dinner plate I felt like a small pampered child, my feet swinging above the floor beneath my chair.

Afterwards, I attempted to help her with the dishes, to fill the time, but she would have none of it. The set of her shoulders at the sink warned me against insisting. Soon she had to open the store, which was at the other end of her lot, facing the high street. She let me sit on the high stool behind the counter while she measured out flour expertly into ten-pound bags and filled sweet jars. It was like being allowed to sit behind Father's counter again.

I laid my notebook on the smooth old wooden counter and tried to record something of what I had witnessed since setting foot on Australian soil two days before. Everything I grasped and pinned to the page represented a dozen more astonishments I could not contain. Every few minutes I checked the large clock above my head. I see in the notebook that my handwriting was even more of a scrawl than usual. It does not matter; I remember. I close my eyes and there is

Mrs Stuart, bending over the flour sack with her metal scoop while past the open door of the store go the girls in their striped dresses and the boys in their shorts to the primary school. There is a girl with dark plaits who reads as she walks. I watch her disappear into the brightness of the street.

Finally, the horn of a car sounded from the street outside. I heard the children's voices calling cheerfully: 'Miss Jacob! Miss Jacob!' and smiled. 'We've got a motorcar!' It seemed Jill had come to some arrangement with the proprietor about another of his vehicles.

'They miss you already!' called Jill from the car. I can't imagine it was true, but she did her best with me.

Mrs Stuart opened the door and clasped my hand in her long, bony fingers. 'Good luck,' she whispered, but in the next moment I was leaping off the verandah without time for reflection into the blinding light of the morning, down to the car, yanking open the heavy door.

Jill laughed. 'Got a sweet old duck to take you in, then? You're a marvel, Hannah.' She looked better for sleep, her old glamorous self, and I felt encouraged too for seeing her restored so. The children were playing a game in the back where one jumped up as the other sank down and vice versa. They had managed to become proficient at it, like circus performers. Jill and I peered up at the guard tower beyond the last house. 'What shall we find here, do you think?' she said quietly as she pulled up the handbrake.

We sat for a moment, contemplating the prospect, now that we were here at last.

Our friend from the previous afternoon emerged from his hut at the sound of our doors slamming and scuffed across the dusty road. The day blazed with heat and the cicadas were deafening as he approached. This time he smiled, and greeted us by name. He made a show of checking his watch. 'On the dot, ladies. Leave the car here and follow me. Don't worry. Bill will keep an eye on it.' He gestured behind him to a man up in the guard tower, who waved at us. The children waved back, smiling.

Our soldier let us inside the fences through two gates and we followed him along a path amid forlorn gardens tended by a young, tragically thin Jewish boy, who looked at the children as they passed with large sad eyes. I thought I heard a cello, and dismissed it as heat-induced imagining until Henry said, 'Mummy, there's music.'

'Heavens,' she said, 'so there is,' and smiled at him.

'That's the Hay–Berlin Chamber Orchestra practising,' said the soldier. 'Lucky to have them.'

We came to a one-roomed building, identical to the sentry office, where the soldier stopped. Beyond it was the inner cluster of huts where the men lived. 'Come and wait in here please, everybody. They won't be long.'

I led the way into the heat of a long room, divided across the centre widthways by a wall of chicken wire. I stared at it. They could not mean to keep us apart with this thing. Close on my heels were Jill and the children. 'You have got to be joking,' Jill whispered. Sweat streamed from my forehead; the tin roof made the place like an oven. We sat down on two benches that faced the wire, the little family on one and me on the second, edging away from each other in readiness. Even so, we were a mere few yards apart, and would be witness to every word of the other's reunion.

In came our digger and stood at the door, his bayonet fixed. For a moment I wanted to laugh. But then, above the faint clatter of tin plates, soldiers shouting orders, the chamber orchestra, footsteps sounded, close in the dirt, and the door at the other end of the hut was opening, letting the sounds in, and he was first to enter, followed by the man I assumed to be Mr Paul Baum. Then there was their own mirror image of our soldier, who closed their door and guarded it with his own bayonet. All this I noted in a fraction of a second; it was such a small space, across which Emil was walking, sitting down opposite me, and I could not breathe or speak. I knew his walk, the dark shape of him, through the mesh that separated us. For a moment the room was absolutely silent but for the muted sounds outside and a fly that had come in with the men.

I stared at him, taking in what I could through the blur of the wire. He did not smile. He was so thin, even in the face, and his hair had greyed shockingly with a new white streak at the temple. I put a hand to the wire. He did the same. I felt pressure, not skin. 'Is that Daddy?' Henry said from their side of the room. I stared at Emil. Elation warred with shock beneath my ribs.

'Emil,' I whispered. 'What has happened to you? Are you ill?'

'Not now. On the ship.' His voice was hoarse. I wondered whether he was sleeping.

'How do they treat you?'

'Well, here. The ship, the British, not so good.'

We were silent for a moment. I looked at his eyes, dark holes, indistinct beyond the mesh. I was looking for a message, the story of everything that had happened to him. Paul sang quietly for the children with the distant orchestra. Suddenly, Emil smiled and in his face the man I had known leaped to life, though I saw, my stomach falling away, that there was a new dark gap amid the lower row of his teeth. 'I cannot believe you are here. In Australia! My own little Hannah. It is a miracle.' His smile disappeared again.

'When can I see you?' I glanced at the soldier who guarded Emil's door. His eyes were concealed beneath the deep brim of his hat. 'Not like this—properly?'

Emil shrugged and looked down at his hands, clasped together between his knees. I could see from the way his clothes hung from his gaunt shape, even through the chicken wire, that he had lost a frightening amount of weight. There was so little of him. Something rose in my chest. I felt an urge to hunt down someone in authority and call for an immediate improvement to conditions. I glanced at Mr Baum. He was of reasonable weight. Why was Emil so dreadfully thin?

'Are you eating?'

'Not much. The food is good though. We have great chefs. Really, you would not believe the things to come out of that kitchen. But I have not recovered from the boat very well.'

I switched to German. Paul would understand, if he was listening, but at least Jill and the children would not. 'I want to touch your skin,' I said quietly, looking into his eyes, the dark shape of them. The guard behind Emil looked up sharply as soon as I spoke in this other language. 'I want to be with you privately.'

'Hannah, Hannah. Keep your wishes small.'

'No, there must be a way. Things can always be arranged.' I lowered my voice, in spite of my German. 'Do they take bribes? Jill tried yesterday but perhaps she did not do it right. Or perhaps she asked the wrong one.'

'I don't think so. Some have tried. Sometimes they'll get you things but mostly not. In any case, have you suddenly become rich since I saw you last?' I laughed grimly and shook my head. 'Then it's more important to worry about how you will live. I'll be fed every day for as long as this goes on. And you are thin. But listen, I must tell you something—I don't know what it means for us. Everything is confusing.' He shook his head. 'I cannot believe that you are here.'

Then I spoke in a rush, in English now, speaking over Paul's singing, Jill's whispers, as though I knew I needed to prevent him saying what he would say next. 'There is a kind woman who owns the store in the town. She has said that I can stay. I will try to pay her for food later, but of course I cannot earn a living here. I have been making notes on everything, my impressions. I thought just at first I might try and offer a piece to the newspapers in Sydney and Melbourne. I know it is a flimsy chance but it is all I have at the moment. I cannot imagine there is much call for translation from French or German at this end of the world.'

He answered in English. 'Oh, good. Good, Hannah. There are refugees here who wrote for the press before they were interned, about the European situation. It's difficult for the papers to get hold of people who know. You are an expert! But soon you must go to a city. You'll suffer out here. It's the end of the earth.' His voice was faint with speaking this much. 'But listen, I've received an official release.'

I found myself on my feet. I gave out a laugh. From the corner of my eye I saw Emil's guard tilt his head back to look at me. 'Whatever do you mean? Then why are you still here?'

'They will only release me to put me on a ship to England.'

I sat slowly. 'What?'

'The Australians will not release me here.'

'Do you mean to say that if I had stayed at home, you would have returned?'

'Hannah, I am so sorry.' He put his hand up to the wire. 'It is astonishing that you came. We will discover what to do. At the least we know, it is a mistake. They have admitted it. Perhaps they will return you too.'

'But I came to be with you. I spent my last penny to come. My union friends, they said you would at some point be released here, with your qualifications. I came all this way to help you. I cannot afford to return.' My voice had risen. I felt a little shift in the room.

The children looked at me. I caught Paul's eye and he looked down quickly. The guard behind Emil looked at his watch and the man behind me shifted his weight on his heels—I felt it through the boards under my feet.

Emil glanced at him for a moment. 'Listen,' he said, leaning forward. 'Find out what you can from the Home Office. Tell them I am an engineer. I can do war work, here or in England. That is what I want to do. To work and to be with you. Will you tell them? Tell them we will do what they say, so long as we can be together. Yes?'

I nodded and felt a sudden hot breeze as our guard opened his door at the same time as his colleague. 'Come on now,' said our man. 'That's it till next week, ladies. The men've got exercise now. Got to keep 'em strong now, hey?'

I felt something jab my hand through the wire. I glanced down—it was a little roll of paper, which I concealed quickly in my palm—then back at Emil. Polly was whining: 'Daddy, another song, please!' and Emil was already gone, the first out the door. Paul, smiling shyly at Jill, and briefly, apologetically at me, followed him.

'Wait just a moment, ladies. Let them go.'

I stood from the bench, staring at the closed door through which he had come and so quickly left. I had never been in such a hot, close room. All of a sudden I could smell bodies: sweaty children, the unwashed hair of the men, carbolic soap. I felt that I could *hear* the heat coming down through the tin roof. Blasts of it, like the sound of my blood surging through my veins as my ear hit the pillow at night.

We were all silent in the car, even, for once, the children. I unscrolled the little roll of paper. It read, in tiny letters: 'I will never again board a ship without you.'

Emil

Even on the river a layer of red dust had settled like a volcanic crust. The men did not care. They knew the water was beneath and that it would be cool and lovely, and they jumped in from high on the banks, calling like birds in the instant before immersion. In seconds the thirty or so men were in the water, paddling and splashing like an outing of schoolchildren.

The previous day they had spent inside the hut, cramming paper in the cracks around the windows, venturing across to the mess with handkerchiefs over their mouths, while the top inch of every paddock for a hundred miles to the west blew across them towards the sea. The sky was red like hell and they sniped at one another in ways no one was proud of, then or afterwards. Two boys stumbled down the hut steps for a fight in the yard and they all went out to watch and shout. Emil saw their shapes clutch one another amid the red cloud and roared until his lungs were tight and dry.

'I'm told they're sending someone to deal with us, case by case,' Solomon said, stretched out on the steep bank in his underwear, brown rivulets streaking his skin as though it were a map of topographical features.

Above them on the bank a digger dozed against a tree, hat tipped over one eye, rifle leaning against the trunk behind him. He was one of those who would not train a gun on the men unless he was at that particular moment observed by a superior officer.

'I try not to listen to these rumours.' Emil was shaving the gluey dust from his calves with a sharp-edged blade of grass.

'Some of the men know him. A Jew. Major Temple. They think he will be sympathetic.'

'He will have no particular reason to be sympathetic to me.'

'But you have Hannah in your corner.'

Emil nodded. Smiled in the shifting shade of the tired old gums. 'I do. This Temple would turn his ship about if he only knew.'

~

That night Emil did not know whether he was hot or very cold. Solomon whispered from his bed, 'You're shivering.'

'Is it cold tonight?'

The moon fell on Solomon's face, casting his cheeks and neck into deep shadow. His bristles made the bottom half of his face black. 'No. Do you want me to get the doctor?'

'I'll sleep it off.'

'Emil, it strikes me that you could return to England, that your Hannah is resourceful enough to follow in her own time.'

'Boats go down every day. We cannot go separately. I will wait.'

~

He dreamed, but he did not only dream. He found himself outside, his cheek against gravel and dust, vest sticking to his skin. I am not in my bed, he told himself, opening his eyes. Bright light from the towers blinded him and he closed them again. *I am out in the night.* He could see the station, where they had come in, beyond the guard towers and the fence. He was panting. *I ran, through woods. I swam through water.* He bent his knees and brought them under himself, rose slowly to his feet. *I am ill. I must walk carefully.*

A man appeared in front of him, a soldier. He knew the uniform. They were kind but they had not always been. There was something else inside them, the men who looked like this. The man took his elbow. 'Becker, hey? Infirmary for you, I reckon.'

He shuffled along, allowed himself to be led, assisted. He could not fathom whether he was a prisoner or a convalescent. In any case he must preserve himself, he must place one foot in front of the other, until his vision cleared.

Hannah

I felt like a tiny, hapless figure whipped by biblical fury during those weeks in Hay. Dust storms were followed by floods, in which the town and the camp became gelatinous with wet, reddish clay. Shrimps, eggs dormant for years, were animated with the sudden deluge and the river and its tributaries were suddenly filled with the little creatures.

Jill moved the children to Melbourne. My last image of them as I stood on the bright street after they waved goodbye: the three of them turning away, holding hands, bent-headed, their necks pale strips of skin exposed to the sun, disappearing into the shade beneath the upstairs verandah of the hotel. Apart from missing them more than I had thought I would, I had now to walk out to the camp pouring with sweat or drenched by a downpour for the single visit I was permitted per week. I vented my frustration in letters to MPs here and at home and attempted to write calmer letters to Mother, about the flowers and the food. To my brothers I made light of my fate, and my own efforts. Geoffrey was we knew not where, because he was not allowed to say, while Benjamin was preparing fighter pilots to face the appalling odds of aerial warfare, and so I just about found the decorum not to wail endlessly of my misfortune.

Christmas drew near and the strangeness of heat and isolation grew with such events as the Griffith truck's delivery of pine trees to the store along with boxes of decorations. One morning the mail delivery came a little earlier than usual. I was sitting on the stool behind the counter and about fell off when I saw my name on the envelope. Here at last, I imagined, was word from one of my MPs informing me he was to take on our case personally, having been outraged by our treatment. It was in fact from the editor of the *Age* in Melbourne, with the news that he would be printing my impressions of Australia. He enclosed a cheque for a pound and three shillings, appearing to be thrilled by my European experience, and invited me to send more work. I sat on the high stool behind Mrs Stuart's counter in the general store and my body vibrated with the fulfilment of an old longing. I thought immediately of my father, who had wanted us all to be writers. At that moment Mrs Stuart entered the store from the house. 'Are you all right, dear?'

'Yes, yes, yes! I have some money for you. I have been paid for a piece. It is to be printed!'

Mrs Stuart was silent for a moment, looking out to the blinding street. 'I don't expect payment, Miss Jacob. Your bed doesn't cost me anything, and you eat like a bird. Save your money. No doubt you'll need it soon enough.'

I could not look at her. I wished I had the means to refuse her kindness. I am afraid at that moment I could not even open my mouth to say thank you.

I wrote a few more pieces for the *Age*: one on what it was like to live in London amid the Battle of Britain, another on the crossing, and one on the life of Hay, a town which had doubled its population overnight with the arrival of two thousand Germans and Austrians and where the locals had to accustom themselves to the towers and floodlights and parades of refugees on their way through town on working parties and excursions to the river. On Saturday nights the townspeople gathered in the street at the front of the store to gossip and I listened to them from the sleep-out at the back, quite unashamedly quoting them in my story.

Just before Christmas, I walked to the camp, my feet for once reluctant and slow. I had forgotten my hat and the sun glared through the clouds. I would be bright red by the time I arrived, but he had seen me in every state now from sodden to wilting. It would have been crueller to arrive with hair just combed and clothes beautifully pressed, while he sat there in his mismatched clothes, hair greying by the moment.

They brought him out and there seemed a difference in him. He moved easily, gracefully again. He smiled as he sat down. Still I felt that urge to touch him that made me want to scream, that I had to press down in order to speak, to make the most of our few minutes. At least now Jill had gone it was just us and the soldiers. I had learned not to care what they heard, or at least to speak in German when I did. 'You look well,' I said.

'Really? Well, I feel not so bad. The food is making me fat. But you look anxious. What's the matter?'

And I was saying it, without having known that it was what I planned. 'I think that I must after all go to Melbourne. I must find reliable work.' I could not look at him.

He sighed. 'That's good news. This place does not suit you.'

'Oh, but I feel dreadful. It seems terrible to think of leaving you. I thought with Mrs Stuart's help I might stay until they released you.'

'They feed me. I don't need money. I have conversation and chess and a job in the workshop. This could take years. How long does a war last? You cannot wait in this town.'

'I'll come back, as soon as I can afford it.'

'Don't, Hannah. Not out here.'

I was close to tears, though I had disciplined myself to save them for my sleep-out and the cover of night. 'You're giving up, aren't you? That's why you seem different. I'll get an answer soon from my MPs. In Melbourne I'll be able to go and see people, to make our case in person.'

'You need to work. Life is simple for me when I keep calm and quiet. The days pass so slowly, waiting for your visits. The others, they make quiet lives in here.'

'You want to forget about me. It's easier for you.'

'No. No, Hannah.'

The guard behind Emil, whom I had not seen before, was looking at me. They were about to eject me. I knew the signs. He looked away. I put my hand to the mesh, our signal, and felt the paper push against it. 'I will reclaim our lives—you will see,' I whispered as the doors opened. He shook his head and stood. I left quickly with my guard.

At the gate I had to unclench my fist so that the note did not disintegrate in my hot hand. There was a very tall Aboriginal guard who saw me out. He said nothing but from his pocket he drew forth a beautiful peach and handed it to me wordlessly, holding my eye from a full foot and a half above, giving a little nod. Of all the kindnesses, that one returns so vividly. I smell peach when I think of it, and remember his liquid eyes, narrowed in the bright day. As I began my walk I ate the peach, in lieu of a drink, and it was so perfectly ripe that juice ran down my neck as I ate it.

Clear of the gates I read my note. The writing was tinier even than before, as for once he had information to impart: two items, just a few words, but important ones. One was the name and address of a woman from a refugee organisation in Melbourne, Edith Hart. The other was this: *Home Office liaison officer to arrive: Major Temple. Staying in Melbourne.*

Note in one hand, peach in the other, I felt a little steel return to my spine. I walked quickly home and began to pack.

TATURA, 1941

It was green in this place to which they had all been moved; vegetables were growing, and he could hear and occasionally saw children in the family camp, when they ventured to the fence. Through a gap, a little boy had given him a green tin plate on which he had painted flowers. He had thought of Hans more than usual, the day the boy had given it to him. Fifteen now. Young enough, still, to be at home with Ava, to be off to school every day with satchel and scuffed shoes.

The food was very good and they were well organised here, as in Hay. There were the theatre groups and the café and the lectures. But Solomon had been moved to a different hut. It made his days a little heavier, longer, though he ran into him from time to time moving about the camp and it had something of the feel of being young and wandering about town, stumbling across a friend, filling an hour with talk. In this camp there were Nazis mixed in with them and it was a constant effort to avoid run-ins. He did not want fights with them here, where it did no good, where any argument was theoretical and could only disturb the equilibrium he had gained. He must avoid large emotions in order to keep himself intact. Hannah, so far as he knew, did not yet know where he was. The minutes went by at a distance from him. He watched the activities in the camp, did his job in the workshop—mending things: bed legs, dental tools, spectacles—ate and slept. He tried to remember passages from books and he kept his eye out for an engine to fix, but he no longer played chess. He helped a young man secretly build a radio on the proviso that he brought him no news of outside, whatever he might pick up on the airwaves. He must shelter himself from time, for now.

One day at the workshop his colleague came in and said, 'There was a package for you, Becker. I'll look after things here if you want.'

He left without speaking and went to the administration block. The strange milky lake beyond the huts shone faintly. A soldier gave him a packet with her handwriting on it. It was fat and held together with a much-taped sheet of brown paper. He slipped it under his arm and went back to his hut, lay on the bed to open it.

'What you got there?' called a talkative man from Stuttgart, cutting his toenails at his bunk. 'Food parcel?'

Emil ignored him. He had made his privacy through reticence.

He took a knife from his soap crate, began to slit open the package. Onto his chest slid a number of folded wads of paper. He began to unfold one, and another: copies of Hannah's correspondence with Temple. He let them lie there, slipping off his body and onto the bed. Do I wish to know? he thought, but already he was beginning to arrange them, in date order, to find out what was happening to him out there, to the status of his name.

They started off politely enough. They told his story in a way he did not entirely recognise, although the facts were true. If the world of one's life were a fat sphere, these fragments she described were the point where the ball touched the ground. But she arranged them well for the purpose. You could hear the stump speech in the way she addressed herself to officialdom.

It seemed Temple would not grant her an interview. Emil had had his own interview with him in Hay. He seemed a decent man, sympathetic, but he could not alter the parameters of their dilemma. Emil must go home alone, if a passage could be found, or stay behind the wire. The Australians had not asked for him and did not want him. Hannah could do as she pleased; she was British, after all. Temple had said to him, softly, echoing Solomon, 'If you would consider returning alone, she might find her own way later.'

In the first few letters, Hannah had just about held back her temper. There was cajoling and charm, and then, when she did not get satisfaction: 'My life—or what the British authorities have made of it—means nothing to me. I am familiar with your appearance from the daily press. I am also familiar with the appearance of your car. As a last resort I shall place myself directly in its path.'

His body became rigid. Why have I been sent these now? What has she done? But then his pulse slowed, his body relaxed. The parcel was addressed by her hand, and that clumsy taping was her work too. She was given to the dramatic turn of phrase, he reminded himself. And it was almost funny, what she had threatened. She was the last person in the world to stop fighting and lie down in the road. If Hitler himself were coming down the street she'd be demanding an account of what he thought he was doing.

She bullied Temple with the names of those she knew in England, with friends in the Melbourne press. Temple's brief, polite notes acknowledged her letters, restating the position of the Australian government, retreating into official blankness. Then, finally, a note to Emil from Hannah.

> *Emil—Harts continue to be kindest souls imaginable. However did you get on to them? Dear Edith has found me a job on a university survey. Will leave me less time to haunt Temple and none for pieces for paper but is solid means of support. Will use in argument for your release—that I can now support us both. Another piece of goodish news: some talk of releasing men for skilled war work. Will push this line as hard as possible.*
>
> *Love and fortitude,*
> *Hannah*

He went out and looked over the grey-blue dish of water lining the shallow valley beneath the clouds. The shadow of the guard tower passed across his neck as he walked back to the workshop. At his bench was the toy he was making in his spare time. He had taken the wind-up mechanism of a broken toy discarded from the family camp and fitted it to the legs of a little marionette he had carved. He'd been working on it for weeks. It was difficult to get the little person to stay up, to balance well enough to be able to manage movement. He felt the weight of the doll in his hands, tightened the screws that held it balanced in position, carefully wound the key and watched it walk across the bench, the full length of it, straight and steady, before falling onto the ground. He laughed and picked it up, carved his initials under its foot.

Hannah

MELBOURNE, 1942

At the dawn of 1942 I regarded my most impressive achievement as having survived 1941 without quite succumbing to despair. I was staying in a tiny room at the back of the Australia Hotel in Collins Street and had been found a full-time job by the refugee people, helping to carry out a university survey on housing in which I interviewed working and unemployed people in Fitzroy and Collingwood and other suburbs close to the city about housing conditions. Thrilling as it had been to be paid to write, freelance wages kept me reliant on the charity of my friends and did not permit me easy sleep.

I arrived one January afternoon at the tiny slum cottage of a Polish refugee in his seventies to discover that he was out. I sat on his low brick wall, happy to rest my feet for a while. My refugee was fifteen minutes late, and I was stunned to see as he shuffled towards me that his face was covered in fresh purple bruises. He apologised to me, his hand shaking. I took hold of it. I remember the bones and the tremor which even my own hand did not still. 'Ruffians give me fright at station. Bad boys punch, call reffo.' He would not let me go to the police, whom he called fascists, or go and fetch ice from Hoddle Street.

We went and sat at the table in his tiny dim kitchen. He could tell me little for coughing and trembling and gingerly touching his puffed-up face, but I made him tea and we chatted in German for a while, which he knew much better than English, and he talked of his beautiful daughter. He lived on meat-paste sandwiches and shakily rolled cigarettes, and his trousers seemed to meet his braces without touching his narrow body. 'You vood *luff* hir,' he said several times, rheumy-eyed, as he followed me to the door. I didn't like to leave him, but I had to be away, and he said that his neighbour was coming at six with beer and soup, so he would not be alone for long.

My room was filled with the narrow bed and the sound of the laundrywomen laughing and gossiping. I backed onto the service rooms of the hotel and along my corridor the maids and waiters slept. On the floor above, I had discovered, slept Major Temple. One of my refugee people had let it slip that he stayed here, and I now spent a good portion of my wages staying in this dismal room and drinking coffee in the café opposite where I could observe his comings and goings.

He generally returned from the barracks at about six or so, and I sat on my bed, scribbling a note at my bedside table, making a carbon copy in my journal. *Dear Major Temple*, I wrote:

> *I have now fulfilled all requirements anyone might make of me in order to get satisfaction in the case of my friend Emil Becker. I have attained a full-time position with the university if he were to be released into Australia and require support. And I have*

had some interest from a munitions firm desperately in need of qualified engineers.

Despairing of a sudden attack of compassion that would lead your employers to fund my passage home, I have done everything anyone might ask of me to have our case viewed favourably. I imagine that I need not remind you that Mr Becker has been officially 'free' for fourteen months now?

I await as always your advice and instruction.

Yours sincerely,

Hannah Jacob

P.S. I suppose you wouldn't have time to see me for just two minutes, would you?

About as soon as I had finished copying the letter there came a knock at the door and I started, feeling caught out at something. My first thought was that it was him, Temple, come somehow to tell me off for the tone of my letter before I had even got it to him. I opened the door, unable to step very far back into the room because of the overwhelming presence of the bed. It was my friend Edith, whose name Emil had miraculously found for me. She was as small as I, as sturdy and determined, clever-looking, with thick glasses and orange hair, interested in the lives of those without power or advantage. Sweeter and gentler though, quietly resolved, diplomatic. She reached a hand forward through the crack to grasp my wrist. 'Another letter! Is it for the fortunate Major Temple?'

I smiled in spite of myself. 'It is. I try not to let a day go by without letting him know I think of him.'

'You have not even taken off your hat, Hannah dear. I'll take it up, if it's finished. You rest for a moment. And then I have something rather wonderful to show you, if you can manage a walk.'

'I couldn't ask you to go sneaking around the corridors.'

'It will be fun. He might catch me at it!'

'You can deliver it if you like, but I shall come with you. I can't send you off on your own.' I folded the letter and handed it to her and she was off smartly ahead of me along the corridor to the back stairs, clutching the letter to her chest like a child with a prize-winning essay approaching the stage. In the stairwell I heard her footsteps release the floorboards as she skipped upwards. I was rather tired from my day walking the streets for the survey and the gap between us grew.

By the time I reached the upper corridor I heard her voice and felt the hair rise at the back of my neck. *He* has *caught her at it!* I thought. I rounded the last stair to see her shape in the dim corridor, looking up at someone beyond a doorway. Temple was tall. Oh dear. My lovely respectable Edith, caught skulking around a hotel on my behalf. 'Perhaps you could talk to her in person, Major Temple,' she was saying. 'Why, here she is now. It would ease her mind no end to have a conversation with you.' She turned and smiled, beckoned me on with the gesture of a traffic policeman. 'Hannah dear. Here's your man. Just on his way out to dinner. We're lucky to catch him!'

Indeed, there he was, my elusive target, whom I had seen only at a distance, in his uniform as always but without jacket or hat, tall, heavy, annoyed with these little ones in his doorway. He smelled of boot polish and tobacco. His thick moustache was somehow more intimidating close up. Behind him was an immaculate room, the long Melbourne evening light thrown across a large, crisply made bed. My letter was in his hand. He had clearly picked it up and opened the door immediately, something I hoped for every time I put a note under his door. Until now he had been too restrained to respond in such a way. But now it struck me—dear Edith had had the gall to knock on the door of his private quarters!

I was too exhausted for niceties, and in any case I had worn them out in my earlier letters. Here we all were. It was now or never. 'Major Temple, I must tell you I cannot bear another day of inaction. What will you do to resolve our case? Mr Becker has been interned now for *twenty months*. I warn you that before I throw myself in front of a tram, as I fear I must soon, I will write an awful lot of letters. It is something I have become proficient at.' I felt Edith's small fingers at the inner crease of my elbow.

'Will you let me speak, Miss Jacob?' Temple said. The annoyed look had gone. He was kind, I see that now. I know that he had his own worries, his own people in France for whom he could do nothing. He would probably have changed my troubles for his gladly.

'Of course. Of course you may speak, Major.'

'I must admit I was never sure if all the claims you made about the quality of your friends were quite true, but I am convinced. The German Refugee Association, under pressure from the Youth Hostel Association, the British Metalworkers' Union and three Labour MPs, have promised to wire funds for your return to England.' Edith squeezed my arm. 'So with your permission, I will advise Mr Becker to apply for a transport.'

'Is this really true?' I found that I had taken the fabric of his sleeve. Edith laughed as Temple looked at the cloth clenched in my fingers and I released it.

'Yes, it is. Although you must bear in mind that transports are unpredictable just now. There's a war on, you may remember.'

'Oh, yes. Thank you, Major. Well, what now? What do I do next?'

'I'll send you a note about arrangements, if you can wait perhaps two days while I make enquiries.'

Edith had a firmer grip of my arm and was steering me away from the door. 'Thank you, Major Temple. I am sure Hannah can wait for your instructions.'

The door was closing. He nodded and was gone and we were scurrying along the corridor, holding hands like children running from the scene of a prank. 'I cannot believe it,' I said. 'Edith, if you were not here to witness it, I *would not* believe it.'

'Well I was, and glad of it. Get your bag. I'll show you my surprise, and then Molly's got some soup on for the refugees. We've got some excellent people at the moment. You must meet them. There's a violinist with the most beautiful instrument. We don't let him in without it. Then dinner is always so good he feels obliged to play until very late.'

It was a warm evening and we walked away from the tall buildings of the city to the east. It was refreshing to be away from the dark corridors of the hotel that I had been haunting for weeks for a sight of him. How revolutionary, simply to knock! Australians could be wonderful. Edith chatted, holding my elbow, while I looked around me at the worried people, the sandbagged doorways, stunned. I was to go home, and see my mother and brothers, *with Emil*. We reached Fitzroy Gardens, where Edith and her family had taken the refugees for a picnic the weekend before. I loved it there. It was a proper city park, in a square, with long avenues of trees, garden beds, people quietly living, walking, unhurried, for a moment or two apparently untroubled. You always saw some soldier or sailor in the shadows on his jacket under the trees with a giggling girl. For once, this evening, I did not begrudge them the touch of each other.

As we emerged at the eastern end of the park and crossed the road into a wide street lined with lovely white, yellow and pink houses and blocks of flats, Edith stopped before a gate, felt about in her bag and held a key before my face, smiling.

'What is this, Edith?'

She said nothing but pushed open the tall black iron gates, took me down a little pathway that ran alongside a pale yellow building, and opened a door at the back. I followed her into a corridor off which we found a bright, clean kitchen, a small sitting room looking out at a lemon tree and the street, a ginger cat in a patch of sun on the wall, and at the side of the building a bedroom with a double bed, made up, a dressing table and plain wooden rack with empty hangers. There was even a bookcase with books that looked rather like novels and poetry. In every room were tall white-framed sash windows that let in the evening light slanting through the trees.

'What do you think?' she asked, looking pleased with herself.

'I'll admit you have me baffled, Edith. You heard Temple. I am to go home. In any case, lovely as it is, I could never afford it.'

She explained to me that the tenant, a tutor of their acquaintance, was off to help with communications in Darwin, and didn't mind receiving just a little rent, if someone could feed his cat.

'But Temple says we can apply for a transport. I can stay at the hotel until then, rather than move again and inconvenience everybody.'

She smiled. She had the patience and bearing of a nun. 'It is wonderful news, of course, but ships are unpredictable. When you have to give up the flat, we have plenty of people who would look after it. The hotel is expensive and your room is *really awful.* We've been plotting to get you out of it since you moved in.'

I gave a forlorn laugh. We were standing in the sitting room. I sat down on one of the old stuffed chairs, looking out to the street. Edith sat on the other, laying her arms along its sides. She looked pleased with herself. A woman walked by on the street with an enormous navy blue pram. The cat got up and arched his back. 'Is that to be my cat? That ginger one on the wall?'

'I believe so. His name is Tigger. I'm told he sleeps on the bed, and that he will not tolerate being put out.'

'Then I suppose I shall have some company at last.'

Emil

Emil, making his bed, saw a familiar head pass the window. The thick wavy hair, round glasses. Then he was in the door, smiling a little sadly, and dressed in a uniform of a similar colour to the Australians who guarded them, but without the hat. Emil waited for him to speak. 'For now, Emil, it is goodbye.' Emil stood from the bed. 'I have been placed in a working party. We leave this afternoon.'

'Well, really, that's wonderful news.' Emil held out a hand to shake. Solomon looked efficient and handsome in his uniform. He'd not seen him in clothes that fitted him for a long time. 'What do they have you doing? Picking fruit?'

'We are to load and unload freight where the rails meet at the state border.'

'Explain to me this piece of nonsense.'

'Apparently, New South Wales and Victoria have differently gauged tracks.'

Emil stared at his friend, who was smiling. 'This is true?' Solomon nodded. 'I would like to meet these Australian engineers and ask them where they went to school.'

'It's work. I'd like to thank them.'

'Where do you stay?'

'Albury. In digs. A farm I think.'

'Not a camp.'

'No.' Solomon held out his hand once more. 'It cannot be long now, Emil. Hannah is unstoppable. And the camp is emptying out.'

'Just we old men left now.'

'I'll see you in Melbourne before Christmas. I'm sure of it.' Solomon put his hand in his pocket and pulled something out, spread his hand before Emil's face. He was holding out the little globe Emil had first seen in the Isle of Man boarding house on Solomon's packing crate. 'For you, Emil.'

'No, Sol.'

Solomon opened Emil's hand and pressed it into his palm. 'It has brought me luck.'

Emil did not watch him leave the hut. Later, through the workshop window, he saw them gathering outside the mess hall in their new uniforms. Young men, laughing, giving one another little shoves, hoisting big bags onto shoulders without effort. A truck sent up dust in front of them, and they lined up to get on. Solomon cast a glance back at the workshop, then jumped up into the back with the others. Beyond the huts the gates swung open, and they were gone.

~

Half the beds in his hut were empty, and he, free for so long now, spent his days wandering the perimeter, listening out for the few children left in the family camp, and avoiding the Nazis who, like the old trade unionists who would or could not return to England, were not allowed out. They were the old men here now, the over-forties, and spent their days gardening or tinkering in the workshop like men who no longer had a proper use. He had not seen Hannah for two months. She was working and it was difficult for her to visit even at the weekend, as the train did not come right to the camp, and she had to write ahead and ask to be met by the camp administration, and they did not always have someone available.

He had a new job in the camp garden since so many had left, and as he crouched among the cabbages, weeding, a soldier, Peebles, approached. Emil was pleased to see him. He was a profoundly grumpy man and Emil found his unremitting sourness and refusal to put on a good front charming and quite fitting, given the circumstances. 'Telegram, Becker. Haven't read it. Bound to be bad news. Just warning you.'

Emil stood, took the piece of paper.

Money wired from England for my passage. Temple arranging transport for both of us. Awaiting details. Really true. Love, Hannah.

'Bad news, is it?'

Emil laughed. 'Yes, terrible.'

'Thought so. Sorry. I did warn you.' And he was off, mooching towards the offices, hands in his pockets.

Emil crouched back down in the earth, its smell lifting in the warm day. He felt the sun on his neck, gave in at last to his imaginings. He was in a cabin with her on a cargo boat. Their bodies were together. They would sleep, they would eat, they would wash, some part of themselves touching. In the dark of the cabin, in the light on deck. And if they were torpedoed, they would never be apart again.

Digging in the garden, in the quiet of the emptying camp, he thought to himself: I must write and tell Solomon. His little globe has brought me luck already.

~

He sat on his bed at half past two, Hannah's battered case next to him, retrieved at Hay from a shed piled high with the remnants of the refugees' possessions stolen on the *Dunera*. He could no longer do up one of the catches because of a dent in the top of the case but he could not leave it behind, it was hers. In any case, he had nothing else in which to put his things.

There were two sets of clothes given to him by the Refugee Emergency Council, the plate with the painted flowers, a razor and toothbrush he hoped to replace before the journey if his guard would allow him to stop en route to the port, and a copy of *The Good Soldier Svejk*, given him by Solomon, whom he would not now see before leaving. He had written him a letter, giving Hannah's mother's address, and saying that he would see him after the war, if he had a mind to return to England.

He kept his hands in his lap. He had already smoked two of the cigarettes from the packet in his jacket pocket, and he had only eight remaining. There was a small amount of money left from his claim for goods lost on the ship but he hoped they would not be too expensive on board. The light in the room fell suddenly and then there was a drumming on the tin roof and lightning flashed up the men's things, all their curious little objects: eggs, bright feathers, matchstick boats. On one bedside table there was a tiny replica of Hay camp with a row of trains pulled up nearby. The huts were made of matches, the trains were real toy trains sent from who knows where, and the man who made it had also found real barbed wire to run along the top of his chicken-wire fence. He had sawn off men, the wrong scale, from rows of football players from one of those special tables, and put them on a rush mat, a little ball of dough amid their feet. Emil took in all these things in the flashes of lightning and hoped that the weather would not prevent him being taken to Melbourne in time.

At half past three the men returned from tea and threw themselves on their beds, talked noisily, opened windows and shouted things out to passing friends. His neighbour Kaufmann looked at him curiously. He sat down on the bed opposite Emil's. 'When does your boat sail, Becker?'

'In three hours.'

'You won't make Melbourne in time. Where's your escort?'

'The car was due at three.'

The man put a hand on his shoulder and went out with the others. There was a performance at the café tonight. The cellist Rosen had had his official release, and this was the last time they would hear him play.

Peebles brought a telegram at five. It was still raining and the hut was dim in the light of its bare bulb. The shoulders of his uniform were dark from the storm, his face shining. Emil watched from the bed as he dripped on the wooden floor all the way along the room between the beds. He handed him a wet, blue slip of paper. For once Peebles left without comment. The telegram read: *Last minute hitch in sailing plans. Army had to put on some extras. Trying to get word to Miss Jacob before she leaves for port. Sincerest apologies, Temple.*

Emil stood, put his case under the bed and went out into the rain. He heard the performance. It was Bach. The man played beautifully. He made his way past the huts and café, where the music was too much to bear, and along to his vegetable garden. Here the rain was enough to drown it out. His shovel sat upright in the earth where he had left it the day before upon receiving the telegram that he was to sail. The wooden handle was wet and gleaming in the dusk. He pulled it with a sharp heft from the ground and began to dig new rows, rivulets of water gathering at his collar and pouring down between his shoulder blades until his shirt and jacket stuck to him like burnt skin. He'd been given a broad field in which to grow vegetables for the camp. He could dig for years and not be done.

Hannah

I returned from the port, where Temple had found me and sent me home again. I do not remember it clearly. I did not write about it in my journal—I could not bear to relive it. I can hardly bear to recall it now. Temple, towering over me in the rain-drenched crowd at the dock as I brandished my useless tickets up at him. A mad walk in the rain—I caught the wrong tram and had to walk from the city back to the flat. There was my key, under the mat, where I'd left it for Edith to pass on to the next tenant. The cat, I remember, was beside himself because I had accidentally shut him out. He was spiky with the rain and tried to scratch me when I reached down to pick him up to dry him. From his point of view, it was a fine thing they had given my berth to Liverpool to soldiers.

Later that night Edith and her sister Dorothy came with enormous sandwiches they had made me for the voyage and taken to Port Melbourne, where they had waited until the ship sailed, and had then caught sight of Temple and extracted an explanation. Edith went out and returned miraculously with coal and made a little fire in the grate. We were all soaking and I got us nightdresses and a bottle of sherry and we sat there in a sort of stupor, listening to the rain and the fire. I think that Dorothy read us some of Nettie Palmer's poems. They knew her through their university friends and had given me a collection. When their clothes were dry they put me to bed, borrowed an umbrella and walked to their tram in the dark and rain.

I heard nothing at all from Emil. I resolved to go up there as soon as I could make arrangements for them to pick me up at the other end. I wrote every day to ask but some censor somewhere was having a fine old time with my correspondence and I did not hear back at all.

More weeks of listening in dank cottages to my refugees and sweatshop workers and old women looking after even more ancient mothers. They did not want to complain. They thought they would lose their homes, such as they were. Everyone grim about Japan. Nothing, nothing from Emil.

Then I got a letter from the manager of a munitions factory, with whom the metalworkers' union had been in touch on Emil's behalf. He told me that the men would not work with a day-release internee but that if I could get Emil released properly he could use him. I telephoned work from the box in the park to tell them that I would be late and took the tram to South Melbourne at once. I rang on the bell of a large brick factory and a secretary came to fetch me. She took me through the immense hall of the building; we passed great guns half made on mammoth benches, men working silently at baffling machines. The heat and noise were intense. I was taken in and introduced to the manager, frowning over a ledger, who looked up, astonished to see me. 'A telegram would have been plenty, miss.'

I clutched my gloves before me. 'I wanted to come and to promise you that if you will hold a position, I will do absolutely everything in my power to have Mr Becker released. I wanted you to know that, very definitely. I will be sending your letter to the Department of Labour and National Service, and I shall try and get satisfaction for you as soon as I possibly can. You will not be sorry for giving us this chance.'

He nodded, stunned, looked at his secretary hovering by the door, and she pulled my arm gently, guiding me once more out across the factory floor. She opened the entrance door for me and shook my hand. I was glad of the touch, but could not speak to thank her, and got a tram immediately for the university so that I could be at work without having missed too much of my day.

~

Then, again, things went darkly quiet. I lay awake every night fearing that Emil must be closer and closer to some desperate act. Still no one at the camp would give me news of him or confirm that they could collect me from the station if I went up there on the train. In my bed I thought: I will buy a car, the cheapest available, or steal one, and I will just drive it. Less capable people than I drove all the time. But Emil had tried, briefly, to teach me. The memory of him in Benjamin's car, in a lane in Hampshire, slamming the door, his back disappearing in the rear-vision mirror. *You cannot be this terrible. It is not possible.*

And so every morning I woke to reality and prepared myself for another day of work, and waiting. I ate everything Edith tucked away in the cooler whether I felt like it or not. I took extremely long walks in the evening to pass the time. I had no choice but to survive.

The season began to turn. The lovely flat was dark soon after I got home from work and I had to relinquish my grip on a portion of my savings for some warmer clothes and decent boots. Everything I had brought from England and managed upon had now just about given out. I came home on a Friday, put my key in the door and thought, perhaps I will not go out walking tonight. It is dark already, and I'm tired, and I might just draw a bath and go to bed. As I went to push the door inward it pulled away from me. A little jolt went through my arm and he was there, somehow inside, thin and old and just about smiling. We paused in front of one another on the doorstep, an eerie space between us with no wire screen. I could see the exact shape of him, of his body, of his face. He reached forward and pulled me to him and in spite of his thinness he was all heat. It went through me and around me. I could not let go.

Emil

They would not let him stay with her the night before they married. The Harts conjured him up a room at one of the colleges and in the morning their brother, Max, came with a suit and tie. He stood in the corridor holding it aloft. 'It's not exactly a morning suit,' he said. 'But I hope it will be all right for you.'

Emil nodded and closed the door, took in the suit. Old but not worn bare. It smelled very clean. He had lost the capacity for casual conversation in the last quiet months at Tatura. The world seemed unpredictably noisy, and he had no wish to add to it. And he must learn again that habit of responding in English without long reflection first. Solomon would come soon, he was due at any moment. They would talk for a while, he would be at ease, be himself.

He liked the park near the flat and he and Hannah went for quiet walks during which he had to still the flutter in his heart when she withdrew her hand to look for her glasses in her bag, or get the matches for him. The roar of the factory had been a shock. He had not been able to sleep the first night for the headache. But after a week of it he found it restful to be at work, to smoke a cigarette when the break bell went, standing in the sunlight of the dusty street with all the others, beginning to recognise the faces, watching women take their small children up the road to the market. The rhythm of it, rising early to catch the right tram, pouring onto the street with the others as the sun was sinking, this was the correct shape to a day. These movements helped him back into his body.

When Max had knocked he had expected trouble of some kind. He had learned to keep his hopes small and not far distant and now he must learn again to make them large and confident, to become himself again, the man who had hopes for himself and the world, who made his plans and followed them through. The boy without shoes who becomes an engineer. *The one who comes back.*

'I will marry today,' he said quietly into the room, looking out at the chapel, covered in ivy, and there were Edith and Dorothy and old Mrs Hart in their pale dresses and gloves and hats, waiting for Max beside a glossy black car. They're going to fetch her, he thought. He felt light, like laughing, but carried the echo of that knock at the door: that at any moment there would be a telegram saying that his release was a mistake, that the wedding banns were not really posted, that he was the wrong Emil Becker and must go back to his place in the camp. He closed his hand on a piece of paper in his pocket, his landing permit, which gave him the right to live, work, marry.

He did his tie in the mirror and combed out his curls. One of the Harts' refugees had cut his hair for him the day before in their garden and there were strips of white skin in front of his ears and at his neck where the skin was still young and naked-looking. The lines in his forehead were deep and no longer went away when he made himself stop frowning. It is still you, Becker, he told his reflection. Tonight you will take your wife dancing. Your feet will remember what to do.

The knock came and his breathing remained slow. It was his friend, come to take him to his wedding.

Hannah

MELBOURNE, 1945

We married on a beautiful, cold, sunny day in the Harts' garden, surrounded by refugees and kind Australians. I spoke German all day, and swished around the lawn in Edith's lovely grey silk, never letting go of Emil's arm, thin but still strong. As a young woman I had never intended to be a woman who married. It felt that day that these exact circumstances, this man, were the only ones that could have led me here, laughing in the winter sun among these wonderful people. I was very, very happy.

Eighteen months after he was released we had our first child, a boy, Geoffrey, and then fourteen months after that another, Benjamin. And so the second half of the war was not nearly so grim for us as the first. Our flat (the tutor never returned, having married in Darwin), so spacious and serene on that summer night in 1942 when Edith plucked me from my grim cupboard at the Australia, was now cramped, disordered and perennially filled with drying nappies. The babies had curly black hair and were deliciously plump. They clearly didn't know there was a war on. I believe they would have eaten the poor old cat if he hadn't taken to hiding in the airing cupboard for most of the day. Being very close in age they pinched and pulled hair but we put them in the same crib to save space in our bedroom, and that was how they liked to sleep, a little box of fat, pink baby skin, dark curls, long, thick eyelashes that rested on their cheeks when they finally relinquished their sturdy grip on the world and dropped off to sleep.

Overnight I became a housewife. I was astonished in those first few years how much of the day is given over to the care of children and a very small household. The alarm went at six for Emil's shift. I got up, made porridge, and bacon when we could get it, fed them all, found clothes for everyone, saw Emil off to his tram, took the babies out in the pram in Fitzroy Gardens if the weather was fine and let them play on a rug on the grass while I attempted to read a book or at least a portion of the previous day's newspaper. If I stayed in the flat I became mournful and dreary, and so I dreaded bad weather. The rest of the day was washing at the tub at the back door while preventing the boys from pulling the cat's tail when he emerged for food (I recall he got an outraged Geoffrey across the eyeball, leaving a thin red line. That cat was very precise, he knew how not to take an eye out while still having his case heard), preparing the boys to go to market, going to market, bringing them back for a nap. Then I tried to read again but usually fell asleep myself, and then got up and tried to do something with the awful cuts of meat we were allowed to buy with our ration books.

It was a short period, that chaotic blur of tiredness and mess, and we were always glad to be together, slipping exhausted into bed at night and curling up in the heat of one another's bodies, the boys making their little noises in their crib, but I felt a little bewildered too, without time to read, or listen to music, or talk to my friends, or write letters. One had to make the most of the quiet sunlit moments when the little ones played quietly on the floor, and magpies sang at the window, and one caught the lovely smells of the flowers and trees of that city.

I had a job for a while at the ABC on a program called 'Talks', recording short segments in which I spoke to ordinary people about how they managed during wartime. It was a delightful job, a real gift. It fed my curiosity about people, and I loved being on the radio, going into the studio and approaching the big microphone at the centre of the room. It is a particular feeling that I enjoy, of entering a secret professional world, like the translators' booths of the big international conferences, later, after the war. It's something to do with all that specialised equipment and an air of arcane knowledge, worn lightly by a steady stream of clever, friendly people going about their business.

I remember, though, that I worried about leaving the boys; I had not done it before. That first evening, as I pulled on my gloves and adjusted my hat, I went into the sitting room to say goodbye. The boys had colonised Emil's lap as he read the newspaper. They were hiding on his side of it, giggling, and yet he managed to be as absorbed in his article as if he were in a gentlemen's club listening to Mozart. (If that is what they do in gentlemen's clubs. Who of us would know? It's what *I'd* have done then if I got a moment to myself.)

'Well then,' I said to the newspaper, trembling with fat little boys. 'Do you know where everything is? They must be in bed by half past seven or they make life a complete misery in the morning.'

He let the paper dip at the top, revealing the boys tucked into his armpits, curled like ammonites. They were unwilling to look at me, in case I removed them from their father so he could read in peace. 'We are all perfectly happy,' Emil said. 'Go and be on the radio.'

'Is there anything else you need?'

'You will miss your tram, Hannah. Go, I want to read them terrifying stories and feed them jam sandwiches.'

I shook my head, the newspaper becoming once more a tent, and I went off to catch my tram, my chest aching to leave them, and then, by the time I was stepping up onto the tram to town in my smart dress and polished shoes, hands free of small boys, wet nappies, half-eaten sandwiches, beaming with freedom and movement.

~

I also got a very interesting position on Saturdays at the Council to Combat Fascism and Anti-Semitism. I wrote to radio presenters and news editors to remind them of the need not to aid Hitler's efforts with unthinking denigration of the Jewish people. It was surprising how necessary it was. I had some lovely spats with an announcer in Perth who had been brought to my attention. You should have seen the way I went at that typewriter.

Emil and the boys liked to come and collect me at the end of the day. He had to get permission at East Melbourne police station every time they came across town because he only had a regular permit to go to his work in South Melbourne. Anywhere else beyond a two-mile radius of our flat needed a signature on a slip of paper for him to show if stopped. Though Geoffrey loved visiting the police station and had even come to know some of the constables by name and worn their hats, Emil did it grudgingly, and I wonder whether on this particular day someone had said something that got under his skin.

My heart lifted when I saw them at the glass doors, which my desk at reception faced, but then as Geoffrey rushed in I saw that Emil was scowling. He handed Ben to me without speaking. I could not ask him what had happened, or whether his leg was troubling him, because immediately behind them came two old dears from the refugee council who liked to drop in and gossip from time to time. They had got it into their heads that I was German, in spite of my British accent. And many of those who worked in the office were Jewish. When they saw the boys on my lap playing with the typewriter, one of the ladies said, 'Oh my dear, you must be so relieved that you and your children are far from Europe. It is not safe at all for your people over there!'

Then Emil said loudly and without preamble, 'We are not Jews. You are mistaken.'

There was a profound silence among the adults while Geoffrey clattered at the keys. I saw the breath rise and fall in Emil's chest. The ladies looked at me, waiting for me to smooth it over. I was staring at him, waiting too for him to explain his outburst. When it became clear that no one was going to speak before I did, I said, 'Emil left Germany because of his anti-fascist views. I am a British citizen, as are the children.'

'Well, yes, of course,' said the woman. 'We are just—we thought we might find Mr Stern here today? He wanted to discuss something with us . . .' And they were backing out the door into the corridor, Emil peering out after them, stony-faced, as their heels clacked on the hard stairs down to the street.

I spoke to him in German. (Geoffrey was already rather inquisitive.) 'What was that all about?' I asked. 'What does it matter if they assume we are all Jews?'

'I don't wish to explain my entire family history every time some old beetle needs someone to feel sorry for. And you should not have to either. We are not anything to anybody. We are British, for Christ's sake.'

The way he said those last words, *We are British*, in German, made the whole thing seem unreal. I did not know what had just happened, but he was already walking out to the street, so I gathered my things, extracted the boys' fingers from the typewriter so I could put on its cover, and waited while they did all the locks on the door. We were never again publicly referred to as Jews, or Germans, in my hearing, so long as he was alive.

~

In the winter of 1945 the streets of Melbourne filled with GIs and the AIF, returning home. There were those terrible bombs in Japan, that have set me against war forever, and then everyone was out of the buildings, rushing into town, flooding across Fitzroy Gardens, compelled to be where everyone else was, to be certain, to be among the others who had lived through it too. To ask one another whether all those that were unaccounted for might really come home now. As I rushed out of the house with the boys, I thought of Benjamin and Geoffrey—my brothers, that is—and of dear mother who would not now be bombed to smithereens, although of course I had been able to relax about them since VE Day, and had had a letter from Mother since that she had seen both my brothers, that they had been in her house, and were *really* all right.

I caught the eye of my neighbour as I hitched Ben on my hip. She was watering her lovely magnolia tree, on which the first pale buds were showing. I looked away, hurrying Geoffrey on. My upstairs neighbour had told me this young woman had lost her sweetheart in a bloody landing in the Pacific.

I pushed through the waves of people, clutching Ben and gripping Geoffrey's hand so tightly that he tried to pull free, lifting him up onto the tram just as the bell rang. It was filled with people drinking from hipflasks and even straight from beer bottles and the boys pressed against me, turning their serious and huge brown eyes upon the strange crowd. I held onto the leather hoop with my free hand and they hung onto me as we lurched and the people gave out delighted cheers.

We got off amid the warehouses in South Melbourne and saw that already the men were coming out of his factory. I feared we had missed him but he was leaning on the brick wall, smoking, watching them go by. He smiled when he saw the boys and Geoffrey pulled at his hand, trying to get Emil to take him inside. 'I cannot take you in there,' he said, bending down. 'The furnaces require little boys for fuel. Someone is bound to throw you in. I cannot take such a grave risk.'

We took them for lemonade across the street. 'I think it will be perhaps a week or two and they will lay off the refugees.'

'Do you think they'll do it that quickly?'

'Already today they announced we are de-protected. This was a small company before the war.'

I studied his face across the booth in the diner. There was no one but us, everyone was out in the road. The young girl looking after the place was standing on the sunny step, waving at people as they passed. 'Well,' I said, smiling, 'do you want to stick it out here, or should we try and get a passage home? The youth hostel people will take us whenever we say the word. We have the fares, just.'

He nodded. 'Not Winchester. We can ask them for something new?'

'Yes, of course.' I put my hand on his. 'You know, if you wanted to go to Germany—' He shook his head. Geoffrey made a loud sucking noise through his straw as he finished his lemonade. 'I will write straightaway. I will see what they can find us.'

~

I had to support us during the last months. I worked very hard so as not to let the housekeeping eat into our fares home, but Emil's job had indeed disappeared quickly, and we could not get a passage until the English spring of 1946. I lost the 'Talks' position at the ABC to a returning serviceman and found a position as a full-time subeditor at the *Age*. It was hard work but suited my skills. I could look up after a long shift and only then realise my eyes were tired.

I came home in the bright afternoon of an October day to perfect silence. I thought that they must be out. But then, when I had kicked off my shoes in the bedroom and gone through to the sitting room at the front of the house, I saw them in the chair under the window. Emil was absolutely frozen, a boy on each of his knees gripped tightly about the chest. In one hand was a letter. I saw that it was handwritten, in German. After I had been in the room for several seconds he lifted his gaze to me. The rims of his eyes were indistinct and red and his mouth was not quite the right shape. The boys strained against his hold for a moment and then clambered down to get at me. I took them off for a glass of milk at the kitchen table, found each of them a chocolate, and went back in. I kneeled before him and he sobbed on my shoulder, trying to hold in the sounds so that the boys would not be frightened. It was difficult to hold him upright, but he stilled himself and we stayed there for a few moments until there was a crash in the kitchen and Ben began to wail.

That night I woke in the dark and heard a brief sound, a stifled cry, from somewhere hidden, as though there was a sealed chamber at the centre of the building. I lay in blackness and waited for him to return. I slept and stirred, grey light in the room, as he climbed back into bed behind me. His cold legs lay against mine, warming themselves, and I slept again.

Emil

FREETOWN, APRIL 1946

This time he would walk about the streets. He knew he would never be in Africa again. He was no longer in the part of his life where everything was still possible. He left them at a café on the dock saying that he wanted tobacco and would see them back at the ship. He could hear behind him the little one start up that sound like an air-raid siren but he would be all right as soon as Hannah put something sweet and sticky into his hand.

Everything was wonderful in its degeneration back into the too-warm, too-ripe land. From piles of rubbish between little huts burst colourful flowers. The thick orange mud tracks, churned and slippery, went up into the hills behind the houses. The milky sea was lined with coconut palms. The people's teeth when they smiled and murmured at you were large and white in dark mouths. Someone somewhere cooked corn on an outdoor grill. He might never feel such heat again, heat with weight, like a blanket over his skin.

He had not had a moment to himself for weeks with the packing and organising and settling of small boys who must be forced to say goodbye to all their mother's friends and continually be kissed and swept up into the air for squeezes and whispered farewells. Now he was alone with himself at last. His mother had told him in the letter of everyone that they had lost. It was many, too many for one letter. His sister's husband, who on his way home from work was pulled off his bicycle and beaten by a Russian slave worker in the days after Germany's defeat. A number of family friends and relatives crushed beneath their houses by Allied bombs. Ava was among these. He only hoped it was quick and unknown to her, that one moment she was dreaming of the bright hair of her child and the next she was not. He didn't believe she would want to make a life without her boy. Only his new Australian children made it imaginable that there could be a world without him.

All that had come back from the army, his mother wrote, was that he was killed in fighting south of Vienna in May 1945. That May, not a year past, Emil had taken the tram to the factory each morning, autumn colours blazing in the gardens of the cottages. In the afternoons Hannah and the boys had waited for him in their own courtyard, Geoffrey breaking free from Hannah as Emil turned the corner onto their street. He and Hannah had gone to bed early as the nights drew in, sinking against each other in their warm bed. In which of these moments had it happened?

He remembered every day their pale heads leaning towards one another on an English train, murmuring, nodding, the fields blurring past the window; that time, in which they were safe, that he could not keep from passing.

Soon, he would be able to visit his mother. He had no desire to go to Germany and see his town separated to individual bricks in the road, but she would not leave, and neither would his sister. A woman in bright clothes smiled as she passed, carrying a dead chicken by its neck.

Solomon had said before he left, 'On a journey, you must think of all the things that you look forward to about your destination.'

'You did this on the *Dunera*?' Emil laughed.

'I did. I spent a lot of time thinking about the absence of British officers and the plentiful nature of lamb.'

He had reached the back of the houses and not seen a store so he turned and walked down through the streets towards the sea. They had been sent a photograph of the hostel. An old manor on the edge of a village in Kent, standing on enormous grounds. The boys could roam in secret places among the hedgerows without ever leaving the garden. They could build little huts and hiding places, squirrel away the secret objects belonging to boys. Hannah could go to London on the train and see her mother and brothers who, thank God, were still here, and go to the theatre, and to Europe to work. She was talking about teaching herself Swedish. The Youth Hostel Association seemed to like to give him places that needed a substantial amount of maintenance. He would have a garden and many sheds. Perhaps he could build a car or a motorcycle, if he could get his hands on the parts in battered old Britain.

There was a store down a side street that he had missed on the way up. He was paying the shopkeeper for his tobacco as the ship sounded its horn. The man smiled and gestured for him to hurry. He walked quickly down to the dock, slipping in the red clay. As he came out of the streets near the ship he was not sure what he was seeing at first, but then it was clear that it was their three little dark shapes against the bright dock. Hannah, hair wild, holding their suitcases, flanked by the boys, who ran to him as soon as they set eyes on him and buried their faces against his legs. 'What is this?' he asked Hannah. 'Why do you have the luggage?'

'The ship is about to leave.' She set down the cases, laid a small hand on his chest, seemed to catch her breath for a moment. 'We thought you would not make it back in time. We did not want to sail without you. I'm afraid the boys rather caught my fear.'

'Come, come.' He shooed the boys onto the gangway where a sailor beckoned them along. He took the cases and they hurried onto the bridge between the land and the ship, stumbling quickly inside the boat as the sailor pulled up the gangway after them.

Part V

Hannah

KENT, 1958

The boys grew older, and so of course did we. They ran around the grounds, finding sheds for their exhibitions and projects. Emil walked and mended things and spoke German, finally, to those groups when they came. I travelled, of course, and became one of the first of the simultaneous interpreters. There were very few of us then who could perform this task, though everyone is used to seeing it on the television now. A delegate speaks and the translator's voice comes over the top in English, as though it is the easiest thing in the world. Well, it was not, and there was as much work as those of us who could manage it could take on. For myself, I was happy enough to miss the large groups of guests at the hostel. They became a bit much for me. I remember in those years that I was always trying to find a quiet corner of the house in which to study some specialist language before a conference or simply to write letters or read a book.

One afternoon, after returning from a few days' work in London, I had met the boys from the bus stop after school. They were too old to need collecting by then but my bus arrived shortly before theirs, and I was eager to see them. As we approached the warden's quarters, I heard music playing. It was Sutherland, singing Rossini, a gift sent us by the Harts, who have never in all these years forgotten the boys on their birthdays or at Christmas. Music seemed to me a good sign. When we went in we found Emil sitting at the big table dressing a hare and talking in German to his friend Solomon Lek, who was growing old very dashingly, with streaks of grey in his thick hair and lovely gold-rimmed glasses on his delicate nose. He was a professor of philosophy at Goldsmiths now but when he came to see us he talked mostly of his old love, literature, asking me every time when I would write my memoirs and dazzle the world.

Solomon stood at once as we entered and the boys shook his hand. His eyes twinkled behind his glasses. 'The unstoppable Hannah Becker,' he sighed, as he always did, and we embraced. Why did you never marry, Solomon? I wondered. Any young woman would fall over herself. But he was one of those with a private life that was just that. He made it his job to ask about you, and so one never probed. When he kissed me he smelled of rosemary and tobacco. They have been smoking, I thought. The doctor had forbidden it, but Emil took less and less notice of what such people—indeed, anyone—had to say on the matter.

The boys went off to their project, a wheelbarrow with a lawn-mower engine on it that they were attempting to turn into some sort of vehicle. I had seen no evidence of brakes. Emil had given them a shed and left them to it, having built them a thousand such things during their childhood, but they were big now, and he insisted they be left to manage their projects themselves, occasionally offering advice or a brief comment over the top of the newspaper.

Emil too stood and embraced me. 'What is this?' I said. 'My birthday?'

'My *Wiedergutmachung* cheque has arrived from the Germans.'

What a phrase. *Making good again*. 'Really? Is that really true?' I glanced at Solomon, who was smiling. 'I thought it would never happen.'

'I have learned this from you. I make their lives difficult until they move the world to get rid of me.' He took the cheque from his pocket to show me. It was a good sum of money, enough to put something down on our own little place. He was sixty-one, and had some money in his hand. We stood in a little triangle, close together, like refugees again, peering at the cheque.

The boys came over too to take a look. 'My sainted aunt,' said Geoffrey. 'Have we done someone in?'

'Where *do* you get such turns of phrase?' I asked.

'Can we go on holiday?' Ben said. 'I'd like to practise my French.'

'I'd like to practise my French too,' I said.

'Why not?' Emil said. He put the cheque in his pocket and went outside, leaving us sitting around the hare in its tray of rosemary and claret, the boys peering macabrely into its eye sockets and mugging at each other across the table. I saw through the tall bay windows that Emil was smoking a cigarette on his own at the raspberry brambles, not caring who saw or scolded him, looking out over the English fields, thinking, I imagine, of his father, for whose life he was being compensated. But I cannot know such things, and should not like to say.

~

It was so agreeable to be near the sea when we were in France and it had such a beneficial effect on Emil's chest that we decided when we returned that we would pack up over the next winter and retire from the hostel to a flat in Brighton. Emil would miss the young people, but his chest was simply not up to the work anymore, and I was looking forward to a little peace.

First, we had to clear out the house and all the sheds. After thirteen years of bringing up the boys we had to pack up Geoffrey's museum displays of botany and animal life and Ben's various attempts at motorised transport. Then there were all my papers. I assumed I would be left to deal with these when I was ready. My journals, translation documents and dictionaries were in my little study in the house. Outside, though, I had a shed that smelled faintly of bone meal, which I had chosen because it had a window and a long bench at desk height where a previous inhabitant had done their potting. I put my spare typewriter out there and when I had a day to myself with the boys at school, guests out and Emil off on some errand, I worked on my project. I did not necessarily admit to myself that it was secret, and yet I told no one of its existence, saying, if asked, that I liked to do my correspondence out there, away from the noise of the house. I was, as Solomon had mysteriously intuited, writing a memoir, but it was a joint memoir, of both of our lives, a frustrating but compulsive undertaking, which forced me to ask Emil carefully framed questions about his childhood and youth. For the most part he did not answer them, preferring to narrow his eyes at me and make a little harrumphing sound. I could not have said what my plans for this work were. I am certain that I did not know. I only knew that it was work I felt compelled to do, now that I had a place in which to do it.

One morning in autumn I woke to the smell of a bonfire, a not-unusual smell for the time of year—it was a smell that went with the fogs of October and November—but who would start a fire at this hour? Before I had even opened my eyes I had managed to conjure an entire scenario in which one of the boys had left a lantern going near some wood shavings the night before, and I rose expecting to discover a conflagration, the sheds providing kindling for the denser fuel of the main house. It was early, the sky still almost dark, and the house appeared to be intact as I slid my feet onto the cool boards and went over to the window to see. Our quarters were contained in a small wing of the house on the ground floor, and our room looked straight out to the gardens and sheds. In the dawn fog there glowed a bonfire, against it the shape of Emil loading material onto it from a pile of fuel that I could not see, blocked from sight as it was by my shed. I watched him for a moment and saw that he was hefting a rectangular shape like a small box onto the fire, where it separated into sheets and floated upwards. It was paper. '*Emil!*' I was outside in a moment, running across the freezing wet grass in bare feet and thin nightdress, bellowing his name before I could find the composure to articulate further. When I got to him he was emptying a cardboard box of the last of its load, casting the container on after it.

'Those are my *manuscripts*! What is wrong with you?'

He spoke in German. 'Not yours.' He turned to face me. His eyes were like coals.

'These are the drafts of my book. How *could* you?' I glanced behind him. I saw that he had finished the job he had set out to do. 'How could you be so *vicious*? I was almost there. I just about had the thing done!'

'My life is my own.'

'Speak in English, damn you!'

He was poking the black cinders into the flames with a shovel, just to be sure. They curled up into the foggy blue sky, irretrievable. He threw the spade onto the ground and marched back to the house, as though it was me who had been shovelling his two years of work onto a bonfire. 'Of all people!' I shouted. 'You, who had your books burned by Nazis!' I saw the shapes of the boys' curly heads at the window, the light on in the kitchen. Let him explain himself to them.

Later, when I was a fraction calmer, he came to me where I sat on a chair outside in the cold light. I was packing Geoffrey's eggs in tissue, exhaling fog. I had planned to throw them out, but I had decided now to make a point about the care of another's treasures. 'I wish you had told me you were doing this thing,' he said, standing behind me.

'You would have approved?'

'I could have stopped you before you wasted the time.'

I stood up. No doubt my eyes were red. I had been grieving for hours without cease. 'It was my life too. You threw it all in. You had absolutely no right.'

'I am sorry for all your work. But if you told me, I would not let you begin.'

'It would never have been published. It was just something I wanted to do.'

'Publish or don't publish. It's the same.'

'I just wanted it not to be lost. Don't you feel that? That it is too much to lose?'

'I am sorry, Hannah,' he said again. 'I could not bear to see it.'

He took ill soon after that, again and again. His chest kept him in bed, and when he was better I spent every spare penny on packing him off to Switzerland to take cures. I tried not to be away as much as I was before, and there was no time to restore those lost pages, or do anything much but worry and work and watch him minutely, as though by casting my gaze across his face and hair and clothes and hands I could head off any threat. If only I could maintain the proper vigilance, I could protect him, and myself, from the future.

BRIGHTON, 1963

One morning in November of 1963, the telephone rang while I was at my desk. I was mid-sentence in a tricky technical translation full of agricultural-economic vocabulary and I tried to ignore it. I remember looking out the window to the flats opposite for a moment, trying to retain my sense of the sentence. It won't hurt you to get that, Emil, I thought. The boys were away at university by then. The telephone continued to ring in the hallway. The sentence was gone. I remembered now that he had gone for a walk. It was part of the routine since we had moved here. His doctor had him taking a daily constitutional, rain or shine, and he was not back yet. I looked at the clock in the hall behind me. It was half past ten. He'd been out rather a long time; I tend not to notice such things when I am working. I went out into the dark passage. I remember looking at my hand as it reached out to the receiver. 'Becker,' I said. 'Mrs Becker?' a woman asked. 'We have your husband.' It sounded like something the police would say, but it was a nurse. Her name was Archer. Funny what you remember. They had him in emergency. He had collapsed at the seafront, unable to breathe. A motorist had heaved him into his car and deposited him at the hospital. I had not been with him. A stranger took his weight and felt him labour for breath. But I was fortunate; at least I was not abroad. I put down the receiver, lifted it again, called for a taxi.

I went into Emil's bedroom. His breathing was too noisy at night for us to sleep in the same room. It was a bare space with a neatly made single bed, wardrobe in the corner, enough room only to walk along between the window and the bed and make it up. A box room we used to call those little leftover spaces between the other rooms. I stood at his window for a moment. You caught a glimpse of the sea from this side of the building, down the hill, between the houses. It was why he chose this room rather than moving into the boys' bigger room at the front. The water was navy blue today under a moody sky. I pulled his case out from under the bed. It was my old battered one, that he had adopted as his own and taken to Australia. I had a smarter, more suitably sized one in my own room but last time he had gone into hospital and I had taken in my case for him he had scolded me. He wanted this one.

I packed his pyjamas, a few changes of clothes, his underwear, toothbrush, shaving kit. As I moved around the flat I had the feeling that I was being entrusted with a task too large for me. I had difficulty making decisions, in spite of the modesty of his belongings. Will he want the blue pyjamas or the burgundy? I worried about the bottle of aftershave. Might the glass bottle break and ruin his clothes? And which scent would not be too much for hospital? In the end I was saved by the tooting of the taxi on the street. I bundled the last few things into the case and struggled with the clasp. My fingers have been losing dexterity for these past years; I seem to have inherited my father's arthritis, a curse for one who relies on a typewriter as much as I do. As I grappled the too-large case down the narrow stairs and felt the chilly draft from under the front door, I realised I had forgotten my overcoat. But it would have to wait now.

When I saw him, lying in the bed in a row of five or six elderly men, I knew that he was worse than he had been before. The condition of the others was in no way reassuring—they are finished, I remember thinking—and the little glances the nurses shot my way each time Emil coughed gave the whole scene and period that same atmosphere as at the end with Father. It's *your turn*, the nurses' looks said. I asked Emil whether I should get the boys. Geoffrey was in his last year at university by then and had exams looming. 'Stop trying to get rid of me,' he grumbled. 'I'll be home next week.'

~

In the beginning, I steeled myself to be civil, lightweight, even among the smells of decaying bodies overlaid with bleach and institution food ripened by the stifling central heating. There were long silences while he read the newspaper, or asked me to read to him. I worried over this. Sometimes I could only get hold of the *Express* on the ward, and he frequently hauled himself upright and shouted when he felt a Tory was on his soapbox. In the end I resolved this situation by pretending I could not find any newspapers and bringing him in some Conrad. He asked me to bring him other things, usually cigarettes, and for the first day or so I held out. Eventually, as his skin took on a strange pallor and he ceased to speak above a murmur, I relented.

Late one afternoon, dusk falling earlier and earlier as the winter closed in, I walked down to the tobacconist on the High Street. I had never been there before. A beautifully painted red and green sign above the door, reading SCHWARTZ'S TOBACCO, gleamed dully in the light from the streetlamp. It gave me a strange feeling for a moment, like missing a stair, and having to catch your balance quickly. I stepped inside, the bell ringing, and the feeling continued. It was larger than Father's shop, but the mixture of smells, the jars of sweets, the crowded shelves, assaulted me as though I had been whisked up in a time machine and set down in an approximate version of my early childhood. The tobacconist, a stooped man with only a little black hair left around his ears and the back of his slightly egg-like head, climbed down from a ladder behind the counter and turned to me. He peered at me for a moment. 'Mrs Becker, isn't it?' He had a German accent. 'I have seen you walk past with your husband. He has not visited for a while.'

I did not ask why my husband should visit a tobacconist when he had officially been a non-smoker for the past three years. 'He is not well, I'm afraid.'

'He is not quite so youthful as you, Mrs Becker, I think. We old men have seen something of life.' He was already reaching up behind him, laying out on the counter a tin of tobacco with a green lid, some Rizla rolling papers. He began to slide his treasures into a small brown paper bag, and then flipped it over so the corners were sealed. Even that movement seemed stolen from Father.

'How much do I owe you, Mr Schwartz?'

'Please.' He lifted a hand in the air. 'Mr Becker himself may settle his account when he is better.'

'But you see, I really don't know when that will be. It would be better to settle it now so that I don't have to worry about it later.' He looked at me kindly. My voice was a little shriller than I had intended. Then he was emerging from behind the counter to open the door.

'Goodbye, Mrs Becker. It was a pleasure to meet you. Please tell Mr Becker I look forward to his next visit. I miss our discussions. Such an interesting man, your husband. So many ideas about the world.'

~

That evening I wheeled him wordlessly out into the grounds and across the grass in spite of a light rain and it being dark. It was a great pre-war contraption I had to push him in and I was warm and breathless by the time I had positioned him behind a little shrub, out of sight of the bossy nurses. Of course I had forgotten to bring matches. He waited silently while I remonstrated with myself. It seemed as though his mind was elsewhere. Don't go yet, I wanted to say, when I am right here, next to you still.

'Look, there's a visitor,' I said at last. 'I'll see if he has matches.' A dark-coated man, hunched into his collar, was crunching across the gravel under the streetlight between the car park and the door to reception. As I grew closer in the icy rain I discovered it was Emil's doctor, but by now he had seen me and I had to say something; there was no sense in subterfuge. 'Dr Elliot, I wonder if you have a box of matches you could lend me for a moment.'

He peered past me to make out Emil in his wheelchair in the dark and rain. 'It is no good for his health, you know.'

'I believe he is past caring, Doctor.'

He nodded, and drew from his coat pocket a box of Swan Vestas. He rattled them as he handed them to me. An odd, jaunty gesture, like children laughing in church. 'Tell him he may keep them.'

I watched Emil in the weak light from the building smoke his cigarette, which I had inexpertly rolled for him. It kept going out in the rain, growing heavier by the moment. 'Thank you, Hannah,' he said, and smiled as he threw the butt onto the grass. We stayed in the rain for a few moments. I held his cold, wet hand where it lay on the arm of the wheelchair. His fingers were permanently nicked from his years of working with his hands. I could feel those old grooves, like weathered wood. I wanted to tell him something but my mind was empty and my throat thick. His face was wet with the rain, his hair stringy and awry. His smile had gone. It had been only a brief interruption to the expression he had worn most of the time since he had come to this place, an appearance of having just been told something he could not quite comprehend. He looked—unravelled. I stared for a moment at his tired old face and tried to imprint it on my memory, his real face, how it was for me, not what I would see later in a photograph. I saw in it for the briefest instant the man who had stood under the window at the Maison du Peuple in his ill-matched clothes. Something closed like clasped hands, pressing together, at the centre of me. I saw that he was getting terribly wet, and wheeled him back inside.

There was a commotion on the ward. The sister was running towards us, a nurse at her back, calling, 'In the common room, Sister!' I had a mad thought that we had set off some sort of alarm with our disappearance, but the sister rushed past us along the tiles, ignoring us altogether. The nurse reached us a moment later, flushed with news. 'Sister is going to bring out the television,' she said. 'They've shot the president! Kennedy is dead!'

Emil made a noise that I realised after a moment was laughter, setting off a coughing fit. 'What on earth is there to laugh about?' I said as I pushed him back into the ward to await the arrival of the sister with the television set. 'Do you think it can really be true?'

When he had finished coughing, he said, 'I have outlived Kennedy!' and then looked lost again. He liked Kennedy very much, especially since he had gone to Berlin. He had listened to him on the radio, and heard the cheering Berlin crowds, smiling to himself.

The television arrived and people came from all over the hospital, it seemed, to gather round. We watched the news, the American newsreaders stunned, round-eyed, two of our nurses crying. For myself I could barely take it in. What might it all mean? It was troubling in the way that it made life strange suddenly, unstable and unfamiliar.

I went home soon after to sleep for a while. I had barely rested since he had come in here, and the nurse told me she would telephone me if he looked any worse. I returned in the morning with a paper for him to see what we could find out about Kennedy, but it was all over of course. They even had the man who fired the shots. When I went back into the ward it was quiet, one old fellow snoring gently, the dirty breakfast trays not yet collected. Emil's eyes were closed. This was how he rested, even though he was not one to nap. It was his way of ignoring the complaining old men, as he called them, of creating privacy. I so wish I could have afforded a private clinic for him, some quiet place of peace and calm. The National Health is a marvel, of course, but still.

I sat on the plastic chair beside him, unfolding *The Times*, readying myself to read him the article. I glanced at his tray on the bedside table where his breakfast sat untouched. I began to read, '*As the citizens of the United States mourn the violent death*—' I stopped. I don't know how one knows these things, but as I looked at Emil's face, waiting for him to open his eyes, I saw that the man I knew, beneath the skin, had gone. The moment had come in which it was too much, finally, to draw another breath, and so he had not. The newspaper crumpled in my lap as I leaned over him, crushing it between us, laid my head on his body, still warm, still mine. You are still here, Emil, I thought. I will not say goodbye.

Later, I felt a nurse's fingers close around my wrist. She whispered to me for a while, until I heard her and allowed her to lead me away.

~

At home, I gathered the last things and put them in a box that he had made for me to house my passport and documents when I was not travelling, so that I could always find them. He had kept his bits and pieces in a drawer in his room. It was not much to stand as proof of a life. No papers, except for his notice of reparations from the German government, which stated that his wife was entitled to a German widow's pension. An ancient copy of Grimm, in old German script. Two medals. A compass. A green tin plate with childish flowers painted on it. A small globe. I added to these things a tape. He had made up a silly song for me on our anniversary and sang it at the hostel, all the young people laughing and clapping. I could not listen to it just then and I am still afraid to wear it out or break it. When it is gone his voice shall be irretrievably lost from the world. And then I saw poking out from under the other things a dull silver key. I know this key, I thought, the layers of time clearing. I saw it again in my hand, held up under a streetlight outside a Brussels pension, and I found that my heart was beating as quickly as it did then, thirty years before.

WEST HAMPSTEAD, 1972

When everyone had gone, I realised I was free to do as I chose, to make my home where I wanted it to be, not where the fates decided to set me down. I found a flat that I could afford, and from which I could walk to the heath, and it is truly my home. My desk is in the window of my lovely, light sitting room and I sit at it and watch the interesting people that still love this part of the world go by. My desk and the dining table are covered in papers and books. I like to see them, to have them close. Emil would think it a disgrace. There is a bedroom for the boys, when they visit, amid their work and travels and busy lives. Geoffrey is here now, with his new wife and the baby girl. I hear them, the little one is crying, they make gentle noises and walk her about, as we did with him when he was small.

This morning I took my daily walk on the heath. It is well into spring and the air felt clean and refreshing. I looked forward to Geoffrey's arrival, with the new baby, my first grandchild, as I walked past the pond, and Mother's old house, Mother gone too, not long after Emil. I walked past a young woman. She was smiling as she walked, either a little mad or brimming over with some new experience. Probably a man, but I like to think she might have just got herself a really excellent job, for which she was superbly qualified. After she had passed, and I was thinking of that smile and what it might signify, I caught the scent of the soap she used, an old kind, lemony in a very particular way, and I was flooded with memories of a hundred places. Though it was the soap I used as a young woman travelling alone, it was a whole life that rushed at me, and a thought: I have made a home in movement. That is what I would say about myself, about my life.

I sat on a bench and looked at London, changed now, with that odd space-age Post Office tower. These past months I have spent separating the details of my life, itemising them, and now, sitting on that bench, they all surged over me together in an irresistible wave. I felt very weak, that I must eat, and so I stopped at the bakery on the way home for a wonderful buttery croissant.

So, I find, I have just about finished. I have written it again. In all this life, I have at last written a book. It is not someone else's that I have translated. It is mine. When I first ran home from school, saying, 'Father, I know what the letters mean,' and he put the chocolate upon my tongue, and I saw in my mind my name on the blackboard, the sweet dissolved and I began. Now this last sheet of paper rolled into the typewriter will be enough.

This afternoon, after lunch, we sat on the lawn at the back of the flats, Geoffrey and his wife with their long hair, their odd perfume, their loudly patterned clothes, chatting and laughing, the baby between us. She rolled on her blanket, mesmerised by the movement of the trees above. I watched her, astonished by her toes, and her laugh. Emil once said that we should have more children until we had a girl, but two noisy, relentlessly curious boys were enough for me.

If the young people were to wander off for a moment or two into the gardens, I thought, I would lift her up, stand her soft feet on my knees and speak closely into her ear: Little one, I would tell her, it is a gift to live life as a clever, beloved girl. Here is what I have to send you on your way: half a story, the half that is mine to give. Of the rest, make what you will.

ACKNOWLEDGEMENTS

I wish to thank the Australia Council for a grant that made the initial travel and research for this project possible. I would also like to thank Varuna, the Writers' House for the space and time to write large sections of this book.

While I have drawn from many sources for historical detail, I would like to acknowledge the use in the last pages of the novel of the phrase 'a home in movement' from *The Holocaust and the Postmodern* by Robert Eaglestone.

Ivor Indyk and Gail Jones have read my drafts with enthusiasm and insight and have always given me something new to take into my writing. My publisher Annette Barlow has been a model of patience and my editors Catherine Milne and Ali Lavau have approached the manuscript with impressive care and sensitivity.

My cousin Freyja Castles provided translation and company during a crucial early trip to Duisburg. On that trip, my grandfather's cousin

Helmut Schmitz generously shared his memories of our grandfather's life, without which we would know very much less. He also made valuable comments on a late draft of the novel. Also on that trip, Mr Dzudzek of IG Metall took us to the memorials to the murdered unionists, including my great-grandfather Johann Schlösser, and told us much about this episode in our family and the town's history.

I am very grateful to my father Frank Castles and my uncle Stephen Castles for their memories, papers and photographs and for their encouragement in writing a fictional version of the lives of their parents. It must be very strange to read such a thing. Thanks too to Dad and Beth for the use of the Moruya house. According to Philip Pullman, 'We need books, time, and silence.' Thank you for those. For time and silence I must also thank the lovely Gail Shiach who regularly looked after my daughters while I was writing.

To Brad Shiach and Ellie and Olive Castles for their unwavering patience and love: thank you. I never forget it.

And finally to my grandparents, Heinz and Fay, I hope this is all right. Thank you for your story.